Don't be afraid.
Don't resist.
Open yourself up to the wild pleasures
of four authors who will take you where
you've never been before . . .

CHRISTINE FEEHAN
". . . does not disappoint."
—*Under the Covers Book Reviews*

MAGGIE SHAYNE
". . . is better than chocolate.
She satisfies every wicked craving."
—Suzanne Forster

EMMA HOLLY
". . . brings a level of sensuality to her storytelling
that may shock the uninitiated."
—*Publishers Weekly*

ANGELA KNIGHT
". . . has seduced readers with [her] stories."
—*Sensuous Romance Reviews*

Hot BLOODED

CHRISTINE FEEHAN

MAGGIE SHAYNE

EMMA HOLLY

ANGELA KNIGHT

JOVE BOOKS, NEW YORK

HOT BLOODED

A Jove Book / published by arrangement with the authors

Cover design by Erika Fusari.
Cover photo by Robin Davis.
Book design by Kristin del Rosario.

ISBN: 0-7394-4608-8

A JOVE BOOK®
Jove Books are published by The Berkley Publishing Group,
a division of Penguin Group (USA) Inc.,
375 Hudson Street, New York, New York 10014.
JOVE and the "J" design
are trademarks belonging to Penguin Group (USA) Inc.

PRINTED IN THE UNITED STATES OF AMERICA

CONTENTS

Dark Hunger

•

CHRISTINE FEEHAN

This story is dedicated to Diane Trudeau
and all the ladies at the RBL board.
May you always know how to live life to the fullest!

Chapter 1

"YOU would have to pick the most humid night of the year," Juliette Sangria whispered to her sister. She wiped sweat from her forehead and crouched lower in the shrubbery to keep from being seen.

A spotlight swept the area of thick vegetation where the two girls were hidden, but it couldn't penetrate the lush shrubbery and multitude of vines and creepers hanging from the trees. Jasmine waited for the light to pass before shrugging. "I saw them bring in three animals tonight. We have to get them out before they hurt them or perform experiments on them. You know that's what this place is all about."

Juliette swore under her breath and melted back into the shadows as the spotlight slid by them in a long sweep. She was certain the light was more for the superstitious guards, always afraid of the encroaching jungle. She knew from experience the jungle never slept and always tried to regain what man took away.

The building was concrete and mortar, fairly new, but already covered with moss and fungi, a dark, moldy green as the jungle crept back. Creeper vines climbed the walls and wound around the top of the building as if seeking a way in. There were no windows, and Juliette could imagine how hot it was inside for the animals, even with the thick walls. Humidity was always high here, and the research center had been built in the most unlikely of places. She knew it was built in this remote location simply to hide the fact that animals on the endangered species list were being used for illegal research.

"Jazz, we'll only have six minutes to get as many animals out as possible. Some of them will be highly agitated. If any are beyond our help, you have to leave them. Is that understood?" She knew her sister's affinity for wildlife. "These people play for keeps. I think they'd kill us, Jazz. Promise me, no matter what, you'll get out in six minutes and head for home and stay there. I'll hang back and make sure they don't recapture any of the animals."

"You'll lay a false trail into the jungle to keep them off of me," Jasmine said.

"That too. We both know I can lose them. Yes or no, Jazz, do you give me your word? We aren't going in otherwise." Juliette would take her younger sister home and come back another night if she didn't promise. She detested that these men could come into her jungle and capture and torture animals and get away with it, but she wasn't losing her sister over it.

"Six minutes," Jasmine confirmed and set the alarm on her watch.

"Then let's do it. I'll take out the guard at the main entrance and you cut into the security system."

Jasmine frowned as she nodded her acceptance of the plan. Juliette always made it sound so easy. Distracting and taking out the guard was always dangerous. She moved into a better position, covering her sister and getting closer to the main box where the wires were stored. Few people paid attention to that little box, but Juliette and Jasmine knew it contained the highway for the main alarms. At night, only the guards were in attendance and they were always nervous and highly superstitious. They seemed as afraid of what was out in the dark interior of the jungle as they were afraid of what was inside the building they guarded.

Juliette unbuttoned her blouse to just below her breasts so that the thin material gaped open, revealing the generous swell of soft, inviting skin. She pulled a thick banana from her pack and slipped around the building, slowly unpeeling the fruit as she went. As she emerged from the thick shrubbery, she paused deliberately in the sliver of moonlight, bringing the banana to her mouth and running her tongue over the tip of it. The light shone through the thin fabric of her blouse, caressing her rounded breasts so that her dark nipples thrust invitingly against the fabric.

The guard's attention was immediately riveted to her breasts. He licked his lips and stared. Juliette smiled at him around the banana. "I had no idea this building was here. I'm camping with a small party of friends just beyond the stream." She used tentative Spanish as if she didn't know the local dialect. Juliette turned slightly, giving him a more intriguing view of her body, and pointed back into the darkened vegetation. She turned back to him, allowing her gaze to sweep him up and down, to linger for just a moment on the sudden bulge growing in his trousers. "Oh, my, I certainly didn't expect such a big, strong man as you."

He couldn't talk, staring at her mouth as she sucked on the fruit, her lips sliding up and down suggestively. Juliette pulled the banana from her mouth, gaining ground, her hips swaying, her smile flirtatious. "Are you hungry? I'll share." She held out the banana and seemed to notice her blouse gaping open for the first time. "Oh, I'm sorry, it was so steamy in the jungle, I can hardly stand having clothes on. Doesn't the heat bother you? It makes me feel . . . soooo hot." One hand went to her blouse as if to close it, but her fingers trailed over the ripe swell of her breast.

The guard swallowed hard, staring at her. She held the banana to his mouth. "Are all the men in the jungle as handsome as you?"

He took a bite of the offered fruit, he couldn't help himself. He was smiling down at her, still staring at her breasts when she used the pressure syringe on him, tranquilizing him. He was heavy, but Juliette was strong, and she dragged him into the cover of the bushes, sending up a small prayer that no predatory animal would find him defenseless, propped up against a broad tree trunk. She hastily prepared the scene while Jasmine penetrated the alarm system. From her pack, Juliette spilled a small amount of liquor on the guard's clothes, settled the flask in his hand and removed the bullets from his gun, flinging them into the dense undergrowth.

Juliette and Jasmine stayed in the shadows, avoiding the open where a camera might pick them up as they hurried through the large building. The first few rooms appeared to be empty offices, but just beyond them, they could hear the uneasy sounds of animals in distress. The laboratories were fairly large, each holding several cages. They separated, glancing quickly at their watches and blowing a kiss for luck as they took separate sides of the huge building in the hopes of freeing as many animals as possible.

Both had the ability to calm and control even the largest of cats. It was more difficult when the animals had been teased and abused or tortured, but both women were certain of their talents and they moved fast and efficiently, their teamwork well practiced.

Juliette kept an eye on the time as she opened cages and directed animals. The last laboratory held the biggest animals. A sun bear, a jaguar, and a sloth. She cursed under her breath as she saw that the sloth was beyond all help. The sun bear had several injuries from someone poking it with a sharp instrument, but the jaguar was still in good shape, one of the newest animals the laboratory had acquired. She spoke softly, soothing the pacing animal, growling once low in her throat when it leapt at the cage walls in agitation. It took a bit longer to manage the lock and herd him out of the room down toward the entrance, using her telepathic link to guide him. She took three steps after the cat when she felt a tremendous draw toward her left. To her dismay there was another door.

The door was heavy, a thick, soundproof vault with several bars and locks. Juliette glanced at her watch a second time. She should be running to get out, but something outside herself demanded she investigate. Praying Jasmine kept her promise to depart and head home immediately, Juliette set to work on the door.

RIORDAN lay on the cement floor in a pool of blood, dispassionately watching as it seeped toward the built-in drain. His blood looked like a thin, pale gray trail of liquid pooling in an ever-widening puddle. It was unthinkable that he had been trapped like this, that one of his kind could be shamed and dying at the hands of his enemies. He was an immortal, a Carpathian male, no fledgling, but a man of honor and skill. He lay in a pitiful heap, unable to gather the strength needed to move. Unable to summon help from his own kind.

His brothers would be seeking him now, wondering why his mind was closed to them. He dared not draw another into the trap as he had been drawn. He would not be bait to ensnare more of his kind. The enemy had found a way to poison the blood of their people, to immobilize them long enough to drain their blood and keep them weak. He had thought he was skilled enough to push the poison from his body. In the past he had done so on numerous occasions, but the new poison held him helpless and weak and paralyzed against the continual torture.

There was no way to transmit the news to his prince, no way to warn of this new, even more lethal drug their enemies had devised. Riordan struggled into a sitting position until he lay, propped against the wall he was chained to, examining the compounds racing through his system. They had used some sort of electrical charge to stimulate the cell deterioration in his blood. He allowed his breath to escape in a long, slow hiss of deadly promise. Of deadly despair.

He would not die easily—his body would continually regenerate—but without the necessary blood, without the healing earth, it would happen, slowly and painfully. It was the last death he had ever envisioned for himself.

The drug was crawling through his body, a chemical monster nearly as lethal as the dark demon lurking deep within him. Before he died, he intended to transmit as much information on the poisonous compound as he could to his brothers. He would issue a warning, but he would not do so until his death was imminent. He would not betray his kin. He would not be used as bait to draw in the others. His prince needed to know that a master vampire was using the humans, playing puppet master. Riordan had to find a way to escape, there was no other option. He could not allow his life to end until he carried the vital information of this treachery to his people. He could not let pain and despair, his ever-present companions, weaken his resolve.

Riordan closed his eyes and crawled deep into his mind. Almost at once he heard the soft click of the lock at the heavy metal door. Fearing his immense power, his captors never came to him at night. He did a cursory scanning to touch the mind of the human entering the laboratory, his prison, but to his shock, he could not read the thoughts. He had the impression of a human female.

He sat very still, his mind working at a furious rate. Had his captors managed to find a way to shield their thoughts? They were protected most of the time by his own weakness. During the daylight hours he was helpless and vulnerable, but at night they had been cunning enough to stay away. Although they had drained his blood and his strength, he was mentally strong enough to command one of them should they venture near at night. This was his chance to escape or seek a way to end his life before they could use him against his own species.

He studied the mind of the single person entering his prison. She was a young female. He kept his eyes closed, conserving his strength, waiting for that one moment he knew would come. He would reach past the strange barriers in her mind, rip past each strange compartment until he had total control. He would force the human female to do his bidding. Escape or death, whichever it took to win this battle. He could smell her now, a clean, fresh fragrance suggesting the outdoors, the rain forest after a cleansing downpour. A hint of exotic flowers, and something else— something wild. Something not quite human. Riordan felt his muscles tense at the unfamiliar odor, a strange quickening, a heat spreading throughout his body, but he held himself under control.

Nothing could prevent his attack. It was the first mistake any of them had made, and he would use it, capitalize on it. The demon in him was struggling to break free, listening to the steady heartbeat, the ebb and flow of blood in her veins. Hunger gnawed at him endlessly, mindlessly, brutally. He waited, unmoving, listening to the soft padding of her steps. There was only a whisper of sound, yet he smelled her excitement, the edge of fear and adrenaline. She was moving closer.

All at once the soft footfall ceased, her breath exploding out of her in a soft hiss of shock. "Oh no!" There was a rush of movement toward him, the rustle of clothes. Riordan clearly heard the shocked horror in her voice. She had not been expecting him.

Juliette couldn't believe the terrible sight, the man pale beyond imagining, his blood draining away on the floor. The heavy chains wrapped around his chest seemed burned into his very flesh. His hands were manacled, and blood seeped from a multitude of wounds. She couldn't believe he could suffer so much and still live. She knelt beside him and felt for his pulse.

Riordan opened his eyes to stare into her face as she squatted beside him, heedless of the blood smearing her clothing as she leaned in close. Her fingers settled gently against his neck. Her large, strangely turquoise eyes filled with compassion. "Who did this to you?" Even as she whispered the question, she was pulling out a small instrument from a tool belt hooked around her waist to work at the lock on the heavy cuffs. She carefully avoided looking at the cameras she knew were locked on him.

"We don't have too long. Can you walk? They'll send security after us and we'll have to run." He was a big man and Juliette didn't think she had a prayer of packing him out in a fireman's carry. She would try it though. She had come to this place thinking it was a research lab for exotic jungle cats. She had never expected to find a half-dead, obviously tortured man imprisoned within the walls. She had never seen so much blood, such a ravaged face, such intense eyes. The cuff dropped off of his left hand, and she stretched around him to work at the second one.

Her hair fell across her face in a silky fall of blue-black strands. Faintly shocked that he could see the individual colors, Riordan could only stare at her hair. For one moment he couldn't think, couldn't even breathe, drag air into his lungs. It was impossible, yet the hand he raised to the fall of black hair was smeared red with blood. Red, not a muddy gray. His fingers brushed her hair back over her shoulder with exquisite gentleness, an instinct bred into his bones, exposing the line of her neck to him. She didn't seem to notice, working meticulously on the lock of the thick steel cuff. Her skin was soft and inviting. Like satin. He bent his head forward, slowly, steadily, the fangs lengthening, the demon roaring, his body clenching. His breath was warm against her skin. His teeth almost touched her pulse, that vulnerable pinpoint beckoning seductively.

Her blouse gaped open, revealing exquisite breasts, lush and full and soft enough to pillow his head. He wanted to slip his hand inside her shirt and hold warm flesh as he bent to her neck.

She made a sound, frowning, still absorbed in her work. Riordan inhaled, taking the scent of her deep into his body. He didn't have control of her mind, and he was too weak to waste what was left of his strength on working out the intricate puzzle. The moment the heavy steel dropped from his wrist, he whipped up his arms, locking her body to his as his teeth sank deep into her neck.

White-hot pain lashed through Juliette's body, danced like a whip of lightning through her bloodstream, heating her body so that every nerve ending was alive and pulsing with fire. The pain gave way to a dark, erotic, slumberous ecstasy she was helpless to resist. Juliette was certain she struggled, but he was like iron, her softer body battering itself against his hard one, and he didn't seem to notice. She felt the strength growing in him, spreading through him, even as her own strength seemed to slide away from her. There was a part of her that seemed to be separate, standing apart, watching and feeling in a kind of horror. There was fire in her blood, moving through her body, muscles clenching, tightening, going boneless, pliant in his ironlike grip.

Riordan glanced up at the camera trained on him, his mouth twisting in a humorless smile, flashing his white teeth. With his eyes staring straight at the lens, he lowered his head and stroked a caress across the pinpricks on her neck with his tongue. That look would tell them everything. He knew each of them, knew their scent; he knew his enemies. Their stench was in his very lungs, and he was a hunter. He had gone from prey to predator with one small infusion of blood. It wasn't enough to completely heal him, but it was enough to allow his escape.

He lifted the woman's limp body easily to his shoulder, moving with a graceful show of strength. He had every intention of drawing his enemies to him and away from his family. But first he would destroy everything they had built out in the jungle. They hid their laboratory away from prying eyes. They hid their hideous torture chamber deep within the jungle, thinking they were far from the law, far from justice, but he would show them who owned this part of the world, who had owned it for a long, long time.

The woman erupted into a wild struggle, attempting to squirm away from him.

Riordan tightened his hold on her. "Stop it," he ordered. "You have no way to escape. It is impossible. Lie still." His voice was a soft, menacing command.

Juliette lay quietly, feeling the enormous strength in his arms. She fought down her panic, trying desperately to think. Her body had become lead. It was an effort to lift her arm, make a fist, pound on his back. She was dizzy and sick. His emotions were swamping her, a wild swirling of dark danger beating at her. She had never come close to feeling such overwhelming emotions. They welled up like a volcano, explosive, violent, very intense. She sensed something wild and untamed, a predator without equal. Her neck throbbed and burned and she wondered what manner of demon she had unleashed.

She actually felt the strength gathering in him. *Felt* it. A seething cauldron of enormous power. It built in him and seemed to spill out of him, out of his pores, bursting from his masculine body so that the building frame shook and creaked ominously, until the very air was so filled, the walls actually bulged outward in an attempt to contain such power. Juliette clutched at the tattered remains of his shirt, her fist bunching the material in her palm, needing something, anything to hang on to.

"My sister might be in here." She managed to whisper the words, terrified Jasmine would be caught in the massive destruction of cement and mortar.

"No one is in the building but us," he assured. He moved then, his speed so incredible everything around her blurred. Juliette squeezed her eyes shut tightly to prevent the dizziness from overcoming her. Her stomach lurched and she clung grimly. She could feel the powerful muscles bunching beneath her, the rush of air over her body. She could have sworn at one point they left the ground, moving through space so quickly they were flying.

Chapter 2

FEAR amounting to terror tore at Juliette. She had no idea what she was dealing with, but he was a powerful predator and from the condition she found him in, his anger was justified. She could feel a controlled rage simmering deep within him. Shockingly, they seemed linked together, she feeling his emotions, he feeling hers. She summoned her courage, her eyes still held tightly shut to keep dizziness at bay, keep from being overwhelmed with fear and the rush of wind in her face as they raced through the chamber of horrors. She needed all of her senses working if she was going to escape. She had to be alert for that one moment, that one chance when he would momentarily be distracted. She tried to gather her strength.

It seemed a monumental task in the face of being upside, her stomach rammed hard against his shoulder. He held her with one arm tightly across her buttocks, easily, casually, as if he barely remembered she was there. Her stomach rebelled and she was weak and light-headed. *But his touch seemed familiar, intimate even.* His fingers were splayed across her bottom, absently caressing the roundness of her muscles even as he was striding quickly through the building. Almost as if his touch remembered her body, knew her intimately in some way. Juliette couldn't focus properly no matter how hard she tried, aware of his fingers more than she would have liked.

The very foundation of the building shook; wrenching apart, the earth beneath them buckled and rippled violently. Sparks began to snap and crackle around them as the wiring popped from the beams, cracking and splintering overhead. Light fixtures swayed precariously. Fissures appeared in the floor, along the wall, great, ominous cracks.

There was a roaring in her ears, loud and insistent. The man locking her to him moved smoothly, fluidly, a certain poetry to his motion, not jarring her badly knotted stomach. *Breathe.* She heard the word as a soft whisper in her mind. Almost a caress, intimate. *Breathe.* As if warm air from his mouth was breathed into her ear. As if his lungs moved for her lungs. Her body still felt leaden, her arms hanging heavily down his back. She tried to concentrate, tried to gather her strength to wait for her moment, but that single word had disturbed her. Changed her. *Breathe.* It whispered through her body, swam in her bloodstream, spread insidiously throughout her body so that her very heart beat the rhythm of his heart. And the word was in her mind, not spoken aloud.

As the building vibrated, he took stairs three and four at a time. He leapt from the crumbling cement wall, a good twenty feet in the air, landing easily on the balls of his feet, still careful not to jar her. Flames were licking at the blocks of concrete, trying to find fuel, greedily looking for something to devour as he took her into the shelter of the jungle.

At once the dark green leaves enfolded them, swallowed them, a haven of rich, lush vegetation. The darkness was nearly inpenetrable beneath the heavy canopy of foliage overhead. The fallen trees and thick shrubbery didn't slow him down. He moved as one born and bred in the jungle, silent and deadly, protecting her with his body as he raced through the darkened interior, putting distance between them and the crumbling laboratory. He seemed to know exactly where he was going, when most were disoriented deep within the forest. Before he had run with speed and power, now he began to falter, his legs shaking as if he were suddenly weak. Blood still ran from his wounds and trickled down his body from the many lacerations.

Juliette flexed her fingers, grasping his tattered shirt. She didn't have the energy to cry out a protest, limp and lifeless, hanging like a sack over his shoulder, but she was certain he was half-mad with pain. All at once they were back on the edge of the trees where civilization had hacked the jungle back to build small townships and villages. The jungle, as always, was creeping forward to reclaim what had been taken, providing cover all the way to the very edge of the village.

He stopped near a thick tree trunk, a shadow in the darkness. She felt his stillness, his gathering of information, scenting the wind. Her heart began to pound in anticipation, a loud, terrifying beat. He was hunting prey. Deep within her very soul, she knew he was hunting human prey with her leaden body draped casually over his shoulder. She wanted to struggle, to scream, to warn his victim. No sound emerged; her body refused to obey her. Her heart nearly exploded in her chest, wild and frightened.

Breathe. It came again. A soft command in her mind— gentle, intimate. A caress she felt on her skin, a stroke she felt in her hair. On her bare breast. Air moved through her lungs, through his, and her heart found the steady, natural beat of his.

She heard the padding of footsteps, the murmur of voices carrying in the night. Coming closer. Closer still. Who would be so foolish as to wander near the jungle this late at night? There were many predators in the forest. He moved then, shifting her into his arms, cradling her close to his chest, his black eyes burning deeply into hers for a long moment. She could only stare helplessly, half mesmerized, half paralyzed. Slowly he lowered her feet to the ground, keeping his arm around her to hold her to him. To hold her up. She was dizzy and weak.

His dark examination was the most intimate thing she
had ever experienced. The connection between them was
growing. His gaze drifted over her body, touched her exposed breasts with the heat of a flame. Juliette couldn't summon the strength to button her blouse so she stood swaying
and vulnerable in front of him. As if reading her mind, her
captor drew the edges of the material together and slipped
the buttons in place. His knuckles brushed against her skin,
sending a shiver of awareness down her spine. He bent his
dark head toward her, a slow, almost seductive movement.
Her heart thundered in her ears as his sculpted mouth came
close to hers. A whisper away, no more. Mesmerized, she
could only stare at him, waiting, forgetting to breathe.
Abruptly, he turned his head toward the small group of
houses.

Juliette saw two men moving toward them, walking
straight as if on a path, yet they were walking through dense
shrubbery. Neither spoke, nor looked right or left. Neither
seemed to be aware they were close to the jungle where
predators lurked. Juliette tipped her head back. It fell against
his chest, too heavy for her to hold up on her own. His arm
tightened, locking her even closer to him so that the heat of
his body seeped into the cold of hers.

She could only stand there helplessly as the two victims
walked closer and closer. There was a stillness in her captor,
the coiling of a snake. She felt him gathering his strength,
holding it in place while his prey came closer. The two men
walked right up to him as if drawn, as if programmed. A
shudder ran through her as one tipped his head back, exposing his throat. Her captor bent his dark head in that same,
unhurried, almost casual manner, and sank his fangs deep
and drank.

Juliette's heart pounded frantically, adrenaline racing
through her bloodstream. *They cannot feel. They are not
afraid, why should you be afraid for them? I am not hurting
them. You always forget to breathe.* There was the merest
hint of amusement in his melodic voice, an intimacy that
took her breath away.

Her entire body clenched, searing heat touching her in places like the stroke of fingertips. Her breath caught in her throat. He was dangerous, far more than she first thought. His voice was a weapon, seduction a tool. And she was susceptible to his sensual mouth, his burning eyes and his velvet voice.

Juliette forced energy into her body, using her fear, her adrenaline and his momentary distraction while feeding. She attempted to jerk out of his arms, using the sudden surge of built-up terror. His arm remained clamped around her like a steel trap, unmoving, almost as if he didn't feel her resistance.

Riordan allowed the first human male to sit down on the ground, swaying weakly, and he reached for the second one. He needed fresh blood to replace the enormous loss he had suffered through his confinement and torture within the walls of the laboratory. With the infusion of blood, he hoped to heal enough to begin restoring his body to full power. With renewed power and without the constant electrical charges to stimulate the artificial poison he might be able to remove the substance from his system. Carefully, he helped the second human to the ground, retaining possession of the woman by holding her body close to his. He felt her. Every inch, every curve. Her skin was unbelievably soft. He bent his head to her thick mane of flowing hair, inhaling the scent of her. It took a tremendous amount of self-control not to bury his face in the silken strands.

She was very frightened, the fear swamping her despite the fact that he had tried to soothe her. Her brain patterns were different, the most difficult he had ever encountered. He caught her chin firmly in his hand and tipped her head back so her strange eyes were forced to meet his gaze. Her eyes were shaped liked a cat's, a deep turquoise in color, and he could tell by her pupils she had excellent night vision. Her lashes were long and the same inky black color as her hair. He stared down into her eyes, a simple hypnotic technique that should have calmed her instantly, but instead he could hear the frantic rhythm of her heart pick up.

"You rescued me. Thank you," he said softly, gently, compulsion buried in the silvery tones of his voice.

Juliette tried desperately to regain her energy. Her legs were very heavy, her arms still leaden. He was the only thing holding her up. She was dizzy, and every time she stared into his black eyes she felt as if she were falling forward. She blinked rapidly, trying to find a way to regain her ability to think clearly. "What's wrong with me?" Her mouth was dry and her voice sounded far away to her own ears.

"I took too much of your blood," he answered softly, honestly. "It was the only way I could escape from that hellhole. There is no need to fear me, I will replace what was lost." His arms tightened possessively.

Juliette pushed ineffectually at him. "Just go away. I don't want you to replace anything at all."

"I am Riordan, your lifemate. I have searched these long years to find you."

"You are some kind of bloodsucking something or other and I just want you to go away." Juliette nearly sank into the bushes, but he lifted her, preventing her from falling. It disturbed her that he had such strength when he had been so brutally tortured. Blood or no blood, he should have been as weak as a kitten. His chest held long, raw burn marks, almost as if the chains holding him had been made of acid. "You have to take care of these wounds. They'll get infected in the jungle. You can't have any open wounds at all." Why she cared made no sense. She just wanted him to go away. He cradled her as if she were a child hanging limply in his arms, her head lolling back on her neck. She was very aware of her throat, so vulnerable to his sharp teeth.

Riordan stared down into her peculiar eyes, searching her mind for a way to calm her fears. He heard a soft grunting cough coming from the darkened interior not very far from them. She reacted. She tried not to, but there was elation, hastily suppressed in her mind, and her body tensed for the briefest of moments. He felt her response beginning in her mind, he was already that tuned to her and they hadn't shared his blood yet. She took a breath. Before she could make a sound his hand clamped around her throat. Her frightened gaze jumped to his. Riordan shook his head.

You will remain silent. I will kill anything that comes to your aid. Is that understood?

Juliette nodded. She didn't understand the tremendous connection between them. She felt what he felt. She could almost see the black, volcanic thoughts swirling in his mind to match the dark violence churning in his belly. He frightened her in a way that had nothing to do with his teeth and evident abilities. Long ago she had heard the whisper of another race of beings, and she suspected he was of that race. Carpathians. Nearly immortal. Hunters of the vampire, guardians of the many species, yet always alone, always apart. She knew little about them, only that they were extremely dangerous to her kind.

He had not killed either man he had fed on, even with the black anger stirring in his gut and the terrible need for vengeance riding him hard. She should have feared for her life, but it was something altogether different that frightened her. The way he looked at her was entirely predatory. Entirely sexual. Entirely possessive. And her whole being responded with heat and fire and secret longing and shocked terror.

Riordan allowed his hand to slip from her throat. He bent to place his mouth beside her ear, although when he spoke he used telepathic communication rather than speaking aloud. *I am taking you far from this place. The hunters will know I am weak. I must rid my body of their toxins before I can attend you. Close your eyes if traveling through the air frightens you.*

You frighten me. Leave me here.

He made a sound. Not out loud, but deep in his mind—a snort of derision. His face was an implacable mask, lines of weariness and pain were etched deep. If she could have, Juliette would have touched those small lines with gentle fingers. She wanted to take that look of bleak loneliness from his face forever.

You only fear that you have lost your freedom. You do not fear that I will harm you. You feel my need of you, do not pretend you cannot.

Juliette turned his words over in her mind. He couldn't read her as clearly as he pretended, which was a good thing. He was torn up, a stranger, a demon for all she knew, but something deep and feminine and animalistic responded to him with every fiber of her being.

She watched the earth drop away, the clouds whiten and mist form around them. Below her the canopy looked unbroken and impenetrable. He knew the jungle nearly as well as she knew it. He had a specific goal in mind. She rarely left her part of the forest to explore the deeper more mountainous areas, but she knew that was where he was taking her. She would be a hundred miles from home, maybe more. Juliette hugged her secrets to her. She just needed to find her strength, go along with whatever he wanted until she was able to make her escape.

His laughter was low and without humor. *I am not in the mood to go chasing you through the forest.*

What good news. She looked up at masculine face. He looked a man, not a boy, one who could be frightening, even a little cruel should he choose. Why would she be remotely attracted to such a man? It was unthinkable, yet she couldn't look at him without feeling the effects.

Maybe you should be afraid of me. He sounded more weary than sarcastic. *Are you going to tell me your name?*

She tried to think clearly, tried to remember the old legends told around the campfires, told by her mother's people about such a race. Did giving her name give him more power over her? She couldn't sort through the haze in her mind quickly enough.

I think it essential to know your name. Are you going to give me something to call you or shall I make it up?

Juliette. My name is Juliette. She didn't want him calling her some endearment in his mesmerizing voice that she might come to believe. In any case, she couldn't imagine him having any more power over her than he already did.

Thunder rolled over their heads, booming through the clouds so that the tree branches below them shook and the

space they traveled through vibrated in alarm. Juliette felt
Riordan's body jerk. She clutched at his arms.

I will not drop you, we are being pursued by the undead.

I don't like the sound of that. If only she wasn't so weak.
She didn't have a weapon, nothing at all that could help. *Is
the undead what I think it is?*

I will not be trapped twice. There was such finality in his
voice she shivered. *And yes, it is a vampire tracking us.*

How is he trailing us? You aren't leaving tracks behind.

He smells my blood. His voice was grim.

Juliette was silent, sensing Riordan was growing tired
with the effort he was making. Her stomach flipped when he
dropped unexpectedly to the ground below. The canopy was
thick and leaves slapped at them as they plummeted through,
skimming branches and hurtling toward the ground at such a
fast speed she thought they would crash. She kept her eyes
closed tight and only the thought of a vampire hearing her
kept her from screaming.

Suddenly they were floating, coming to a halt. Riordan
placed Juliette on the ground, her back against a tree. Her
eyes widened with horror as he stared at his hand, his fingernail growing to a lethal-looking length. Juliette drew in her
legs, stifling a gasp as he tore a long cut in his own wrist.
Blood dripping, he flung droplets in all directions and took
off running with blurring speed, away from her, winding
through the trees, spreading the scent along the leaves and
shrubbery over a long distance.

Juliette held her breath for a long moment, waiting to be
certain she was alone. For some reason, Riordan shocked
her by abandoning her to the vampire. He was clearly using
her as bait. She dragged herself to her feet. So much for
sexy, brooding heroes. Obviously the more tortured, the less
heroic. "Maybe you weren't really all that sexy after all," she
muttered out loud, furious that he would leave her. Her legs
were wobbly and she was dizzy, the ground tilting and
rolling. It didn't matter. She was not going to wait for the
vampire to descend from the clouds and find a helpless vic-

tim. If she had to crawl, she would find a way to escape. She let go of the tree and took two tentative steps. The ground rushed up to meet her. Before she hit the ground, a strong arm circled her waist and she was dragged up against Riordan's hard body.

Chapter 3

"WHAT are you doing?" Riordan hissed the words at her, clearly annoyed.

Juliette glared at him. "I thought you left me."

"I am your lifemate. Your protection and health must be placed above all things. I would never leave you."

If she weren't so tired, she would have rolled her eyes in exasperation. She did the mental equivalent just to let him know he was an idiot for not explaining things she had no hope of understanding on her own. She glanced down at his wrist. The jagged tear was closed but looked raw and angry. "You laid a false trail of blood for the vampire, one stronger and fresher, didn't you?"

"Of course. It will hopefully delay him long enough for me to regain more strength and remove the poison from my body." He gathered her into his arms. "He will attack the skies blindly in hopes of finding us. You must remain silent."

Juliette was becoming annoyed at being hauled around like a sack of potatoes. "I'm not exactly a cringing baby. I got you out of that place, didn't I?"

For the first time a faint smile flitted across his face. It nearly stopped her heart. "That was before I showed you my teeth."

"Is that a little vampire humor?" she asked, but her stomach was doing a curious little flip. He looked so weary. She might have given in and put her arms around him to comfort him if she weren't so certain touching him was dangerous.

He bent his head to hers, his breath warm against her skin. When he smiled, she could see no signs of his incisors, but it didn't stop a small shiver from running down her spine. Unexpectedly her womb clenched. She didn't think that was a good sign. There was definite chemistry between them and it seemed to be growing. It wasn't logical and she just wanted to get away from him.

"The vampire will try to attack us in the air. He will not really know where we are, but he will hope to score a hit. It is essential you remain quiet. It will be very frightening."

She snorted derisively. "And you aren't? Let's get out of here."

He took to the skies again with dizzying speed. She felt him stirring in her mind, an attempt to reassure her, but she wanted to keep him out. Mind-to-mind contact was far too intimate. He could read her thoughts and even, possibly, her strange attraction to him. It bothered her that she was susceptible to him. There was no way to tell whether it was physical attraction or whether he was manipulating her in some way. She definitely had no intention of sticking around long enough to find out which it was.

Without warning the clouds rained sparks, red-hot embers, slivers of molten fire that fell like raindrops in a steady barrage. Riordan bent his body protectively over Juliette, cursing that he wasn't at full strength and couldn't provide the shelter they needed as they streaked through the sky. Despite his best efforts, several slivers penetrated her arm and burned through her skin nearly to the bone. He heard her gasp, but she turned her face against his chest, against the terrible burn marks there, and remained silent. The embers burned his back and shoulders, raised welts and stung like angry bees along his arms. He was infinitely weary and wanted desperately to go to the healing ground in the way of his people, but Juliette could not do that, and he would not leave her unprotected while human and vampire enemies searched for them.

She was an unexpected gift, drawn to him by their connection, two halves of the same soul. She didn't want the connection, but it was there and it was explosive. In spite of the relentless pain, he was all too aware of her soft, generous curves and the heat and scent of her body. It only added to his physical discomfort and raised the level of her wariness. With her face nuzzling his bare chest, his insides were turning to mush. She had no idea how much faith and trust she showed him with that simple gesture.

I'm hiding from the embers. She denied his thoughts.

You are hiding from yourself, from the truth.

You could be the most infuriating, exasperating creature on the face of this earth.

Perhaps, but nevertheless, you find yourself inexplicably attracted to me. There was purring satisfaction in his voice.

Riordan took them lower into the comparative shelter of the jungle canopy and made his way toward the small forest stream where the plants he needed grew in abundance. Lightning slashed the night skies, lighting up the forests in flashes, sending animals scurrying for shelter. He moved through the trees until he found the darker, overgrown spot he needed for safety.

"If we are lucky, the vampire is weaving his way through the forest miles from here. Let me look at those burns." Riordan set her down and crouched beside her, drawing her arm straight out to examine it.

"You're hurt worse than I am," Juliette objected, her heart pounding. It was the way he was looking at her wound, his black eyes moving over her skin as if he took it as a personal affront that she'd been scored by the slivers of fire. "I can live with it."

"I cannot," he said simply and bent his head so that his dark hair, wild and tangled from the journey through the sky, cascaded around him, hiding his face.

She felt the warmth of his breath first. His lips, feather-light, a mere brush so that her heart quickened and her body tensed. His tongue swirled over the blackened welt. Electricity sizzled through her entire body. The breath went out of her lungs and her mouth went dry. She jerked her arm in reaction, but he held on firmly.

"I am sorry if this hurts, but I have a healing agent in my saliva. It should remove all pain. Just relax." He didn't just say the words, he breathed them against her skin. She felt his voice crawling through her pores, winding around her heart and lungs and every other vital organ.

Juliette closed her eyes against the waves of heat coursing through her bloodstream. Bloody and torn, swaying with weariness, Riordan was still the sexiest man she'd ever encountered. There was his voice, his eyes, the way he looked at her, the way he turned his head, his hard, masculine body, but most of all, the danger emanating from him. He was a powerful predator and it showed, yet his touch with her was amazingly gentle, almost tender.

She swallowed hard. "It isn't right that you're trying to heal me when your body is so torn up. I can wait."

"I feel your pain beating at me."

She made an attempt at finding humor when her body was stirring to life and her thoughts were turning to things better left alone. "See why we shouldn't share minds? It would be so much easier if you didn't have to feel my pain on top of yours." She frowned. "I'm in your mind, why can't I feel your pain?" She could feel how tired he was, but he had to feel pain with all the lacerations and burns.

His tongue swirled a second time. Then a third. "I am shielding you."

He could rob a woman of sanity. Juliette couldn't look at his gorgeous face without wanting to wipe away those terrible lines. His touch was beyond gentle, was causing her stomach to do flips and somersaults. Beads of sweat trickled down the valley between her breasts, and she was certain it had nothing to do with the humidity. The small burns miraculously stopped stinging under his ministrations. When he finally lifted his head and looked at her with his dark eyes, she saw the stark hunger smoldering there.

Riordan allowed her arm to slip from his fingers before moving a short distance away from her to the stream.

Juliette half sat with her back against the tree trunk watching Riordan carefully. "Thank you. It really does feel much better." She studied the lines in his face. "Is there really poison in your system?"

He glanced at her, his black, black eyes blazing a trail right to her heart . . . or her body. He began to carefully ease out of the bloodstained and tattered shirt. All the while his gaze remained on her, making it difficult to breathe. "Unfortunately, yes."

"Why? Why would they do that to you?"

"Because I am different. I am a creature to be loathed and hated. And because, I fear, they wish to kill our prince."

The burns on his skin were horrible to see. "Did they heat the chains? Is that how those burns got there?" Juliette wanted to rush to him, press her lips to those terrible marks. He had to be in such pain, yet he had attended to her first.

"They had vampire blood and they painted the chains regularly with it. They knew the blood was toxic and would burn as acid does. And they hoped the scent of blood, when I was drained and starving, would drive me out of my mind." He gave her a faint smile. "Perhaps they succeeded."

Juliette shook her head. "You're saner than they will ever be. We're both a bit shaky, but we made it out of there."

"Thanks to you. I am sorry you have to see me this way. As soon as I remove the poison, I'll restore your strength to you."

"I'm not as dizzy. I think my body's already recovering. You just worry about you." She wanted to look away as his face grew paler, as he made a tremendous effort, using every ounce of reserve strength in an attempt to analyze the poisonous compound used to paralyze him. A part of her mind was merged with his, or perhaps it was the other way around, but she could see the data flowing through his mind and was amazed that he understood each separate composite. "Who are you? How do you know all this?"

He leaned back against a moss-covered boulder. "I have lived a long life and learned much over the years. There is little else to do when you have nothing to live for. Knowledge is power and it keeps one alive, even when one no longer wishes to remain in a barren world." His dark eyes slid over her. He reached out his hand.

Juliette had no idea why she put her hand in his. The moment his fingers closed around hers her body came alive, and it felt right. Juliette wanted to pull her hand away from the heat of his, but he looked bone weary and tormented and she didn't have the heart.

"You changed that for me. You gave me back colors and emotions. I have four brothers. I have lived with them for years with only the memory of my affection for them, yet in that one moment when you spoke to me, I *felt* that deep love for them again. How could I ever repay such a gift?" His voice was soft, almost as if he were talking to himself.

"I love my sister and cousin so much. I can't imagine not being able to feel my love for them. I'm glad I could, in some way, restore those feelings to you." She tightened her fingers around his. "Have you always lived in South America? You're obviously familiar with the jungle." She knew he was resting, gathering his strength to break down the poison and push it from his system. She could feel him continually scanning the skies, worried the vampire might have tracked them in spite of his sacrifice of precious blood to lay a false trail. He had fought vampires on many occasions and she briefly touched on those hideous battles through their link. The creatures were grotesque and evil and worse than the human monsters she'd encountered.

"Many years ago, when our current prince was still young, his father sent many of us out in the hopes we could stop the spread of evil. I was fortunate that my family was sent together. It made it easier to endure being so far from our kind, so far from our homeland. We made this our home." He squeezed her fingers as if for courage and started to let go.

Juliette tightened her grip, tugging until he looked at her.

"I'm strong enough to help you. I'm keeping you out of my mind, but I can let you use my strength."

"You do not have to, Juliette." He liked saying her name, was pleased she wanted to aid him, but he was not the gentle man she believed he was in her mind. He was far more ruthless than she knew, and he had no intention of allowing her to escape him. "I would not want you to expend energy you cannot afford."

He was warning her. Juliette felt a chill go through her body, but she chose to ignore it. He was drooping with pain. His wounds seeped and wept and every now and then, in spite of his efforts to shield her, she glimpsed the torment he was in. "I don't mind. I'm just sitting here anyway." She gave him a tentative smile. "How did they manage to capture you?"

His expression darkened. "I heard a cry for help on the common telepathic link all Carpathians use. When I followed the cry back to its source, I found a vampire, not a Carpathian. Unfortunately it was impossible to tell that he was vampire until it was too late. I was injected with the paralyzing formula and drained of blood to keep me weak." His gaze settled on hers, stayed there, a hypnotic, mesmerizing stare. "You are not shocked to hear of my species. You were frightened of me because I took your blood in such a manner, and for that I apologize, but the fact that I needed it did not fully surprise you. How is that?"

She was silent for a moment, weighing her words carefully. She felt him in her mind, seeking answers, but he was not nearly at full strength and the poison was hideously painful. With her brain patterns so different and the strength of her protective walls, he simply waited for her spoken answer. "When I was a child we often spent long periods of time in the jungle. At night my mother would build a campfire and we'd tell stories. She told us of a great people, Carpathians from the mountains in Europe with extraordinary skills and gifts. They were blood-drinkers."

"How did she know of them?"

"Our family goes back hundreds of years. Apparently my

ancestor met a small group of Carpathians here in the jungle." She looked at him steadily. "Five brothers. They were said to have a vast cattle estate and human family to work their lands while they slept beneath the ground during the sunlight hours."

Juliette waited for a response to her revelation, but Riordan only stared at her for a few more moments in silence, then simply withdrew, pulling back into himself. He moved outside his own body, gathering himself into a ball of pure energy. It was fascinating to observe his healing abilities. She stayed merged with his mind, watching him not only break down the chemical compound so he could view each separate element and identify it, but also send the information to someone else with a warning to pass it on to the prince of their people and as many of their hunters as possible.

Sending the information over a distance was draining and Riordan faltered.

Where are you? The demand was strong in her mind. Male and frightening, it carried a command, a hypnotic draw that was very powerful and sent shivers of fear down Juliette's spine. *Riordan. I feel your pain.*

Riordan hesitated. *Do not come to me. I will be able to push the poison from my body and replenish myself.*

Juliette found herself holding her breath. She didn't want to meet the man behind that voice. There was a merciless, ruthless, frightening quality to the voice.

She felt Riordan touch her with his mind, a reassuring, caressing stroke.

I will not allow you to be recaptured. You were sent to check out the research lab to see what they were doing.

The Morrison research laboratory was a front for a vampire controlling the human society that hunts our people. I have destroyed the building. The animals they captured on pretense were allowed to go free. I will come home when I have healed.

Where is the vampire?

He is hunting us. Riordan broke off the communication

and glanced over at Juliette. "My eldest brother is very exacting about our staying alive."

"Families are like that. My sister will probably be worried about me. I need to get back home." She watched his face, hoping to read his response, but his sculptured features went carefully blank.

Riordan stared down at his arms. She felt the gathering of his strength. Very slowly the poison began to respond, moving with reluctance as he shepherded the damaging compound toward his pores. Some of the droplets oozed through his skin, golden, thick liquid carrying the ability to paralyze his race.

Juliette pulled a small plastic container from the bag hanging around her waist. She leaned forward and pressed the lip of the container to his arm, capturing as much of the liquid as possible before she screwed the lid on tight. "This might come in handy if your people need to study this."

He leaned against the boulder, his head back, fighting for air, his strength gone. Juliette immediately opened her mind to his, sending him as much of her remaining strength as she could give. She knew the jungle, better than most, every rustle in the undergrowth, every sound the birds made. Something evil was stalking them, and the jungle was alive with the news. In her present state she couldn't escape, but she had no doubt Riordan could fight if given the strength.

He wasted no time removing every drop of the toxic compound as quickly as possible. The moment he was certain he had gotten rid of all of it, he dunked his head into the stream, rubbed the cold water over his arms to scrub off the thick, sticky residue. Riordan spun around and reached for Juliette, dragging her onto his lap, cradling her against his chest.

She felt a jolt through her body, an electric shock as their bodies came into contact. Her mouth went dry. "What are you going to do?"

"Exchange our blood. Your blood will help me get us somewhere safe where I can heal, and my blood is ancient and will restore the strength you have so generously given to me."

"Will it tie us together?" Her voice might have been an invitation, but her palm went up in a defensive gesture, fingers splayed wide against his chest.

"Yes." His strong fingers slid over her chin, pushed stray tendrils of hair from her shoulder. "But we are already tied together." He bent his head, his face buried in the warmth of her soft, vulnerable neck. The water from the small stream was cold as it dripped from him, down her skin, cooling the heat from the oppressive humidity.

A soft moan of pleasure escaped as his teeth sank deep. She settled deeper into his hard frame, moving with restless urgency as her blood went thick with heat. Her lashes drifted down, her hands sliding limply into her lap.

"I claim you as my lifemate. I belong to you. I offer my life for you. I give to you my protection, my allegiance, my heart, my soul and my body. I take into my keeping the same that is yours. Your life, happiness and welfare will be cherished and placed above my own for all time. You are my lifemate, bound to me for all eternity and always in my care." Riordan spoke the words in a black velvet voice.

Juliette felt his voice vibrate through her body, touch her deep inside. Somehow his words brought them together, skin to skin, organ to organ so that they breathed with the same lungs, shared the same heartbeat, possessed the same soul. He flowed through her, a dark temptation, learning her secrets, sharing his. Kissing her until her body caught fire and ached for his. There were hot blood and flames licking at her. She shook her head, suddenly caught by the ritual of the entire thing. A ceremony as old as time.

Chapter 4

JULIETTE opened her eyes cautiously in the hopes that none of her recent experiences had been real, that she'd just been having nightmares. She had participated all too eagerly in the exchange of blood, in the exchange of kisses. "Damn, damn, damn," she muttered and pushed herself up from the bed of foliage she was lying on.

She could hear the steady drip of water. She was in a cave, and the leaves and twigs that formed her bed were man-made, not at all natural. Riordan had provided her with the safety of a shelter and a soft bed while he had "gone to ground." She carefully avoided walking over the spot where she was certain he lay in a bed of rich soil. She felt him there beneath the dirt and leaves, buried deep. Still, not breathing.

Juliette dragged air into her burning lungs and backed away from the spot. She had a mad desire to fling herself to the ground and claw the dirt away to get to him. A sob welled up in her throat. She took another step back. "It was a ceremony of some kind, wasn't it?" She whispered. "My people do not marry." She backed up another step, although this time her feet dragged. "You're an extraordinary man, but I'm not what you think and I never could be."

She had no choice; she had to get home to her sister. Juliette tugged off her boots and tied the laces together. She shrugged out of her blouse and then her jeans, tying the two garments tightly together with the boots. She stood there completely naked, holding one hand over her throbbing neck. Her body called to him. Her mind called. Her very heart tried to find the beat of his. Hastily, before she gave into the grief and madness welling up in her, Juliette tied the clothes securely around her neck.

She closed her eyes to block out all visual distractions and calm her mind. She would need every ounce of strength to leave him. When he had recited those ritual words, Riordan had carefully explained that they were tied together and should she wake without him she would feel the separation as intense grief. "And you weren't kidding," she said aloud. "I feel like my heart's been torn out. Whatever it is you are, whatever it is you did, it definitely works on me."

What are you doing? There was alarm in his voice. She could almost feel his fingers brush over her face, trail down her throat, slip over her breast. Her entire body reacted, recognizing his touch, reacting with heat and need.

Her eyes opened wide and she looked wildly around. *Where are you? Why can't I see you? How can you touch me when you aren't here?*

I am locked beneath the earth until the sun sets. You cannot leave me, Juliette. You know you must not.

Another gift? You can touch me, but I can't reach you? It was shocking that his touch seemed so real, could arouse her body and affect her heart when he wasn't even a substantial presence.

Tell me what you are doing. Why would you leave when you feel that we belong?

You don't know me. He had his secrets, but so did she.

You refuse to allow me into your mind and heart.

I can't. Her hand went to her suddenly raw throat. The thought of leaving him was painful. Hearing his voice only added to her torment, but she had obligations and she couldn't put them aside because her heart and soul and body cried out for his.

You can't escape me. Your blood flows in me and mine in you. He sighed. *I can see your mind is made up. When it becomes too difficult, reach for me, I will answer. In the meantime, try not to get into too much trouble.* Abruptly he broke the connection between them.

Juliette felt the loss like a physical blow. She took a deep breath and released the air slowly, calling up her other self, calling up the part of her that could give her the strength to go home where she belonged, when she really wanted to crawl into the earth with Riordan.

The change took her slowly, almost reluctantly, as if a part of her brain was fighting rather than embracing her other form. Spotted fur slid over her skin, muscles and tendons contracted and stretched. Stiletto-sharp claws sprang from her curving hands. She landed heavily on all fours while her body went through the change. It was always a slow process and somewhat painful, but never like this time. Juliette wept as the jaguar took her over.

The cat was small and stocky. Roped muscles and a flexible spine allowed her to flow across the cavern floor, seeking a way out to the jungle where she belonged. Rain fell softly as she emerged from the damp cave. She paused to get her bearings before taking to the trees and running along the twisting highway of branches high above the forest floor. She couldn't maintain this form for long periods of time, so she had to use it efficiently to travel across the greatest distance before shedding it. She ran as quickly as possible, threading her way through the leaves and foliage.

The rain barely penetrated the canopy, dripping steadily on the leaves but rarely touching her fur. Steam rose from the forest floor, but the jaguar didn't feel the heat the way Juliette would have. The boots banged against her neck and chest as she made her way through the trees and shrubbery. The birds screamed a warning to one another at her approach and monkeys chattered and threw sticks and leaves at her. She snarled at them, but hurried onward, not stopping to teach them manners.

After a time, she began to shake, her legs suddenly growing weak. She stumbled twice, tripped on a branch and leapt hastily to the ground. She was miles from the cave; the sun was setting and Riordan would be rising. Hopefully he would only find the scent of a large cat and she would be gone. Even if her blood called to him, she was a great distance away with a good head start.

She shifted into her human form, her sides heaving and her lungs burning for air. Leaves and twigs scraped her bare flesh. She looked hastily around to make certain she wasn't crouching in anything poisonous. The last thing she wanted was blisters on her skin. More than once she'd managed to shift at the most inappropriate time. She had little control when the form became too difficult to hold.

With a sigh she dragged on her clothes. Humidity was so high the material clung to her skin. Juliette was skilled in the jungle, but without the jaguar's fur and claws, it was much more difficult to make her way through the trees. The canopy kept out much of the light, and with the sun setting, the interior went dark quickly. She had excellent night vision, but it wasn't going to help much with night predators.

She passed the miles alternating between a run and walk. She tried to listen to the steady rhythm of the rain, but it sounded like a heartbeat. She tried to block out the scent of Riordan, but it clung to her body. Tears made a relentless path down her face, blurring her vision. Grief was a heavy weight that slowed her steps and robbed her of air.

Every step was a fight to go forward, to keep from turning around and running back to find Riordan. Worse, her mind continually tried to tune itself to his. Fighting herself was more exhausting than fighting the jungle. She needed a place to rest. Juliette found a small circle of boulders, nearly hidden by overgrown ferns. Within the ring of boulders a deep pool fed by a small stream shimmered in the moonlight. She sat down, lifted her face to catch the mistlike drops that managed to work through the thick foliage overhead. Thunder rolled. Lightning lined the clouds. A roar shook the ground, the trees, caused small waves to race across the surface of the water. Juliette's hand fluttered over her heart. He had risen.

JULIETTE was gone. His first reaction was to roar out his pain and frustration. Now Riordan let out his breath in a long, slow hiss of exasperation. He wanted to shake her. The physical attraction between them was a wildfire. That alone should have been enough to bind her to him. She was in for a long, difficult time, out there alone without him. The ritual bonding words would force her mind to attempt to connect with his. He had explained it to her, had tried to spare her the misery he knew she would be going through.

He was already feeling the effects of their separation. Worse, he was feeling her grief, a torrent of emotion every bit as deep as the well of passion he touched in her. She felt things intensely. Riordan raked his fingers through his long hair. He needed to find prey fast. He needed more time in the ground to heal, but more than anything, he needed Juliette. He lifted his head toward the heavens and roared a second time. She had opened the dam of his emotions. He remembered nothing of anger and jealousy and fear, but now the feelings were crowding into his mind mixed with grief. It was a potent combination and a dangerous one.

He found the tracks of a large cat, but not the footprints of a woman. His heart beat hard in his chest, pounded with fear for her, with need for her. She had managed to disguise herself, leave no trace behind, but the call of blood and the ties that bound them together were far too strong to ever break. He moved quickly through the cave, shifting on the run, bursting into the air as a thick stream of white mist. The sky was orange and red, dazzling and vivid and near blinding to a man who had seen only shades of gray for so long. Even with the heavy mist for protection, his head burst with the sheer brilliance of color. He streaked through the trees, staying below the canopy, using the protection of the foliage while he acclimated himself to his new sight.

A bird shrieked, his only warning. He hit something and bounced backward. Droplets shimmered briefly through a dropping silver net, falling through on the outside. Instincts took over. He shot upward, through and above the silver. In his present form he was able to slip through, but he felt the thin blades, razor-sharp, cutting deep.

Riordan! Juliette sounded panic-stricken.

The trap had been set specifically for him. Juliette knew he would come after her. He had not fully penetrated the barriers in her mind. Could she betray him? Was it even possible for one lifemate to betray another? Riordan doubted it, but he didn't have time to think so he simply didn't answer, pulling his mind from hers. The echo of her anguished cry tore at his heart, but he refused to be swayed, streaking through the canopy and shifting into the form of a bird. He went still, hiding among the birds in the tree, examining the trap that had been set for him.

It had been sprung without an operator. He had merely flown into it, which meant there might be other traps out there waiting for him. Blood trickled down his beak and seeped through his feathers. Far below, on the forest floor, the silver net lay tangled in a heap. He could see traces of his blood on the thin wires.

Humans, puppets of a vampire, had constructed the trap, and only a master vampire could have kept his presence from Riordan. He was dealing with something extremely powerful and evil. Something willing to mingle with humans and use them for its own ruthless purposes.

Fear for his lifemate clawed at him. She was somewhere alone and unprotected. It couldn't have been Juliette. What would be the point of rescuing him only to lead him into a trap? He touched her mind, heard her weeping. His heart shattered. For a moment he couldn't breathe, couldn't drag air into his lungs. How could her soft weeping affect him so deeply?

Juliette, it is nothing, a trap that failed.

There was a small silence. He pictured her wiping at her tears, felt the anger stirring in her mind. *I hate that you did this to us. Tied us together until we can't breathe without each other.*

Destiny tied us together, Juliette.

You had a choice.

I did not have a choice. I was shocked to find you. I had never expected to find you. Tell me why you are so resistant. I can help you with whatever it is you feel the need to do. You are not so opposed to our joining as you want me to believe.

He felt her shock that he had penetrated her barriers to such an extent. He felt her hurt that he might think she was part of a larger conspiracy to harm him when she had risked her life to get him out of the laboratory. He felt her withdrawal, but he could not let it matter. He would find her. He had no other choice.

Carpathians often traveled in the form of an owl. The vampire had prepared to capture him in the form of mist, knowing hunters often used the fog to travel in. The vampire could very well have planned a trap for a bird winging through the sky. Riordan chose the shape of a smaller cat, a civet, able to move fast on the highway of branches above the forest floor. Any trap designed for an animal would be for a wolf or the much heavier leopard, forms routinely used for fast travel.

He was much more cautious as he leapt from branch to branch. His mind continually tuned itself toward Juliette. Riordan was used to being in complete control, without the danger of intense emotions, and his newly acquired feelings threw his normal balance. He sighed. *I am as ensnared as you.*

The silence was so long, he feared she would refuse to answer. *I would not say ensnared. I am merely obsessed, and obsession is very disturbing.*

I do not mind if I am the object of your obsession.

I mind. I refuse to be obsessed over anything, or anyone, let alone a man.

He felt the heat in her voice, the raw desire. Somewhere,

Juliette was thinking of him, fantasizing over him. There was a silence, and he caught the shimmer of images in her mind. Their mouths welded together, her hands stroking his body, her lips traveling over the terrible burns on his chest. Riordan's temperature rose sharply. Thunder pounded in his head. His body went tight and uncomfortable. The small cat stumbled as the sexual drive hit it hard.

You cannot do this to me. He knew his voice was husky and slightly harsh but he couldn't help it. His body burned, was on fire. Each step was painful and mixed with the cat's animalistic emotions, his own beast roared for his mate.

Why not? You did it to me. I don't think my fantasy about touching your body or kissing you is nearly as bad as you touching me without physically laying a finger on me.

The little cat leapt over a twig holding a spray of leaves and nearly didn't make it, almost somersaulting into a thick snake coiled around a branch. The cat hissed and spit as it gave the snake a wide berth.

Riordan nearly groaned. Juliette wasn't stopping her fantasy at touching his body or kissing him. She was doing delicious things with her lips, working her way deliberately down his body to engulf him in the heated silk of her mouth. He groaned aloud, the small cat shuddering. It was becoming an effort to hold the form while hunger beat at him and desire swamped him. He had not taken the time to fully heal himself and if he were to regain his strength he would need sustenance.

More than anything he wanted to find Juliette, to bury his body deep in the haven of hers, relieve the terrible pressure building with unrelenting madness in his body. He could almost feel her mouth gliding over him. He could taste her heat and spice, feel her soft skin beneath his fingers.

A sound shook him out of his reverie and the small cat went instantly still, crouching low high in the forest canopy. He heard a soft sound in the distance, muted by the natural sounds of the night. Insects hummed. The sap ran in trees. Bats dipped and wheeled in the air. Bushes rustled as small rodents dashed around looking for safety. Larger predators hunted. But the sound was human—and feminine.

Riordan remained still, allowing his senses to flair out into the night, scanning the area for intruders, for traps, for the identity of the human hidden a few miles from him.

Juliette. His heart accelerated. He shifted to his natural form as his incisors lengthened in anticipation. She was close, just ahead near the stream. He could hear the water bubbling over rocks and emptying into a pool of sorts. She had to be there, cooling her body from the heat of the jungle, from the fire raging out of control between them. When he was absolutely certain they were alone, with no one near them for miles, he began to make his way toward her, using the foliage for cover.

I want you. He breathed the words into her mind. Meaning them. Needing her.

There was the smallest of hesitations. *Well, maybe I want you too, but I have things that I have to do, obligations to fulfill. I can't just change my life to suit you.*

Her voice was breathless, sensual. She was feeling the same heat, the same needs. Riordan was beginning to understand what lifemates were all about. He had been away from his people too long and he had forgotten the close bonds. He had forgotten whatever one lifemate was feeling, so did the other. Relationships were highly sexual and always intense.

He found his way to the small grotto where she rested. He sat above her, high in the trees, pleasure blossoming deep and wild just looking at her. She was so beautiful she robbed him of speech, of breath. He could look at her for eternity and never tire of it.

Chapter 5

JULIETTE lifted her hair from the nape of her neck and wiped the sweat gleaming on her body. It was very hot and her clothes were sticking to her skin. The moon's reflection in the deep pool shimmered with cool invitation. She slowly unbuttoned her blouse and allowed it to fall to her elbows.

Riordan's breath caught in his lungs. She shrugged the top off and tossed it to land on a large fern growing out of the boulders. Juliette dipped her hand in the cool pool and poured the water down the valley between her breasts. Her head was thrown back and her breasts jutted forward, high and firm and enticing in the moonlight. Her body was no girl's, but that of a woman, with generous curves a man could lose himself in. She looked a night temptress, a woods fairy, nearly insubstantial as the water ran down her soft alluring skin to her belly and lower still, disappearing beneath the darker material of her jeans.

His body tightened into a hard, painful ache just looking at her. Her hands were graceful as she pulled the pins from her hair and the thick braid tumbled down well below her waist. There was something terribly sensual about a woman unbraiding her hair, Riordan decided. His chest hurt it was so tight, his lungs burning for air. Her hair floated free, a mass of blue-black silk he longed to crush in his fingers, to bury his face in.

She crouched by the pool, threw water on her face. Droplets ran down her throat, down to the creamy swell of her breasts, and lay on her skin waiting to be licked off. Riordan shifted his weight in an attempt to ease the fullness of his clothes. He didn't dare warn her she wasn't alone: she would try to run from him, and it was necessary to find out the secrets she kept locked away from him.

A faint breeze fingered the leaves of the trees so that they glittered silver and black in the night. Her scent was ripe and feminine, an allure all its own. He felt a growl rising in his throat, the beast roaring for freedom. Temptation was a woman cooling the heat of her body there by the pool in the moonlight. Riordan sank his nails deep into the branch to keep from going to her. His head pounded, his blood thick and hot. Every movement she made was a seduction. And what the hell was she doing walking around half-naked all alone where any predator could come upon her?

Juliette rose with her lithe, sensuous grace, her breasts swaying in time with the seductive movement of her hips. He couldn't take his hungry gaze off of her. Honor and gentlemanly behavior were completely overridden by primitive possessiveness. She was his lifemate. She belonged to him. Her lush body was everything he could ever want. He wanted to start at the top of her head and kiss his way down to her toes, lingering in every intriguing shadow and hollow along the way. His gaze narrowed as he saw her look around, scrutinizing the trees and bushes before stepping up on the highest boulder. She lifted her face into the air and sniffed, as if scenting the wind. Apparently satisfied she was alone, she stepped back to the edge of the pool, her hands going to the zipper of her jeans.

Riordan bit down hard on his bottom lip, hoping the pain would distract him. He couldn't have looked away if his life depended on it. She tugged at her jeans. The humidity was high and the material clung to her skin, so she had to squirm and shimmy to get them over her hips and down her thighs. Her breasts jiggled invitingly as she did a little dance to rid herself of her clothes. Tight dark curls formed a vee at the junction of her legs, a tempting arrow to draw his attention. At once he caught her feminine fragrance, the call of woman to man. Her body was burning, catching fire from his thoughts. He was broadcasting his hunger far too loudly.

Juliette was very susceptible to his needs. Dark cravings ate at him, hardened his body and sent erotic images teasing his brain. She was there waiting for him, her body open for his, craving his with the same terrible need that could never be assuaged. He closed his eyes and thought about how it would feel to plunge inside of her welcoming sheath, hot and tight and wet, slick with need for him.

Juliette made a single sound of distress as her body reacted to the waves of sexual hunger, the lust rising in him, lust she'd helped to create with her blatant fantasies. Riordan drank her in through half-closed eyes, his lids heavy and his body on fire. He wanted to see her hands travel over her soft skin, taking the path his hands would take. Up her thighs, over her rounded belly, up her narrow rib cage to cup the weight of her breasts in his palms. He wanted her thumbs to tease and flick her dark nipples, bring them to a heated peak in anticipation of his hot mouth suckling strongly.

He could already taste her, feel the soft mound of flesh in his mouth. He needed to pillow his head there, spend the night lavishing attention on each breast, on the dark inviting nipples, yet it wasn't enough. He wanted to feel how hot she was. How wet. How much she needed his body deep inside of her. His palms itched to feel her thighs, soft and rounded with firm muscles. He would slide his palms upward, feel the heat of her entrance before widening her stance, wanting her legs open to him. Gently he would slide one finger deep inside of her. He actually felt fiery heat, slick and moist, and it nearly stopped his heart. He wanted more. Wanted to feel her body grip and hold, clamp tightly around his.

He couldn't bear the feel of his clothes another moment

and he dispensed with them easily with a single thought in the way of his people. The small breeze instantly caressed his body, touching him all over, adding to his sensitivity. He wished it were her fingers wrapping around the hard length of him. His erection was full and heavy and merciless, a pulsing, throbbing pain he could hardly endure.

Damn you, what are you doing to me? Her voice was breathless in his mind. Husky. Sexy. Fraught with an elemental need.

Damn you back. My body is on fire. I want your mouth on me. I want to be inside of you. I do not want illusion. Your stubbornness is going to kill us both.

Juliette had never felt such unbearable lust. It rose up from the very depths of her being and consumed her. She had always known there was passion deep inside of her. The heat of the jungle made her feel sensual when others found it oppressive. She often felt sexy, even seductive around men, but never had she felt such building heat. It was uncomfortable and unsettling, an edgy pressure demanding urgent relief. Her breasts ached for the feel of his mouth. She didn't want a gentle lover, she wanted him to feel the same smoldering, dangerous passion welling up in her. She wanted an explosive joining, his hard body driving deep and mercilessly into her. She itched and burned and hungered and there was no relief, no matter what she did.

Are you near me? She couldn't keep the invitation out of her voice. She looked around her, unconsciously enticing him with her body. She stretched her arms over her head, turned slowly in a circle. She knew she had a beautiful body and she wanted him to see it. He had done this to her, put her in this terrible state of passion, and it was up to him to assuage her unrelenting lust.

I am watching you. Can't you feel my eyes on you? You are so beautiful. Touch yourself for me.

There was seduction in his voice. A purring command, a promise of exactly what she needed. Sex—hot, elemental. A fierce lover who would slake her burning need. Juliette turned her head so that her silken hair flew around her like a cape, settling over her shoulders and body, sliding over her sensitive skin. She felt his heated gaze burning over her and she smiled.

I'm so much hotter than you can imagine. I'm slick and wet, dripping for you. She licked her fingers, a slow deliberate curl of her tongue before sucking her own tangy juice from her fingers. *I'm burning up. Are you going to just watch me all night or are you going to do something about it?* Juliette had never been so bold in her life, but then she'd never felt such intense pressure. She was angry with him for making her so out of control, and if she was out of control, she was determined he would feel the same. And she wanted him right there, right now, and didn't care that he knew it.

Riordan didn't wait for a second invitation. He floated across the sky toward the pool, settling to earth behind her. She had a beautiful back and a perfect, rounded bottom. His hands slid over the curve of her hips, starkly possessive, and he dragged her roughly against him, wanting her to feel the thick, hard length of his erection pressed tightly against her bottom.

The breath slammed out of her lungs and hot fluid rushed to pool between her legs. His teeth skimmed the nape of her neck, her shoulder, and his hands slid up to cup her aching breasts. The soft weight filled his palms, his thumbs slid over her taut nipples, stroking caresses.

"I never thought I would find you. I spent centuries without hope, and you came to me in my darkest hour." His lips drifted up her neck to her ear, whispering the words while his hips pushed into her, rubbed to try, unsuccessfully, to ease some of the pressure.

His touch set every nerve ending screaming for relief. "I found you." Juliette didn't recognize her own voice. She shook with hunger. His body was everything to her, his mind thrust deep inside of hers, heightening her pleasure at his touch, sharing her passion, the intensity of her desire until she couldn't tell where hers began or where his left off. "I can't wait anymore. I want you inside of me."

His hand slid between her legs, felt her wet welcome. She

nearly sobbed with pleasure, pushing against his hand. Her arm went back, circled his neck, dragged his head around so she could find his mouth, drown in his kisses, devour him, her teeth nibbling at his lips, her tongue dueling and dancing wildly with his. "I *need* you inside of me, Riordan. I'm going to burn up if you don't hurry."

He bit wildly at her mouth, her neck, bent her back so he could get to her breasts. He'd been fantasizing about her breasts for so long he couldn't stand not tasting them, drawing her into his mouth, suckling strongly, while his hips frantically surged against her enticing buttocks.

She screamed at the pull of his mouth, her hand tunneling in his hair, clutching his head to her while he devoured her breast. Every pull of his mouth sent wet heat pulsating through her body and trickling down her leg. Her cries nearly sent him over the edge. He bent her body forward, planting her hands on the boulders while he thrust his fingers deep into her to test her readiness. She pushed back into his hand, riding, bucking, sobbing for him enter her.

He caught her hips and held her, looking down at her beautiful body. His lifemate. Sultry, sexy—everything he could ever want. Crying out for him. Pleading for him to take her, to unite them. *Demanding* he take her. He was so hard he thought he might shatter. He surged into her thick wetness, one long stroke that felt as if it blew the top of his head off. Fire raced up his penis, spread through his body, a volcanic eruption that reached all the way to his toes.

Juliette's body was tight and hot and gripping his as he withdrew so that he shuddered with pleasure. She sobbed again, pushing eagerly back onto him as he thrust forward. He was large and thick, and driving through the soft folds was sweet torture. "Are you all right?" He was so large and she felt so small. He pressed her forward, adjusting their positions so she could take more of him. "I want all of me inside of you."

"I want every last bit of you in me too," Juliette answered. "Can't you feel what I'm feeling? Harder. Faster. I need you to be crazy, because I feel crazy." And she did. She felt wild and heated and sensual and she wanted him out of control and driving into her with everything he was. Pouring his heart and soul and his very essence into her. "More, I want more."

Juliette gave herself up to the wild pounding. Every hard stroke sent vibrations of sheer pleasure rushing through her body. Every cell, every nerve ending, every tiny part of her burned and blazed. Her breasts ached and swung with every thrust, her hair brushed the ground and silky strands fell in her face. Her body was hot and sweaty and exploding in ecstasy. She took him with her over the edge, her muscles clamping around his thick erection and dragging every last drop of his seed out of him.

For Juliette it didn't end, her body rippling with aftershocks, colors bursting behind her eyes and fireworks going off in her mind. She didn't want him to move, wanted to savor their joined bodies. He was magnificent, long and thick and more than she could possibly have imagined.

Riordan slid out of her body reluctantly. When she made a soft sound of protest he drew her back into his arms. "We have time. All the time in the world, and I want to touch you. I love kissing you." His hands skimmed her breasts, moved up to frame her face. "And I hunger for the taste of you. I want to bring you more fully into my world."

She turned her face up to nuzzle his throat. "Do you know what I am?" She kissed the hollow of his throat, her hands sliding possessively over his body. Stroking his flat stomach and kissing her way along his chest. Her hands caressed his penis, shaping and teasing and memorizing the long line of him. "I'm jaguar. A shape-shifter. Are you certain I am what you want?"

Riordan answered her in the only way he could. His body was sensitized and reacting with more demands. His incisors lengthened as his penis did. He bent his head and buried his teeth in the pulse beating so strongly in her neck.

She cried out, threw her head back and circled his neck with her arms, pressing her body closer to his. He had not used his tongue to prepare her for the shock of the connection, but Juliette felt it only as white-hot heat coursing through her bloodstream, as whips of lightning lashed every nerve ending into a sexual frenzy.

He held her possessively, his hands tender, but commanding, shifting her so that the tips of her breasts rubbed against his chest and her hair was out of the way. So that his straining groin pressed against her soft belly. *You taste like an exotic fruit, tangy and spicy and hot. I wonder what you'll taste like when I crawl between your legs and drink my fill there.*

Her entire body clenched. She closed her eyes and pressed closer to him. She wanted everything from him, with him. She wanted it all.

His tongue swept across the pinpricks on her neck. His hand circled her throat, his thumb tipping up her face so that she was compelled to look into his eyes. *See what I taste like.* He commanded it in a purring, velvet voice, so mesmerizing she half fell into a dream. Riordan opened a line with a sharp fingernail, caught the back of her head in his palm and pressed her face forward until her mouth was pressed to the heavy muscles of his chest, just above his heart. She could feel it beating, accelerating as her lips moved over his skin, as she drew his dark gift into her body.

He brought her out of her enthrallment when she had taken enough for their second exchange, his mouth ravishing hers. He could kiss her forever, over and over and never get enough. Their mouths clung, tongues tangling wildly. Abruptly he pulled away, scowling at her. There was an ominous danger to his smoldering gaze.

"What?"

"Do not *what* me. You were thinking of another man."

Juliette ran her tongue over her bottom lip. "I was not thinking of another man. I merely thought I'd never been with a man as sexy as you. There's a difference."

His hand circled her bare arm, brought her close to him. "You have been with another man."

"Jaguars are sexual creatures, Riordan. We need sex at times." She leaned forward and lapped at his chest, right above his heart. "Why should that bother you?"

"Juliette, we are bound together. I would know if you had sex with another man. You could not hide it from me."

"I wouldn't try to hide it from you." She pushed at the wall of his chest but he was a rock, and even with her unusual strength, she couldn't move him.

"I would kill him."

"Why would you kill him? He isn't the one bound to you."

"Exactly." Riordan turned away from her, a black anger he didn't understand enveloping him. To cool off, he waded into the pool and looked back at her. She stood there with the moonlight spilling over her luscious body, her expression a mixture of amusement and exasperation. She was so beautiful he hurt just looking at her. "I am not human, Juliette and you can never think for one moment that I am. I am a predator and I will protect what is mine."

"Did I say I wanted another man? No! I was thinking no one else could compare with you. I was *not* thinking I wanted someone else. How could I, after what we just shared? Are you going to be an idiot and act jealous all the time? That would make me crazy."

He ducked under the water to rinse the heat from his skin. He stood up, the water lapping at his hips. "Come here."

"You didn't answer me."

He sighed. "Yes, I am going to be an idiot and act jealous all the time. The idea of another man touching you, making love to you, makes me want to tear out his heart."

"Well." Juliette smiled and waded out to him. "I'd want to tear out the heart of any woman that tried to seduce you." She reached him, tipping up her face for his searing kiss. "We'll both have to work not to be jealous idiots. I can't see myself wanting anyone else when I have you."

"I will not mind if you wish to seduce me." He kissed her again, long, addictive kisses that had a bite to them.

"How lucky for me." She bent down and hit the water with her hand, sending up a spray that doused him thoroughly. Laughing, she dove away from him, swimming beneath the water to the center of the pond.

Chapter 6

RIORDAN watched her swim, her pale body slipping sensuously through the water. The clear liquid shimmered over her feminine form, enhancing every curve and secret hollow. Catching the glimpse of another man in her mind had been a shock, and he wasn't certain why it would be. She was a very sexual woman. She was bold and knew what she wanted. He wanted that kind of woman, as sexual as he knew himself to be, yet the thought of another man leaning down to suckle her breast or plunge deep into her body made the beast in him rise. It was dark and ugly and utterly dangerous.

Juliette would attract the attention of men with her shapely body. She was the epitome of a sexual creature. Riordan dove under water and began to swim laps, back and forth, driving himself to keep his fury at bay. If she ever wanted another man . . .

I thought lifemates wanted only each other. There was curiosity in her voice.

You are the only lifemate I have ever had. I am new at this.

He sounded so disgruntled she laughed and swam to the other side of the pool. There was a smooth shelf formed from boulders beneath the surface near the edge of the water. Juliette sat on it and watched him swim back and forth like a shark. *Does it really bother you so much?*

Riordan heard the soft tremor in her voice. *Of course it bothers me. I am a possessive man. But it matters little, Juliette. We are lifemates. We are bound from this time forward and there will be no other.*

Is that a decree? She didn't know why she was suddenly close to tears. She wasn't ashamed of her past. She didn't want any other men now, but she couldn't help that she had been born into a species that made it nearly impossible not to have sex at certain times. She wasn't about to apologize for who she was.

Riordan caught the echo of her thoughts, the painful tightness in her chest, and knew he hurt her. Had that been his intention? He hoped not. He would despise himself if his newly acquired emotions were so out of control that he could punish his lifemate for something she did before he met her.

He swam slowly across the pool until he was directly in front of her. "I do believe I am the idiot you called me. I apologize for my jealous streak. I also find I have a rotten temper which I shall do my best to control." He grinned at her, a sudden melting smile that brought life to his dark eyes. "It is the passion in me. My blood runs hot and I am caught. Fortunately . . ." He moved closer to her, his hands circling her ankles. "I can make up for my shortcomings in other ways."

"Don't you dare." She could see the mischief on his face.

He yanked on her legs, catching her by surprise, so that she slid toward him, her legs over his shoulders. *I thought I would find out how you taste. If you're as tangy and spicy all over as I imagine you are.* Without giving her the slightest opportunity to squirm away, he lowered his head between her thighs.

Juliette jumped, but his hands cupped her bare buttocks,

fingers digging deep to hold her still. His teeth scraped the inside of her thigh. She heard herself moan softly. Felt the first surge of moist welcoming heat.

"Lie back for me," he said softly, "relax, float. Just feel. Just feel this time, Juliette."

She loved the way he said her name with his peculiar, very sexy accent. She loved the way his eyes went dark and smoldered and hungered and burned over her body. His hair touched her sensitive skin, her body trembled. She felt his hand pushing against her heat. She stared up at the night sky, watched the droplets of rain come down in slow motion. Some landed on her face, some on her bare breasts. Water from the pool slid over her stomach, a silken blanket arousing her further. Juliette gave herself to him completely.

His finger pushed into her, stroking deep caresses, teasing and dancing until she moaned with pleasure. His mouth replaced his hand, a hot pulsing of fire that left her breathless, unable to scream, unable to breathe. Pressure built fast and hard and raged through her body for release. When her orgasm hit, it was explosive and violent and shook her to the very core of her being.

Riordan slowly lifted his head from between her thighs, holding her secure when she might have drowned, might have just sunk to the bottom in a heap of heated feminine flesh. He pulled her through the water to him, rocked her gently while her body continued to sizzle and spark and ripple with pleasure.

Juliette wrapped her arms around his neck and laid her head on his shoulder. "I accept your apology."

His arms tightened possessively. He floated over to the small shelf near the water's edge. "I hoped you would feel my sincerity."

"Do you think a woman can fall in love with a man she barely knows?"

"I do not know, but she can fall in love with a man after she has walked in his mind and knows who he is and what he stands for."

She kissed his neck. "I never once dreamed I would have a man in my life. Never once."

"That is only because you could not conjure up the image of such a charming man." He sank down onto the shelf looking pleased with himself and pulled her onto his lap, cradling her close. "I have four brothers." He pushed the wet hair from the side of her neck and threw it back in a long, wet trail over her shoulder. "Our prince sent us out so many years ago this country has become our home. I am the youngest in the family, and my brothers worry for me, all of them. Nicolas and Rafael are out of the country at the moment so you are safe from meeting them en masse. We have very close ties to a family of humans. . . ."

"The ones who work your cattle empire," she interrupted.

"Ranch. It is large, but it is no empire. Yes, they run the ranch. They have young orphaned relatives in the United States and two of my brothers went to help them smooth the way to bring them home."

She looked up at him suspiciously. "What does that mean? Smooth the way. By using their voices with hypnotic suggestions? Their eyes mesmerizing people?"

He grinned again, softening the lines in his face. "Is that what you think I do?"

"You're shameless about it," she confirmed.

"It worked on you, and that is all that matters."

"You wish it worked on me. I just happen to like the way you're put together." She laced her fingers through his. "So you have a big ranch and live there with four overprotective brothers and a human family as well."

"My other brothers, Manolito and Zacarias, the eldest, are probably heading this way as we speak to check on me as if I were an infant."

She brought his hand to her mouth. "I'll testify you're long past the infant stage if you'd like."

"I doubt if it will be helpful. I can handle my brothers. I am just warning you that their protection will extend to you. We have to avoid them until I know you're so completely captivated by my charm, you will not run away from them."

"I live with my younger sister, and my cousin. Jasmine, my little sister, is beautiful inside and out." Juliette frowned. "She is able to shift once in a while if she is under tremendous stress, but she can't count on the ability as I do. My cousin and I are the protectors in my family. Not just in my family but for all women in our bloodline."

He was silent, waiting for her to continue. He sensed a terrible sadness and tightened his arms around her to give her comfort and support.

Juliette leaned her head against his shoulder, her hair floating on the water around them like seaweed. "I have to go back home and make certain my sister and my cousin are safe. I have a duty to my family, Riordan, just as you have one to your people. We don't have men to protect us. Our men do not mate for life, nor do they stay with us. Some of the men try to kidnap and hold our women prisoners just to be able to keep the bloodline pure. Very few of us are capable of shifting into our other form. And it will continue to become fewer and fewer. They treat these women like breeding machines. It's a horrible thing. They don't love them or try to create an atmosphere of happiness, they simply force them to produce babies."

"And what is it you think you can do to stop them?" His voice was utterly devoid of expression.

Juliette felt a chill go down her spine. She sensed his sudden stillness. She had been in his mind and there was a ruthless, merciless quality buried deep inside of him that alarmed her. "Someone has to rescue the women. I'm strong. I'm capable of shifting, and I'm not afraid of those bastards. I can protect my sister and cousin. Well, maybe Solange protects me." She turned her head to look up at his face. "They took my mother. She was held in a tiny room, and several men raped her to get her pregnant. It didn't happen immediately so they had her for a long time. It took us two years to find her."

"Juliette." He breathed her name. Her sorrow beat at him, tore at his heart and soul. He nuzzled the top of her head. "I am so sorry." She didn't need to tell him the rest. He saw it

in her mind. Her mother had died in childbirth, too long neg-
lected by the men who held her prisoner. The child had died
as well, and Juliette felt responsible because it had taken so
long to find her mother.

Riordan had been prepared to forbid her to assume the
part of a warrior woman, but he couldn't speak, couldn't issue commands even though it might keep her safe. Her pain
ran too deep. He understood the need to protect others. He
understood honor and responsibility. His fingers crushed her
hair in his fist. "Did you find the men who took her? You
must know them by scent."

Tears burned behind her eyelids, tears she vowed would
never be shed. She refused to spend her time crying. There
were very few women capable of shifting and the jaguar
males who had banded together were determined to possess
them. She was every bit as determined that they would never
get their hands on them.

"Jasmine may not be able to shift on command, but even
the small ability she has places her in danger. She has other
gifts to aid her, but she couldn't fight against the males if
they captured her. I live with Jasmine and my cousin.
Solange is my mother's sister's daughter and my mother
raised her after my aunt was killed when several males tried
to capture us. She fought them off, giving my mother time to
escape with the three of us girls."

"So now you and your sister and cousin live in fear of
these men coming after you. Why did you stay in the jungle
where there is danger?"

"Why do you hunt the vampire?" she fired back. "This is
our home. We're not the only women these men are after, but
we have skills. After what they did to our mothers, we don't
plan to just let them steal and kill other women. We know the
way the men think now, and we've successfully taken back
several women."

"Juliette, what you do is very dangerous. These males are
not right. I have known some of the jaguar race and the men
did not commit these crimes against their women. Something is wrong."

"It isn't all the men. It is only a small group, yet they are very powerful because they have banded together." She turned in his arms. "Do you understand why I have to stay with these women? They have no other protection. Jasmine and I feared the males were in league with someone at the new Morrison laboratory. Too many animals on the endangered species list were being captured. We thought the jaguar males were trading animals for help in finding the females. That was one of the reasons we broke into the laboratory."

"Is it possible a vampire has connected with a jaguar male and corrupted him?"

"I think these males have corrupted themselves."

"We will return to your family and make certain they are safe, Juliette. If you care about them, then, of course, I care about them. There is no question this practice must be stopped."

"I tried not to blame the males, I really did. Our species is dying out, but they don't care at all about the females, only that they want the race to go on." She shook her head sadly. "It isn't right. We have a right to our lives."

He kissed her temple, the corner of her mouth. "I understand their desperation. Our species is nearly extinct also." He tipped her chin up so he could capture her mouth. His kiss was gentle, tender. "I bound you to me with no thought of your feelings, Juliette. Perhaps I am as guilty as these males." His arms circled her waist, pulled her onto his lap so that they half floated in the water, her body fitting into the cradle of his hips. "I never thought how selfish that would be. In my culture, lifemates are destined and must be together for survival. It is another world now, one where our women, perhaps, are not even from the same species. I should have thought more of what you wished to accomplish in your life and less of what I needed to survive."

Juliette lay back against him, resting her head in the niche of his sternum. His hands cupped her full breasts, taking the weight in his palms, his fingers gently massaging her almost without thought. Pleasure shot through her. She thought she might never want to move again, yet his hands on her body created a molten heat that moved slowly through her bloodstream and licked at her skin.

"I wasn't thinking either, Riordan, only how much I wanted you. I could barely think straight with wanting you. You hadn't bound us together at that point so I'm not so certain I would have said no." She turned over lazily and slid down his body, skin to skin, rubbing along his chest and rib cage, delighting in the differences between men and women. His belly was flat and ridged with muscles. She licked off droplets of water. The rain fell gently, cool drops that seemed to sizzle against her hot skin. She wrapped her arms around his hips, nuzzling his navel lazily. Her teeth nipped his skin.

Riordan felt his body harden in response. Looking down at the clean line of her back, the rounded enticement of her bottom, her legs floating over his in the cool waters of the pool was enough to give any man pleasure. Her mouth wandered over him, tasting and licking. There was nothing inhibited about Juliette. She loved having sex with him, loved his body, and in her mind she let him know. With her body she let him know. It was exciting to have a woman so completely open and natural with him.

"I should have given you the opportunity to at least discuss what it meant, Juliette," he said. His voice was husky. Her mouth was doing delicious things to his body and it was becoming much more difficult to think straight.

"I don't think I wanted to discuss it." She slipped a little lower so she could breathe hot air over his heavy erection. She smiled when she felt his muscles contract and his hands clamp over her arms in reaction. Juliette lifted her chin so she could meet his gaze, reveling in the hunger darkening his eyes. "If I'd thought too much, I wouldn't have been able to have you. And I really, really wanted you." She lowered her head so she could lick along the head of his penis, a slow, leisurely exploration of the shape and texture of his body.

His breath slammed out of his lungs. "I have to admit, I

am eternally grateful you want me. I do not think we will ever have enough time to do all the things I have in my mind." Deliberately he let her see his every desire, his every need.

Juliette laughed softly. "It's good we think along the same lines. I would hate to be tied to someone who isn't adventurous. I definitely need adventurous."

It was his turn to yell. The sound ripped from his throat when her mouth engulfed him, took him deep into her throat and began a slow, sensuous foray. *I thought I would find out how you taste. Whether you're hot and spicy and tangy.* Her teasing laughter played over his senses and stroked at his body. He lost time, drifting in the waves of the pool lapping at his body, with her hot mouth and tongue bringing him to a fever pitch. When he could no longer stay still, he moved his hips into her, letting her take charge of the rhythm, set the pace. She teased him to the brink of an orgasm, sucking hard and lavishing attention with her tongue, only to slide her mouth loosely over him, her teeth gentle. *I love to feel what you feel. I love to hear the roar in your head and know I can put it there just by doing this.* Her mouth pulled at him. His hands fisted in her hair, his hips growing more urgent, more frantic in his response. She took him deep, working him until he was so caught in her spell, so far gone with pleasure he couldn't think straight.

"Finish it or let me have you," he managed to hiss out between his teeth.

She complied, her soft, taunting laughter only teasing his senses more. Juliette reveled in her power. He was enormously strong and dangerous, and yet he needed her. *You need fun in your life, Riordan. You really do need me.*

Damn it. He growled it in her mind, his hands bunching in her hair.

Her mouth sent him deliberately over the edge, milking him as her teasing laughter burned in his brain. She was etched in his very bones for all time. He would never be able to go back to what he had been. And he would never be able to be without her. She carried light with her and she made him feel it in the unrelenting darkness that had been his home.

She ducked under the water, pushing away from him. Riordan reached out and caught her, dragging her back. He pushed the wet hair from her face and stared down at her. His miracle. "I do need you," he admitted. If she could be brave and honest and admit what she wanted and needed he could do no less. "You are everything."

Chapter 7

"I need blood, Juliette. The night is slipping away from us. We must return to your family at full strength. I would love to spend the rest of my days here, making love to you and discovering the secrets of my lifemate, but I must have sustenance to renew my strength." Riordan waded out of the pool and held out his hand to her.

Juliette took her time, her eyes taking her fill of him. "I swore I would never have anything to do with a man. The men I've known have no knowledge of caring." She looked down at the ground. "It's a terrible thing to grow up being ashamed of what you are, knowing you might give birth to a male of the species and no matter what you do, how much you love him, how you raise him, his nature will always prevent him from loving you back."

His fingers settled around her wrist and he drew her to him. "I have lived many years and have found that each species has both strengths and weaknesses. The males of the jaguar race are wanderers, but the ones I encountered cared about their women. They could not settle down and the continual drive to perpetuate their race became their downfall.

They would not stay with one female, though I believe many of them tried and were very distressed that they could not." He drew her into his arms to comfort her. "The rain forest here in South America is very large and there are no borders in the jungle. We settled in Brazil, on the edge of the forest, but we travel from country to country to insure the safety of the inhabitants. In our travels we often encounter the males. They are all solitary creatures. We had been instructed by our prince to avoid them if possible, but often we spoke with them. Jaguars, like our species, are on the verge of extinction. They are intelligent and know they contributed to their own extinction, yet they still could not stop what nature dictated." And a part of him felt very much as if they deserved their fate when they refused to treasure their women and children.

"You're saying it's not their fault." Juliette pulled out of his arms, turning her face away from him as she gathered her clothes with shaking hands. She stepped into her jeans and dragged them up over her bare skin, blinking back tears. That was twice she'd nearly cried in front of him. She didn't cry. Not because of a man.

"We are not talking about the rogue males, the ones out of control and doing harm to their women. They should be brought to justice, not allowed to be kidnapping and raping women with the idea of creating baby machines." He took the shirt from her hands and turned her around to face him, tipping up her chin so she had to meet his dark gaze. "I may be rough, Juliette, and I will admit I have long ago forgotten how to be gentle, but I would never harm a woman unless she threatened my life or my people. It is not done."

She framed his face, her palms resting along his shadowed jaw. "You're gentle enough for me." And he was. He moved her like no other man had ever done—or ever could. They had come together in fire, burning hot and out of control, yet then he had stroked tender caresses down her body with a trembling hand, sitting her on his lap, cupping her breasts reverently.

Riordan leaned down to kiss her upturned face, taking his

time, lingering over it. His heart found the rhythm of hers. "You are an unexpected gift. I am not a man to throw such things away."

She took her shirt from him and slipped into it.

He reached out to pull the edges of the material together over her generous breasts. "Even in your clothes, you look so sexy I am uncertain whether or not I can keep my hands off of you." He lifted the soft weight of her breast, his fingers sliding over creamy skin. "Your skin is so soft and warm and inviting." He bent down and drew her nipple into the heat of his mouth, unable to resist the temptation.

Juliette closed her eyes, pressing closer to him, wrapping her arms around his head, holding him to her while waves of pleasure coursed through her body, swamped her utterly and completely. She loved the way he indulged himself with her body. She loved that he enjoyed her so much and that he obviously wanted her to feel the same about him. "We're never going to leave this spot if we keep this up," she murmured, wanting to strip off her jeans and wrap her legs firmly around his waist. "I think sex with you is addicting."

"I cannot help myself." His tongue teased her nipple into a hard peak before reluctantly releasing her. "Your body is such a temptation."

Her fingers drifted over his heavy erection. "There you go again, blaming it on me. I see you like this, hard and thick and so in need, and naturally I want to do something about it."

He groaned. "I have no discipline around you." He tugged at the jeans until they were down around her ankles and she could kick them aside. "If I do not get some relief, I doubt I will be able to walk, let alone battle any vampires. What do you intend to do about it?"

She circled his neck with her arms and pulled herself up his body, wrapping her legs tightly around his waist. "I thought I would just take a ride," she whispered and licked his ear with a teasing tongue. Very slowly she settled over his penis, lowering herself with slow deliberation. As he began to push his way through her tight folds she shivered with pleasure. "It's always so perfect with you." She waited to move until he had filled her completely, sinking down onto his shaft so that she was impaled and full and every nerve ending was alive and sizzling with flames.

Riordan didn't wait for her, catching her hips in his hands and helping her with her sensuous ride; long, hard thrusts that went deep inside of her, joining them together. He loved the way her breasts rubbed against his chest, the way she threw her head back, obvious pleasure lighting her face. She purred, just like a cat, deepening the movement, as wild and uninhibited as he was. He was so tuned to her mind now, he could adjust his every movement to better give her pleasure. He knew the moment she wanted him to be slow and deep and he knew when she needed the hard, long strokes that sent fiery friction whipping through both of them.

Night shadows hid them in the small grotto. The wind rustled in the canopy overhead. Bats fluttered above the water, hitting insects just above the surface. Raindrops splattered into the pool. Juliette inhaled the scents of the night, the combined scent of man and woman. Her nails dug into Riordan's shoulders and back as wave after wave of orgasm burst through her. He shared the experience in her mind and the riptide of ecstasy coursing through her sent him over the edge. Juliette, merged so completely with Riordan, felt the pressure start deep in his core and explode through his body with the force of a locomotive. They fed each other passion and heat, a firestorm of pleasure that washed over and through them and left them breathless and clinging to one another.

Juliette fastened her mouth to his—hot, wet, hungry. She tried to crawl inside of him, share the same body, the same mind. Kisses went from greedy lust to slower, calmer, leisurely exploration, to long, lingering enjoyment. She lifted her head and looked into his eyes. They stared at one another for a long time, drinking each other in, falling into the depths of each other's eyes. "I look at you and everything just comes together, Riordan. I don't know why, and I don't think I want to question it too closely. I'm just going to take what fate offered me and grab on with both hands."

"You will never be sorry, Juliette," he promised, raining kisses over her face, her eyes, down her neck and throat. "You will never be sorry."

"I can feel your hunger now, the call inside you. It's a frightening thing. How can you keep it at bay the way you do? If I felt like that, I would be devouring something." She swept back his hair and slowly allowed her legs to drop to the ground. "You have to get some nourishment. I don't mind, Riordan. I'm not in the least bit hungry and the thought of food makes me want to gag, but it's sort of sexy when you take my blood. I think I'm getting a bit kinky." She looked around for her clothes, missing the look of wonderment on his face.

He reached down to snag her blouse from where it had been carelessly tossed aside. He didn't even remember stripping it off of her. "You are a very generous woman, but I think I will refrain from the temptation of your blood." This time he firmly buttoned the blouse. "You know I am going to think of your breasts just waiting behind this very thin barrier. If I am distracted later, you will know why."

Juliette laughed. She couldn't remember being so happy. "That's all right, you go ahead and think about my breasts. I'll be thinking of your very nicely put together anatomy." She yanked her jeans on and deftly braided her hair. "How much time do we have for traveling tonight?"

He glanced at the sky. "A few hours. We should be able to cover many miles. I will have to carry you, and that means I will have to find blood." He glanced down at the terrible marks on his chest. "Carpathians heal in the ground and yet I did not. I need to get back to full strength for the coming battle, and that means I need to find people."

She suddenly went still. "Not my sister or cousin." There was a warning note in her voice.

He grinned at her. "I do not think you have to worry. I would not risk your wrath." He tugged playfully at her braid. "You sound so fierce."

Juliette watched him clothe himself. It was done with a simple wave of his hand as if he'd manufactured the clothes from thin air. His hair was neatly brushed back away from his face and tied with a leather thong. There wasn't a drop of water on him anywhere and his hair was dry. "Oh, that is cheating. Look at me, I look like a drowned rat." She flipped her thick wet braid over her shoulder. "I want to be able to do that."

"You will," he assured. "Come here. We need to get started."

"You aren't going to throw me over your shoulder like you did last time, are you?" she asked suspiciously.

He grinned at her, his teeth very white. "Well, I was thinking about it."

"Refrain. Last time I considered getting sick all over you."

"I am so glad you didn't." Riordan gathered her to him, holding her close, and took to the air, shifting into his favorite form of a bird as he rose. It was easier to fly above the canopy then to try to wind his way through the thick branches and leaves. And he was wary of traps. They were nearing the area where he had first heard the voice of the vampire calling to him for help. He was certain the vampire and his human accomplices were responsible for the net that had nearly claimed him a second time.

Juliette laughed aloud as Riordan raced across the sky. Twice she reached out, trying to touch a cloud, unable to resist. *This is astonishing.* She felt a part of the night sky, the stars and the clouds and even the rain. It was as though she had merged with nature. She expected to feel fear, but she felt elation, joy, completely alive. It was every bit as wonderful as running through the jungle in the form of a jaguar.

Do not ever feel regret, Juliette. You will be able to shift into many forms and effortlessly hold those forms.

I have to tell you something. The smile faded from Juliette's face. Riordan caught the uneasiness rising as he followed the directions in her mind. *We have to move often. We have several homes.*

He waited. It wasn't what she wanted to tell him. She was hesitant, very unlike his bold Juliette. She carefully turned over her words, trying to formulate the best way to get him to understand.

Juliette. You must trust me. Just say what you need to say and trust me to understand.

She could see the canopy far below her. The leaves of the trees were silver-black in the moonlight. The raindrops dazzled her eyes, glittering like diamonds as they fell from the clouds. *We have seen terrible things from the males. Young girls unable to shape-shift beaten and abused. Solange, Jasmine and I vowed never to have anything to do with a man other than the necessities.*

Necessities? She meant sex. Riordan felt his heart pound. Something black and dangerous swirled in his gut. It was ugly and volcanic, and he was ashamed of his reaction. She was telling him something terribly important, not only to her, but to her life, and his first thought had been that the necessity was sex with another man. He despised himself for being so petty. She was a beautiful and sensual woman. Many men would find her attractive, and he should be proud of her. Lifemates trusted one another implicitly. It was impossible to lie to one another or hide anything, and as they grew to know each other better it would be natural to spend more and more time in one another's mind.

I am not such a man, Juliette. At my worst, I would not harm a woman or child. It is abhorrent to me. I had no idea my returning emotions would be so overwhelming and intense, but I know myself well. I would never, I could never hurt you or your sister and cousin.

Juliette leaned into him, felt the tickle of feathers and immediately wanted to be able to join him in the form of a bird. *You don't have to tell me that. I already know you wouldn't ever hurt a woman or I would never be with you. I'm concerned my family won't be very accepting of our relationship.*

I will win them over.

Far below them, near the edge of the rain forest, was a

small settlement. Riordan began his descent cautiously, one part of him scanning the area below for signs of the vampire. *Always scan to look for danger before revealing yourself.*

It feels a bit intrusive. You pick up random thoughts. She was studying his ways carefully, trying to learn as much as possible. *I would hate to pick up my sister's thoughts or worse, my cousin's.*

He laughed as he set her gently on the ground, shifting back to his natural form as he planted his feet in the thick vegetation. "You can avoid scanning the thoughts of your family. You will learn to tune things out once you refine the process. Start experimenting now with volume and reading the air. You can feel danger vibrating. If there is a blank spot where what seems natural to you is not there, a vampire is attempting to hide his presence from you."

"Do you always know a vampire is a vampire?"

"Unfortunately, no. If a vampire is skilled, such as a master vampire, he could easily walk up to one of the hunters, greet him in the way of our people and go on his way unscathed."

"How frightening."

"Stay here while I feed. You should be safe for the moment. There is a feel to the forest, as if the animals are in hiding."

Juliette went still. She had been so busy trying to think as a Carpathian, so wrapped up in Riordan as a man, that she had forgotten the first rule of living in the jungle. She hadn't paid attention to the warning system of the inhabitants. Riordan strode away from her, melting into the shadows so that it was impossible to see him, even when she was looking directly at him.

She lifted her face to the wind. She was jaguar. And her senses were enhanced by ancient Carpathian blood. She could read the forest news. Animals were hiding, lying low and trembling, waiting until a night bird signaled they were once again safe from predators. Juliette turned her head this way and that, on the alert, feeling the vibration of danger moving through the air. Something was wrong. They were a few miles from the laboratory and several miles from her home.

Her heart jumped. "Jasmine." A large predator or a hunting party had passed through the area and frightened the inhabitants. A sudden chill went down her spine. Or a *group* of predators. She was supposed to lead the guards from the Morrison laboratory away from the direction of her home, but Riordan had carried her off instead. Had they found Jasmine's trail? Jasmine might not have been as cautious as she should have, thinking Juliette would be drawing the guards away from her. What if it was worse than the human guards? What if the male jaguars had cut across Jasmine's trail? Solange was on a scouting mission, hunting for any news of missing females. Jasmine had been alone.

Juliette didn't hesitate, she turned and ran, following the small animal trail through the brush. *I think my sister's in trouble.*

I am feeding, near full strength. Wait for me. I will get us to her.

She couldn't wait. She knew it didn't make sense, but she had to do something. Adrenaline was pouring through her body. Fear took hold of her mind. What if Jasmine had been taken the night before and the males had her already for nearly twenty-four hours? *Please God, please God.* She chanted the plea, her chest burning, her throat closing. The more she ran, the more she was certain the jaguars had been on her sister's trail, tracking her.

"Juliette," Riordan caught her in strong arms, in front of her, blocking her way. She hit his chest hard, but his larger frame barely rocked under her assault. "We have to be cautious. And we do not want to ruin any tracks. If they have her, it is better to slow down and find her trail, than to go running around without direction."

"You don't know what they do," she hissed, pulling away from him.

"We will find her and get her back."

She stepped away from him and wrapped her arms

around her body, hunching. "You have no idea what she will suffer, and I can never take it back."

He led the way, moving fluidly, so silent not even the leaves rustled. Juliette tried to breathe, to get her brain functioning again. *I couldn't bear it if something happened to Jasmine. It's my fault. I was supposed to draw the guards away. I wasn't here to do it, and she probably left tracks. The males would be able to follow her easily.*

This is not your fault Juliette. Riordan could smell them now. He didn't want to tell her, but he knew as they approached the small hut covered over with vines and creepers. The structure was difficult to see through all the foliage. He reached for her hand. The door was splintered down the middle, one half cracked and broken out, leaving a large hole.

A terrible cry welled up in Juliette. She couldn't stop it, couldn't repress it. The sound tore through her body, raw and horrible, tearing her throat. It was an agonized cry of pain and heartache and grief. It was a cry of revenge, of promise, a vow of absolute retribution.

Chapter 8

RIORDAN went through the door first. The stench of terror permeated the room. The pungent odor of large cats was overpowering. A table was overturned. There was a smear of blood on the wall and another on a broken chair.

Juliette pressed her hand to her mouth, choking back a sob. "She's just a child, Riordan. She's just turned twenty." She pushed past Riordan and hurried across the room to the wall. She inhaled deeply, scenting the blood. "This isn't from Jasmine. It's Solange. She was here."

Riordan was examining the room and the forest floor just outside. "She came when they were taking Jasmine and she must have shifted on the run. Can she do that? See, here are her footprints, and here are ripped clothes and claw marks. She did not have time to shed her clothes and shifted with them on. The seams of the material separated and she ripped the rest away from her so she could fight. She was the one who destroyed the door trying to get to your sister. They barred it from the inside and took your sister out the back. One was carrying her. They were in the form of men. See," he crouched beside the tracks. "This one is suddenly heavier, and he's bearing a weight. Jasmine is not struggling."

"She's unconscious," Juliette said. "She would fight them with her last breath. We all watched my mother die. Solange saw them kill her mother and yet she raced in, without hesitation, to try to stop them." She turned back to study the blood. "She isn't hurt too bad."

"One remained behind, a big male, and he shifted into jaguar form. He probably didn't want to harm her when he saw she was female and she shifted on the run. After all, she is probably extremely rare." Riordan followed the tracks. "She got away, into the forest. The big male is after her." He turned back to Juliette. "Which one do we go after?"

"Maybe we should split up. I'll follow Solange. We've fought together before, and I know how she thinks. She'll accept me. You go after Jasmine. You're far stronger and can travel faster. You have a chance of getting to her before they hurt her."

"Dawn will be breaking soon, Juliette. I will have to go to ground. If I do not reach your sister before that time, she will spend another day in torment." Riordan cursed the vulnerability of his heritage. "I cannot walk in the sun." His fingers brushed her cheek. "You will burn, Juliette. Your skin is no longer able to stand intense sunlight and your eyes will burn."

"I don't care about my skin." Juliette pushed past him and studied the ground, the direction the group of men had taken. She tried to think who would need her the most. Riordan was fast; he could get her close to her sister before he would have to get away from the sun. "Jasmine's already been with them for hours. If you don't think you'll have enough time to get to her then I'll have to trust Solange to get away from her attacker alone. We have to find Jasmine fast, Riordan."

Riordan circled her waist with one arm, lifting her. The surrounding jungle was a blur as he raced through it. She had no idea how he could focus on the tracks, on the small bruised leaves, snapped twigs, and occasional footprint when he moved so quickly. She didn't need to tell him her younger sister was in dire trouble; he could read every worry in her mind. When the males shifted form, they were without clothes. Jasmine was alone and without protection. Juliette could only pray that the males would want to get her as far from help as possible. She tried not to think of her cousin— alone, hurt, running for her life.

I can send for my brothers, but they are hundreds of miles away. They would not be here for several risings.

Solange will fight. They will not take her easily. Even as she thought it, a wave of hope went through her. It was true, Solange was a fighter. She would never surrender, never give up, no matter how injured she was. *I feel as if I'm deserting her, but she has a much better chance than Jasmine.*

From what I have seen of your cousin in your mind, she would want you to go after Jasmine.

Riordan was all too aware of the time slipping away from them. The jaguar males were adept at losing themselves in the forest. They had spread out, weaving through the trees, more cunning now, obviously certain there would be an attempt to follow them.

The wind rose in a sudden rush off the forest floor, carrying a swirling eddy of vegetation, leaves and twigs and petals of flowers in a dark funnel straight toward the sky. The debris burst over them, a cloud of missiles hurled from the ground by unseen hands. Riordan reacted instantly, instinctively swinging his body around in midair to better protect Juliette. Debris embedded in his skin, drove for his heart. He swore in several languages as he raced to get them to earth where he could fight without the burden of Juliette's human form hampering him.

Remove your clothes now and as soon as you feel the ground under your feet, shift and blend into the trees. Hide your true self deep within the animal.

It was the grimness in his voice that had her obeying without hesitation. She couldn't always shift to her other form, certainly not at will in the way he did, or even the way Solange was able to do, but she recognized they were in mortal danger. She managed to wiggle out of her jeans and unbutton her blouse before they were on the ground. She tossed her clothes away from her, willing the change, embracing it.

Riordan moved in her mind, picking up the image, lending his strength. The shifting was slightly different from that of Carpathians, but he was deep in her mind and knew how it worked now so he was able to provide the extra speed. The jaguar sprang into the lower branches of a tree and disappeared entirely into the canopy. Riordan turned to face his enemy.

A shadowy figure exploded out of the ground, erupting directly in front of Riordan, fist slamming into his chest and driving deep. Riordan twisted slightly, taking the pain and letting it go, sweeping with one leg to send his attacker sprawling. There was no sound, and no face. The vampire was nothing more than black smoke dissolving rapidly. It was eerily silent. Not even the insects hummed.

Zacarias. Riordan reached along his private mental path for his older brother. *A master vampire is here, one with powers beyond all imagining. I cannot spot him. I cannot attack him. Should I fall, you must find and protect my lifemate.* Riordan crouched low, restless eyes searching, every sense on full alert. He dug into the forest floor and scooped handfuls of rich soil. He was losing blood fast. The vampire had deliberately weakened him. To preserve his strength, Riordan didn't move, other than to pack his wounds. He heard Juliette's distress in his mind, knew she remained close in hopes of aiding him, but there was no way to fight the unseen.

Riordan felt his brother moving through him, examining the terrible hole opened in his chest, estimating his strength, searching through his memories to replay the attack. *Get out of there. No lone hunter will take this one down alone.* Even as he sent the command, he was working to repair his younger brother's injury from a distance. Riordan could feel the warmth moving through his body, hear the healing chant in his mind.

He felt the air stir around him and immediately flung himself away from the disturbance, rolling to his left and coming up to face the shadowy figure. Riordan managed to deflect the jagged bolt of lightning before it struck him. The energy slammed into the ground, shaking the earth. He raised his arms and the ground continued to roll and pitch. Great cracks opened up, one rushing toward the insubstantial figure with ominous speed. Riordan felt the exact moment when both Juliette and Zacarias threw their strength in with his. The crack widened and split the ground and the vampire fell into the hole. Riordan sent the bolts of lightning streaking down after him, spear after spear, driving each deep in an effort to score a blind hit.

Riordan staggered as he moved to get away from where the vampire had last seen him. There was stillness now, as if the forest held its breath. Riordan realized the sky was dark due to storm clouds. Dawn was only a matter of minutes away. The vampire had struck fast and ferociously in the hopes of defeating him quickly.

He felt me with you. Zacarias thought it over. *He will not return to fight. He will most likely go to ground for a long period of time or leave our area. Whatever he wished to accomplish here is not worth his life. Whatever brought such a powerful enemy to our lands had to be important.*

I believe he has tainted some of the jaguar males. They have been capturing women and forcing them to mate for the purpose of breeding. Their women all have psychic abilities and are capable of becoming lifemates to our males. Riordan was certain a powerful vampire would only come to the jungle if it profited him. If the vampire could prevent the Carpathians from finding lifemates, more and more of their males would turn vampire or walk into the sun.

You are thinking this is a very defined conspiracy. Zacarias turned the idea over in his mind. *This must be reported to our brethren in our homeland. I will send Manolito. We will deal with the jaguar males who are abusing their women. You must go to ground quickly, Riordan. Put your lifemate in the ground and stay until you are fully healed. I will begin the hunt for the women.*

The sister of my lifemate has been taken.

You must heal or we will lose both of you. That cannot happen. Without children our race faces extinction, just as the jaguar.

Riordan abruptly broke off contact with his brother, despising the truth, despising the command in his brother's voice. It made them no different than the jaguar males.

"That isn't true." Juliette was at his side, pushing him onto the ground while she examined the blood-soaked pack in his chest. She pressed him to lie flat while she gathered more rich soil and healing herbs and mixed them with his saliva. "I learn fast. This ugly little recipe was in your mind while you were trying to do it yourself."

"It is true, Juliette. We need women desperately, and we need them to give birth to female children." He couldn't stop looking at her, bending over him with her beautiful feminine body. She was naked, crouched beside him, anxiety on her face, her incredible breasts swaying with every movement. He felt as if he were in a dream. She couldn't possibly be real. Women like Juliette didn't exist in his world.

"Riordan." She said his name sharply. "You're fading on me. Don't you dare pass out. Let me pack this tight and then I'll provide you with blood." She looked around nervously. "Are you certain he's gone? I never saw him. I couldn't help you because I never got a clear glimpse of him."

"It is dawn." Riordan sounded far away. He lifted his hand and touched her breast, barely skimming the soft skin to confirm that she was real. "He had no choice but to go to ground."

"Riordan, take my blood."

He shook his head. "You will be left weak and dizzy with no one to protect you."

She ignored the hand cupping her breast, massaging her flesh with gentle fingers. She caught his face and forced him to look at her. "Do as I tell you and take my blood. You can't die, and you will if you don't have blood. I need you to help me get Jasmine back. I want you to live for me. Forget everything else, Riordan."

"I cannot protect you while I lie beneath the earth these long hours."

"I can protect myself. Please take my blood, Riordan." She was beginning to feel desperate.

There was a faint stirring in her mind. Another voice swirled there for a time, whispering with the same accent, far away and distant as if it was difficult to find the exact path. And then it was suddenly clear. *I am Zacarias. He will never willingly put you in more danger by weakening you. I will aid you, but you must remember, should anything happen to you while he rests beneath the earth, he will rise vampire and I will be forced to destroy him. You must stay alive.*

"Somebody ought to lay out the rules ahead of time," Juliette muttered under her breath, but gave the mental nod to Riordan's brother. She couldn't bear the idea of losing Riordan, and she could clearly see he was going to be stubborn and combative if she persisted without help.

She knew the exact moment Zacarias struck, taking hold of Riordan and forcing him to bite deep into Juliette's wrist. Even though he was under strong compulsion, she felt Riordan striving to protect her, swirling his tongue over her skin to lessen the pain. A surge of anger went through him briefly at what Juliette and Zacarias were doing, but his temper died a quick death. Juliette went her own way when she felt justified. If Riordan wanted to spend a lifetime with her, he had better get used to who she was.

Riordan pulled away from Zacarias's control the moment the blood gave him enough strength. He took only enough from Juliette to aid his healing before closing the wound with his tongue. He brushed his thumb over the pinpricks. "I want to spend several lifetimes with you, and I know exactly who you are, Juliette." He loved every inch of her, loved looking at her with her bare feminine curves, but time was slipping away and he was far weaker than he should be.

He fashioned jeans and a blouse for her, a soft lightweight material that wouldn't cling so much in the high humidity. "You must protect your eyes as best you can. I made the shirt long-sleeved to protect your skin. Try to stay under cover as much as possible. I know you will continue to track Jasmine, but do not put yourself in danger until I can aid you. It will not help your sister to have you killed or captured."

She pulled on the clothes, a little shaky from the blood

loss and the terrible fear that welled up each time she looked at the shocking hole in his chest. "I'll be careful." She ran her fingers through his hair. "Do what you have to do. I'll see you as soon as the sun sets."

Riordan glanced around him, his fingers suddenly shackling her wrist, halting all movement. Uneasiness was beginning to creep into his mind. Scanning didn't connect with enemies, human or otherwise in the area. It would be impossible for a vampire to stand the rising of the sun. Although most Carpathians could take the early morning hours, Riordan was severely injured and the light was already affecting his body. He rolled over to stare up into the canopy, unable to shake the sudden alarm coursing through his body. The leaves rustled and swayed with the mild wind. Every kind of plant climbed the trunks of the trees and twisted around branches, creating a jungle of foliage. The wind touched the leaves, the smallest of brushes, but it was enough to reveal turquoise eyes, gleaming like rare gems, glittering down at them.

The jaguar sprang, its stocky, compact body hurtling through the air, claws extended, eyes focused on its prey. Riordan shoved Juliette hard enough to send her sprawling and dissolved into mist, so that the cat hit the ground where he had been. The cat whirled, using its flexible spine, swiping with large claws at empty space.

"Solange! No!" Juliette rushed to grab the cat, running her hands through the soft fur, looking for damage. There were several lacerations, a series of ragged, gaping wounds where a cat had obviously raked her side. "You're hurt, these are deep." She turned to look for Riordan, felt his fingertips brush her cheek.

She meant to kill me, Juliette. I feel it in her mind. I must go to ground. She is enraged over the taking of her cousin. You stay safe and do your best to settle her down.

She heard the regret in his voice, the weariness and pain. "Go, Riordan. I'll see you at sunset."

Clothes floated to earth as he streaked away. The jeans were for someone with longer legs and a smaller waist. The shirt would cover Solange's well-endowed body. It had been easy enough to catch her exact proportions from Juliette's memories.

"He's gone, Solange. Tell me what happened."

Solange shifted to her natural form, remaining crouched on the ground, facing Juliette. "They already had her before I reached the house. I couldn't stop them, I'm sorry. I'm so sorry." She shook back her heavy fall of dark hair. "One stayed behind to try to give the others a head start. Once he realized I was female, and capable of shifting fast, with a more pure bloodline, I had a very real advantage. He didn't want to hurt me." Blood was dripping from the wounds in her side. "He did this before he realized what I was. I'm afraid it puts Jasmine in more trouble. They'll guard her much more carefully."

Juliette hugged Solange. "We'll find her and take her back."

"Who was that man?"

"Not one of them. He is Carpathian. Riordan. You heard Mom talk about them before." She couldn't help the defensive note in her voice.

"He's still a man, and they can't be trusted, Juliette. What does he want us for? Isn't the Carpathian race in the same trouble as the jaguar race?" Solange took the clothes from Juliette's hands and knotted them together before tying them around her neck. "They need babies to keep their race alive."

"They at least respect women and want them to be happy, Solange. All men are not responsible for what a few have done. And there is some suspicion that the jaguar males have come into contact with a master vampire. I saw one, and if that is so, I felt how evil he was. The males may very well have been influenced by him."

"It matters little to me why they do what they do. They cannot have Jasmine," Solange said. "Get rid of the clothes and let's get out of here." She studied Juliette as her cousin stripped. "You're very pale." There was suspicion in her voice.

"I don't want to argue with you, Solange. Let's find Jasmine before we do anything else."

"We don't argue," Solange objected. "At least we didn't before you took up with a man." She studied her cousin's pale body. "A man who takes blood from others."

Juliette ignored the implication. "Is the jaguar still on your trail?"

"I doubled back and led him near the laboratory just to see if he would ask for assistance. A bunch of men are sifting through what's left of the building. It completely collapsed. Did the Carpathian have something to do with that?"

Juliette nodded. "I found him there, chained in a cell, and got him free. He was in bad shape. They'd tortured him."

Solange swore. "I suppose that makes me like him more. At least he knows a little bit of what our women go through."

Chapter 9

"THE sun is burning my eyes," Juliette said, pressing her fingertips to her face. "No matter what I do they weep. My skin feels like it's blistering."

"It is. Shift, Juliette, hurry before you're a mass of blisters. We'll talk about this later." Solange looked at her closely. "You can tell me what that man has done after we get Jasmine back."

"Tell me whether or not the jaguar male went near the humans," Juliette encouraged as she tied her own clothes in knots and looped them around her neck.

"He did. He spoke briefly with them, although he didn't reveal his body to them. He was able to half shift. *Half* of his body human and the other half jaguar. I can't do that. None of us can."

"You come from the purest bloodline we know of," Juliette pointed out. "Mom referred to you as a princess once."

Solange made a face. "Somehow I don't consider myself very lucky. I wouldn't want to be the princess of the jaguar people." She glanced around her. "Are you ready? We have to get out of here. Those men have had Jasmine far too long." She was already shifting, fur bursting through her skin, rippling over her face while her muzzle elongated to accommodate teeth.

Juliette closed her burning eyes and reached for Riordan. *Tell me you are safe.*

I am deep in the arms of the earth. Let me help you shift. He sensed how tired she was, how weak. He stifled the need to keep her with him. Greater than his own need, there was hers. She had to find her sister, and he understood that. He didn't like it, but he understood it.

Juliette called up her large cat, concentrating on the shifting of muscle and bone. She felt Riordan moving within her, lending her power and strength when he didn't have it to give. A part of her wanted to weep when she felt his pain. She feared the coming separation from him, but she had to find Jasmine.

The change took her rapidly. Juliette touched muzzles with Solange and they turned together and raced off into the darkened interior. Using the jaguar's highly acute sense of smell they found Jasmine's trail immediately and hurried after her. They took to the overhead highway, the tangle of branches high up in the canopy that allowed them to travel fast and in secret.

Birds took to the air, shrieked warnings at their passing, but neither jaguar paid any attention, and after a moment the birds settled back into the tops of the trees, ignoring them. The forest had stirred to life, insects humming, frogs croaking and deer barking to warn of the larger predators.

Juliette knew the exact moment when Riordan succumbed to the climbing sun and his heart stopped beating. The breath went out of her lungs, her heart stuttered in reaction, and she was suddenly and utterly alone—bereaved, grief-stricken. The jaguar stumbled, nearly tumbling from the branches. Claws dug into bark, scattering leaves and twigs and sending the birds once more shrieking. Solange turned sharply to growl a warning for stealth. They did not want to alert any of the males that might be guarding the back-trail.

The heavy canopy protected her from the sun, but Juliette still felt the rays piercing her skin through the thick fur. Her eyes wept continually, burning in the light. None of it mattered—not her grief, not her discomfort. Not the separation from her other half. She focused on her beloved sister. Jasmine was all that mattered. Juliette followed Solange.

The trail grew warmer in early afternoon. The pungent odor of the jaguar males was easier to follow. They were taking turns, hurrying through the forest, four in jaguar form and one in human form carrying Jasmine.

In spite of her determination, Juliette found she was having trouble keeping up with Solange. Her body, even in the form of the jaguar, demanded she sleep and worse, wanted to shift back into her human form. She'd always had trouble holding her animal shape for long periods of time. She had never gone from early dawn to early afternoon and it was nearly impossible to continue.

Solange stopped abruptly, her animal form suddenly stiffening. Juliette caught the scent of fear, of violence, of sexual predation. She lost her jaguar self, gagging, choking, catching the branch of the tree for support to keep from falling. Solange shifted into her human shape, holding Juliette as she was violently ill.

For a few minutes, Juliette's head roared with protest, with rage. She pounded at the bark of the trees until her fists were bruised and bleeding, weeping uncontrollably. "She fought them. She fought them, and I wasn't here. How could they do such a thing to her?"

Solange wept silently, the anger in her deep and firm and enduring. "We will get her back, Juliette. Be strong. You have to be strong for her. We can't let this slow us down. They wanted her docile and shocked. This was to show domination. This was to strip her of dignity and hope. But she knows we'll come. She knows we'll never stop until we have her back or we're dead." Solange brushed the hair from Juliette's eyes. "I see the sun is hurting you, that your body needs rest, but you haven't given in to it. You haven't stopped no matter what the cost to you. Jasmine knows what we're like. She will count on that and she will endure."

Juliette allowed her cousin to hold her, to comfort her for a brief moment. "We have to hurry, Solange. They can't do this to her a second time."

Neither woman wanted to think about their mothers, but it was inevitable. "Can you hold the jaguar form?" Solange asked.

Juliette nodded. "I don't know how long, but I'll do my best. Do you have any weapons stashed in this area?"

"About a mile from here. I think we're close to one of our caches. Clothes, food, drinking water, meds and knives. They have to stop soon. They're big males and they'll want to rest."

Juliette reached for her other form. It was easier not to think about Jasmine and what the males had done to her. She didn't want to see the smears of blood on the ground and the signs of struggle. It only weakened her. Her fury needed to burn bright and strong, and vengeful.

She struggled through the next couple of hours, pushing her body when it desperately needed sleep. Her eyes streamed every step of the way, but this time she was uncertain if it was the affects of the sun, or the grief raging in her. She knew by the way Solange carried her body that she felt the same intense emotions, a mixture of rage and sorrow that might never go away. She tried not to think of the girl Jasmine had been, her pixie smile and gentle kindnesses. Solange and Juliette burned with passion, hot and fiery with strong emotions. Jasmine was sweet and steady and irresistible.

Juliette felt a scream of denial welling up and just managed to choke it down as Solange veered from their path to indicate where the cache of weapons and food was stored. In human form, they dressed, strapping on knives with the same ease they dragged on clothes.

"They're close," Solange said, her voice very low. "I feel them. We're downwind of them." She drank water from the bottle stored with her supplies. It was brackish from age, but it was wet. She passed it to Juliette. "Are you up for this? It won't be easy."

Their eyes met. Juliette nodded. "We will succeed, there is no other alternative."

Solange took back the water bottle. "They outnumber us and they're strong, incredibly strong. I've heard Carpathians can perform incredible feats. Obviously if the man can become mist when under attack, it's true. Can he aid us, even from beneath the ground?"

Juliette reached for Riordan eagerly. Her mind had continually tuned itself to his, needing to touch him, compounding her sorrow when she couldn't. This time she was demanding, her call to him edged with need.

Juliette? His voice was faint and far away, but it was there, and relief swept through her heart and soul.

She replayed the events of the day in her mind. He went very still, withdrawing, but not before she felt the impact of his black, dark rage. It boiled up, dangerous and deadly and far more lethal than her own. She should have been frightened, but she was comforted by his anger on her sister's behalf.

When he managed to get his anger under control, Riordan reached for her. The connection was much stronger. *These males are dangerous, perhaps their behavior is tainted by the vampire, perhaps they are a group of deviants who have banded together. They must be stopped, but two women against such odds is ludicrous and you know it. It will not help your sister if you are dead.*

We have no choice but to go in after her now, Riordan. We cannot subject her to more of their violence. Please understand I have no other choice. Can you help?

It is two hours until the setting of the sun. I can rise early. Give me another hour. He wanted to claw his way through the earth to get to her, but his body lay leaden.

Solange will scout them, but if they are raping her, we cannot sit back while they brutalize her. You can't ask that of us.

He swore softly. *I should have converted you immediately and you would be fully under my protection.* It was far too late to correct his mistake now. He was locked beneath the earth, and she was in terrible danger. He switched tactics, feeling her slight withdrawal. He didn't dare lose their connection. *Zacarias, awaken. I need your help. Manolito, we need you.*

Juliette held her breath, waiting. She knew Riordan was powerful, and she had already experienced his eldest brother's tremendous abilities. Hope surged through her.

Manolito is traveling to the Carpathian Mountains. Zacarias answered his call. *I will feed you my strength when needed. Warn the women that should your lifemate fall, so will you, and in such a way that they cannot conceive of the monster that will be unleashed.*

She understood more than they realized. She was already adept at reading Riordan's memories. She honestly didn't know whether or not she would have bound Riordan to her and converted him immediately if she were the one that could be consumed by the madness of the vampire. Juliette sent him as much reassurance as she could. *Thank you, Riordan. Please thank your brother.*

She turned to her cousin. "They are with us, Solange."

Solange handed her back the water bottle. "I'll trust your man if you do. Stay here and wait for the signal. I'll see what we're up against. That should give you another few minutes to rest."

"We go back-to-back, Solange, like we always do. If Jasmine is safe, we stall until Riordan is able to rise. If not, hopefully they can help us." Already she noted the storm clouds floating above them, helping block the sun and protect her eyes. The wind shifted completely, bringing the strong scent of the jaguar male to them. Juliette turned and pushed her way through the shrubbery, careful to keep from making noise. Solange had already melted away, lost in the forest of orchids and fungi and fern. Few could surpass Solange's ability to blend into the forest and remain unseen. Juliette had complete faith in her cousin. She moved into position, a distance from the small encampment.

The jaguars were using a small cave, man-made, dug into

the side of the embankment. The opening was a mere slit between two boulders. Solange worked her way in a circle
around the area, knowing there had to be a back entrance.
The jaguars would never risk being trapped in the cave. The
wind shifted as she moved, always in front of her, giving her
the exact location of the sentries. A jaguar male, obviously
trusting in the forest warning system, rested in the tree
branches to the left of the cave, sleeping in the late afternoon, tired from the two-day rush through the forest. The
second guard crouched in human form near a large group of
ferns. Solange was certain it was the bolt-hole for emergen-
cies. She made her way back to Juliette to confer.

The two lay side by side in the grasses. Solange pressed
her mouth to Juliette's ear. "I couldn't hear anything in the
cave. I think they're resting. I'm fairly certain I can get close
enough to the guard in his human form to kill him, but neither of us is going to be able to do much with the jaguar. He's
big and he's a fighter." She touched her side. "He's fast too."

"We don't stand much of a chance inside," Juliette
pointed out. "With the one up in the tree, I counted five.
We're not going to win against five fully grown jaguars."

"Four," Solange said firmly. "After I take out the guard.
You're right though, we have to draw the others out of the
cave to have any chance at all."

"I can do that," Juliette said with confidence.

No! Riordan's harsh command was sharp. She heard the
echo of Zacarias's protest. *Wait as long as possible.*

"Riordan wants us to wait, Solange," Juliette reported un-
easily. She had no idea how her cousin would react. "He will
try to rise before sunset to help us."

Solange nodded slowly. "I guess it makes sense, Juliette.
We don't have to like it, but we don't have much chance
against five males."

"I want to get closer, just to make certain they aren't
touching her," Juliette said.

"I'll go. I can be invisible." A small, humorless smile
tugged at Solange's mouth. "Well, not like your Carpathian,
but I manage."

"You have a gift," Juliette acknowledged.

Solange began to circle back around toward the rear entrance, presuming Jasmine was being held as deep in the cave as possible. Once the jaguar in the tree stirred, yawned, his mouth gaping open to show sharp teeth. Solange sank into the bushes, going completely still. Juliette slid a knife into her palm. The jaguar stretched, looked around and sniffed the air, testing with his tongue and sensitive whiskers. The wind carried the scent of the women away from him. The jaguar dropped his head back onto his leg and closed his eyes.

Juliette let her breath out slowly. Solange waited a few more minutes before continuing to creep forward again. Juliette strained to watch her cousin's process. The fronds of a fern swayed slightly, in tune with the wind. Juliette couldn't understand how Riordan and Zacarias had the strength to guide the wind and follow Solange's progress. She could almost feel Riordan moving through her, attempting to get the layout of the battlefield through her eyes. He was waiting, much like a coiled snake, waiting for that moment when he could explode into the sky and come to her. Riordan's concern was comforting, and she sent him her appreciation.

Juliette's first warning was the way the human guard at the back entrance suddenly turned his head toward the cave with an evil smile. He walked a few steps and peered into the collection of shrubbery, his hand absently rubbing his crotch. She saw Solange move in behind him. A scream, a mixture of anger, terror and pain came from the interior of the cave. It was choked off abruptly. *I have no choice, Riordan.* It was her only apology for whatever might happen. Using higher ground, she ran to the entrance of the cave, catching a brief glimpse of Solange and the guard, the man falling to the ground, the bloodstained knife in Solange's hand.

Riordan was calm. He didn't protest, he simply waited, watching the events unfold through her eyes. Juliette could feel the presence of his elder brother. They coiled in her waiting their moment.

Stay to the side, hold the blade edge up. Riordan instructed as she neared the cave's entrance. Juliette didn't argue; she already knew his plan, catching the details in their shared minds. She called out Jasmine's name to let her know she wasn't alone and to draw the men from the cave. She had to trust Solange to watch her back and keep the jaguar off of her. Her arm flashed, faster than she knew how to move, an instinctual, timed movement that brought down the first man rushing from the cavern. Blood soaked the ground, but Juliette couldn't look, didn't dare look. She heard the roar of the jaguar as it leapt from the branches onto Solange.

Juliette turned to help her cousin, sprinting with a burst of speed not her own. Solange shifted on the run, coming together in fury with the heavy male cat, raking and biting, fur and material flying everywhere. Juliette skidded to a halt. She had no chance to help Solange, to try to kill the jaguar with the knife. The two cats rolled over and over in a terrible fury making it impossible to aid her cousin.

Juliette! Riordan was rising. She felt him bursting through soil and leaves to take to the air. At his warning she spun around, knife held low and close to her body, meeting the rush of the jaguar as it burst from the cave. The heavy cat hit her chest hard, driving her backward, the jaguar's foul breath hot in her face. Pain ripped through her as the sharp claws tore through her skin to the bone. She felt Zacarias and Riordan moving in her, the knife plunging into the cat's sides and chest as his teeth drove at her throat. Breathing was difficult, but Riordan forced the air through her burning lungs. She slammed into the ground hard and lay pinned beneath the heavier body. Leaves and twigs soaked red with blood beneath but she couldn't tell whose blood it was. The cat's teeth were embedded in her throat and her arms were leaden, making it impossible to push the heavy body off of her.

Look at Solange. Riordan, so calm it was frightening. There was a command in his voice she couldn't disobey.

Jasmine screamed again, and Juliette's body jerked at the sound.

Look at Solange. Riordan repeated it. He was much closer and gaining in strength as the sun began to set.

Juliette couldn't move her head, so she shifted her gaze to see the male cat clawing Solange viciously. Blood seeped through fur and Solange staggered under the assault. A white haze was forming over Juliette's eyes. She blinked rapidly to clear her vision. Jaşmine screamed again. Juliette could hear her weeping.

Stay focused on Solange. Riordan's voice softened. *Hold on for me. Just hold on, Juliette.*

Flames ran over the male jaguar's fur. Bright red and orange flames tipping the ends of the spotted coat and engulfing the animal. The two jaguars rolled on the ground in a terrible frenzy of claws and teeth, but not a single flame touched the female. The male howled and broke away.

Chapter 10

Riordan erupted out of the sky, a demon with red eyes, his black hair unbound and streaming in the wind. He materialized directly behind the man holding Jasmine as a shield. Juliette actually felt the man's head as if she had grabbed him. Riordan twisted hard. The frightening crack was loud as he snapped the man's neck and dropped him carelessly to the ground.

Jasmine ran to kneel by Solange while Riordan eased the teeth of the jaguar carefully out of Juliette's neck and tossed the heavy body of the cat away as if it were no more than a bothersome branch. Pain engulfed her, rushed through her body now that it was over and he was there. He pressed his hands to the puncture wounds on either side of her throat, clamping down hard to prevent her from bleeding to death.

Juliette began to choke. *Is my sister okay? Solange? I can't see them.*

Riordan glanced over his shoulder toward the two women. Jasmine's face was swollen and black and blue. Her clothes hung in shreds. There was blood smeared on her body, but she was alive and trying desperately to staunch the flow of blood from her cousin's many lacerations. Solange was naked and bloody, lying on the ground, but she was alert, watching Riordan as he bent over Juliette.

They are both alive, Juliette. Lie still for me. He trusted his brother to remain alert for further trouble as he went outside his body and into hers to attempt to heal her from the inside out. Juliette gurgled, choked and coughed up blood.

"Save her. Damn you, I know you can save her," Solange called to him. "Do whatever you have to do." She attempted to rise, pushed feebly at Jasmine, who held her down.

"I have to convert her."

"What does that mean?" Jasmine asked fearfully.

"Who cares," Solange snapped. "Hurry, before it's too late."

Riordan ignored everything and everyone around him. Juliette was slipping away from him. He bent his head to her throat and drank, taking more of her precious fluid for an exchange. Riordan gathered her into his arms, slashed his chest and pressed her mouth to the wound. Deep within Riordan's mind, Zacarias gathered his spirit into a healing ball of energy and moving through Riordan, found the puncture wounds and torn arteries in Juliette's throat and began to repair them from the inside out. He took his time, making no mistakes, closing the gaping holes and removing foreign bacteria from her system.

Juliette felt both men from a distance. Zacarias broke off abruptly as if the connection between them had grown too difficult to maintain. She felt the lack of warmth immediately and shivered. Riordan leaned down and whispered to her, ending the flow of nourishing strength pouring into her body. She tried to lift her hand to his face. He looked so worried. Her hand fluttered next to her thigh but didn't quite make it into the air. Someone was crying. She turned her head toward the sound.

Jasmine sat beside Solange, wiping ineffectually at the bloody wounds and weeping softly. She was barely recognizable with her swollen face. "Is my sister going to live?"

Her voice was very soft and shaky. She didn't look at Riordan, but kept her gaze fixed on her cousin.

"Yes, little one," Riordan answered gently. "She will live. I have to take her away for a short time. I would like you and your cousin to go to my ranch where you will be safe until I can bring her back to you."

Jasmine shifted closer to Solange. It was a small movement for protection, but Riordan noted it immediately.

Can you take it away from her? What they did? Can you undo it?

Riordan lifted Juliette and carried her to her sister and cousin. "We can't stay long. I need to get Juliette to a place where she is safe while the conversion takes place and where I can heal her fully." *You know I cannot undo what has been done.*

Solange reached out to take Jasmine's hand. Jasmine twined her fingers through Juliette's. "Together we get through," Solange whispered.

Juliette tried to speak, but her throat was too swollen and raw. *Ask Solange if you can heal her.*

Riordan could feel the waves of distaste and fear coming from both women. They were doing their best to tolerate him and trust him because they loved Juliette. "She wants me to heal your wounds, Solange. I do not think she will leave this place and be calm without me doing so." It was the only leverage he had. If Solange didn't comply he would have no choice but to use his other gifts.

"Get it over with then." Solange never took her eyes from her cousin. "I am not going to your ranch. I'll destroy these bodies so our race remains secret, and Jasmine and I will go to our home at the edge of the rain forest, far from this place. We'll wait there for Juliette's return. Jasmine and Juliette will not be happy being apart." It was a clear warning.

Riordan nodded. "I am fully aware of that." Not wanting to waste any more time on talking, Riordan immediately allowed his physical self to fall away, called his spirit into a strong ball of healing energy and entered Solange. She had many wounds. Most were superficial, but some went bone deep, just as he had found in Juliette. He spent precious time healing from the inside out, shocked at how difficult it was to keep his mind from Juliette and the fact that time was slipping away from him. He was always focused, yet it required a tremendous discipline to shut out all thoughts and concentrate on his task.

Solange lay watching him. Her gaze never wavered. Her eyes never blinked. Her hand remained in Jasmine's, but her attention was fixed on Riordan. When his body swayed and the soothing warmth disappeared from inside of her she let out her breath. "Jasmine, he's got to take Juliette now. We have to be strong a little longer."

Jasmine leaned over immediately and kissed Juliette. She didn't look at Riordan when she spoke. "Thank you."

"You two must be safe. If you go to my ranch—"

Solange shook her head. "No, I can't. Please try to understand. I know you've helped us, but we haven't had very good experiences with men and we feel safer alone."

Riordan couldn't help but see the shudder that went through Jasmine. Juliette squeezed her sister's fingers. "I am sorry. I really have to take her to a safer place for the conversion. I do not like leaving the two of you alone and unprotected."

"Thanks to your healing skills, I'm able to protect us." Solange looked around her at the bodies lying on the ground. "Most of our enemies are dead. Take her before we lose her."

Riordan gathered Juliette in his arms but stopped when Jasmine made a soft sound of distress. "What is it, little one?" He used his most gentle voice.

"How long?" Jasmine clung to Juliette as if she couldn't let her go.

"Can you be separated two days? That will give her time to heal enough to be safe rising. Solange knows of my people. Our word is our honor. I give you my word, we will return at once to you, the moment we rise. Juliette would want nothing else."

Jasmine nodded and reluctantly allowed her sister's hand to drop limply from hers. She leaned into Solange for protection. Solange wrapped her arms around Jasmine. "Go now, we can be unselfish enough to let you take her. I'll take care of things here."

Riordan didn't wait for a second invitation. He already felt the first stirrings in Juliette's fragile body, a wave of unease, a ripple of fire. Time was running out. He launched himself skyward, hugging Juliette to him, hearing Jasmine gasp then begin to sob. Glancing down he could see Solange sitting up slowly and gathering her young cousin to her.

I should be with her, with Jasmine.

It should never have happened, Riordan replied grimly. He had no idea how he managed to keep the black anger swirling inside him at bay. He had Juliette's memories now, the intensity of her love for her sister and cousin. The memories of her aunt and her mother dying at the hands of deviant males. His every protective instinct was aroused, and rage lived and breathed inside of him.

Thank you for caring about them. And thank you for what you did for my cousin. I know it was uncomfortable not being accepted.

Fire blossomed in her stomach, spread through her body, engulfing every organ. He shared the pain, shocked at the intensity. He was as unprepared as Juliette for the violence of it. She shivered in his arms, biting back the cry of pain and trying to break the merge between their minds.

Riordan increased his speed. He couldn't make the protection of his ranch, or even get close to his home range, but after centuries living and hunting vampires in South America he was very familiar with their current surroundings. He dropped to earth in the rise of mountains, heading for a deep cave with natural hot springs. The soil was rich with minerals and the cave would be a natural protection against enemies. He could set strong safeguards and know humans and animals were safe from accidental encounters.

It took only minutes to prepare the cavern. Candles sprang to life, casting eerie lights across the shimmering pools. He placed Juliette on a soft bed he'd fashioned of rich soil that cushioned her body in welcoming arms. "I know it hurts, Juliette. I had no idea it was so painful."

We really didn't have much of a choice. Juliette didn't try to speak. Her raw throat wouldn't allow it, and in any case it was too tiring. She could feel the beast in her fighting for life, resisting the change in her body. The jaguar didn't want the reshaping of organs and tissue. Juliette was just too weary and in too much pain to care.

I would have converted you without the attack from the male. He felt compelled to confess it, settling next to her, holding her in his arms, lifting her fingers to his mouth. *I would not have been able to continue without you*. Riordan wasn't certain it was an apology, only that he wanted her to understand his conflicting emotions.

I would have been unable to continue without you. Riordan, so stop beating yourself up. Get my clothes off, I can't stand the weight of them against my skin. The last was said in desperation.

He stripped her clothes away without a thought for the material, shredding it from her body as quickly as possible. Her skin was hot to the touch. Riordan dipped his shirt into the coolest of the pools and bathed her face and wrists.

"I dreamt of you once," he said softly as he squeezed droplets of water over her throat and down the valley between her breasts. "You were laughing. I remembered the sound of your laughter for years afterward. It kept me going at times when I could not find a reason to continue." He pushed the hair from her face. She was sweating. The beads of sweat mixed with tiny beads of blood.

I dreamt of you, too. There was happiness in her voice, the only thing that kept him from crying when a convulsion took hold of her and pain lashed for what seemed an eternity. She gripped his wrist, held on, trying to breathe through it, stay on top of it. When the wave released her she sighed. *I still think you're a dream*.

He had to swallow several times before he could speak. "Even now, with what I'm putting you through?"

Her eyes flashed, a reminder of her passionate nature, the fire contained in her feminine body. *I am jaguar. I have choices, and I make them. I wanted you from the first moment I saw you. As a jaguar, I have no future. With you I do. As a jaguar, there is no happiness, with you there is. I know the difference, Riordan.*

Before she could say more, the next wave hit her, even stronger than the last. The jaguar was not going to let Riordan have her without a fight. Riordan ground his teeth together, trying to take the pain from her, the bursting fire that rushed through her body and seared her insides. She was stoic about it, enduring the pain without a complaint. There wasn't a hint of blame in her mind. When the wave passed she inhaled the scent of the healing candles. *I'm going to be sick.*

It was his only warning and he moved quickly, holding her while her body rid itself of toxins. She was violently ill even as another wave of pain raced through her. Riordan was cursing when it ebbed away.

Wrapping her in his arms, he carried her into the coolest pool, submerging both of them up to their necks. He buried his face against her neck. "Are we going to survive this?"

She smiled. Not physically, but he felt it in his mind. *You are such a baby when it comes to me. I see you all rough and tough when you're scaring everyone around you with your bad-boy image and you fall apart because I'm in pain.* She caught a glimpse of something else and it brought tears to her eyes. *You're falling apart because of what happened to Jasmine. Riordan, it wasn't your fault. How could you think that?*

Before he could answer, the blowtorch blossomed in her stomach and lungs, eating through her until it was so great she convulsed again, her brain shutting off to prevent her from overload. All Riordan could do was hold her, feeling helpless and guilty and angry for not understanding what would occur.

Juliette opened her eyes and looked up at him. *You're crying blood, Riordan. Don't cry for me. I chose this path and I didn't expect my passing from one to the other to be easy. I feel the jaguar fading in strength. I knew from your memories that human women with psychic abilities could be converted, and all the jaguar women, and hopefully the descendents with more diluted blood, are psychic. I had hoped Solange would find a Carpathian to bring her the same happiness, and even, eventually, Jasmine, but I fear the jaguar in Solange is far too strong. It would never let her go.*

Had I not taken you when you saved me from the laboratory, you would have been home to aid your sister. He couldn't say the words aloud to her. He whispered them in her mind. The idea that a male would commit such atrocities against a woman burned like a hole in his belly.

I was not expected back that night, Riordan. Jasmine knew I would draw the human trackers away. Neither of us expected an attack by the jaguars. I didn't even know they were in our part of the forest. I wasn't worried about the males.

He forced air though his lungs, so much rage in him the ground shook. *I know her through you. A younger sister who will remain scarred for life. I wanted to insist she come home with us to the ranch, but I have brought you fully into my world. Who will be with her in the hours when she is alone?*

The next wave was even longer, her thrashing body creating waves in the pool. Water splashed in agitation. The flames from the candles leapt as if a wind rushed through the cavern. The lights flickered, and the scents mingled to bring healing aroma wafting over the pool.

Juliette's nails dug deep into Riordan's skin. It took a few moments to find her breath again. *She'll always have me. And now you. She's uneasy with your presence, and so is Solange, but they'll get better with time. We'll be more able to watch over them. Two of us with the Carpathian gifts will be able to guard them more carefully.*

He bathed her, taking his time, cleaning her skin thoroughly, his hands lingering in places he sensed soothed her. The water helped to keep her skin cool.

The water helps. And the feel of your hands. When I dreamt of you, I dreamt of your hands touching me. I knew what they'd feel like on my body before you actually touched me physically.

"When did you dream about me? Did I look the same?"

Your hair was flowing in the wind, and you had that same incredible smile. I couldn't see your eyes as clearly because you were touching me and I was feeling rather than looking.

His heart nearly stopped beating. He remembered his dream vividly. He had awakened with a terrible hunger and his body alive with heat. He hardly recognized the sexual urges, he hadn't experienced them in centuries. He heard her in his mind, laughing softly, sensuously, calling to him. She was running just ahead of him, her scent ripe with heat. In his dream he had no choice but to follow her. She was always just out of reach, a tantalizing temptation, leaving in the air behind her a trail of sexual excitement.

We must have been close to one another and I was telegraphing my need. The purer the blood of the jaguar, the more the sexual heats hit us hard. Fortunately, there aren't many of us women left. We stay as far away from the males as possible.

Riordan closed his eyes against the next wave of pain. The convulsion actually took her out of his arms, so that she nearly sank beneath the agitated water. He cursed his people, even his God, everything he could think of, then began to pray, promising everything he could think of if only her ordeal would be over.

He heard her soft laughter in his mind even before the pain leeched from her body. *You're going to save the world if this stops?*

He rubbed his chin over the top of her head. "I was desperate. It has to be over soon."

No wonder women have all the babies.

"Not you, not if it is anything like this. We will do without babies. I am serious, Juliette. I think I am going to be sick."

Well don't. I'm sick enough for both of us. I'm so tired. I just want to sleep.

He waded out of the pool, bringing her back to the rich, welcoming soil. "I can send you to sleep the moment it is safe to do so." He kissed her eyes closed. Kissed the corners of her mouth. "I love you."

How strange. I love you too.

It took two more intense waves of burning fire and convulsions before the jaguar was gone, the conversion was complete, and he could issue the command for healing sleep. He wrapped his arms and body protectively around hers and wept while the candles burned brightly and the water lapped at the edges of the pool.

Chapter 11

RIORDAN paced back and forth, his restless nature showing through his normally calm demeanor. Juliette had been in the house with her sister and cousin for most of the night. Dawn was only a couple of hours away, and he had yet to spend time with her. He understood completely the need to be with her sister after such a trauma, and he tried hard to suppress the selfish part of his nature, but fear was an ugly, clawing thing that kept him on edge. Solange and Jasmine wanted nothing to do with men. Riordan didn't blame them. Jasmine's gentle nature could barely tolerate what had happened to her. She was hanging on to her sanity by a thread. Juliette would help with her healing skills, strengthened by Riordan, but he knew the two women were a tremendous influence on Juliette. She also had a nature that demanded loyalty and responsibility. Jasmine was in pain, was terribly wounded. Juliette might feel she needed to stay with her.

The moment they had risen, he had fed, taken care of her needs and kept his promise to her family, bringing her straight to them. He knew they needed to be alone, and he had been the one to suggest he wait outside, but he couldn't help wanting to protect her from the pain of what Jasmine had gone through. It was difficult in the ensuing hours to keep his mind firmly away from hers to give Juliette and her family complete privacy, but he managed by pacing restlessly back and forth just in front of the small house.

He heard the door and spun around. Juliette was framed there, holding Jasmine and Solange to her, hugging them hard. She emerged with a bright smile on her face and tears in her eyes. It was obvious she had been weeping on and off for hours. Riordan's heart moved in his chest. He opened his arms, and she came into the shelter of his body.

He glanced over her head, nodded when Solange and Jasmine both lifted a tentative hand before closing the door. "I am so sorry I could not be there to comfort you," he whispered, brushing soothing kisses along her temple and down her tear-stained cheek. "I wanted to be there for you."

"I know. I carried you with me and leaned on your strength more than once. She needs time, Riordan. Please don't take the way they are personally. They'll come to love you, I know they will."

"They have given me acceptance," he pointed out. "I did not even expect that much, so I am grateful."

"I want to shift into another form and run away for awhile. I want it to be just you and me somewhere beautiful where I can't think about terrible things happening to people I love. Take me away, Riordan. Let's go find our pool. Let's just be together where I can't think anymore."

"Would you like to try a leopard form? I often use it to travel through the forest."

She tugged until he let her loose. "That might be best. I still feel like a cat inside." Being close to Riordan definitely brought cat traits out in her. "Let's try." The thought of losing herself in an animal form was enticing. It had been wearing, all those long hours, holding her baby sister, rocking her, crying with her. She looked up at Riordan. "In the end, there's no real way to take it back. No way to help her." Juliette looked ashamed for a moment. "I almost asked you if you could remove her memories."

"Not with that large of a trauma. I could perhaps lessen the impact, but it would be in her memories and she might not know why she had reactions to things that were upsetting to her. If you want me to try—"

Juliette shook her head. "Jasmine is strong. She can survive this, maybe better than the rest of us. I've never seen Solange so filled with sorrow. We chose to remain here, moving from place to place because mom told us the males were kidnapping women they suspected of being of jaguar blood and bringing them here. They have no one else, no hope of rescue other than us. So we stayed."

"Now there are others to help, Juliette. I will. My brothers will. My people will."

She smiled at him, for the first time, her heart lightening. "Our people, Riordan. I'm Carpathian now."

He trailed his fingers over her cheek, framed her face with his hands and bent his head to find her mouth with his. His kiss was gentle, loving, tender even. "Absolutely, you are Carpathian."

"So how do I make the change?"

"In much the same way as before. I have the image and structure in my head. Study it, focus on it and reach for it. I will help. With us, we actually have to hold the image in our mind the entire time we stay in the form. You become the jaguar. We are the image of the animal. We have all of its senses and abilities, but we must maintain the outer shell."

She liked the idea. It would occupy her thoughts entirely. And she found she wasn't quite ready to give up the freedom she always felt running in her jaguar form through the heavy canopy. Juliette stretched her arms up to the night sky. "Show me the leopard."

"The leopard is in your mind. Hold its form, Juliette, do not think you can forget it as you did the jaguar," he cautioned.

"With you to remind me, I doubt I would have a chance," she teased, already reaching for the image. It wasn't all that different from her own unique beginnings, but it was complex. As she changed form, so did Riordan. He made it seem easy and natural and fun.

The moment Juliette felt the familiar ropes of muscle, joy spread through her. She turned her head to look at the large cat beside her. He was big and shiny black with darker rosettes covering his body. He looked powerful and muscular and very alluring. She rubbed against him, body to body, a long affectionate signal to play. Whirling, she took off running in the direction of their private grotto.

Riordan, deep inside the body of the leopard, paced just behind her, admiring her sleek lines and beautiful curves. They leapt over fallen logs, rousted rodents from the shrubbery, chased a small squirrel through several trees and splashed through two creeks and up an embankment. Both raked the bark from the trees, Juliette trying to reach higher than the much larger male.

He rubbed his muzzle along her face and neck. His teeth playfully bit at her neck and shoulder. Her fragrance was ripe and enthralling, captivating him until all he could do was think about her. She teased him openly, running away, waiting for him to catch up, crouching temptingly in front of him, only to leap away before he could blanket her.

Riordan was grateful to see the shimmering pool of water waiting for them in the natural rock grotto. The high ferns screened the lush oasis from prying eyes, making it a virtual paradise.

They shifted together, Juliette laughing with glee. "That was so fun." Her gaze drifted boldly, possessively over him. "I see the experience was particularly arousing to you." Juliette stepped close to him, inhaling his scent. Her fingers trailed with tantalizing expertise over his aching erection.

Before he could react, she shifted her palms to his bare chest, "I don't think the change completely took the cat out of me." She ran her hands over his chest, feeling every defined muscle. "I thought I wanted all of it gone, every last bit of that DNA from my body, but I've changed my mind."

Her fingers rubbed over his skin in small, demanding caresses, transmitting a certain urgency. "What part of the cat remained behind?" It was hard to breathe when she was so close to him. When he was already throbbing and mercilessly hard for her touch. For her taste. He closed his eyes briefly. For the feel of her tight hot sheath surrounding his body and milking him dry.

She leaned forward and lapped at his chest, rubbed her body the length of his. "Touch. Touch is very important to cats." Her hand slid down his body, over his belly, wrapped around his thickened penis. Her thumb rubbed the sensitive tip gently. "Like this. Cats love to touch and feel. We like to be stroked." She smiled up at him. "Do you think you can manage a little stroking?"

She didn't give him the chance, kissing his chest, her mouth open and wet, her tongue working along his ribs and her teeth nipping until he thought he might go out of his mind. Riordan stood it as long as he could, with his body growing harder and the pressure building with every touch of her fingers and lips. He tunneled his hands into her hair and pulled her head up to fasten his mouth on hers. He devoured her, kiss after kiss, unable to stop to take a breath, his tongue dueling with hers.

The roaring could have been in his head, maybe it was hers, the roaring was so loud he couldn't tell. His body burned and ached and demanded relief. He kissed his way from her mouth to her throat, laved the valley between her breasts before stopping there, lavishing attention while he brought her body more fully into his.

Juliette twined one leg around him, aligning their bodies so the head of his penis was pressed tightly into her wet, welcoming entrance. "I don't want to wait anymore," she said, tugging at his hair. "I want to feel you inside of me."

He stroked her nipple with his tongue. "When?"

"Right now, this minute."

She tried to impale her body on his, but he moved, his mouth pulling strongly at her breast. With each strong pull a wave of liquid heat pushed over the head of his erection and trickled down the shaft.

"Are you certain?" When she squirmed again, he abandoned all pretense of teasing, caught her bottom in both hands and lifted her up onto him.

She cried out, sliding over him, fitting like the proverbial glove, contracting her muscles around him to hold him to her. She moved with him, meeting him stroke for stroke, urging him to move into her harder and faster. Her breath came in ragged gasps, but pleasure burst through her like a rainbow, beautiful after what seemed like endless darkness. She wanted their ride to be wild and abandoned and to go on forever.

Riordan, so tuned to her, drove into her body, going deeper with each stroke. He urged her hips into the rhythm of his. Juliette went unexpectedly over the edge, her body shuddering with pleasure, the intensity of her orgasm shaking them both. Riordan slowed the pace, heightening her enjoyment, drawing it out so that she had a series of strong orgasms. She moaned softly then cried his name, her nails digging into his shoulder. He allowed himself to go over with her, exploding with passion, riding the wave of pleasure until for the moment he was somewhat sated.

They clung to one another, her head on his shoulder, their arms around each other, as close as they could get. It took a few minutes before they could make their way to the inviting coolness of the pool, slipping into the water.

"I love this place, Riordan. Do you? Do you want to remain here in South America, or do you long to travel back to the place you were born?"

His white teeth flashed, robbing her of breath. It was always so unexpected, her reaction to his genuine smile. "I love this land. It has become my home, Juliette. And I would never take you far from you sister and cousin. You forget I am in your mind and can read your fears."

She grinned at him, looking mischievous, but obviously relieved. "What am I thinking now?"

His entire body tightened. "What you are thinking is anatomically impossible, but we can try variations."

She laughed at him, fully aware of his growing fascination with her. She hoped it would continue to grow for all eternity.

"It is obsession, not fascination," he pointed out.

She turned over to lie floating on her back, drifting with the small waves, staring up at the stars glittering over her head. "I'd like to think that somewhere out there is a man for Solange and another one for Jasmine. Good men." She turned her head to look at him as he paced slowly beside her.

Riordan scooped her up in his arms, unable to bear the melancholy in her voice. He wrapped her up tightly, holding her against his body, wanting to protect her from everything evil in the world.

Juliette brushed back his hair to look into his eyes. "Someone like you, capable of loving them no matter what. Someone capable of understanding what our lives have been like and the trauma they've been through. Do you think that will ever happen for them?"

"It really will come out right," he whispered, burying kisses in her hair. "Everything will be all right."

"I almost feel as if it will never be right again," she said and buried her face against his shoulder.

"They have us, Juliette. It will not happen overnight, but we can help them rebuild their lives. They are my family now, too. And they are under the protection of the Carpathian people."

She turned her mouth blindly to his, nearly sinking them beneath the lapping water. He responded, kissing her over and over again. His hands stroked her hair. "It will be all right, Juliette. I promise you, and I take my promises very seriously." He rested his cheek on the top of her wet hair, nuzzling her, making every effort to console and comfort her.

Juliette snuggled deeper against his body, tightening her hold on him. "I know as long as I have you with me, I'll be happy. With the two of us working together, I can only believe that the people I love will find happiness too. I'm not afraid of our life."

He lifted her chin and took possession of her mouth with his. They still had a few hours until they absolutely had to go to ground and he was determined to make the most of his time.

Awaiting Moonrise

•

MAGGIE SHAYNE

Chapter 1

MIST rose from the rain-soaked pavement and wound its way upward, tangling in the endless veils of Spanish moss. A Hollywood director couldn't have come up with a more likely setting, although Jenny supposed she should be wearing heels that would *tap-tap-tap* over the macadam and turn her ankle when she ran, instead of her royal and teal Nike cross trainers. And a flowing white dress would be more atmospheric than the jeans and loose, gauzy top. The blouse *was* white, though, and floaty enough to create the right affect. It was important to wear white. She wanted to be seen.

The plantation house was a solid half-mile back along the narrow road that meandered through the dark bayou. There wasn't a streetlight or a vehicle in sight, and the moon was full, though tough to see through the low-level fog. The air was so heavy that her skin and hair had been wet as soon as she'd left the house. Not with sweat, though that followed soon enough. Midsummer in Louisiana had the same feeling she imagined swimming in a bowl of hot soup would have.

Something rustled in the trees.

She stopped, turned to look toward the trees along the

roadside, where the sound seemed to have come from, as she slowly unzipped the waist-pack that was concealed by the loose material of her blouse. She couldn't see a damned thing, though the mists seemed to move differently there.

Her hand closed around the cool metal of her flashlight, but she didn't take it out. Shining a light in the creature's eyes would only frighten it away. She let the flashlight go and dug deeper, finding the rough diamond-patterned grip of the gun instead. She tugged it out of the bag, but not out from under the soft white gauze of the blouse. If the beast saw it, would it know it for what it was? She couldn't be sure.

So she stood there, with deer scent wafting from her shoes, and she waited. Human bait.

The wind, as heavy and hot as a lover's breath, picked up, causing the mists around her feet to swirl and rise. Her heart beat faster. The grasses and brush moved—or something moved them. She strained her eyes to see. And then, in one burst of motion, the animal exploded out of the trees and raced toward her. She jerked the gun up fast, and damn near darted the wild boar before she realized what it was and stopped herself. The barrel-shaped animal, grunting and snuffling, scuttled past her and crossed the road, vanishing into the swamp on the other side.

She stood there, the tranquilizer gun still in her hands, arms outstretched as if about to fire, and felt the nervous laughter bubble up in her chest. Slowly, she lowered her head, her arms. God, she'd almost bagged herself a pig.

The low, deep growl came from behind her, and her laughter froze in her throat. It was close. Dammit, why had she let her guard down? She lifted the gun again, turning at the same time.

Too late. The thing hit her like a linebacker, bringing a set of razor-sharp claws across her chest even as her back slammed onto the hot pavement. The gun went skidding across the road. She lay there, staring up at the thing, as amazed and awestruck as she was afraid. Maybe more.

It half crouched over her, panting quickly, a soft growl

emerging with every exhalation. The face was misshapen, the jaw elongated while the nose seemed abbreviated. Its face wasn't as hair-covered as she'd expected. The eyebrows were full and thick, the eyes deep set and dark. The hairline seemed to extend further down onto the face than it would on a human, and its chin was covered in hair, like a beard. It was dark, coarse hair. Not fur, not exactly.

It had, she realized as she lay there, waiting for death, beautiful eyes.

But was it human?

She forced her own eyes away from its dark brown ones, and examined the rest of its body. Hands, very humanlike, except for the thick layer of hair coating the backs of them. The palms were smooth, hairless. Claws curled from the ends of the fingers. Claws that cut, she thought, momentarily acknowledging the pain in her chest. Its torso was unclothed, muscular, hairy, with bits of tattered white material clinging here and there. Its lower extremities—wore jeans.

She blinked and looked again, but they remained. Denim jeans, torn and dirty, but there. So much for her theory that the sightings were of some previously undiscovered species. The jeans told her otherwise. Animals didn't routinely wear human clothing.

But just how human was it?

"Can you understand me?" she asked, forcing her voice to come out clearly, if not quite calmly.

The beast leaned closer, its dark eyes moving over her body. It seemed, she thought, to be looking her over as thoroughly as she'd been doing to it. But its gaze stopped on the front of her, and she glanced down and saw three bloody tears in her blouse, and in the flesh beneath.

She lifted her head, found those eyes waiting there. It bent still closer. She thought it might be catching the scent of her blood. Of her. And it was changing, even as she watched, the body altering in the darkness, the snout elongating.

"I mean you no harm," she said.

It growled loudly and leapt at her, would have landed

fully upon her if she hadn't reacted instantly. She lifted both her legs and thrust her feet against its chest with all her might. Its forward momentum halted, the creature shot backward so fast that its feet—paws—left the pavement a second before its entire body landed there. It didn't look like it had before. It was a wolf now, and she wondered vaguely if it had been all along. But she knew better than to question her own senses.

She jumped to her feet, scrambled for her tranq gun and spun around with it aimed and ready.

The creature was gone. She caught a glimpse of the wolf leaping a ditch with a graceful power that took her breath away. It landed easily, never breaking its stride. The bayou and the mists soon swallowed it up.

"My God," she whispered. "It's real."

She touched the wounds on her chest, wincing in pain as she did. Damn, those cuts were painful. They were also fabulous. Physical evidence!

Looking around the road, seeing no sign of danger, she replaced the gun in her pack as she dug for the more important items. The flashlight, a mini-camera, sterile bags to collect samples. Maybe the creature had left a few hairs behind. She photographed the area, marked it with a discreet orange chalk X, noted the time. She was disappointed when she found no samples. She had been so close, too. Why the hell hadn't she reached out and plucked a few hairs when it had been leaning over her?

As she packed her stuff back up, she went still as an unearthly howl came floating on the night from somewhere far away. It was, she thought, the most heartbreaking sound she had ever heard.

AT 8 A.M. when the doctor arrived at the small town's only clinic, carrying a half-full cup of coffee and looking a bit bleary-eyed, she was there waiting. He glanced at her when he walked through the reception area. She wasn't sitting, but instead pacing the waiting room. He stopped short, eying her from head to toe, and making her so self-conscious she ran a hand through her short red curls and wondered if they were standing on end.

"I hope you're the doctor," she said. *And damn,* she thought, *I really mean that.* He was the best-looking man she'd seen in six months.

He held her eyes as if he'd heard her thoughts, then turned away to glance toward the receptionist behind her desk.

"She was waiting outside when I got in, and that was a half-hour ago," the woman, whose nameplate read SALLY HAYNES, told him, shaking her head.

He looked back at Jenny again, and she shivered just a little. "If it was an emergency you should have gone to the—"

"The ER, I know. It isn't that kind of an emergency."

"What kind? Medical?"

"Could we talk in an exam room?"

He lowered his head. "Sure. Follow me."

Sally held out a fresh white lab coat, and he took it as he passed, pulling it on as he led the way to the first exam room. He tugged a stethoscope from his shirt pocket and draped it around his neck on the way. Once in the room, he nodded at the paper-covered table. "Have a seat while I wash my hands." Then he glanced at her. "I do have time to wash my hands, don't I?"

She nodded once, so he went ahead and scrubbed, dried with paper towels, tossed them and finally turned to face her again. Then he went still, seeming surprised that she had taken off her blouse. The way he looked at her, you'd have thought she was wearing a black lace negligee instead of a serviceable white bra and a pair of blue jeans.

"What, you've never seen a half-dressed female before, Doc?"

He didn't even pretend not to look his fill. "It's just that patients usually wait until I tell them to undress before doing it. Not that I'm complaining."

She should have been offended. She really should. "I'm in a little bit of a hurry."

"Shame," he muttered. Then, frowning, he moved closer, and she thought he was finally seeing the angry red scratches across her chest. "That looks nasty. What happened?" He moved still closer, leaning in. She felt his breath across her breasts and told herself it was not turning her on.

She knew what the scratches looked like. There were three of them, deep enough in places to qualify as cuts, raked across her skin, from just above the left clavicle to the upper part of the right breast.

"Something with big claws took a swipe at me."

"That much I could have guessed." He turned away from her to open a cabinet, and began setting items on the stainless steel tray beside her. Gauze pads, sterile water and alcohol, antibiotic ointment. "What was it, a dog?"

"Not exactly."

He pulled on latex gloves and began carefully cleaning the cuts. She winced as he worked, but was secretly glad of the sting. Without it, she'd have been enjoying his touch way more than she should. "So what, exactly, was it?"

"I don't know yet. But if pressed, Doc, I'd say it was a lycanthrope."

He grinned suddenly, tried not to let the chuckle escape. "You're another werewolf hunter, hmm? Come down here looking for the loup-garou?"

"I'm a professor at Dunkirk University. I'm here doing research."

"A professor of what?"

She cleared her throat. "Cryptozoology."

This time he couldn't contain the laugh. It escaped, and she flinched and shot him an angry look. He stopped in midchuckle. "I'm sorry. It's just—you didn't really come down her to research werewolves, did you?"

"I came down to determine whether there might be a previously unknown species of mammal hiding out in the Louisiana bayou."

"Sounds so much more rational your way," he told her.

She shrugged. "Well, rational or not, something attacked

me on the road last night. And I can tell you, Doc, whatever it was, it was no *known* species."

"And the moon *was* full."

"Are you making fun?"

"Just stating a fact." He frowned, more serious now. "Whatever it was, it did a number on you. This is no laughing matter. It could have been rabid."

"It wasn't."

"You can't know that for sure."

"Doesn't matter. I've been immunized."

"Against rabies?"

"Of course. I have a masters in zoology and a Ph.D. in veterinary medicine. I have been immunized against just about anything you can think of that can be transmitted from animal to human."

He took a step back, seemingly satisfied that the wound was thoroughly clean. "You're a vet, huh?"

"Mmm-hmm."

Pursing his lips, nodding slowly, he reached for the ointment. "So it's safe to say you could have patched this up yourself."

"Could have. Didn't want to."

"Why don't you stop playing games and tell me why you're really here?"

She was surprised. She felt her eyes widen as they shot to his. He'd startled her by being so direct. "I wasn't playing games, doctor. I had planned to come and see you anyway, and I simply thought as long as I was here, I'd get myself patched up. Okay?"

"Okay." He began smearing ointment over the cuts. She began wishing the latex gloves were not between his fingertips and her flesh. "Why were you coming to see me anyway?"

"To ask you how often you see patients with marks like the ones on my chest."

He shrugged. "I haven't seen a chest quite like yours in a long time," he said, without cracking a smile. Totally inappropriate—the way he was looking at her breasts where they swelled over the top of the bra. And yet it made her warm all over.

"You know that's not what I was asking."

He didn't look away from his work. She thought his hands were moving way more slowly than necessary, smoothing that ointment on her cuts, rubbing it in, his touch soft and erotic. "How often, Doctor?" she managed to ask. Did her voice sound slightly hoarse to him?

"Not more often than would be considered normal."

"These kinds of attacks are what you call normal?"

"Scratches are normal. People get them in numerous ways. Tangling with thorny bushes, angry cats or rambunctious dogs, falling on a lawn rake. Getting a little carried away during sex." He pushed a bra strap down over her shoulder, then pulled the cup away and downward, exposing her breast completely.

It wasn't exactly unnecessary, she told herself. The scratches did continue an inch or so beyond the fabric. What was unnecessary was the way her body reacted to his intense scrutiny, and the way her nipple tightened in the chilled air of the exam room.

When he licked his lips, she almost moaned.

"Did any of those other patients with scratches ever claim they were attacked by a werewolf?" she asked, but her voice was barely more than a whisper.

His eyes still on her breast, he put a little more ointment on his gloved hand. "Not a one. Until now."

She blinked slowly. "You wouldn't lie to me about that, now, would you?"

"Not on your life." He met her eyes, held them as his hand moved to massage the ointment over her breast. He had, she thought, beautiful eyes. Dark and intense and full of sexual promises that didn't need to be spoken aloud. His fingers brushed her nipple and she bit her bottom lip.

"So do you suppose you'll turn into a werewolf now, too?"

His voice, too, had lowered, turned rough.

He was teasing her now, with his words as well as his fingers, and she wasn't objecting. Shivers tiptoed up her spine. "I don't know. The mythology says it has to be a bite for that to happen, but—"

"He didn't bite you, then?"

"N-no."

"Damn stupid werewolf, if you ask me." Again his fingers flicked across her nipple.

She sucked in a breath and drew back, just a little. With more regret than she could even believe, she tugged the bra's cup back into place.

He sighed as if he regretted it, too. "So just what does a hundred-pound redhead do with a werewolf, once she finds it?"

"Study it. Talk to it, if that's possible. Try to learn what it is, how much of the folklore is true and how much isn't."

He smirked a little, lowering his eyes.

"I take it you don't approve of those goals?"

He shrugged. "Lie back and I'll bind you up." He caught her quick look. She knew damn well he'd intended the double entendre. "Bandage your cuts," he corrected.

She laid down on the table, and he unrolled soft gauze over the ointment-daubed scratches. "What would *you* do?"

He smoothed tape over the gauze to hold it in place. "I'm a doctor," he said. "I suppose I'd try to help it, if that were possible. Cure it, if that was what it wanted. And I'd keep its secrets, either way. Not write them up for some scientific journal and my own fame and glory."

"Is that what you think I'm after? Fame and glory?"

"Isn't it?"

"No," she said. He finished with the bandages, never baring her breast again. She sat up, and he handed her the blouse.

"Well, that's good to know." He didn't sound as if he believed her. And he watched her while she pulled her blouse on, watched her while she buttoned it.

"Thank you for patching me up," she said.

"It was my pleasure." He put extra emphasis on the word "pleasure."

"Don't be too sure about that."

He met her eyes, silently acknowledging that he got the message, loud and clear.

Chapter 2

JENNY walked back to the sprawling white plantation house and went inside to find the crew—three grad students who thought they were smarter than her and one department head who knew he was—gathered in the dining room, munching on pastries and slugging down coffee.

"Where have you been all morning?" Professor Hinkle asked in his usual tone—the one that always seemed to insinuate something, never quite letting on what.

"Interviewing some of the locals in town. No hits, so far." She wasn't about to tell him about her lycanthropic encounter and subsequent visit to the hotter-than-hell doctor. He wouldn't believe her about the werewolf anyway. No, not until she had *proof*.

"Did you see anything last night?" Carrie asked. She was the most gullible. Believed everything until it was proven false, when the ideal cryptozoologist practiced the opposite. She had a long way to go.

"Wild boar," she replied. "Ran out of the woods at me so suddenly, I almost darted it."

Carrie grinned. Mike and Toby exchanged smirks that

said only a woman would be so jumpy. Right, she'd like to see one of the "twins" come face-to-face with that thing from last night. They'd have jumped right out of their matching chinos and Ralph Lauren polo shirts. They were unrelated, but wore nearly identical ultrashort, slightly gelled hairstyles, one a little blonder than the other. The two were practically clones as far as she was concerned. Not only in style choices, but in attitude and arrogance. She was well aware they'd only signed up for this program because they thought it would give them four easy credits. Or maybe they were both planning a masters thesis that would attempt to debunk her profession.

They wouldn't succeed.

"So, how's the research coming?" she asked, turning her attention to the eager pupil.

"I found tons of stuff!" Carrie said, reaching for the notebook that was never far from her side with one hand and flipping her expertly cut hair with the other.

"Yeah. Fairy tales and folklore," Toby sneered. "Nothing legitimate."

"Folklore is what led us to the giant gorillas, Toby."

"Here we go with the giant gorillas again."

"Until scientists began taking the local legends seriously, no one believed they existed, but they do. They'd been living in the jungles for centuries, and only those natives who lived among them knew the truth. No one believed them, just as no one believes people today when they see something strange and have the nerve to tell someone about it."

"Right."

Carrie shot the boys a killing look, and opened her notebook to a page of neatly typed text. "I've got reams of stuff here. Most of the sources include legends about how to kill them with a silver bullet, but some take that a lot further. They have to be decapitated and burned afterward."

Jenny shot her a look. "Carrie, if we find a specimen we certainly won't be looking for ways to kill it."

"I figured—you know, just in case."

Jenny moved closer, taking Carrie's notebook from her

and carrying it to the table. She grabbed a beignet from the tray of pastries on the table, filled an empty china cup with fragrant, steaming coffee and flipped through pages.

"To become a werewolf," she read.

"Oh, great," Toby said. "Recipes."

Jenny smiled a little, because it was close. " 'On the night of the dark moon, or the third night of the full, betake thyself to a place far from the haunts of man—deep in the forest. There, draw a circle no less than seven feet in diameter, and within it draw another of three feet. Within the smaller circle, erect a tripod of iron, and from it suspend a cauldron of iron, and fill the cauldron with water taken from a stream in which three wolves have been seen to drink. Build a fire beneath, and when the water boils, add to it any three of the following herbs: blind bluff, devil's eye, bittersweet, devil's dung, beaver poison or opium.' "

"I daresay," Professor Hinkle remarked, "a few whiffs of the steam from that brew might convince any of us we'd become a werewolf."

Jenny almost gasped. Had the old sourpuss actually made a joke?

"The only real ingredient in there is the opium," Toby said. "That other stuff is made up."

"Oh, you're dead wrong there," Jenny corrected. "These are folk names. Blind bluff is poppy. Devil's eye is henbane. Bittersweet is solanum. Devil's dung is aesophetida, named quite aptly, for its smell."

"And beaver poison is hemlock," Carrie put in. "Keep reading, Professor Rose. It's fascinating."

She shrugged. "After that it says to strip naked and rub your body all over with an ointment made from," she glanced at the page to find her place, "the fat of a freshly killed feline, mixed with opium, camphor and anise seed."

"Clever," the professor said. "The camphor would open the pores, allowing one to absorb the opium more quickly."

"Then 'wrap thy loins in the hide of a wolf, speak the charm and await the advent of the unknown.' " She nodded. "How many of you have taken anthropology classes?"

All hands went up, including the professor's, though his came with a sarcastic look.

"Good. Now, think back and tell me what this recipe reminds you of."

"Oh, oh, I know!" Carrie said. "It's just like what some shamans of various cultures do. They ingest a hallucinogenic, and go on a journey into the other realms. Shapeshifting is often a part of the experience."

Jenny nodded. "Good. Any other similar examples?"

Mike raised a reluctant hand, then looked at it sheepishly and spoke up. "The so-called flying ointments used by witches?"

"Bingo. Animal-fat base, fly agaric being the most commonly used active ingredient. So what does this tell us about this particular account of turning oneself into a werewolf? Where did this author get his information?"

They looked at each other blankly.

"He got it from someone who was into magic. A shaman or sage or village witch. What he's talking about is magic, not reality. We are scientists. Is the creature we're looking for something that was created by cat fat and opium? No. The only things created by that blend were hallucinations. What is our werewolf, then?"

She held out her hands, palms up.

All together, the three students intoned, "A previously undiscovered species."

"Precisely. So what can we get out of this?"

"Not a hell of a lot?" Toby suggested.

"Not a lot, but some. We can learn that the creature in question dwells in very deep forests, avoids humans when possible and is somewhat manlike in appearance. See that's the key. Take the folklore, sift out the impossible and take a look at what's left. The solid stuff that can lead you to the truth."

"But, Professor Rose," Carrie asked, "what if the werewolf really was created by some kind of curse, some kind of magic?"

"Carrie, you're a science student. There is no such thing

as magic. The sooner you get that through your head, the better you'll do." She shut the notebook. "Now, I want you to go through these notes, pick out all the fantasy and magic and compile what's left for me."

"I'd like copies of those notes as well, Carrie," Dr. Hinkle added. "Before you do any deleting."

"What about us?" Mike asked.

"You and Toby do some more canvassing of the locals. Ask them what they've heard about the loup-garou. Tape-record their answers so you don't inadvertantly leave out something I can use," Jenny told him.

"And what do you plan to spend *your* morning doing, Professor Rose?" Hinkle asked.

"I'm going out into the woods to see if I can find any sign of an unknown species. You're welcome to come along, professor, but you'll need good hiking shoes and a backpack for supplies. I plan to go deep into the forests, and the terrain won't be gentle."

" 'Far from the haunts of man?' " he asked, smirking.

"Exactly."

It was, of course, an outright lie. She was going into the woods along the roadside, where she'd encountered that beast last night. She might be able to see clues in daylight that she hadn't seen in the darkness. She didn't want or need Hinkle looking over her shoulder, second-guessing her every move and constantly looking for something to use against her.

It would suit him just fine if her proposal of a cryptozoology department at Dunkirk University—a department she proposed to head up herself—be annihilated as soon as possible. He hated the idea.

He hated her.

"You coming?" she asked, glancing at him.

"Of course not. You know better. I'll just stay here and read through your notes."

She smiled as if that thought didn't make her nervous. It shouldn't. Like Al Capone's accountant, she kept two sets of books. No one saw her private thoughts.

"I'll see you later then," she said, turning to go.

"Don't forget the feline fat," he called after her, then he chuckled at his own lame joke, while Toby and Mike laughed obediently.

Puppies, Jenny thought. She would have called them were-pups, but that would imply they were half-man, and she didn't think they qualified.

She jogged up the stairs to her rooms to change clothes before heading back to the place where she'd seen—what she'd seen last night.

Mamma Louisa was in the bedroom, busily making the bed, her head wrapped in a pure white turban, her blouse and skirt just as white. Spotless, bleached and in stark contrast to her dark skin.

Women of her size didn't wear a lot of white up north. Jenny thought it was a shame. Mamma Louisa looked good. Big and beautiful and proud. She carried herself like royalty.

She looked up when Jenny walked in and sent her a smile. "I can come back later," she said, the bayou thick in her voice.

"No, no, don't stop. I'm just grabbing a few things and heading back out."

"All right, then. How is de research goin'?"

"Fine. Better than fine, actually." Jenny turned to the dresser, tugged open a drawer and found a T-shirt. Then she peeled her blouse over her head, facing the mirror.

"Osé, osé, osé," Mamma Louisa whispered urgently, and when Jenny met her eyes in the mirror, she saw that the other woman's gaze was on her own bandaged chest. "What happened to you last night, *chère?*"

Dammit, how could she be so careless? She pulled the T-shirt over her head quickly. "Nothing—it's just a scratch. I brushed up against a thorn tree."

"Did you, now?" The woman eyed the blouse that was lying on the floor beside the bed—white fabric with a few tears and some dried blood. She took a single step toward it, and Jenny rushed forward, getting there first and snatching it off the floor and wadding it up.

"Somethin' there you don't want me to see, child?"

"I'm not used to being waited on, Mamma Louisa. It makes me uncomfortable to have someone picking up after me."

"You prefer to tend your own bedroom from now on, then?"

"Yes. Yes, actually, I do."

Mamma shrugged. "Well, I be paid good money to keep the house and do the cookin' for the guests here, Miss Jenny. But if it makes you uneasy, I stay clear of your room . . . and your secrets."

"I have no secrets."

She nodded. "I'll let Eva Lynn know, so she'll stay out of your rooms as well." She started for the door, leaving the bed half-made, but when she reached the door, she paused.

"There be things out there, *chère*. Things you would never believe. Things that ought to be left alone."

Blinking out of the shock those words caused, Jenny raced forward after Mamma Louisa left the room and closed the door behind her.

She yanked the door open and lunged into the long corridor. "Wait. What do you know about this?"

But Mamma Louisa was nowhere in sight.

Chapter 3

JENNY knelt on the spongelike ground and forcibly resisted the urge to release a shriek of joy. In front of her, clear as day, was a footprint sunken into the moist earth. It was too large and too oblong to belong to an animal, she thought. The creature hadn't been a wolf when it had left this track, but it hadn't been a man, either. She supposed the print might belong to a bear, though that would be more rounded. Perhaps a gorilla, but there were no gorillas running wild in the bayou. None she knew of, at least. She would run it through the computer to make sure, and she was trying hard not to jump to conclusions in the meantime. It was tough, though, to maintain her scientific skepticism in the face of such a discovery.

This could be major.

She shrugged off her backpack, unzipped it and removed supplies. She mixed the powdered plaster with bottled water until it was just the right consistency, then carefully she brushed loose bits of grass and dirt from the print. Finally, she poured the plaster into it and stood back to wait for it to harden.

As she waited, she looked around. She stood in a wooded area several yards from the road. She'd started off in the direction she thought the creature had come from last night, then moved in a half-circle around the spot where she'd first seen it, increasing the size of her search area, inspecting the ground and trees for any sign at all of wildlife. And she'd found it, too. A raven feather. The tracks of a wild pig, probably the one she'd encountered last night. A few bristly hairs stuck in the bark of a tree, probably where that same pig had scratched a pesky itch. And near the place where the swamp met the dry land, a long, smooth patch of mud that was probably a gator slide.

And then, the footprint.

Kneeling, she checked the plaster. Still wet.

The sound of a vehicle's motor brought her head up again, and as she searched for the source, she frowned. It wasn't coming from the road, which was behind her, but from somewhere ahead. Was there another road skirting this patch of swamp and woods?

As she strained to listen, the motor cut off, then a door slammed.

Someone was out there. She gathered a few large, leafy plants and laid them over her plaster cast to keep it out of sight, then shouldered her pack and started forward, deeper into the woods. Fifty yards, then sixty, and just when she thought was going to find nothing, she saw it. A square shape within the trees, almost perfectly camouflaged—a log cabin.

Frowning, she moved closer, peering through the trees until she had a clear view of the little house. It was charming, with a cobblestone chimney and green painted window shutters, with moon-shaped cutouts in each of them. The door was green, too, a deep, piney color that blended well with the surrounding foliage.

The car in the driveway was a familiar one—the same dark-brown jeep she'd seen when she'd left the doctor's office this morning. Frowning, she double-checked the plates, saw the MD tag on the corner.

"Did you come for me?" a deep voice asked.

The voice came from right behind her, and startled her so much she nearly jumped out of her skin as she spun around. He stood there, looking at her, not even cracking a smile.

"What are you doing here, Professor Rose?"

She released the breath she'd sucked in, before it could burst her lungs. "Sheesh, you scared the daylights out of me."

"That's what happens, I suppose, when you are caught sneaking around on private property."

"I wasn't sneaking around! I was working. And what are you doing out here, anyway, making a house call?"

He shook his head slowly, holding her eyes. "I came home for lunch. I do that sometimes."

Jenny licked her lips and tried to calm her racing heart. "You . . . live here?"

"And you don't. So again, I have to ask, what are you doing here?"

He seemed awfully irritated for someone who'd seemed as into her as he had earlier. She couldn't hide her disappointment. "Look, I didn't know it was private property. There are no signs—"

He pointed, and she turned her head to see a POSTED: NO TRESPASSING sign tacked to a nearby tree.

"Okay, so I wasn't looking for signs, or maybe I would have seen them."

"Then what were you looking for?"

She didn't answer.

"The loup-garou?" She didn't miss the sarcasm loaded onto the word. "They only come out at night, Professor Rose. But I would have thought a woman of your expertise would know that."

"That's what the folklore says. I don't take anything as fact until I've found proof of it, though."

He nodded slowly. "So is that what you're out here looking for? Proof?" He narrowed his eyes. "Or is this where you had your . . . encounter last night?"

"Not far from here," she said. "Out on the road."

"I see."

She drew a deep breath, then sighed. "I've really pissed you off, haven't I? I'm really sorry about the trespassing, Doctor . . ." she searched her memory for his last name. She was sure she'd seen or heard it this morning, but—

"La Roque," he said.

"Right. La Roque. It's not my habit to traipse around on private property. It really isn't. I always ask permission before walking on private land. I insist my students do the same. I just—I was overzealous and forgot my protocol." She held his eyes, hoping he could see the sincerity in hers.

He studied her face as if weighing her words. When he spoke again, he said the last thing she expected to hear. "You want to come in? Join me for lunch?"

For some reason she thought of Little Red Riding Hood and the Big Bad Wolf. At least he didn't say he wanted to have her for lunch, she thought grimly. She wanted to get back to her plaster cast, which should be hard enough by now, but he lived here. He could have seen or heard something, especially if the creature frequented this area. She couldn't pass up the opportunity to pick his brain, and she thought he knew it.

Besides, now that he'd decided to accept her apology, that look was creeping back into his eyes. The one that heated her blood.

"Sure," she said at last. "I'm kind of surprised you would ask."

"You shouldn't be. Or didn't you get the message back there in my office that I would like to see you again while you're in town?"

She licked her lips. "I . . . yeah, I did."

With a nod, he moved past her, leading the way out of the trees and into the clearing that surrounded his cabin. She noticed that the long driveway angled back out, probably to the road. She scanned the ground as they walked, straining her eyes in search of any other odd tracks, but the ground was hard and dry. Not a good medium for footprints.

He opened the door, then stood aside to let her enter first. She did, and stopped just inside, looking around at the cozy cabin. The living and dining rooms were combined in one large, open space, with a cobblestone fireplace at one end. The room was open to the peak, log rafters at intervals. A loft took up half of the upper part, its floor forming the ceiling of the small kitchen.

"This is a great cabin."

"It suits me."

"Very private, out of the way."

"That's what I like best about it." He walked into the kitchen, opened the fridge and began taking items out of it. "I'm having a ham sandwich. That okay with you?"

"Fine, if you hold the ham."

"What?" He looked at her, puzzled.

"I'm a vegetarian."

He blinked slowly. Then, finally, he smiled. It was like a light dawning on his face, and it reached his eyes. "That's almost funny. A vegetarian werewolf hunter."

"I'm no hunter, Dr. La—"

"Call me Samuel. We don't stand much on formality in these parts." He yanked tomatoes and lettuce out of the fridge, a brick of cheese, a jar of locally produced gourmet mayonnaise, and a package of deli-sliced ham.

"Samuel. Is that what your patients call you?"

"Only the ones I all but seduce during an exam," he said softly.

She shot him a look. His eyes were smoky. "And are there a lot of those?"

"You were the first. Should I apologize for being so far out of line?"

Holding his gaze, she shook her head slowly.

"That's good, because I wouldn't mean it if I did."

She had to avert her eyes, it was getting so hot, and the way his hard, strong hand was cupping the tomato was making her shake. "So what do your patients call you?" she asked, just to break the tension.

"Mostly they call me Doc Rock. They think it's funny."

"But you don't?"

He shrugged. "Call me Samuel."

"Okay. So Samuel, were you home last night?"

He put her sandwich together first, slicing hunks from a huge loaf of bread, and laying them on a paper plate, before adding the mayo, veggies and cheese. "What time?" he asked, not even glancing at her as he worked.

"Must have been around nine or a little after."

He nodded, putting the top slice of bread on the sandwich, slicing it diagonally, setting the plate aside and beginning work on his own. "Is that what time you bumped into the werewolf?"

"That's what time I encountered an unknown species of mammal. What it is, remains to be determined."

He nodded slowly, finishing his sandwich and then bringing both plates to the table and setting them down. "I was sound asleep. No witnesses of course."

"You live alone, then," she asked.

He met her eyes, a little spark appearing in their dark-brown depths. "Yeah. You?"

"Yeah. I mean, I do when I'm home. Right now I'm sharing a house with three grad students and a doctor of zoology with an attitude."

"The Branson Estate, right?"

She nodded.

"Have you seen anything . . . interesting there yet?"

Frowning, she searched his face. "Like what?"

He turned away, returning the veggies and meat to the fridge and removing two cold beers while he was there, opening them both. He didn't answer, only shrugged.

"Come on, Sam, spill it."

"Samuel." He sat down, handed her a bottle of beer, took a swig of his own. "I'd rather show you than tell you."

"Now you're just teasing me. Not to mention changing the subject."

"I didn't see or hear anything out of the ordinary last night, Jenny."

She warmed a little at his use of her first name. "Oh." She took a bite of her sandwich.

"Aren't you going to ask me the rest?"

She chewed, swallowed, washed the food down with a swig of beer. "What do you mean?"

"You know exactly what I mean. You want to know if I changed under the light of the full moon, went out on the hunt. You want to know if I chased a wild boar out of the woods, then changed my mind about my prey when I caught a glimpse of you out there, all alone."

She swallowed hard, her blood having gone cold. "That's silly."

"Is it?"

She shrugged, lowering her gaze. "D-did you?"

He licked his lips. "What makes you think I'd remember it if I had?"

She shrugged and looked away, but when she looked back again he was probing her eyes with his.

"You really shouldn't walk that road alone at night, Jenny," he said. "It's not playing fair."

"What . . . what do you mean?"

He reached across the table, stroked a little path over her cheek with the tip of one finger. "You're beautiful, young, tender . . . I don't know a wolf who could resist just a little taste."

Blinking fast, shivering from the power of that touch—just one finger trailing over her skin shouldn't make her shiver like that!—she lowered her eyes. "Are you coming on to me, Samuel?"

He drew a deep breath, lowered his hand. "As hard as I can, Jenny. Do you mind?"

Lifting her eyes again, she met his. He was smiling now, that intense, almost predatory look gone. "You're handsome, and single, and a doctor. Why would I mind?"

His smile grew. "This is unusual for me. I don't usually get to see a woman naked before asking her out."

"I was only half naked."

"Well, there's always the follow-up appointment."

She laughed softly, warming to his teasing tone. "Tell me again that you really don't behave this way with all your patients."

"If I did, I wouldn't have a license for long. No, Jenny, I'm not nearly this unprofessional. I swear it. I guess there's just something about you." He smiled again, slowly this time. "You bring out the beast in me."

She tried to laugh it off, but a chill raced right up her spine. She returned to eating her sandwich, and he watched her. Watched every bite she took, watched her chew, watched her swallow and lick her lips. He watched her like no one had ever watched her before. When she put the beer bottle to her lips and tipped it up to drink, his eyes were glued to her mouth, and she felt almost stripped naked the way they looked at her.

He made every single part of her body tingle with awareness, all without even touching her. Those eyes—they were powerful.

She set the bottle down. "I should go."

"You haven't agreed to go out with me yet."

She thought maybe she'd rather stay in with him, but she couldn't very well say so. "How about tonight?"

He nodded. "I'll be at your place at six. We'll have dinner. And maybe I'll show you some of the secrets of the Branson Estate."

"There's a full moon tonight," she whispered. "I really should be out patrolling, keeping an eye for the werewolf."

"The moon rises at nine twenty-two tonight. I promise I'll kiss you goodnight long before then."

Her stomach knotted. "What makes you think I'm going to let you kiss me?"

"Oh, I'm going to kiss you. Consider yourself fore-warned."

His eyes were on her mouth, and she was fighting the urge to lean across the table and press it to his. She pushed her chair away from the table, got to her feet. "I really have to go." Because if she stayed here much longer she was go-ing to start tearing off her clothes.

"Have a good afternoon, Jenny. I'll see you at six."

She started for the door, then paused. "Samuel, the oth-ers—the grad students and Dr. Hinkle—they don't know about what happened last night. I'd just as soon keep it that way."

"You didn't tell them?" he asked, getting to his feet, coming with her to the door. "Why not?"

She shrugged. "I wanted to have proof first."

"You think they won't believe you."

"I don't know if they would or not. Just—don't say anything about it if you see any of them tonight, okay?"

"Your secret's safe with me," he murmured. Then he opened the door and was distracted by something beyond her. When she turned and saw the giant dog loping toward them she almost jumped. Then she looked again and realized it wasn't a dog at all. It was a large black wolf.

"Mojo! There you are. You're late for lunch," Samuel called.

She stepped out of the way as the wolf raced past her into the house and leapt on Samuel, standing on its hind legs, paws to his chest. Samuel ran his hands through the animal's lush, deep fur.

"My pet, Mojo."

"He's a wolf."

"Just garden variety, I swear."

She nodded, patting the dog on the head with a hesitant hand before turning to go.

"See you later, Jenny."

"Thanks for lunch." She left the cabin in a rush, hurried back into the woods and as soon as she was out of sight, stopped to lean back against a tree, hug her arms, close her eyes and ask herself just when in her life she had ever been as turned on as she had been just now. He had barely touched her. My God, she was trembling.

She took a few breaths, tried to steady her frayed, tingling nerves and finally got moving again, heading back to the site where she'd left her plaster to dry.

When she got there, the leaves she'd placed over the footprint were gone. The plaster was missing as well, and the footprint itself had been smeared beyond recognition.

Chapter 4

W HEN she returned to the plantation house, she crept in quietly, using a side door and hoping not to encounter anyone on the way to her rooms. She was upset, shaken and still trying to remember the events of the day exactly as they'd happened. First, she'd created the plaster cast. Second, she'd heard the vehicle. Third, she'd moved away from her precious footprint, leaving it unguarded, in order to find the source of the noise, and she'd crept up on the little cabin in the woods, and the by-then-silent Jeep. And fourth, Samuel La Roque had come up behind her.

Behind her.

Why hadn't he just got out of his Jeep and gone into his house? It wasn't as if she'd made any noise that would have alerted him to her presence. What had possessed him to creep into the woods, past her, and then come up behind her? And most important of all, had he been the one who'd sabotaged what might have been the most important discovery of her career?

She moved through the kitchen, where Eva Lynn was

mixing some thick, fragrant batter in a big metal bowl. She smiled hello, her face a younger version of her mother's flawless complexion, her body more slender and willowy. Like her mother, she dressed all in white, right to the turban on her head. She didn't say a word, sensing, perhaps, that Jenny wished to slip in unseen. She just nodded knowingly and returned her attention to her batter.

Jenny pushed open the swinging door to the back stairs and took them up to the second floor. The stairs continued on to the third floor, where Eva Lynn and Mamma Louisa lived. But Jenny stopped at the second-floor landing, pushed open the door and stepped into the massive hall, with its black and red velvet runner, its gold-painted stands, mirrors and vases and its mini-chandeliers dangling every few yards from the high ceilings. She crept along the hallway to her room, wiping sweat from her brow. No AC in the hallways. Just the rooms themselves. The hallways were like saunas, almost as thick with wet heat as the outdoors.

She stopped outside the door to her room. It was standing slightly open, and she was certain she had closed it when she'd left.

Frowning, Jenny pushed the door gently, opening it a little farther. Dr. Hinkle sat at the small table in the sitting room portion of her suite, squinting at the screen of her laptop, which hadn't been left on.

She stepped inside and cleared her throat.

He looked up fast, clearly startled. For just an instant, guilt clouded his pinched face, but it vanished just as quickly. "Have a pleasant expedition?" he asked, as if he hadn't been doing anything so much as out of the ordinary, much less dead wrong.

"What the hell are you doing in my rooms?"

He lifted his brows. "Going over your notes, supervising your handling of this project, which is exactly what I was sent here to do, Professor Rose."

"You could do that without invading my privacy and going through my personal things."

"How?" he asked with an innocent shrug that was

patently false. "The files are on the computer, and the computer was in here."

"I would be happy to provide you with a copy of all my files on diskette or CD, whichever you prefer: all you have to do is ask. But my room, Dr. Hinkle, is off-limits."

"I am the ranking scientist on this mission," he reminded her. "Not to mention the head of the department."

"But how long would you be, if I were to call the dean right now and tell him I caught you sneaking around in my bedroom?" She smiled slowly. "Sexual harassment is such an ugly term. I'd hate to use it if I didn't have to."

He lowered the lid on the laptop while rising to his feet. "You win, this round at least. I'll stay out of your rooms."

"I think I'll keep them locked from now on, just to make sure."

"One would almost think you had something to hide, Professor Rose."

She stepped aside, opening her door wider so he could leave.

"Why are there password-protected files on your hard drive?"

She shrugged. "Those are my diaries. I fill those files with romantic daydreams and other girlish things that wouldn't interest you in the least."

"Why am I certain you're lying?"

"Maybe you just have a suspicious mind. At any rate, it's no concern of mine. I'd like to shower and change clothes now, if you don't mind. . . ."

"What did you find on your expedition this morning?"

She met his eyes and kept her gaze steady and strong. "Not a thing."

He smirked, then turned and left her bedroom. She closed the door, intending to do exactly what she'd told him she would do, take a shower and rinse away the sticky heat of the bayou. But as she started across the room, something crunched under her shoes, making her look down. Mud, dried mud. Cussing silently, she heeled off her shoes and wished she had taken them off when she'd first come into the house. Shame on her for tracking up the place like that. She left her shoes near the door and started across the room again, but more dried mud crumbled under her socks, and she realized it was scattered in places where her muddy shoes had never been.

Narrowing her eyes, she scanned the sitting room, and then the bedroom floor, seeing bits of it everywhere. That nosy old buzzard had been all through her rooms. What the hell was he looking for?

And where had he been, that he'd managed to get swamp mud on his boots?

Maybe it hadn't been Samuel La Roque who'd sabotaged her and stolen her evidence today, after all.

ON Saturdays, Mamma Louisa and Eva Lynn went off duty at noon and didn't have to work again until Monday morning. When there were guests in residence, the two spent all Saturday morning cooking and baking and shopping to be sure there was plenty of food in the house while they were off duty. After all this was Louisiana: there wasn't much that was more important to a host than keeping the guests well fed.

So they were already gone when Jenny came down the stairs at 5:50 p.m. She'd spent the afternoon making notes of everything that had happened that day and storing them in one of the password-protected files on her laptop. She'd located the key to her suite of rooms, hanging from a hook just inside the bedroom door, and she'd locked the rooms up when she'd left.

She thought her privacy would be safe tonight. It had better be.

"Wow," Carrie said when she reached the bottom of the stairs. "You look great. What's the occasion?" She wiggled her eyebrows. "Hot date?"

"What are you talking about?" She glanced down at her clothes, a simple, tank-style dress in white cotton: a belt made of turquoise beads hung loosely around her waist and dipped downward at one side; a matching strand of the big turquoise stones around her throat, and one at each ear; flat, brown sandals that didn't go with anything, and no nylons at all. It was too hot for nylons.

"You put your hair up," Carrie said, nodding toward the normally wild red curls that Jenny had scooped into a comb. They tumbled from it like a waterfall, but were at least out of her eyes. "And . . . you're wearing makeup."

"I am not wearing makeup. What would be the point, it would only melt off in ten minutes."

She was lying. She'd applied a very light touch of shadow, slightly darker than flesh toned, and a coat of mascara. She'd darkened her lips with tinted lip gloss that tasted like cherries, and told herself it was because *she* liked the taste.

"So who's the lucky guy?"

She shrugged and was saved from having to answer when the twins walked in from the kitchen, each carrying a plate of leftovers. They stopped when they saw her, and Mike said, "Holy shit," and Toby said, "Are you wearing anything under that?"

"Keep it up, you two, and I'll toss you out on your asses without a credit to show for it."

They grinned, exchanged glances, shrugged and continued on their way.

"This is strictly business," she told Carrie, who was now eyeing the dress as if she too wondered what was underneath. "This guy lives near . . . one of the areas where our creature has allegedly been sighted. I am having dinner with him so I can pick his brain, and that's all."

"Sure it is. Is he gorgeous?"

Jenny pursed her lips. "Where is Dr. Hinkle, anyway?"

"Took his dinner up to his room. Said he needed quiet time tonight. And I'm not gonna say a word to him about this, because it's none of his business. But I wouldn't count on the same from those two morons. So *is* he gorgeous?"

The doorbell chimed. Carrie spun around and ran for it so fast her hair flew like a comet's tail behind her. She jerked the heavy door open without even asking who was there, and stood there blinking up at Samuel. "Yep. He is," she said.

"Pardon me?" he asked.

"Nothing," she said quickly, and stepped aside. "Come on in."

He did, then he saw Jenny coming across the room toward him, and he stopped moving, maybe even stopped breathing. He just stared at her, and when his eyes slid down the soft, clingy dress, she got the feeling he didn't have to wonder what she wore underneath. She got the feeling he knew what was under there. Or more accurately, what wasn't.

"Hello, Jenny," he said. But the tone of his voice and the look in his eyes said more.

"Hi." Since when did she speak in a throaty whisper?

"You look—" He shook his head, licked his lips.

"Thanks."

He slid a hand around her bare upper arm and led her out the door. As soon as they were out of earshot, he leaned close to her. "Hungry?"

"Yeah, I am."

"For food?"

She looked at him quickly, and he gave her an evil smile. " 'Cause the way you look tonight, Jenny, I'm thinking I'd be happy with you as the main course."

"Let's just start with dinner, Sam."

"Samuel."

"Right." He opened the passenger door of his Jeep and she slid inside. He watched her move, stared at her legs, then leaned in so close she thought he might kiss her right there, only to buckle the seat belt around her.

The breath stuttered out of her.

"You smell like cherries," he whispered. "I love cherries." Then he closed her door and went to his own, got behind the wheel and drove.

Chapter 5

THE restaurant was quiet and dark, even though the sun hadn't yet set outside. The dinner rush hadn't begun, but for the doctor, a table was ready and waiting in a dim corner where not another table was occupied. Candles glowed on the table, and soft music wafted from unseen speakers.

She noticed when Samuel met the waiter's eyes, nodded and mouthed the word "perfect."

The waiter held out her chair for her, and Samuel stood until she was seated. Then he took his own seat and ordered wine. The way the candlelight lit his eyes was almost eerie. They glowed.

"This is a beautiful restaurant," she said, trying to break the tension that seemed to hover in the air between them. The car had been filled with it.

"For a beautiful woman."

She smiled a little. "You don't waste any time, do you?"

"I don't believe in wasting time. I used to. Used to wait for things to happen at their own pace and try to be patient, and calm. Keep things . . . toned down."

"And that changed?"

He nodded.

"Why?"

With a little shrug, he said, "Because I changed, I guess. I learned the thrill of going after what I wanted, no holds barred. And of living life in a way that lends itself to relishing every single moment. There's a lot to be said for instant gratification."

"That might be true. But what happens when you can't get what you want?"

He smiled slowly. "I always get what I want."

The waiter returned with the wine, showed Samuel the bottle then poured a bit into his glass. Samuel sniffed it, swirled it, tasted it and then gave a nod. The waiter filled both glasses and left the bottle, in its ice-filled silver bucket, on the table.

"Try the wine."

She took a sip. "It's good."

"No. Not like that. Experience the wine, Jenny. Smell it, taste it. Feel it sliding over your tongue and down your throat—relish the moment."

She lifted her glass again.

"Close your eyes, think of nothing but the wine. Open your senses."

She did as he said, trying to focus everything on the wine, though it was difficult with the man sitting across from her, absorbing her attention in a way no wine would ever do. She smelled the wine, let its scent fill her, then took a slow sip and held it in her mouth to taste it thoroughly before swallowing. The wine's taste remained on her tongue even as its warmth spread through her belly.

"Mmm." She opened her eyes to see his fixed on her face.

A throat cleared nearby, and Jenny looked up to see the waiter standing ready with two menus in his hands. "May I tell you about our specials?" he asked.

Samuel let his eyes tell her to answer for them both. She said, "No, I know what I want. I've been dying for some authentic gumbo. Do you make a vegetarian version?"

"Of course. A wonderful choice," he said, then turned to Samuel.

"Steak. Rare."

"And which of our sides do you want with that?"

"None. Just bring the steak."

The waiter turned and hurried away.

Jenny watched the doctor closely throughout the meal, and she found that his words were more than just talk. He really *did* seem to relish every taste, every smell, every sound. He seemed to relish *her*. Looking at her. Watching her.

"Dessert?" he asked when he'd finished the entire steak and pushed the plate aside.

"No, I couldn't even finish this vat of gumbo they brought me." She glanced down at the food remaining and felt a little guilty. "It was delicious, though."

He smiled. "I'm glad you enjoyed it." He lifted a hand without turning his head, catching the attention of the waiter, who was facing in their direction, across the room. Whether he somehow knew the man was looking at them, or just got lucky, she couldn't guess.

"Yes, is everything all right?"

Samuel nodded. "We're ready to leave now." He slipped a bill into the man's hand. Jenny couldn't see what it was. "We're taking the bottle with us. Tally it up and keep the change."

"Yes, sir," the waiter said. From the look on his face as he tucked the money away, it must have been plenty. "It's been a pleasure serving you, Dr. La Roque." He nodded at Jenny. "And you, Professor Rose."

She was surprised he knew her name, but she only smiled back at him and slid out of her chair. Samuel came around the table, slid a hand around her waist and let it rest on her hip as he walked close beside her, out to the Jeep.

"You don't believe in lingering over dinner, do you, Samuel?"

He looked down at her. "I hope you didn't feel rushed. It's just—I'm eager to show you around the plantation, and we don't have all that much time."

"It's fine. I'm eager to see it. I've been staying there several days, and I really haven't had a free second to explore

the grounds. What I have seen is breathtaking, though."
Somehow, she thought it would be even more so in this
man's company. "How is it you're so familiar with the
place?"

"I've lived here all my life," he told her matter-of-factly.
"And . . . it once belonged to my family."

She turned toward him, surprised. "I didn't know that."

He nodded. "A hundred years ago. My great-grandfather
lost it. It had been in the family since the eighteenth cen-
tury."

"How? What happened?"

He shrugged, sending her a sidelong glance. "Gossip, rumors. He was driven out of town for his alleged crimes. Had
he returned he'd have faced a hangman's noose. The place
was deemed abandoned and confiscated by the state, then
sold at auction."

"That's terrible." She tipped her head to one side. "What
was he accused of doing?"

He paused, not answering right away.

"I'm sorry. Was that a rude question?"

"No. Not at all. I just . . . prefer not to sully our time together with talk of past tragedies."

She nodded slowly. "I doubt anything could spoil this
evening for me, Samuel." She could hardly believe the
words came from her mouth, almost bit her tongue. But then
again, why be coy about it? She enjoyed being with him.

He reached across the car to stroke a slow path down her
cheek with the backs of his fingers. "Don't be so sure," he
whispered. And before she could ask what he meant by that,
he said, "Here we are."

She looked out her window, but saw only rolling fields
lined by woods. "This isn't the plantation."

"It's the southernmost border. And the most interesting
spot." He got out, came around to open her door and took
her hand. She hesitated. "What's wrong, Jenny? You think
I've brought you out here to hurt you?"

"Of course I don't think that." She got out of the car,
rubbed her arms. "It's just . . . kind of creepy out here."

"Alone, with a man you barely know, a man who has been wanting to take you since the moment he laid eyes on you."

She met his eyes. "I'm not the kind of woman who has sex with strangers."

"I never thought you were." He moved a step closer. "But I'm no stranger, am I Jenny? Something inside you knows something inside me. Something inside you craves me, just the way I crave you."

She lowered her head. He moved closer, lifted her chin, stared into her eyes. "You do, don't you?"

She nodded mutely.

"Good," he said. "That's good." And then he pulled her hard against him and kissed her. His mouth covered hers, pushed hers open. He closed his hands on her backside and held her tight to his groin, so she could feel how hard he was, how badly he wanted her.

She couldn't resist the heat flooding her—God, he set her on fire. She twined her arms around his neck and wriggled her hips against him. She opened her mouth, and let his tongue probe and taste and lick all it wanted. This was madness—sweet, hot, delicious madness.

Finally, with a deep growl, he lifted his mouth from hers, dragged his gaze from her eyes to look past her, at the sky. "It's dark. The stars will be coming out soon."

"I've changed my mind. I don't have to work tonight, I—"

"Ssshh." He stroked her hair, her face. "Of course you do. You have a commitment to keep, and so do I. And that leaves us no time to do what we both want to do. But there will be another time. I promise you that."

She wasn't sure she would live that long.

"Besides, I haven't shown you what I promised. One of the secrets of this place. Come."

He turned, taking her by the hand and leading her across the field, through a patch of woods.

"Listen," he said.

She stopped walking, listened. At first, she thought she was hearing a heartbeat, a deep, pulsing heartbeat as if of the earth itself. But then it came more clearly, and she frowned up at him. "Is that . . . a drum?"

He nodded, tugging her forward. Soon they were walking along the banks of a river, wide and deep, and there were voices floating on the night air in addition to the beat of the drums. She saw light in the distance, the light of a fire.

"What is this?" she whispered.

"Shhh. You must be quiet now. Come."

He led her closer, until they were both crouching in the trees just beyond the glowing circle of firelight. She saw men beating huge, painted drums in a rhythm so compelling she felt her body tugged to move. She saw women, wearing white skirts and turbans, dancing. And then she caught her breath, because one of those women was Mamma Louisa.

She leaned closer, only to feel a strong hand on her shoulder, tugging her back into a hidden position.

"Is that . . . Voodoo?"

He nodded. "Mamma Louisa is a Voudon priestess." He nodded. "See how the others give her plenty of space? Watch, they won't stop the dancing until she does."

She watched Mamma Louisa, glorious and beautiful, round and lush, moving as if she'd become one with the driving beat of the drums. She was incredible. Her dance, beautiful and erotic.

"She's the housekeeper at the plantation."

"I know. Her family has always worked there."

She swallowed hard. "Should I be worried?"

He frowned at her. "I thought you were an educated woman, Jenny. It's only a religion. Don't you know that?"

"Knowing it and living under the same roof with it are slightly different things, Samuel." She looked longingly at the firelight, the dancers moving around it, the glow it cast on their faces. "Can we let them know we're here? Talk to them?"

He shook his head. "It would be an invasion. We're uninvited."

"It isn't an invasion to be out here watching them like this?"

"It is. But it's the kind of thing I figured you'd have to see to believe. Besides," he said, tracing a slow path along her forearm with his fingertips. "It made a great excuse to get you out in the middle of nowhere alone."

The drummers pounded faster, harder.

"It worked," she whispered, and she felt the reverberations of the drums echoing in her chest. The drums and the firelight, the sight of the wild dancing, were heady. It made her want to join in the movement. Her body rocked a little in time, hips twitching irresistibly as she crouched in the bushes beside Samuel.

"There's something compelling about it, isn't there?" he asked her, leaning so close she could feel his breath on her neck.

"It's enticing. Almost . . . irresistible."

"Yes."

Again his breath was warm—hot—on her neck. She turned her head just a little, to look into his eyes, and she found him so close her lips brushed his with the movement.

He made a sound deep in his throat, and kissed her.

Chapter 6

HE drew her up until she was standing, all the while exploring her mouth with his tongue. He moved her backward until her back was pressed to a tree, and he crushed his body to hers, pinning her there.

His breathing was harsh and heavy. Hers was rapid and shallow. She threaded her fingers into his hair as his mouth moved, hot and hungry, from her lips to her jaw, to her neck, where he sucked at her skin, bit it gently.

He'd said there was no time for this tonight. But, God, she was going to go up in flames if she didn't make love to him soon.

He seemed to have forgotten his earlier words anyway, as his hands moved between them to cup her breasts through the dress she wore. Then he shoved the straps from her shoulders and pushed the dress downward, baring her breasts to his rough hands. He covered them, squeezed them, lifted them as he slid his mouth lower over her skin, sliding from her neck, to her chest, to her breast. He took it into his mouth, sucking until she moaned softly. When her fingers tangled in his hair, pulling his head harder to her, he bit down, teeth closing sharply on her nipple. Then he did it again, and matched the sweet pain with his fingers on the other breast, pinching, tugging until she was shaking all over and wriggling her hips shamelessly against his erection.

One hand slid up under her dress, found her center, and didn't even hesitate to invade. Shocking, the sudden feeling of his callused fingers on her, opening her, entering her. She rocked with the invasion, taking as much as he gave her. Three fingers, four, she didn't know. She only knew his thumb was ruthlessly working her while his fingers drove in and out, and his mouth and teeth tormented her breast. His teeth bit down hard, then his tongue licked away the hurt, and then he bit down again, harder than before. She rocked her hips, taking his fingers in and out, riding his hand.

His mouth left her breast, but his free hand took its place there, pinching and twisting and pulling. He leaned close to her, whispered in her ear, saying things that made her even hotter. And when she exploded with the force of the orgasm, he kept working her, making it go on and on and on.

He was still holding her, still kissing her, when the blood stopped pounding in her ears, and it occurred to her that the drumbeat no longer echoed in her chest. It was just her heart pounding now. She was standing with her back braced against a tree, and his body was pressed tight to hers. Her dress was hiked up higher than her hips, and she was breathless and burning. He'd returned his hands to her hips, and his mouth to her mouth.

She didn't remember pushing his shirt off his shoulders, but it was. Her hands ran over his hard shoulders and chest, and then her lips followed suit. He moaned, his fingers dragging through her hair.

She lifted her head away. "The Voudons have gone home."

His eyes opened slowly, revealing a predatory gleam.

"My heart's pounding so hard, I thought the drums were still beating."

His gaze seemed to clear, his brows drawing together. Passion faded slightly, and some kind of worry replaced it.

He withdrew his arms from around her, and she shivered in the sudden chill while he squinted down at his wristwatch in the darkness. Jenny righted her dress. "What's wrong, Samuel?"

"The time . . . I—"

"Look," she whispered. "The moon's rising."

His head came up fast, eyes spearing her, then he turned to follow her gaze. "No . . ."

Jenny put her hand on his shoulder, longing for his touch, his arms around her. "It's all right."

"I . . . lost track of the time."

"I did, too. It's my fault as much as yours." She moved in front of him, sliding her hands up his chest.

He turned away again, this time pushing his hands through his hair as he lowered his head. "Go back to the car, Jenny."

She frowned. "But—I don't understand."

"Go!" His hands clenched in his hair, his face pulling into a tight grimace.

"God, Samuel, what's wrong? Are you all right?"

He dropped to his knees, right there in the forest. He seemed, suddenly, to be in excruciating pain. Jenny hovered nearby, unsure what to do. Every time she touched him he jerked away as if her touch burned. "Samuel?"

He fell forward, hands pressing to the soil, head hanging down between his arms.

"Samuel, what can I do to help you? Please." Tears choked her. She got in front of him, crouching low, running a hand over his hair. "Please, let me help you. What can I do, Samuel?"

He lifted his head, and his eyes gleamed with yellow light. He uttered a single word, that drew out into a growl. "Run."

His face—God, his face was . . . changing.

Jenny backed away, one step, then two. She couldn't take her eyes from him. His hair twisted and lengthened. His face contorted, deep wrinkles appearing where none had been before. His lips pulled away from his teeth, and incisors, no—canines—gleamed in the moonlight.

She turned, and she ran. Roots sprang up to trip her. Limbs swiped at her face from every tree. She crashed through the woods headlong, unsure which way to go, thinking only of escape. She couldn't tell if he—or it—was pursuing her, but she felt as if it was. Chills raced up her spine, the back of her neck tingling as the fine hairs there stood on end.

Which way is the road? God, where the hell is the car? Did he leave the keys?

Her foot caught on a root and she smashed face-first into the ground. Scrambling to get to her feet again, she heard a low growl at her back.

"Oh, God!" She rolled onto her back, and saw it. A huge black wolf, front paws splayed widely, back legs bent, ready to spring. Its teeth were bared, its eyes on her.

Never taking her eyes from the wolf, she clawed the ground, her hand closing around a limb. She brought it upward, knowing by its lack of weight that it would make a poor weapon against such a powerful animal.

And then, suddenly, the wolf's stance changed. It shifted its gaze upward, looking at something beyond Jenny.

"Go, now!" a woman's voice said. "Oya commands it! Go!"

The wolf's ears perked forward, and then suddenly, it turned and loped gracefully into the dark woods.

Only then did Jenny dare to turn and look at the woman who stood behind her. Mamma Louisa stood there, looking like a tribal angel. She held something in her hand, a red pouch of some kind that bulged with its contents and had feathers and stones dangling from its drawstrings.

"Come, child. Get up on your feet. We're not safe, even now."

She hurried to obey, while Mamma Louisa stood there, eyes scanning the trees around them, the pouch held up like a weapon. When Jenny was beside her, she turned. "This way."

She followed the woman in white over a path that meandered through the woods, along the river's edge, wondering where on earth they were going, right until she saw the welcoming lights gleaming from the windows of the plantation house up ahead. Mamma Louisa led her right to the back of the house, through the kitchen entrance door and up the back stairs to the third floor. As they moved through the door at the top, she found herself in a cozy living room. Rattan furnishings, stained a deep brown color and stacked with jewel-toned cushions, littered the room. One wall sported a hardwood stand, draped in a brightly colored cloth, its entire surface filled with fascinating objects, statues, stones, crosses. In its very center was a shrine with a dark-skinned Madonna enthroned within it.

"Sit, child," Mamma Louisa said, nodding toward one of the comfy-looking chairs. She locked the door behind them and then turned and came to her, eyes concerned. "Are you hurt?" she asked.

"No. I don't think so."

All the same, the woman was examining her. She ran her hands over Jenny's arms, eyes sharp and probing. She repeated the process with her other arm, then lifted her hair and examined her neck and ears. Kneeling, she inspected Jenny's legs, even her ankles. Every bit of exposed skin was subjected to her scrutiny.

"What are you looking for?"

"The mark of the wolf." She nodded as if satisfied. "Your dress is torn here. Better let me see the skin underneath."

Jenny didn't know why she complied so easily, but she did. She lowered the strap of the dress, exposing her shoulder to Mamma Louisa's steady gaze.

Finally, the woman nodded. "Nothing, it's good, you escaped without injury." She met Jenny's eyes. "The wolf didn't harm you, then."

"But it was no ordinary wolf, was it Mamma Louisa?"

The woman's gaze shifted so quickly Jenny knew she was going to lie. "What else could it have been?"

"A werewolf. The loup-garou."

"Every child knows there's no such thing."

"But you know different."

She moved to her altar, then opened a cupboard under-neath. Jenny saw mason jars, filled with herbs and roots and other things she couldn't identify.

"You've seen the wolf before, haven't you? You know about it."

The other woman shrugged, removing several jars and setting them upon the altar. "I know some things."

"Will you tell me? The things you know?"

She straightened, closing the cupboard, a small red pouch in her hands. It was empty. "Some things are better left alone, *chère*." She opened her jars, taking a pinch of this and a bit of that and dropping it into the red pouch. She added a gleaming black stone and then knotted the draw-strings while chanting something in a language Jenny didn't know. She held her hands over the bag and whis-pered what sounded like "Ah-say, ah-say, ah-say." Then she bought the pouch to Jenny, pressed it into her hands. "Keep this with you. Don't be without it. It will keep the wolf away."

Jenny looked down at the pouch. "What if I don't want to keep it away?" She lifted her eyes to Mamma Louisa's. "I came here to find the werewolf, to prove it exists. I can't do that unless I see it again."

"You saw the wolf with your own eyes, *chère*. What more proof do you need?"

She shrugged. "Photographs. A sample of its fur, or its blood. A footprint." She shook her head. "If I could get hold of the carcass from one of its kills, something it's fed on, I might be able to extract a DNA sample from the saliva."

"Mmm," Mamma Louisa said slowly. "If it kills you, maybe it leaves some spit on your remains, eh?"

"It's not going to kill me."

"It's a wolf. It's nature is to hunt, to kill."

"It's also a man."

She blinked, but didn't look away this time. "Your sci-ence tells you that?"

"No. My science tells me that would be impossible. But I saw it. I saw it change . . ."

"Then you know who he is? The loup-garou?"

It was Jenny's turn to avert her eyes. "You mean you don't?"

"I'm a powerful woman. What I know puts me in no danger. What you know—might. He's a killer, a predator."

"How do you know he's preyed on anyone?"

Mamma Louisa shrugged. "It's as I said. It's the nature of the wolf to hunt, to kill."

"But that's not the nature of the man."

The older woman arched her brow. "You wish to think of this thing as harmless, then?"

"I only want to know the truth before I judge a man a killer."

"That kind of thinking will only make you his next victim, *chère*. Take the 'gree-gree.' "

"The what?"

"The gris-gris bag, take it. Keep it tucked inside a pocket and take it out only if your life is in danger."

She nodded, getting to her feet and taking the bag. "I have to get to work," she said. "I've got a lot to do tonight." She rose and started for the door.

"Take the other door, *chère*. It leads down to the main house." Mamma Louisa pointed at a second door, on the opposite side of the room.

Turning, Jenny paused. "I don't quite know how to thank you. If you hadn't shown up when you had—I don't know what might have happened."

"You do," she said. "You just wish you didn't."

Chapter 7

SHE entered every detail of her encounter—except for the name of the shape-shifting doctor—in her computer's password-protected files, watching the clock the entire time. Maybe, she thought, she ought to take the precaution of telling someone what her passwords were, just in case anything happened to her. Just in case Mamma Louisa was right, and Samuel was a killer.

She closed her eyes, battling the shiver that chilled her marrow. In her mind's eye she saw him, Samuel, the man, his eyes burning with passion, hunger, longing—for her. And then she saw the wolf, with its teeth bared, and its eyes gleaming with a far different sort of hunger.

Which was real? Which was true? Could both of them truly live within one being? One man? Was it a constant struggle—the animal against the human? Would one eventually win out over the other? And if so, which would win?

She had to know. Not only because it was her job, her life's work, but because—because she cared about Samuel. And maybe that made no sense, and maybe she'd only just met him and all of this was based on nothing more than the most intense chemistry she'd ever felt with any man in her life. Or maybe it was something more. Samuel told her that there was something inside her that recognized something inside him. It felt—it felt very much as if that were true.

When she finished entering all the data, describing all she'd seen in as much detail as she could, she changed her clothes, donning a comfy pair of jeans and a ribbed baby-blue tank top. She pulled thick cushy socks and running shoes onto her feet.

Then she took out her trusty backpack and double-checked its contents. The good camera, with high-speed, low-light film. The bottles of water, compass, flashlight. The plaster-cast kit, plastic bags and test tubes for collecting samples, tweezers, sticky-tape. And most important of all—the guns. One, the tranquilizer gun, was already near at hand, but the other was locked away in her briefcase, pro-tected by a combination dial lock.

She spun the lock open and retrieved the revolver. She flipped open the cylinder and checked the six rounds she'd had specially made. While the bullet casings looked per-fectly ordinary, with their coppery hue, the tips of the bul-lets—the parts that actually flew toward a target when the trigger was pulled—were pure silver.

Clapping the cylinder closed again, she tucked the gun into the most easily accessible side pocket of her pack and yanked it up over her shoulders, but then she paused. Almost as an afterthought, she picked up the red gris-gris bag, and added that to the backpack as well. Finally, she headed out of the house.

Long before dawn, Jenny had gained entry to Samuel La Roque's cabin. The door had been locked, but she had no compunction about breaking in, especially after knocking and making enough racket that he would have surely come to the door had he been home. She entered through a side window, breaking the glass from a single pane, and reaching through to free the latch to open it. Before climbing inside, she whistled, called for Mojo, the doc's oversized wolf-dog, but there was no sign of the animal around. Then and only then did she clamber through the window, closing it behind her. She took a look around, just to assure herself that she was alone, and even took the time to sweep up the broken glass, before tossing a log on the fire, and finding a comfy spot to wait out the remainder of the night with her backpack right at her side.

Unfortunately, it was a little too comfy in Samuel's over-stuffed easy chair. Especially with the fire's warmth reaching out and wrapping around her like a warm blanket. She only realized she'd fallen asleep when the dull thump at the front door startled her right out of her chair. She was on her feet before she even came fully awake. When she did, all was silent. She hugged herself, eyes glued to the door, every sense on alert.

The knob jiggled just a little. Then there was a low moan, and a soft sound, as if something slid over the door.

Swallowing her fear, Jenny yanked the gun from the backpack at her side, then moved forward very slowly. She reached for the doorknob.

A soft snuffling sound, then a low bark almost made her hit the ceiling. She jerked backward three steps, then hurried to a side window to peer out.

She could see the wagging tail of Samuel's pet. It was standing on the door-stoop, head down, but she could only see the back of it.

Dare she open that door to see what was going on outside? It was still dark, but not fully. The distant sky was beginning to pale to gray, and the moon was nowhere in sight. Not that she'd ever once believed the moon had to be visible in order for a man to assume wolf form. Nor even that a man *could* assume wolf form under any circumstances. Still . . .

Mojo had been friendly before. It might be different now, however.

The wolf barked again. A friendly, if urgent-sounding yip, aimed at the door, from the sounds of it.

"He's a wolf," she told herself aloud. "It's not as if he doesn't already know I'm in here."

Tucking the gun into the back of her jeans, she moved to the door, gripped the knob and opened it just a crack.

Then she flung it open the rest of the way, because Samuel was lying at her feet, completely naked, his pet nuzzling and licking at his face, pushing him as if to get him up.

For just an instant she could only stand there, staring at him. He looked like a fallen, battered God—Lucifer after the fall. The lines of him, the planes and angles—he was stunning; he was perfect.

She dropped to her knees, hands gripping Samuel's warm, hard shoulders, rolling him carefully onto his back. His chest was sculpted, powerful, his belly lean. "Samuel? Are you all right?"

His eyes were closed, but she wasn't sure if that was because he was unconscious, or because they were cut and bruised and swollen. "My God, what happened to you?"

"Why are . . . you here?" he asked, his words broken, hoarse.

"Waiting for you."

He tried to get into a sitting position, and she gripped his forearms and helped him as he struggled to his feet and limped into the house with his dog dancing around his feet. She winced in sympathy with his pain and closed the door. He said, "It's nothing, I'll be fine in a few hours."

"Some doctor you are. It'll be more like a few weeks."

"I need . . . my bed."

"You need a hospital bed. Yours will have to do for now." She kept hold of him as they made their way to his bedroom. "Hold on." She peeled back the covers on the huge bed, a rustic four-poster made of knotty pine logs.

As soon as the blankets were out of the way, he fell face-down onto the bed, his head turned away from her.

Jenny tugged the covers over him again. "Is anything broken, do you think? Is there anything more serious than cuts and bruises?"

He said nothing. Not a word.

"Samuel?"

Nothing.

She rounded the bed so she could see his face, and watched the slow, steady rise and fall of his powerful back as he breathed. Gently, she reached out, brushed a wisp of dark hair away from his forehead.

"Samuel."

She didn't know what had happened to him, but she could guess. She imagined that the same kind of behavior that would constitute hunting, or even frolicking for a wild wolf, would mean physical exhaustion for a human being. The branches and twigs that snapped against the fur-covered hide of a wolf would leave welts on a human.

But it looked as if more than that had happened. It looked as if he'd run a gauntlet of sadists armed with whips and clubs. It looked as if he'd been beaten to within an inch of his life.

Sighing, she got to her feet, only to feel the brush of Mojo's head on her leg. She looked down at the animal, and it whined plaintively. Jenny stroked the dog's head. "It's okay, Mojo. I'm not going to leave him, if that's what you're asking."

The animal seemed relieved, its jaw falling open and tongue lolling between sharp teeth, almost like a doggie smile.

Jenny went into the bathroom just off the bedroom, found a washcloth, towels, soap and some antiseptic ointments. There was even a tube of old-fashioned liniment. Carrying them all back into the bedroom, she dumped them on the bedside stand. Then she hurried out to the kitchen, rummaged in the cupboards until she located a large basin and filled it with the hottest water she could bear on her skin.

She took the water with her back to the bedroom, set it on a chair and poured antiseptic into it until it turned a mustard-tinted brown. She settled herself on the edge of his mattress, shaking her head at the scratches and cuts on his back as she pulled the covers away. Then she dipped the washcloth into the hot water, squeezed it out and began the slow, gentle work of washing him.

The cuts, scratches and scrapes on his back were numerous. There were a couple of punctures, tiny ones, and she even found a thorn poking from one of them. That put a delay on her work as she paused to locate tweezers, then removed the offending thorn, and made sure plenty of the antiseptic got into the tiny wound it left behind.

After washing one section of his body, she applied ointment to every scrape and scratch, ointment and bandages to the larger cuts. She paused over each bruise to gently rub liniment into it.

When she finished with his back, shoulders and arms, she moved lower. His buttocks were covered in injuries as well, mostly bruises, and she worked there just as diligently, even if not quite as calmly. He had a perfectly shaped butt and rock-solid thighs. She couldn't resist touching him as she worked, running her hands over him, knowing he would never know the difference, and wouldn't mind if he did.

He felt good. She liked the smooth feel of his toned skin and hard muscle beneath her palms.

Finally, she moved on to his feet, the soles of which were not a pretty sight. Nothing more sensitive than the sole of a man's foot. Well, almost nothing.

She worked on him for a long, long time, losing herself to an almost hypnotic state induced by the act of rubbing, caressing, healing him.

She rolled him onto his back, as carefully as she could, and started all over again. And ministering to the front of him was even more interesting, even more arousing and exciting. She ran her washcloth, and then her hands, over his chest, exploring and touching every inch of it. Touching him this way, this freely, this boldly, made every part of her body come alive. Every nerve ending tingled. She savored him, the way he had taught her to savor her meal last night. The feel of him, the sight of him, the smell of him. The sound of her palms brushing over his skin. The sound of her heart pounding in her chest. The sound of him sighing in contentment in his sleep.

Carefully, she leaned closer, pressing her lips to his chest, daring to part them, to taste him, just a little flick of her tongue. He would want her to do it. She knew he would.

He groaned deep in his throat, and his arms came around her, pulling her into the bed. He was hard and far stronger than she'd have given him credit for being, as he rolled her over and covered her body with his. He took her mouth, and even while she began to protest that he shouldn't, that he was hurt, and should wait, he began working her clothing free.

His strong hands slid over her waist, to the bottom of her tank top, then slid upward again, lifting the fabric with them higher, baring her belly, and then her breasts. He pressed her arms upward, so he could strip the blouse away, and then he paused, staring down at her.

"You're hurt," he whispered.

"It's nothing—branches and briars when I ran through the woods."

"I frightened you."

"Not you," she told him, pressing her hand to his cheek. "The wolf."

"But I *am* the wolf." He closed his eyes and lowered his head until his lips brushed gently over the scratch on her collarbone. He kissed the length of it, then kept moving, finding her breast and kissing it as well. When he tended the nipple with soft, teasing kisses, her blood heated beyond endurance.

"Samuel," she whispered.

He took that as encouragement, changed tactics, taking her nipple into his mouth, suckling now, tugging and nibbling.

She threaded her hands in his hair to urge him onward. And he obliged her, even while he slid his hand over her belly and undid her jeans. Then he kept going, down the front of them, inside her panties. His fingers found their target, and parted and probed.

She moved against his hand, even as her own hands traced the contours of his skin, his back and shoulders, so broad and firm, smooth beneath her palms.

He slid her jeans lower, and she kicked free of them, as eager as he was to be rid of any barrier between his flesh and hers. Then he lowered himself between her thighs, and she wrapped her legs around him. His hardness pressed to her center, but he paused, waited there, and he kissed her mouth and then opened his eyes. "Don't be afraid of me, Jenny. I'd never hurt you."

"I'm not afraid of you."

He sighed as if in relief, and then gently slid inside her. Jenny felt the very breath driven from her lungs as he filled her, and she held him tighter, tipping her hips to receive him.

After that, she lost her ability to think or reason. There was only pleasure, the delicious friction and stroking rhythm of the two of them, moving within and around each other. He moved faster, held her to him more tightly. His kisses grew more feverish and the words he whispered into her ear hotter as her body twisted into a tight little knot of need. And finally, he pushed her over the edge of release. Every part of her quivered and trembled. She cried his name out loud and clung to him while the waves of pleasure washed through her. And she felt the same intense sensations rippling through him as he held her beneath him.

Finally, her body uncoiled, the muscles relaxing as warmth and a sense of perfection suffused her.

"My God," Samuel whispered, carefully rolling to one side and then gathering her into his arms as if she were something too fragile to be real. "My God, it's never been like that before."

She snuggled in his embrace, nodding her agreement, and knowing that it would never be like this again, either. Not with any other man but him.

Chapter 8

JENNY lay cradled in Samuel's arms as the sun rose higher, slanting its beams through the windows to paint her skin in heat and light. Sex with Samuel had been the most intense experience of her life. Desperate, even rough, at times, and then so tender it brought tears to her eyes at others.

"How do you do it?" she asked him softly.

He'd opened the bedroom window. As the sun heated the room, a warm bayou breeze played with the sheer white curtains. "Do what?"

She shrugged. "You were exhausted, hurt."

"Not anymore."

She averted her eyes, fighting a blush.

"I'm not kidding, Jenny. Look at me. Look." He sat up, letting the sheets fall away from his powerful chest, lifting her with him. When she was upright, she let her gaze travel over his chest, and then she frowned. Lifting her hands, she touched the spots where, only a few hours earlier, cuts, scrapes and bruises had made her wince in sympathy. But there was nothing there. The places where she'd rubbed ointment and liniment, looked as perfect, as flawless, as the rest of him.

Frowning even more deeply, she put a hand on his shoulder, turning him so she could see his back. But it was the same there. Even the worst of the bruises, a huge purple blotch on his hip, had faded until it was barely visible.

Blinking in confusion, she let him return to his former position.

He was staring at her face, but she couldn't hold his gaze.

"We haven't talked about . . . about what you saw happening to me, last night. I never . . . I never meant for you to see that."

"What, exactly, *did* I see, Samuel?"

He looked away. "You know what you saw. You saw me, changing forms. Becoming . . . the wolf. I'm the one you've been looking for."

She closed her eyes. "Then it's true. It's . . . you're a . . . God, I can't even say it. It's too outlandish to be real."

"I'm the werewolf, the loup-garou, the shape-shifter. It's me. I'm the one you've been looking for, Jenny. The only question is, now that you've found me, what do you plan to do about it?"

She lifted her eyes slowly, met his and was amazed at the amount of courage it took to do so, and not look away. "Will you cooperate with me? Help me with my research?"

"By answering your questions? Yes, if you'll keep my name out of it."

She swallowed hard. "What about videotape?"

He held her gaze steadily. "You think I'm insane? Or just suicidal?"

"Samuel, I'd protect you. I'd never let anyone—"

"No. What I go through, what I become—no, it's personal. I can't think of a moment more private than those three nights a month, when . . . when it happens. I can hardly stand the idea that you watched it happen. I couldn't bear to let you tape it."

"Samuel, you don't understand. This is my life's work."

"Jenny, *you* don't understand." He cupped her cheek in

one hand, gently, lovingly. His eyes beamed his feelings into hers. "This is my *life*."

She lowered her head, drew her knees up to her chest, sitting up in the bed. "If you don't cooperate with my research, how can you ever hope to find a cure?"

"Who says I *want* a cure?"

She looked him, wide-eyed. "Don't you?"

He was quiet for a moment, his gaze turning inward. "Samuel?"

"I don't know. I don't . . . I just don't know, all right?"

"My God, Samuel, how on earth could you even consider wanting to stay like this if you don't have to?"

He shook his head slowly. "How could I not? Look at me, Jenny. My senses are sharper than they've ever been. Sharper than they ever could have been, if the family curse hadn't found its way to me. Before the changes began, I was . . . I was barely alive. Going through life in a kind of a complacent daze. Now, I experience everything, I *feel* everything."

His eyes sparkled when he talked about this thing. She couldn't believe it, hadn't even considered that he might see this affliction as having a positive side. "Are you in control of what you do, when you . . . change?"

He lowered his gaze. "I don't know. Afterward, it's . . . it's difficult to remember what I've done. But don't think I'm not watching for signs. There have been no unexplained injuries, no violent deaths, no one reporting that they were attacked. I have to believe that, even as the wolf, I'm incapable of causing harm to another human being."

"But you don't know that for sure."

With a heavy sigh, he conceded the point. Then he lifted his eyes to hers. "I could have hurt you, that night on the road. But I didn't."

"I guess the scratches across my chest don't count, then."

"I can't believe I intended to harm you. Not you, Jenny." He made a halfhearted attempt at a smile. "Maybe I was just trying to get your blouse off."

The joke fell flat for her. "I'm sorry, Samuel, but I can't

laugh about this. You came after me in the woods last night. If Mamma Louisa hadn't come along when she did—I don't know. I don't know what might have happened."

"Mamma Louisa?" She heard the change in his tone when he repeated the woman's name. He sounded . . . angry. "Tell me what happened," he said.

"I fell. You—the wolf was crouching, poised as if to spring. Its teeth were bared, hair on its neck bristling up, and it was growling. It did not appear to be friendly, Samuel. Not like . . ." She glanced at the floor, where Mojo lay napping on a braided throw rug. "Not like Mojo. I was sure I was done for."

"But it didn't hurt you. I didn't hurt you."

She nodded, admitting that much was true.

"What happened next?"

"Mamma Louisa said something—an incantation or something. She waved her little red gris-gris bag around, and the wolf just ran away."

He sighed, shaking his head. "Ironic that she should be the one to step in."

Jenny frowned. "Why?"

He didn't answer, and she touched his face, turned it toward hers. "What has she got to do with this, Samuel?"

"Everything. It was her family who put this curse on mine. Her great-grandmother started it all, taking out her vengeance against my great-grandfather with Voodoo magic."

"Vengeance?"

He nodded. "God knows he had it coming if he did what . . . what her family claimed he did. My great-grandfather, Beckett Branson La Roque owned the plantation back then. He inherited it from his mother's family, the Bransons. Mamma Louisa's family, the DuVal's, worked for him just as they'd worked for his mother's family. Her great-grandmother, Celeste, was the matriarch of the clan then, and she was also a Voudon priestess."

She nodded, listening, rapt.

"They said my great-grandfather raped a girl, Alana

DuVal, Celeste's daughter. Mamma Louisa's grandmother. She was only sixteen."

"Do you believe it?"

He shrugged. "I don't know why she would have made it up. My grandfather never admitted it, but more importantly, he never denied it." There was a long pause. "Yeah, I believe it. But it doesn't really matter what I believe. Celeste believed it, and she avenged her daughter's innocence by cursing my ancestor and my line. In each generation, a La Roque male will be possessed by the spirit of the loup-garou, until there are no more males born."

"The curse dies with the line."

He nodded.

"Do you think Mamma Louisa knows how to remove it?"

"Of course she knows how—but she won't. I've asked her, believe me."

"Then you *do* want to be rid of it." He shot her a look. "You said you'd asked her," she rushed on. "You wouldn't have asked if you didn't want it gone."

"Early on, I thought the curse was the end of my life. I hated it. I fought it. I raged against it. But over time, I learned to live with it. And over a little more time, I began to realize that it wasn't all bad. I even learned to . . . to embrace it."

"But you may not have to."

"It's a part of who I am now, Jenny." He climbed out of the bed, paced away from her, then turned suddenly. "It's made me a better doctor."

Jenny frowned. "How?"

"I don't know. The heightened senses, maybe. The sharper instincts. I can tell what a patient's problem is even before I've run tests to confirm it. I spot potentially fatal complications before they happen, and I'm able to avert them." He shook his head. "I don't want to give that up."

"And you don't want anyone to know. But they will, Samuel. Eventually, the people around you are going to catch on. How are you going to deal with that?"

He shrugged. "I'll cross that bridge when I come to it."

She closed her eyes.

He came back to the bed. "I know you're disappointed, Jenny. I know it would mean a lot to your career to make a case study out of me—but it would be the end for me. I'd be hunted by superstitious fools wanting to kill me and pursued by scientists wanting to study me. My life would be over."

She couldn't argue with him. "When I came here, searching for the creature, I was convinced all I would find, if anything, would be an animal. An unknown species. I never for one minute thought the myths would be true—that a human being could change forms, or that a curse could be the cause. I've never believed in magic."

"And now that you've seen the living proof of it? How is that going to change your approach to this, Jenny?"

"I don't know. I have . . . I have to rethink everything." She got to her feet. "I should go." She got out of the bed, tugging the sheet around her, then bent to retrieve her clothes from the floor.

"Jenny."

She paused, not looking at him. "I won't tell anyone, Samuel. When I decide what I have to do, I'll let you know first. Before I do anything at all, I'll talk to you. I promise."

He nodded. "For some reason, I believe you." Then he came closer, slid his hands over her bare shoulders, squeezed gently. "But that's not what I was going to say."

"It isn't?"

"No."

"Then . . . what?"

He turned her to face him. "Just . . . this." He kissed her, softly, slowly and thoroughly. When their lips slid apart, she relaxed against his chest and he held her to him. "It hasn't been this way for me in a long time. With a woman, I mean. I've . . . I've been afraid to let anyone get too close. But with you, I just—it was like I had no choice. Something else took over."

"The wolf?" she asked softly.

He tipped her chin up, looked her in the eye. "My heart, I think."

A lump formed in her throat, making it hard to breathe and impossible to speak.

"I've handed you the loaded gun, Jenny, with the silver bullet already in the chamber. I'm trusting you not to pull the trigger."

He kissed her again, then with a sigh, walked into the bathroom.

Jenny heard the shower running a few minutes later. She didn't want to see him again before she left, because she still didn't know what the hell she was going to do. She would keep her word to him, she vowed. She would tell him her decision, once it was made.

God, she felt like an assassin for even considering moving forward with her work, making a study of him, perhaps without his consent. There had to be some way she could keep his identity secret. She had to at least consider the possibility, weigh the options. How could she not?

She threw her clothes on quickly and headed back to the plantation while he was still in the shower.

Chapter 9

"WHAT are you working on?"

The voice, coming from so close behind her, made her jerk her pencil across the sketchbook. She drew it to her chest protectively and shot a look over her shoulder. "Dr. Hinkle. What are you doing in here?"

"I'm the project supervisor, Professor Rose. I'm supervising." He nodded at the pad. "No use hiding it, I've already seen." Then he yanked it from her and took a closer look.

"My door was locked."

"I have keys to every door in this house." He was staring at the sketchbook where she'd been drawing, from memory, the way Samuel had looked as he'd changed. She wasn't certain why she'd been drawing it. She just had to get it down, to get the image out of her head and to try to make sense of it all.

"So you saw it again last night?" Hinkle asked.

"I didn't see anything. This is just doodling." She took the pad back. "And I thought I made it clear that I didn't want you in my rooms."

"Is the drawing based on . . . anyone you know?"

"You're changing the subject. I'm going to file a complaint with the university if you don't stay out of my rooms."

"Bears a striking resemblance to the town doctor. What's his name? La Roque?"

"You're being ridiculous."

He shrugged. "You went out to dinner with him last night, according to Toby. Did you spend the night, Professor?"

"What are you talking about? I came home last night."

"Yes, after your date."

"It wasn't a date. It was research. I wanted to know if there had been any patients coming in with unexplained injuries."

"And have there?"

"No. None."

He nodded. "I never saw him drop you off."

"I felt like a walk." *God, he was catching on.* More than before, she realized Samuel was right. If she pursued this, it would impossible to protect his identity for very long. And she wasn't sure why, but she felt an instinctive fear of Dr. Hinkle learning the truth.

"And then you left again," he said. "I checked, later on. You didn't sleep here."

"So you were sneaking around in my bedroom in the middle of the night, when you thought I'd be sound asleep? God, what were you thinking?"

"Where did you spend the night, Jenny?"

She bit back her anger—it wasn't going to dissuade him. "I went back out to the woods. According to all we've got so far, this creature—if it exists at all, which I'm beginning to doubt—is nocturnal. I was hoping to spot it." She shrugged, sighed. "No sign of it, though. I say it reluctantly, Dr. Hinkle, but I'm ready to concede that you may be right. We might be just wasting our time down here."

He shrugged. "We have one more night to produce results. The moon is still full, you know."

"Yes. I know."

"If there are no results, I'm pulling the plug on this project. We'll pack up and head back to the university tomorrow."

She nodded, and tried to hide her relief. If he knew—if he had an inkling, there would be no way he would consider ending the project. Then again, why would any sane person believe a man could become a wolf? "Maybe that's for the best." She felt like crying. All her work, all her research; just when she was so close to success, she was throwing it all away. But she couldn't base her personal success on the destruction of Samuel's life. It would be unfair. Besides, as illogical as it seemed—she felt something for him. Something powerful.

"I must say, Jenny, I'm surprised. You don't usually give up so easily."

She shrugged and tried to inject her demeanor with some enthusiasm. "Who says I've given up? There's always tonight."

"Yes. There's always tonight."

There was something in his eyes when he said it, something that frightened her.

As soon as he left the room, Jenny pulled up every one of her password-protected files and deleted them. She'd made her decision. She would make her name, her career by discovering some legitimate unknown species of animal. Not by exploiting a man who was doing his best to live his life under the heavy burden of a curse.

She wasn't even sure she believed in curses, but she knew who to ask. And while she'd decided not to continue her research using Samuel as a subject, she hadn't decided to leave him alone entirely.

She thought she just might be able to help him.

Tucking her laptop into her shoulder bag, she took it with her. She wouldn't let it out of her sight again until she'd had the hard drive replaced and demolished the old one. Traces of her files would remain there, even though she'd deleted them. She knew that. She headed to the kitchen, where she found Mamma Louisa kneading bread dough.

Without even looking up, the older woman said, "Hello, *chère*. I suppose you're lookin' for me?"

"Yes."

"He know you're talkin' to me?"

There was no point in asking who she meant. Jenny was well aware by now that Mamma Louisa knew the identity of the loup-garou. "No. He says there's no point in talking to you, that you've already refused to help him."

Her head came up, eyebrows raised. "He said that?"

She nodded.

"Hmmph. Arrogant, know-it-all doctor, anyway." She made a fist and punched the dough.

"You mean you didn't refuse?"

"I told him the truth. I can't remove the curse. Only one who can is the one who put it on him in the first place. An' my great-grandma Celeste is long dead by now."

"Then there's no hope for him?"

She draped a dishtowel over the ceramic bowl of bread dough and set it near a window where the sun beamed through. Then she grabbed another towel to wipe the dough and flour from her hands. "Always there is hope, *chère*. Your doctor, he stomp away from me when I tell him I can't remove the curse. He didn't ask what I *could* do. I figure he don't want my help—maybe don't deserve it."

Jenny felt hope spark in her heart. "Then there is something you can do?"

"Don't know. Not until I try. Not gonna try until he apologize, and ask me proper."

"That's certainly reasonable."

"Stubborn man don't seem to think so." She shrugged. "Even so, I don't know if I can help him."

"But you'll try?"

"He apologize, I try. It's all I can do."

"It's enough," Jenny said. "It has to be."

JENNY tried phoning Samuel three times, only to be told he was busy with patients and unable to come to the phone. She finally drove to his office, but one look at the packed waiting room was enough to deter that effort. It was crowded with sniffling kids and wheezing elders and everything in between. She was about to leave, when Samuel came out, spotted her and waved her closer.

She wove her way through the waiting patients and wondered why it gave her such a thrill to see him again. "I can see you're busy," she said. "I don't want to interrupt."

"I can take a minute." He smiled at her. "I knew you were here—felt you. That's why I came out." Then he turned to the receptionist. "Sally, get Mrs. Finny set up in room one and tell her I'll be in shortly." Taking Jenny's arm, he led her into a hallway, all the way to the end, and then into a small room where the desk was almost an afterthought to the comfy overstuffed chairs, table and coffeemaker.

She went in before him, but didn't sit, turning to face him instead. As soon as he'd closed the door behind him, she said, "I deleted all my files. I'm not going to pursue this. Not on a research level, at least."

He frowned and studied her face. He looked a little bit wary. "But you *are* going to pursue it."

"Not if you say no. But Samuel, I think I can help you. I spoke to Mamma Louisa, and she—"

"Mamma Louisa won't help me. I already told you that."

She shook her head. "You asked her to cure you, not help you. And she told you she couldn't, not that she wouldn't. There's a big difference between what she said and what you heard."

His frown deepened. "Did she tell you something different?"

"Yes. She said that only Celeste could remove the curse, but that she might be able to do something to help you."

"Help me in what way?"

"She didn't say. She's not even sure she can, but she's willing to try." She shrugged. "*If* you will apologize for losing your temper with her, and ask her nicely."

He looked angry for a moment. Jenny put a hand on his shoulder. "Samuel, she's not the one who put this curse on your family. You can't blame her for that any more than she can blame you for what your great-grandfather did to Alana DuVal."

His face eased slightly. "Yeah. Yeah, you're right. And I did stomp off in a huff when she said she couldn't help me. Haven't spoken to her since." He grimaced. "That was two years ago."

"It's time to let that go. Make amends, if nothing more."

"All right." He sighed. "Jenny, I've been thinking . . . about what I said before, about not wanting a cure." He turned away from her, pushing a hand through his hair. "I want to keep seeing you. I want—I want you in my life. Somehow. And if giving this thing up is what it takes to make that happen, I'll do it."

She smiled a little. "You'd do that for me?"

He shrugged. "I'd miss running wild with Mojo and howling at the moon," he said with a teasing look. "But I'd miss you more. I'd miss never knowing what could have been, what could have happened between us." He lowered his eyes. "I think you might be the one, Jenny."

The words sank into her heart like warm sunlight. Her throat tightened so much she could barely force air through, and when she did speak, her voice was tight with emotion. "I wouldn't ask you to change your life for me, Samuel. This has to be your decision. Not mine."

"But . . ."

"I think you might be the one, too. I'm not going to walk out of your life because of what you are. God, what you are is . . . is what I fell for, you know?"

He seemed relieved. "You really mean that?"

There was a tap on the office door. "Doctor, your patient is waiting."

He licked his lips. "I have to—"

"I know. Look, at least meet with Mamma Louisa. Amends need to be made whether she can help you or not, and whether you decide to accept her help or not. At least talk with her."

He nodded. "I will."

"We'll need privacy," Jenny said quickly. "Come to that same spot where you took me last night. That grove where the Voudons danced. I'll bring Mamma Louisa. Meet us there."

"No later than eight," he said. "Before the moon rises."

"Understood. Eight it is." She started for the door, but he stopped her with an arm around her waist, pulled her close until her body was pressed to the front of his and kissed her mouth. It was a hungry kiss; he used his tongue, probed and delved and tasted. She twined her arms around his neck and kissed him back just as eagerly.

The knock at the door came again, and reluctantly, he let her go.

JENNY went back to the plantation and battled the worst case of nerves she'd ever had in her life. She invented tasks to keep Mike and Toby busy, set Carrie to work doing more research and tried hard to hide her jittery mood from Dr. Hinkle, though he behaved like her shadow all afternoon.

He suspected something—she was sure of it. And the way he stuck to her all day made her wonder how she would manage to slip away from him tonight.

By the time Mamma Louisa was serving them all dinner in the formal dining room, Jenny was ready to climb the walls. She hadn't even managed to let the woman know about tonight's plans. Every time she got Mamma Louisa alone and started to talk to her, Dr. Hinkle showed up like some lurking demon. She would catch a glimpse of him from the corner of her eye, or suddenly feel shivers up her spine, and turn to find him not far away.

During the meal, Jenny managed to catch Mamma Louisa's sharp eye, and she hoped, to send a message, slanting her gaze toward Dr. Hinkle. A moment later, she knew the message have been received. The large woman bent to set a fresh pitcher of ice water on the table and tipped it into Hinkle's lap.

He yelped and jumped to his feet, his pants soaked through. "Damn, woman, what are you thinking?"

"I'm so sorry, mister! Eva Lynn, honey, bring towels!"

Eva Lynn raced in from the kitchen with large white towels in hand. Hinkle snatched one from her and stomped toward the stairs, with the younger woman on his heels dabbing at the back of his pant legs, even as Mamma Louisa glanced at Jenny and inclined her head.

"I'll help you until Eva Lynn gets back," Jenny said, for the benefit of the other three at the table, and then she hurried to the kitchen.

"You wanted to speak to me, yes?" Mamma Louisa said. "Without the old man listenin' in."

"Yes." She glanced back toward the closed door. "I spoke to Samuel, and he admitted he was wrong to have treated you as he did. He wants to apologize, and he'll be grateful to hear about any help you can give him with his . . . problem."

"Mmm. I'm surprised the stubborn fool gave in so easily." She searched Jenny's eyes. "You're good for him, I think. So? When do we meet him?"

The woman's instincts were amazing. "Tonight, eight o'clock, at the grove where I saw you last night."

Her eyes narrowed. "You think it's safe? To be so close to him at night, when the moon is still full?"

"He's fine until moonrise, Mamma Louisa. That won't be until after nine. Is an hour enough time for you to do . . . what you need to do? To help him?"

"If I can't help him in an hour, I can't help him at all. I will go with you, child. Now go, get back to the table before that nosy man comes snooping again. He been watching you like a hawk all the day long."

"I know."

"Don't you worry. We gave him the slip, all right. Whooeee, but how he jump when that ice water hit his man parts!" She smiled from ear to ear.

Jenny grinned, too, but wiped the smile away as she returned to her seat at the table and continued with her meal.

At 7:30, she was in her room getting ready to go, when someone tapped on her door. Fearing it was Dr. Hinkle, she almost didn't answer, then decided she had no choice. When she opened the door, she found Carrie standing there.

"Finished with all that research already?" Jenny asked.

"Um . . . no. I just . . . I wanted you to know something."

Frowning, Jenny let her in. Carrie closed the door, looking nervous. "What is it, Carrie?"

The girl cleared her throat. "When you went into the kitchen, tonight, with Mamma Louisa, Toby left the table."

"Where did he go?"

"I can't be sure," Carrie said. "But he might have gone to the kitchen, too. I started to go for another towel, to mop up the water that was still in Dr. Hinkle's chair. And it looked as if . . . as if he was listening at the door. But like I said, I can't be sure. He saw me and hurried off toward the living room, and I went back to the table."

Jenny closed her eyes. This wasn't good.

"Where is he now?"

"Downstairs, working on his computer."

"And Dr. Hinkle?"

Carrie shrugged. "He went out a few minutes ago. I didn't dare come to you until he left, the way he's been hovering over you all day."

"And now he's suddenly stopped hovering."

"That occurred to me, too," Carrie said. "I think Toby told him whatever he overheard in the kitchen. I saw them talking awhile ago, huddled in a corner, keeping their voices low. Are you in any kind of trouble, Professor Rose? Cause if I can help . . ."

Jenny glanced at her watch. "Keep the twins busy. Downstairs, for the next ten minutes. Can you do that?"

Carrie nodded hard. "Can you tell me what's going on?"

"No. I'm sorry, but it's not my secret to tell."

"Is it . . . the werewolf?"

Jenny smiled and smoothed a hand over Carrie's hair as if she were a small child. "Don't be silly, hon. There are no such things as werewolves."

Carrie looked puzzled but rushed away to do as Jenny asked. Jenny took the back stairs up to the third floor and knocked on Mamma Louisa's door.

When the woman opened it, she said, "Ready to go, then?"

"Not quite. I need to take a look in Dr. Hinkle's room before we leave. But we'll have to be fast."

"I never like that man anyway." Mamma Louisa dipped into a pocket and pulled out a jangling ring of keys. "Let's go see what secrets that man be keepin'."

Chapter 10

JENNY felt as if every hair on her body were standing on end as she crept through Dr. Hinkle's suite of rooms. Mamma Louisa stood just outside the door, in the ornate hallway, keeping watch. Not that it was going to be much help, should the good doctor return. There wasn't any other way out of the rooms, just that one door. But at least she'd have some warning.

She went to the desk that was set up in a window-lined alcove, glanced through the papers that were spread over it but found nothing. She flipped open the laptop computer and checked for the most recently opened files, but again, found only the most mundane reports on the project.

She tried the desk drawer and found it locked.

Turning toward the door, she whisper-shouted for Mamma Louisa, who poked her head into the room, eyebrows raised.

"The keys to this desk. Do you have them?"

"No, missy. The doctor, he make sure he have the only set."

That nailed it, then. If Hinkle had anything he wanted to

hide, the desk had to be where it was. Mamma Louisa came
the rest of the way into the room, eyes on the desk drawer,
lips moving to form soundless words as she reached a hand
out. She leaned over, blew on the drawer's handle and
tugged it open.

"How the hell—"

"You were mistaken, *chère*. The draw' wasn't locked at
all." Turning, she hurried back to her post in the hallway.

Jenny swallowed down the rising sense of disorientation.
She'd seen so many things since coming here—things her
practical mind and her education told her didn't exist—
couldn't exist. And yet, she couldn't deny her own senses.
She'd *seen* Samuel's face and body twisting into something
else. And she knew this drawer had been locked tight moments ago.

Now, she was staring into it, at a leather-bound volume.
Beside it was the plaster cast she'd taken of that paw print in
the woods. Then he *had* been the one who'd stolen it! Carefully, she took the book out and opened it, seeing pages upon
pages of handwritten lines. Each page was dated. It was a
journal.

Frowning, she flipped pages, reading a few lines here and
there. Her own name jumped out at her, catching her eye.
"Jennifer Rose is the best I've ever seen, the best I've ever
worked with. But I must never let her believe I support her
theories. In fact I need to prove them wrong, discredit her,
even while I use her to lead me to what I need."

She blinked. Good God, he'd practically gushed about
her skill in her field. To her face he'd never done anything
but criticize, belittle and condemn her work. It was foolish,
not a real science, fraudulent even.

She flipped more pages.

"I knew she would find it! Here, at last, I have the full
ritual."

Below those words, she saw an outline, like a recipe, ti-
tled, "Becoming a Werewolf."

What the hell?

She read on, recognizing some of the portions from research she'd gleaned, other bits Carrie had ferreted out from various sources; still others were entirely new to her. She skimmed the lines. Third night of the full moon—that was tonight. There was a list of herbs, each one with a checkmark beside it. She knew the rite required a fire, but this list gave the precise instructions for the type of wood to burn, and the kinds of leaves to use to kindle the fire. It gave astrological requirements as well—moon in Scoprio, conjuct to Saturn. Beneath those, today's date was jotted down.

And near the bottom of the list of items needed, was one that made her blood run cold.

The pelt of a werewolf.

Oh my God.

She slammed the book closed and taking it with her, turned and raced out the door and down the hall to the stairs. Mamma Louisa was right on her heels.

"What is it, child?"

"Hinkle—he thinks he can make himself into a were-wolf!"

"But . . . but the only way he can do that is to be bitten by one, and then he'd have as good a chance of dying as of changing . . . unless he's found a spell. But for that he'd have to—"

"To kill Samuel, after the change," Jenny said. "He needs the pelt."

Mamma crossed herself and muttered a prayer as the two women burst into the living room. Carrie leapt up from the couch where she'd been sitting with Mike and Toby. "My God, what's happened?"

Jenny ignored her, going straight to Toby, gripping his shoulder hard. "You followed me to the kitchen earlier tonight. You eavesdropped on my conversation with Mamma Louisa." She held up her free hand as he started to deny it. "Don't even, I don't have time for your lies. Just tell me, did you report what you heard to Dr. Hinkle?"

"I didn't—"

"I swear to God, if you lie to me now I'll get you thrown out of school on charges so scandalous no other university will have you, even if I have to make up every one of them. Don't think I can't do it! This is life and death, Toby, now talk!"

He stared at her, his eyes widening. "You wouldn't—"

"You try me."

Pursing his lips, he swallowed hard. "All right. All right, I listened in. I told Dr. Hinkle what I heard. That you and Mamma Louisa were to meet someone in the grove down by the river at eight."

"He's got a head start," Jenny whispered, releasing him and turning her gaze to Mamma Louisa's. "God, he'll beat us there, and kill Samuel."

Carrie gasped. "Dr. Hinkle's going to kill someone?"

"No, *chère*," Mamma Louisa said. "He can't kill him, not until after the moon comes up. Not until after the change. To kill him before that would serve no purpose."

Jenny nodded. "Then there's still time." She ran for the door as Carrie and the twins shouted questions after her. She made it to her car, surprised when the considerably older, and much heavier woman jumped into the passenger seat only a split second after her. She was fast.

Jenny drove, and watched the sun sink below the horizon. Darkness gathered around them, and she felt as if the entire world were holding its breath, just waiting for moonrise.

THEY'D exited the car and were making their way through the woods to the grove, when Jenny heard the gunshot.

A scream ripped from her throat, and she broke into a run, with Mamma Louisa, a large drawstring bag over her shoulder, racing to keep up.

The path twisted and meandered through the thick, dense forest. She could barely see where she was going, and yet something pulled her on. Some sixth sense, tugging her the way magnetic North tugs a compass needle. She ran, barely able to see her feet hitting the ground ahead of her. She ran, heedless of the branches smacking her face and raking her arms. She ran, and then she saw him.

The wolf lay very still, so still she was nearly upon it before she realized what it was. She fell to her knees, her hands sinking into the thick, soft fur. "Samuel," she whispered. "God, no." She felt warm, thick moisture and lowered her face to the fur, hugging the animal gently. "Samuel, please?"

A soft whimper sounded in response.

Panting, Mamma Louisa caught up, fell to her knees and tore open her bag. She took out flashlight and pointed it at the animal.

"He's still alive," Jenny said softly.

"Mmm, but Hinkle-man got what he wanted, though. Look there." She moved the light, revealing a strip of flesh, red and bleeding, on the wolf's side.

"My God, what did he do? What did he do to you?"

The wolf whined again, a plaintive, pain-racked sound that made her heart twist and her stomach convulse.

"We have to help him, Mamma Louisa."

She nodded, handing the light to Jenny, and taking more items from her bag. Herbs, rattles. She worked over the animal, chanting softly. As she did, Jenny used the light to find the bullet hole, high on the front shoulder. She tore a strip from her own blouse and wrapped the wound. "He'll live," she whispered. "I think it's too high to have hit the heart. I don't think there's internal bleeding." The animal's strong pulse told her as much.

"My God, what's going on out here?"

At the male voice, Jenny looked up, only to see Carrie and the twins standing in the path staring down at the suffering animal in horror. "You followed me?" Jenny asked.

"Of course we did, Carrie said. "You said it was a matter of life and death. She stared at the animal with wide eyes."

"Is that—is that a werewolf?"

"No." Mamma Louisa answered firmly. "This is an ordinary wolf."

Jenny's hands stilled in the deep fur. She looked closer. "My God, you're right. This is Mojo!" She hugged the wolf gently, then lifted her eyes to Mamma Louisa's. "Dr. Hinkle shot the wrong wolf!"

"Dr. Hinkle shot this poor animal?" Mike asked.

"The moon hasn't yet risen," Mamma Louisa explained. "The wolf Hinkle sought is still in human form." She closed her eyes, tipped her head back, rocked slowly on her feet. "Hinkle-man, he realized that even as he tried to skin the poor creature. But the man came. The man came—only moments ago, when the gunshot rang out and the wolf pet cried. The man came, and Hinkle-man hid and waited. When the man bent over the wolf, Hinkle hit him hard, on the head. Knock him out. Took him away."

She took the light from Jenny and shone it on the ground. "Look there. One man, dragging another."

"Hinkle's taken him."

"Mm. He'll hold the man until the moon comes. Until the change comes. And then—"

"Then he'll kill him, and perform his sick ritual." Jenny turned her gaze to the three young people. "Dr. Hinkle plans to turn himself into a werewolf tonight. It's all here, in his journal. Unfortunately, he has to murder an innocent man to do it."

The twins exchanged glances. Toby took the journal from her. "I'm sorry, Professor Rose. We—we trusted him. We had no idea."

"Neither did I."

"What can we do?" Carrie asked. "How can we help?"

Jenny looked down at the suffering animal. "Can you get Mojo to the town vet?"

"Mojo?"

She nodded toward the wolf. "He's a pet. A beautiful animal. Please help him."

"We'll take care of it." The two boys knelt beside Mojo, gently picking him up, one on each end. Mamma Louisa had removed her white bandana and torn it apart to make bandages for the animal's skinned flank. Poor creature. It whimpered as the boys carried it away, but they moved as carefully and gently as they could.

Alone with Mamma Louisa, Jenny faced her. "Where did Hinkle take Samuel?" she asked. "How can we find them?"

The older woman dug in her bag and took out a beautiful, glittering crystal suspended from a string. She let it dangle until it was still, then watched as it began to swing. The motion was barely detectable at first, but grew steadily. Finally, she gave the string a snap, caught the crystal in her hand and said, "This way."

IT seemed to Jenny as if it took forever, before she smelled the smoke. Then, gradually, she saw the faint glow, and then the dancing firelight in the distance. She picked up the pace and tried hard to move quickly, but quietly at the same time. The two of them crept up to the edge of a tiny clearing, and peered from the trees.

Jenny spotted Samuel. He lay on the ground, his hands and feet bound in front of him. He was barely conscious, eyes flickering open and closed, and there was blood coming from his head, glistening in the firelight as it trickled over his face.

A tripod had been erected over the fire, and a cauldron hung from it. Steam rose from the cauldron as its contents boiled, and the scents of herbs filled the air. Close by, Dr. Hinkle sat on the ground, completely naked. He was rubbing something gooey over his arms and chest. Jenny wondered if it were feline fat and felt her stomach lurch. God, how many innocent animals were going to have to suffer to satisfy Hinkle's insanity?

"What do we do?"

"He's made a circle," Mamma Louisa pointed at a ring of what looked like salt, on the ground. "I can break it. Come."

She took a feather fan from her bag and used it like a broom, sweeping the air before her as they crept forward. Hinkle sat with his eyes closed, chanting the words of his spell.

As she reached the ring of salt, Mamma Louisa said, "Open!" and swept the fan in the air and then over the ground, brushing the salt away and stepping inside. Jenny followed, then froze as she saw the glowing sphere of the moon rising above them. She spun around, and saw Samuel, bound there, jerking spasmodically against the ropes as growling sounds emerged from deep in his chest.

At the sound of Mamma Louisa's command, Hinkle's eyes flew wide and he sprang to his feet. "You get out of here!"

Mamma Louisa shook her head.

Beyond her, Samuel was changing. His eyes rolled and his back arched as his facial muscles contorted. The rope at his wrists snapped in two.

"In the name of Oya, in the name of Yemaya, I cast every negative force from this circle! I call in goodness. I call in white light. I call in protection!"

"No! Get out, I say!" Hinkle crouched low, reaching for something, and when he rose again he lifted a gun.

"Look out!" Jenny shouted.

But even as she said it, the wolf leapt, hitting Hinkle squarely in the chest. The gun flew from his hands, and the shot it fired went wild.

Now Hinkle was on his back, with a snarling, fiercely powerful wolf standing on his chest, growling. The two women stood there, staring, and Jenny knew full well there would be nothing either of them could do to prevent the wolf from tearing out Hinkle's throat. Not physically at least.

Swallowing hard, Jenny knew she had to try to reach the man she loved, before he made himself a killer.

"Samuel, I know you're in there," Jenny said softly. "I know you can hear me. Mojo is alive. He's at the vet, getting treatment even now. And this man will never hurt anyone again, not when I testify as to what happened here tonight."

The wolf looked toward her. Its eyes . . . they were Samuel's eyes. Mamma Louisa reached into her bag, and Jenny held up a hand to stop her. "No. No, you don't have to use magic. He won't do harm to a human being, I know it. Just wait."

The wolf growled, deep and low.

"Don't hurt him, Samuel. You're a healer, not a killer."

The animal looked back down at the man on the ground, then at her again.

"I love you, Samuel," she whispered.

The wolf focused on Hinkle's face, leaned very close, so close the man must have felt the animal's hot breath on his skin, then it let loose a series of sharp, angry barks and growls and snapped its jaws within an inch of Hinkle's face, before it turned, and leapt to the ground. It didn't run off as Jenny had expected, but only moved beyond the fire's light and curled on the ground in the shadows.

Jenny ran to snatch up the pieces of fallen rope and the gun. Then she made Hinkle put on his clothes while she held the weapon on him. "What the hell were you thinking?" she demanded as he dressed. "Why would you want to do something so insane?"

He looked up at her as he buttoned his shirt. "I'm aging, Jennifer, or hadn't you noticed that? Young, sharp professors like you are coming in. Pushing me out. I miss my youth, my vitality. I've read the accounts. With the wolf inside me, I'd be young again, strong as a man half my age."

"Wonder how fast you'll age in prison. Maybe you should have considered that."

He shook his head. "You tell anyone about this, I'll reveal Samuel La Roque for what he really is."

"Then you won't end up in prison after all." She smiled softly. "It'll be a mental institution instead."

She handed Mamma Louisa the ropes. The other woman tied him up while Jenny held the gun. Then the two women led him out of the circle of salt and set him on the ground beside a tree. Mamma Louisa returned to the fire in the center of the circle, and using her shawl as a pot holder, took the iron kettle from the tripod. She carried it a few yards away and poured its smelly contents on to the ground. She left the kettle there.

When she returned to the circle, she dug into her bag and tossed handfuls of herbs from various jars onto the glowing fire. The smoke they emitted was fragrant and good.

She turned then, her eyes falling upon the wolf that lay near the circle's edge.

It rose, as if it knew what to do, and paced slowly to her.

Nodding her approval, Mamma Louisa looked to Jenny. "Go, watch over Hinkle-man and let me do my work."

Jenny nodded. "Samuel never got the chance to deliver that apology he owed you," she said.

"He saved me from that one's bullet. I say that's as good as an apology. We be even now. Go."

Jenny left the circle of firelight and stood near Hinkle, the gun still in her hand just in case. Mamma Louisa sprinkled fresh salt in the area where she had brushed it away, completing the ring again. Then she moved to kneel in front of the wolf, her hands pressing to either side of its head as she stared into its eyes and spoke to it earnestly.

The wolf whined as it stared intently back at her, and finally, it lay down at her feet. It didn't fight when she spread her shawl over it, and it lay still there while she moved around it, gesturing and chanting, shaking her rattles, sprinkling it with herbs and salt and lifting her hands skyward to call on her gods. She moved faster, and her voice grew louder and her rattles shook faster, until the noise reached a pitch Jenny was sure could be heard all the way back at the plantation. And then and suddenly, with a loud whoop, Mamma Louisa yanked the shawl from over the wolf.

Samuel lay there, naked, shivering, maybe a little disoriented. He blinked up at Louisa as she nodded in approval. Then she swept an opening in the circle with her feather fan, and waved Jenny closer. Jenny hurried to Samuel. As she sank to her knees beside him, he said "It's still in me. I can still feel the wolf in me."

"Yes," Mamma Louisa told him, handing him the shawl so he could cover himself. He sat up, knotting it around his hips. "The wolf still lives in you. But now, Samuel La Roque, you are in control. You can become the wolf, but only when you want to—or when you lose control of your emotions. It will be difficult at first, as the wolf seeks to take you, especially when the moon is full. But it will grow easier in time, as you make your will stronger and stronger. It is the best I can do for you."

He closed his eyes, drew a deep breath. "Thank you,

Mamma Louisa." Then he opened his eyes and gazed steadily at her. "I'm sorry. For what my great-grandfather did to Alana."

"I'm sorry for what my great-grandmother did to avenge her." She gave him a nod, then took the gun from Jenny's hand. "I take the Hinkle-man from here, *chère*."

"Alone? But . . ."

Mamma Louisa gave her a smile, and nodded at something beyond her where Hinkle sat near the tree. Jenny turned, and saw the entire group of Voudons gathered in the woods nearby, awaiting their priestess's word. "My people, they know when I need them. Don't you worry." She nodded, and two strong men rushed forward, gripping Hinkle's arms and hauling him to his feet and back through the woods.

Mamma Louisa followed and the entire group vanished into the woods.

Samuel got to his feet. He looked like some kind of woodland god, with the white cotton knotted around his hip and his magnificent chest bare. He reached for her.

Jenny went into his arms, relishing the feel of his skin against her body, against her face as she laid her cheek on his shoulder.

He held her for a long time, then he said, "Did you mean what you said before? That you love me?"

She shivered all over. "Yes. I don't know how it happened so fast, Samuel, but it did. I love you."

"Even though I—I might occasionally run with Mojo, and howl at the moon?"

She trailed a hand over his face. "Mojo might have to take a few months off, while he heals. But after that, I may just join you." She stared deeply into his deep, brown eyes. "I love all you are, Samuel. All of you. I love your wolf side, your wild side, and I swear I'll always keep your secrets."

"Just as I'll keep yours. I love you, too, Jenny."

He kissed her deeply, passionately, held her tight to his body as he lowered them both to the ground. As he peeled away her clothes, and she tugged at the shawl that covered him, Jenny heard him growl. She growled right back, and nipped his lip with her teeth as he moved his body to cover hers.

Somewhere in the distance, she heard a wolf howl.

And a few minutes later, she joined in the song.

The Night Owl

·

EMMA HOLLY

To Suzanne Powell,
animal–lover extraordinaire

Chapter 1

THE naked man stood at the edge of the forest, looking back over one broad shoulder at Mariann. His hands were braced on a tree trunk and he was leaning forward, as if he were a runner she'd caught stretching out his calves. Partly obscuring her view, his long, dark hair spilled over rugged musculature to his waist.

It was night. She should not have been able to see him, but light shone from him in the darkness, a scintillation of moonlike shine. Whatever the source of the glow, it made his beautiful form even more distinct. His hips were narrow, his buttocks a tight, lip-licking curve. One of his statue-perfect legs was bent. In the space between his thighs, she could just make out the hang of his scrotum.

Watching him, wanting him, Mariann's body tightened with awareness. Fingers curled against her urge to touch, she swallowed and took a step. She knew there had to be a reason she could not see the rest.

The man knew the reason. He smiled with wicked self-assurance. "I've been waiting for you," he said. "Don't you want to come with me?"

* * *

"CRAP," sighed Mariann O'Faolain as her old-fashioned, windup alarm clock started jangling at 3 A.M.

Her body pulsed with frustration. The last thing she wanted was to shake off her dream. It was, after all, the closest she'd come to getting lucky in the last six months. But that was no reason to hug the pillow. Rolling over, she slapped the ringing silent with a single blow, then blinked into the country dark.

I'm a vampire, she thought, breaking into a crooked grin. Up with the moon and down with the sun.

Her mood improved, she threw the sheets off with a flourish no one was there to see. She had half an hour to shower, dress, suck down a mug of espresso and feed her cat. Then it was off to O'Faolain's, to get in a few uninterrupted hours of baking before the first of the muffin-and-coffee crowd stumbled in. Mariann enjoyed her customers, but she loved baking even more. How could she not? For nearly forty years O'Faolain's had been her second home—more of a home, in fact, than the suburban rambler she'd grown up in. As to that, her current residence, a drafty, nineteenth-century clapboard farmhouse inherited from her grandparents, was much closer to her heart. Fake wood paneling and two-car garages would never be Mariann's style.

Her mind ticking away at her to-do lists, she barely noticed she'd been in and out of the bathroom until she unwound the sopping towel from her mop of tight black curls. A fresh white T-shirt, courtesy of Maynard's Laundry, no-iron chinos, and a pair of sky-blue Keds comprised her uniform for the day—for every day, actually, but Mariann couldn't be bothered to dress like some freaking beanpole out of *Vogue*.

She was a working girl, thank you very much. Comfortable and clean was good enough for her, and naked was strictly for dreams!

Her body still buzzed in memory as she clattered down the creaky stairs. The stove light from the kitchen provided just enough light to see, and she promised herself for the umpteenth time that she'd hire a carpenter to fix the missing spindles on the railing. Her mind skimmed over the vow without a ripple. The peaches had been fantastic this week: juicy, firm, their flesh a rich, ripe yellow that made her mouth water by itself. She'd bake tartlets for the chamber of commerce supper, and maybe whip up a batch of peach caramel ice cream.

Ginger, she thought, pausing on the final tread to have a reverie. Ginger would add the perfect bite.

Coming back to herself with a snap, she skidded across the kitchen's cracked green linoleum and began to hum. With quick, economical movements, she arranged a few chunks of bittersweet Sharffen Berger chocolate onto a heel of crusty French bread, then popped her idea of breakfast into the microwave. Even, as she punched the buttons with her left hand, her right lit the burner beneath her shining Italian pot. Grabbing a mug from its hook, she twirled the handle around her finger like a gunslinger, slammed it on the counter and poured a one-ounce blurp of Vermont cream into its maw. Pirate Vic's bowl and kibble became her next partners in the dance, one she'd performed—at first with forced cheer, but now with real—ever since her husband became her ex.

Five years of her life she'd given to that man, four-and-a-half more than he deserved. She should have known not to trust a broker.

"No more stinking, store-bought granola," she sang to the fading daisy print walls. "No more *Wall Street Journal* and God-darned low-fat milk."

"*Gosh*-darned," she corrected as she finished shaking cat food into the bowl.

She'd been trying to cut back on her cursing. With Tom gone, she thought she shouldn't feel the need.

"Here kitty, kitty," she called as she set the kibble on the dark back porch. Pirate Vic, her black-and-white, one-eyed tom (whom Tom had hated, she reminded herself with satisfaction) usually interrupted his nocturnal rambling long enough to let her feed him. This morning he was either too far away or too entertained by his adventures to heed her call.

She sighed, missing him a little, then decided to eat her breakfast outside. The back steps needed a carpenter's attention as much as her stair rail, but she sat on them all the same. The air was cool and soft, a pleasant start to an August day. Familiar rustles filled the woods that surrounded her scraggly lawn. She owned ten acres, all told, on the southern tail of the Green Mountain spine.

Tom had wanted her to cut down the trees and sell them.

"God bless you, Gramps," she murmured, morning prayers more her style than evening. "Give Grams a kiss for me and, uh, do your bit for world peace."

She was about to try calling Vic again when a shadow slinking through the brambles brought her alert.

"There you are," she cooed, before she realized the intruder could not possibly be a cat.

The shape froze at the sound of her voice, the forward-canted ears obviously canine. It had to be a neighbor's dog. Plenty of folks in Maple Notch let their pets run loose. She expected the dog to flee but, after a pause, it crept foot by silent foot into her yard.

Her first clear sight of it made her pulse patter in her throat.

Her visitor was not dog but wolf, a big, glacial-eyed, gape-jawed beast. Its markings were black, its undercoat a lighter shade she could not make out. Its upcurved tail waved slowly from side to side. It had locked its gaze on hers as if gauging what sort of welcome it would receive. Perhaps unable to decide, it halted midway between the forest and her porch.

It was the wildest, most breathtaking creature she had ever seen. In watching it, she completely forgot her loneliness.

"Omigosh," she whispered, the hair at the nape of her neck prickling like a sunburn. She wasn't sure if she was frightened or simply thrilled. Vermont didn't have wolves. At least, she didn't think they did.

Wherever this one came from, she hoped it hadn't eaten her cat.

The wolf woofed at her as if to object.

"Would you like some kibble?" she offered, thinking the smell of food might have been what drew it. "Or maybe you'd rather try my chocolate?"

The wolf whined at this and resumed its careful forward advance. Maybe it was a crossbreed, or had been raised by humans in a preserve. It certainly didn't appear to be afraid of her. In fact, it was acting like it didn't want to startle her.

The intelligence in its pale, bright eyes made this theory seem less outlandish. At that moment, she wouldn't have been surprised to discover the creature could read her mind.

Trembling, she held her half-eaten bread as far as her arm could reach. When the wolf was close enough to sniff her offering, it sneezed, licked a drip of 62-percent-pure dark chocolate, then delicately took the crust in its teeth. Mariann was almost too shocked to let go, reminded only by a gentle tug. A toss of the wolf's head and a snap of its powerful jaws made the treat disappear.

For a moment, the animal's eyes glowed like hot, green stones. Then, as if all that had gone before hadn't been amazing enough, it crouched down on its forelegs, groveled the tiny distance toward her across the grass, and gave the very tip of her fingers a pink-tongued kiss.

Mariann gasped and snatched back her hand. Immediately the wolf sprang away, trotting toward the trees with its head turned over its shoulder to her. Her imagination lent it a look of regret.

It vanished into the bracken without a sound.

"Wow," she breathed, her hand pressed flat to her pounding chest. Forget sex dreams with naked strangers. This had to be the most exciting morning she'd ever had.

UNDERSTANDABLY, Mariann's quarter-mile bike ride to the bakery passed in a daze. The winding back road she lived on led pretty much nowhere. She didn't see a single car, parked or otherwise, until she hit Maple Notch's main street. City people might have been nervous at the isolation, but Mariann loved it through and through. Because of a promise to her father, she had her cell phone and her pepper spray tucked into her fanny pack. Truth be told, though, in all her time here she'd never come close to needing either one to protect herself—not even in the height of tourist season. No matter her upbringing in the burbs, she'd been born to be a small-town girl.

With an absentminded glow of gratification, she pedaled past the country store and the post office, then turned left at the one stoplight.

O'Faolain's wasn't much farther. Formerly a carriage house, since her grandfather's time the bakery had been an adjunct to the Night Owl Inn—and one of its prime draws. Guests raved about the breakfast baskets left at their doors, often coming back just for them. The current proprietors, who owned the land on which her bakery sat, were continuing the partnership.

The Luces had caused a stir upon their arrival in Maple Notch. With their flowing hair and incredibly fit physiques, either of the tall, dark, handsome cousins could have stepped out of the pages of a magazine. The older one, in particular, dressed like a front man for Armani—perpetually on the verge of looking too cool for the town.

Familial relationship aside, rumors that the Luces were a couple seemed inevitable. Once raised, however, they were quashed with surprising speed. No gay man, common female wisdom decided, could look at a woman like those two did. After encountering the younger Luce on his nightly run, the owner of the Clip 'n' Curl declared rather breathlessly that she thought he had "wanted to eat her up."

That she would willingly have been devoured was understood.

If this influx of testosterone weren't sufficient to set tongues wagging, the cousins were, apparently, filthy rich.

Workers were hired at ungodly wages: architects, plasterers, even a sommelier. The neighboring antique shops were beside themselves trying to supply the inn with period furnishings. No one doubted the Night Owl would be a Victorian showpiece when it was done. Previously a bastion of shabby kitsch, soon it would be a gem to swell the breasts of all and sundry with local pride.

If the Luces sometimes acted as peculiar as they were rich, that was dismissed as "furrin" eccentricity. They were Frenchmen, after all, and to a native Vermonter that was strange indeed. So what if they had never heard of Ben & Jerry's? So what if they slept all day and had some bizarro allergy that kept them out of the sun? The Luces were giving Maple Notch an unexpected shot in the arm. As long as their checks kept clearing, no one gave a darn what they did.

Mariann herself viewed them warily, though the younger of the two, Emile, was extremely charming. Despite her doubts, she helped them redesign their kitchen and promised to continue supplying them with baked goods. O'Faolain's, they assured her, would always be a valued friend to the Night Owl Inn.

Sometimes she thought she'd have trusted them more if they'd been plain. Her ex had been handsome, a golden boy with a heart of brass. After a brief, six-month honeymoon, during which he'd treated her like a queen, he seemed to view cheating on her as his right: life, liberty and the pursuit of secretaries in short skirts. When Mariann looked at Emile and Bastien, she couldn't help thinking: been there, done that.

If she thought it a little more when she looked at Bastien, that was no one's business but hers. It wasn't his fault he'd been creeping into her dreams.

Shaking off the prejudice—which she admitted had no real cause—she noted the removal of the scaffolding that had obscured the inn's facade for the last few months. Built in the 1840s, the Night Owl resembled a castle more than a house, its granite facade and Gothic windows bringing a touch of olde England to their humble burg. The sward of grass it sat on, smooth enough for a round of golf, put her patchy yard to shame.

She had to admit she was impressed. She'd never seen a renovation move so fast. Then again, maybe the heaps of cash the Luces tossed around encouraged even the laid-back locals to get in gear.

Swinging off her old brown Schwinn, Mariann wheeled the bike the last few feet up the gravel drive. Above her head, the O'Faolain's sign clanked on its chains. A second plank hung beneath the first. "Family recipes since 1940," it said, "no matter what anybody claims."

She nodded approvingly at the addendum and leaned her bike beneath the front window. O'Faolain's had a small seating area, a diner-style counter and a kitchen behind that. Since the lights were on, she knew her assistant must have managed to roll out of bed. Heather was just eighteen and had a boyfriend. To Heather's credit, she always showed up . . . just not always on time.

Smiling to herself, Mariann entered and called hello.

"In the kitchen," Heather called back, sounding suspiciously teary.

Mariann found her glaring at six just-baked trays of mini pie shells.

"They're not flaky," Heather moaned with all the drama of her youth. "It looked so easy when you showed me, but no matter what I did, they turned out flat."

Mariann pinched her lower lip and wondered if she should scold. It was good of Heather to anticipate her wanting to make tartlets, but now they'd have to clean up and start from scratch.

"Did you remember to feed the bread starter like I wrote on the prep board?"

"Yes," Heather quavered, her arms crossed protectively at her waist, "and I didn't make a mess."

Mariann had already noticed the counters' gleam. Her admonitions for Heather to tidy behind herself were sinking in. What wasn't sinking in were her reminders not to run before she could walk. A cooking school dropout whose parents played bridge with Mariann's, Heather had been a pity hire. At the time, the teenager could barely be trusted to boil eggs.

As if she knew what her boss was thinking, Heather's chin quivered like a child's.

"Oh, honey," Mariann relented, squeezing the girl's shoulder. The kindness made a tear roll down Heather's cheek. With her shining wheat-brown hair and her peachy skin, she was blooming even more than usual. In truth, she looked like an actress crying for the camera. Appearances notwithstanding, Mariann knew the girl's emotions were as real as a summer storm. She was a babe in the woods, and Mariann hadn't the heart to toughen her up.

Business was slow with the inn shut down for renovations. Heather's trial by fire could wait.

"It's just experience," Mariann said. "And my cold Irish hands. They keep the butter from melting in the flour. When I worked in Boston, I knew an Italian who'd plunge his hands in ice water for two whole minutes before he'd look at a ball of dough."

"Yeah, yeah," said Heather, swiping her sleeve across her eyes. "The few, the proud, the pastry chefs."

Mariann laughed, knowing Heather was all right if she was cracking jokes. Heather smiled shyly back.

"You're late," she pointed out with a sly glance toward the clock. Apparently, this unheard-of occurrence improved her mood.

"Hair emergency," Mariann explained to her own surprise. When she left the house, she'd have sworn her *Wild Kingdom* encounter would have been the first thing out of her mouth. Now—though Heather eyed her curls skeptically—she did not retract the lie.

For reasons she didn't care to examine, Mariann wanted to keep her morning visitor to herself.

Chapter 2

BASTIEN Luce stood in the shadows outside the bakery, looking in at its lights. Perfectly still, with a heart that could beat as seldom as once an hour, he opened his senses to search for threats. Few were great enough to harm him. The night was his dominion, the sun his enemy. Humans—had they known of his existence—would have called him vampire. Among his own kind he was *upyr.*

Theirs was a race of shape-shifting immortal beings, part wolf, part blood-drinker, with a power and beauty no other creature could match. Both power and beauty had to be hidden when *upyr* traveled the mortal realm. These days, few could survive without a knack for glamour and thrall, the gifts that allowed them to look like humans and, when that proved impossible, to convince the humans they had not seen what they thought they had. Sadly, there weren't enough wild places left for them to live wholly apart.

Like their four-footed brethren, *upyr* fought to survive. Immortal did not mean indestructible, especially when modern life held so many dangers. Cameras could watch them without their knowledge, doctors could probe their unique genetics, and swordsmen were hardly necessary when any idiot with a buzz saw could lop off their heads. Even broken hearts could drive his kind to their doom.

Bastien didn't think he was in danger of facing that, but he'd definitely had happier times. Not six months ago, he'd been kicked out of his pack.

For the second time in his life, he'd been forced to leave a country he called home—first by a tyrant, now by a friend.

At least his second exile, from Scotland this time, had been kindly done, complete with murmurings of "time you stretched your legs" and "we could really use your help establishing a power base across the pond." No matter what his pack leader, Ulric, said, Bastien knew the truth in his bones.

He was getting too powerful to keep around, powerful enough to be an elder: one of few who could change human into *upyr*. Bastien couldn't be an underling in someone else's pack when his nature drove him to rule his own. Indeed, as the years went by, it seemed inevitable that he would challenge Ulric for rule of his. Bastien's pack leader was much beloved. Even if Bastien could defeat him, the pack wouldn't want him to. They didn't trust him to rule as well.

For that matter, Bastien didn't trust himself.

This, he thought, was why he'd been drawn so strongly to the bakery. Its warmth, its wonderful, comforting scents, the history that clung to it like a spice, pulled him inexorably. He'd already been thinking he'd buy the Night Owl. The inn had the atmosphere he wanted, and ample surrounding land. He'd believed it would repay his investment and hoped it would tempt visits from his friends. It was the sight of O'Faolain's, however, that sealed the deal.

He only wished the sight of its owner hadn't sealed his fate.

Mariann O'Faolain was as tart as one of her pies—a scrappy little woman with wiry muscles and subtle curves. Though her looks were striking, she appeared to have no vanity. Her unstyled mop of hair was as dark as her favorite drink, her eyes like an April sky. She slaved at her business like no one but humans could, twelve hours at a stretch, as if she feared her life would end too soon for her to work herself into the ground. She had no husband—at the moment, anyway—no child, just a town full of admirers and a chewed-looking cat whose spirit was as fierce as hers.

Bastien wanted her with an intensity that set his blood ablaze: to love with, to hunt with, to make her queen to the king he did not dare be. Centuries would not suffice to slake his thirst for her sweetness.

Unfortunately, it looked like centuries would be required for him to muster the nerve to court her. Since meeting her, he hadn't been able to say two words without tripping over his tongue. The closest he'd come to flirting had been his wolf eating from her hand. He hadn't intended to surprise her. He'd simply been unable to resist going to her house.

The Frenchman in him found his clumsiness pathetic. The man in him just felt lost. As the Americans so colorfully put it, falling in love was a bitch.

His friend, Emile, his sole companion in exile, chose then to appear at his side, probably not by his accident. He wore his usual jeans and polo shirt, and tiny lights blinked in the soles of his running shoes. This was an activity he had taken to with a vengeance. Long ago, Emile had nearly lost his legs. The length to which Bastien had gone to save him was something neither of them spoke about. Brothers at heart, they'd always resembled each other, which had led to the fiction that they were kin. Ironically, almost dying had given Emile a more humorous view of life than his supposed cousin. He took things as they came, and gave thanks for what he had.

For a moment, he was content to stand drinking in the night. Sadly, for Emile peace was never as good as the chance to tease.

"You know," he said, a smile in his voice, "Mariann won't bite you if we go in—unless that is what you are hoping for."

Bastien blushed, no easy feat for his kind. He was glad Emile had not witnessed his ridiculous morning tryst.

"Eff you," he said and, as he'd intended, Emile laughed.

"Very good, *mon ami*. Keep that up and soon no one will guess you were born anywhere but here."

With Emile there watching, it was impossible to hang back. Emile might have been Bastien's best friend for hundreds of years, might have seen him at his very worst, but that didn't mean Bastien wanted to be thought a coward.

He had taken a single step when Emile gave the back of Bastien's suit a shake.

"Hold it," he said. "Leave this off, old friend, and loosen that starchy collar. For once you need to quit pretending you are here on business. No woman wants to be wooed by a stick."

"Fine." Bastien removed his jacket, tossed it into the bushes and attacked the small white button that trapped his neck. Then, to prove he would not do this halfway, he rolled up his sleeves as well.

"*C'est bien*," said Emile. "Now you are casual."

Gritting his teeth to hide his agitation, Bastien pushed through the bakery door. From previous visits, he knew the CLOSED sign did not mean locked. The people of this town were alarmingly unparanoid. Inside, the decor was that of a fifties diner—not re-created but preserved, with all the cracks and worn spots left intact. Bastien had enjoyed the decade as he recalled: the films of Gary Cooper, rock and roll, the smell of cheeseburgers on a grill.

It was odd to think Mariann hadn't been born yet.

He'd been more alone than he knew.

Shivering, he trailed his hand along the counter's silvery trim, his heart thumping faster at the prospect of seeing the object of his dreams. The things he longed to do to her would have made her hair curl even more; his need to possess her was quite savage. Awkward or not, her company had become as necessary to him as food.

"*Bon soir*," Emile called toward the kitchen door. "We have come to keep you lovely ladies company."

"Emile!" Heather exclaimed as she bounded out, her

floppy chef's hat nearly falling off. "You're just in time to get me out of the doghouse."

Unlike himself and Mariann, Heather and Emile had become fast friends within instants of their meeting, as evidenced by the laughing kisses they gave each other's cheeks. As far as Bastien could tell, the girl didn't have a suspicious bone in her body. Emile barely had to use his glamour to trick her into thinking he looked human. Perhaps, young and pretty as she was, she was blasé about handsome men. At the least, Bastien knew she was not cowed by him.

"Late night?" she joked, cocking one brow at him.

"Planning," he said as he tried not to peer too obviously behind her shoulder. "For the leaf peepers in the fall. We're thinking of having a grand opening in time to take advantage of the tourists who come to see the colors change. When we finished brainstorming, we decided to stop by for a cup of joe."

"Sur–re," Heather said in her teenage drawl. "Cuz coffee is what everyone wants before they toddle off to bed."

Bastien wasn't certain, but he thought he saw her exchanging winks with Emile.

"Relax," she said at his frown. "Cinderella has pots to scrub, but I'll get the boss to set you up."

His palms immediately went damp. "Only if she's not too busy."

"We're always busy," Heather teased, "but never too busy to make time for you."

With his keen *upyr* hearing, Bastien couldn't miss the whispered argument that ensued behind the kitchen wall. The words "pretty boy" and "weirdo" were particularly clear. Apparently, Mariann didn't want to see him. His ears grew hot with a shame he hadn't felt since he was human.

"Get out there," the teenager hissed at the last, "and for God's sake get a life!"

When Mariann emerged, Bastien prayed his face was not as pink as hers. He didn't know why, but he found her completely adorable in her buttoned-up baking jacket—not the most opportune reaction, considering her response to him.

"The usual?" she asked, immediately busying herself at the elaborate coffee-making machine.

"Please," he said, then cleared his throat. "With a cup of water."

Emile's interjection was too soft for anyone but him to hear. "Very smooth," he said. "I'm sure you've almost got her now."

Bastien had to admit his friend was right to mock. At this rate, Bastien would be dust before he and Mariann held hands.

"You look pretty today," he blurted out desperately, his eyes honing helplessly on her nape, so slim and bitable. Cursing to himself, he tried to quash his arousal. The last thing he needed was to flash his fangs. "Your hair, um, looks very free."

The sound Mariann made was more snort than laugh. "'Free' is what my hair does best."

To his relief, when she turned to set his coffee and water on the counter, she was smiling. For the first time in what seemed like ages, she met his eyes. Hers were so warm and soft he could have drowned. "You know, Mr. Luce, if the espresso is too strong for you, I can make drip."

"No," he said, his voice gone dark, his hand moving impulsively to cover hers. "I like the way your espresso tastes."

In all their meetings, he had been careful not to thrall her, wanting her to fall for him on her own. Despite his restraint, she went as still at his touch as if he had. Her pupils swelled, her delicate, rosy lips parting for breath. She wore no lipstick. All her colors were her own, from the flush on her cheeks to the tiny freckles on her nose.

I love you, he thought, force of will all that kept the sentiment inside his head. I would do anything to make you mine.

"It's Bastien," he corrected, some scrap of his brain still functioning. "Not Mr. Luce."

"Bastien," she said dazedly.

A smile spread across his face. She might think he was a weirdo, but she was warming to him all the same. He could hear it in her voice. He felt himself all of a sudden confident and masculine. "Mariann," he said, letting his accent soften her name. "Would you like to—"

He would never know if his invitation to dinner would have been accepted. The outside door slammed open and a tall blonde bombshell stalked inside. Shaped like an expensive hourglass from bust to hip, she wore a snug-fitting, ash-gray suit, her debt to Marilyn obvious. A diamond as big as a blueberry sparkled on her left hand. Despite her bursting in like a squall, not a hair on her head was mussed. She was just as fresh as if it were ten in the morning instead of five. Whoever she was, either she got up early herself, or she'd put some planning into this entrance.

At her appearance, Mariann yanked her hand from his.

With one frosted pink nail, the woman pointed at his beloved. "You," she said, "had better stop spreading lies."

Mariann lifted her sharp little chin. "Which lies would those be? That you stole my grandfather's recipes or that you ran off with my husband? You're welcome to him, by the way, with my thanks."

Bastien had tensed in preparation to protect her, but Mariann's quick retort assured him there was no need. The other woman might have been grateful if he'd interfered. An unhealthy shade of brick washed her sculpted cheeks.

"You were always jealous of me," she said. "Always hoarding your little secrets, pretending I wasn't good enough to bake your precious grandfather's pies. But the whole world knows I'm good enough now. If you keep trying to smear my name, the studio's lawyers will sue your stupid, no-iron pants off."

"Really? Even if I can prove every word I say?"

"You can't." The woman's confidence was clear as she tossed her head. "It's your word against mine."

"Not exactly." With a smile that would have done a Borgia proud, Mariann brought a stained leather journal from beneath the counter. She set it on the clean glass top of the display case next to the register. "This is my grandfather's recipe book, which tracks the development of every signature dessert he made, from 1940 on. I had the paper, the handwriting and the ink authenticated by a lab. So you see, Arabella, when I spoke to that reporter at the *Boston Globe*, I had evidence to back up my claims."

Her breath hissing through her nose, the woman grabbed for the book. Bastien slapped his hand on top of it before she could. She gaped at him as if he were mad, then turned dismissively back to Mariann.

"You're nothing," she said. "Just a small-town Betty Crocker who hasn't the sense to hold on to anything she has. I proved it eighteen months ago when we split and, believe me, I will again."

She swept out as regally as she'd swept in, leaving the grounds with a squeal of tires. Bastien broke the silence by sneezing at her perfume. Heather's response was more deliberate.

"So," she said, "that was the famous Arabella Armand. Can't say I'm terribly impressed."

"She's usually more charming," Mariann said tightly. "She saves the Hyde side of her personality for her friends."

Heather laughed, but Mariann made a sound like a hiccup and ran into the kitchen.

"Stay," Bastien said when Heather would have followed. "I'll make certain she is all right."

He put a touch of thrall into the command. The girl fell back like a doll.

"Careful," Emile said as he caught her shoulders.

Bastien knew the warning was meant for him.

He would listen, just not right then.

MARIANN'S kitchen was bigger than her café, with stainless steel cabinets and a terra-cotta floor sloping to a drain. Everything about it was oversized: the overhead lights, the counters, the convection ovens and range. The refrigerated walk-in required a stepladder, and was stocked with hunks of chocolate and butter better fit for giants. That such a tiny female ruled this domain filled him with amusement—not that Mariann ever seemed less than up to the task.

He found her at the butcher-block island, splitting what had to be a real vanilla bean with a knife. As she scraped the seeds the smell overwhelmed his senses: a pungent sweetness that managed to combine homey kitchen and jungle. His body hardened as only an *upyr*'s could, in the space between mortal heartbeats, with a gut-punching thoroughness that nearly buckled his knees. His formerly modest Italian trousers lost their perfect drape, while the itching in his gums warned him his fangs were very close to shooting out.

"I'm fine," she said curtly before he could speak, lifting her elbow high enough to blot her eyes. "I have work to do."

Standing behind her, seeing the prideful stiffness of her spine, he felt as he had been creeping toward her across her yard, desiring contact so badly he would risk frightening her away.

He put his arms around her, gently, slowly, stilling her wrists with his hands. Her fingers were scarred from years of kitchen work: cut, dinged, callused, burned, dried from constant washing and cracked along the seams. He knew she was proud of every imperfection. Many times, when she did not know he watched, he would see her turn them back and forth and smile.

"You're not fine," he said, his nose nudging softly behind her ear. This close to her, with their auras mingling, he could not help but sense her troubled emotions. He had always respected her privacy, but he was too good a mind reader not to catch a wisp of her feelings now. "That woman upset you."

Mariann sniffed out a laugh. "Arabella would be terribly insulted to know you didn't recognize the Cooking Channel's newest darling."

Bastien acknowledged no darling but her. Humming at the pleasure of finally having her in his arms, he drew his lips across the silken skin where his nose had been.

Mariann began to tremble. "You shouldn't be doing this. You're my landlord."

He didn't see what that had to do with anything, but humans did sometimes have strange rules. He slipped his fingertips between the knuckles of her battered hands, which caused her little knife to clatter to the floor. Her head sagged back against his shoulder, baring the line of her throat. Among his kind, this was a gesture of surrender, sexual and otherwise.

His voice sank unavoidably to a growl. "I've been wanting to get close to you since we met."

Her answer was a broken sigh. "You're making it worse."

"How can my holding you cause any harm?"

He kept his tone as soothing as he could, but her neck snapped up again. "The harm is that I don't want to cry!"

He let her turn in his arms, but did not release her from the cage they formed. True to her words, her face was streaked by fresh tears. In spite of this, or possibly because of it, her soft blue eyes blazed with defiance, her passion an aphrodisiac to one like him.

Only her vulnerability called to him more.

"You haven't been held in a while," he said, his blood surging at the thought of everything else she might not have done. "That's why my touch makes you weep."

Sheepish, she ducked her head. "Tom never was much of a hugger."

"An unfortunate trait in a husband."

"I thought so. I mean, I wasn't asking him to hug the world. Only me." She had been gaining in composure, trying to joke, but her voice cracked on the last and she made a face. "Honestly, I don't care. He's a jerk, and I'm better off without him."

"You are," Bastien agreed. "By a thousand times."

"What she did was worse," Mariann said, and Bastien knew she meant Arabella. "We survived the restaurant scene in Boston, two women turning out hundreds of plates a night with those stupid, ass-grabbing line cooks. She convinced me to bring her here as my partner after Grandfather died. We were friends. I thought she liked me. And then she pretends my grandfather's work is her own. 'A little something

I came up with,' she says on her show. The first time I heard it, I thought my head would explode.

"In all the time I worked with her, she never came up with anything. She could cook, but she was lazy. Her first question was always, 'What's the shortcut?' But good baking comes from love, from the desire to create something your customers will really and truly enjoy. You can't take shortcuts with that!"

Disgusted by the memory, Mariann rubbed her nose. When she went on, her tone was resigned. "I never did want to share his recipes with her, but I thought, 'Well, she's not just my partner, she's my friend. I should learn to be more trusting.' Hah. All I did was hand her everything I had."

"Everything you have is here," he said, one hand reaching up to tap her heart. "At least everything that counts."

"Thank you, Zen Master Luce. I'm sure I'd agree with you if I were equally evolved."

"All right," he laughed, enjoying her acerbity. "You have a reason to be mad."

She blinked at him. "Why are you being so nice? You barely said 'boo' to me before today."

Her eyes were wide, her expression willing to hear. Sensing she would allow it, he stroked his fingers through her curls. Though his power undid the tangles, the little twists clung to his hand as if they liked the touch. "Maybe I was waiting for you to think of me as more than a pretty weirdo."

"Yeesh. I'm sorry you heard that. I—"

"No." He touched her lips to hush her apology. "I'm sure I do seem strange. I only hope you'll give me the chance to show you what else I am, what else I'd like to be to you."

"Be?" she repeated. "To me?"

This time he could not miss her breathlessness. Arousal barreled through him in a roaring wave. It was all he could do not to moan.

Oh, Mariann, he thought. I'm going to kiss you to kingdom come.

Chapter 3

SHE knew he was going to kiss her. Worse, she knew she was going to let him. Never mind she'd sworn off unfairly good-looking men. Never mind her schedule barely had room for her schedule. When his hands surrounded her face and his dark, silky hair fell forward, her temperature sizzled like butter set to sauté.

Close as he was, his scent shot up her nose, sending her already buzzing hormones into overdrive. His skin smelled of wood and earth, of mossy water and Beaujolais. He had rolled up his shirtsleeves and opened his collar. She didn't think she'd ever seen him without a jacket. For some reason, she found the sight of his muscled forearms sexier than another man completely bare—not that she hadn't entertained the thought of him that way as well.

To her dismay, he was giving her the laser-beam look he shared with his cousin, like she was the only woman left on the planet and he would give his life to have her. Mariann didn't anticipate that kind of sacrifice being required. She was going to topple quite easily.

"Your hands are cold," she said in a nervous bid for delay. "I should teach *you* to make pie."

"My hands will warm."

He said this with such sensual promise she doubted he'd understood. Up close, his eyes were a pale peridot green, their brilliance heightened by their half-lowered frame of black. Their steadiness unnerved her, the way they seemed to pierce her soul. It was probably her sex-starved imagination, but his gaze looked sad, as if he longed for something he feared he would never find. Without intending to, she held her breath as the look drew out.

He broke the tension before she could.

"Ah, Mariann," he said with an embarrassed laugh. "I've been dreaming of kissing you for so long, I'm almost afraid to do it."

"You better get over that. 'Cause I swear, if you leave me hanging, I'll never give you another chance."

His grin was a blinding flash. "I love your fight," he whispered, "most of all."

She didn't have time to wonder what this meant, because he tipped her head up and lowered his. His mouth molded over her lips, a gentle, testing intimacy. Whatever the test was, she passed it. He moaned low in his chest, the loveliest sound she'd ever heard a person make. His arms slid down her back and tightened as his tongue went deep.

He tasted as good as he smelled. In moments, her head was spinning with the erotic rush. As if he knew, he savored his victory, refusing to hurry a lick or pull, enticing her to respond in kind. She sighed with pleasure as she accepted. To her mind, nothing was better than a man who loved to kiss, and every indication said Bastien did.

She couldn't suppress a whimper when he stopped.

"Touch me," he said, the merest breath against her trembling mouth. "Put your hands on my skin."

"Heather might—"

"Heather is perfectly safe with Emile." His gaze burned into her from inches away, mesmerizing, penetrating, trying to convey some message she could not quite read. "Your touch is what I want most. It's what I crave."

If she'd ever doubted he was strange, this would have capped it. What sort of man talked this way? But his strangeness didn't matter. Directed by cravings of their own, her fingers found the finely woven cotton of his business shirt, smoothing it up his chest. His pecs were steely, his shoulders broad enough to ride. He wore no tie, and at his throat one strong, blue vein pulsed out a wild rhythm.

"Do it," he said, then swallowed hard.

Gripping his shirt at the back, she tugged its tails out from his trousers. For a moment, she thought of ripping it another seam. With shaking hands, she slid her arms beneath.

Whatever she was expecting, it was not this. His back felt like moon-cooled marble under her palms, impossibly smooth, invitingly firm and strong.

He jerked as if her touch had burned him, then closed his eyes. "Yes—s," he hissed, a sound of rapture. "I love your heat."

"You're freezing!" she exclaimed, chafing her hands up his spine.

Swearing softly, he lifted her off her feet.

His next kiss silenced what was left of her yammering brain. It had been ages since anyone had kissed her and, in truth, no one had ever done it with such concentrated, pent-up need. Skill aside, his enthusiasm was flattering: probing, sucking, tilting his head or hers to find new variations of their perfect fit.

When he nipped her lower lip and tugged it, she felt devoured, just as Linda at the Clip 'n' Curl had longed to be. She was glad her nails were short because her fingers dug into his skin. Groaning, he set her on the cutting block, pulled her legs apart and stepped between.

Whoa, thought Mariann, her eyes going wide as she registered the length and breadth of what he was beginning to grind against her, slowly, fiercely, with a gasp that sounded like relief. Her hands clutched his back in amazement. Who'd have expected a man so meticulously put together would sport an erection this rude? The surprise of it aroused her, the thrill as undeniable as it was cheap. Not only was he harder than the eighteen-year-old boys she'd nearly forgotten, Bastien Luce was seriously hung.

Like some dewy-eyed ingenue, she found herself wondering if he would fit.

To hell with that, she decided. She'd make him fit . . . and enjoy every rock-hard inch.

With a curse, he moved his mouth to her neck. "I won't hurt you," he said, panting like a runner against her pulse. "Please do not think it."

"No," she assured him just as heavily. "Never crossed my mind."

This was true, though he was uncannily quick with his hands. She wasn't sure when he had removed it, but her chef's jacket, the one they all called whites, was gone. Now he was pushing her T-shirt up her belly, stroking the skin he uncovered bit by bit. A tingle spread from beneath his fingers, as if he were infused with electricity. She half expected to see sparks.

The effect he had on her was disconcerting. She was no slave to her needs, no silly romantic to go spineless at holding hands. But she squirmed at the sensations, her body growing hotter with every touch. She fought a groan as his palms smoothed around her ribs to pop the clasp of her plain beige bra.

Since Mariann was no centerfold, normally this was the point where she got self-conscious. Bastien didn't give her a chance.

"Look at you," he breathed, both thumbs sweeping arcs across her now bare breasts. Caught at their edges, her areolae swelled and itched. She held her breath as he bent his head.

Even though she was expecting it, her back arched uncontrollably as his mouth fastened on one peak. She barely noticed the caresses of his second hand. His tongue was clearly cleverer than the common run, finding nerves she hadn't known she had. As her muscles threatened to turn to water, he laid her back against the knife-scored wood of her work table. He was suckling strongly, making small, hungry noises as if he liked what he was doing as much as she did.

The vanilla bean she'd been splitting crushed beneath her back.

On top of everything else, the scent was more than she could take, the sense that he had pushed into a sphere no other lover had been a part of. The kitchen was her fortress against the world. Suddenly her heels were locked in the small of his back and she was grinding against him. She'd never been so desperate for a climax, so hot and needy and tight.

"God," he choked, breaking free of her breast and breathing hard. His palm slid smoothly up her hip. "Please. Allow me."

Beyond inhibitions, she ripped her zipper down herself, inviting his hand to slip over her mound and between her folds. He sucked in air as he found her wetness. She was more than slick; she was drowning. Without resistance, two of his fingers slipped inside. His thumb rubbed slow, firm circles against her clit.

"Go ahead," he rasped, reading the way her muscles tensed. "Squeeze your thighs around my wrist."

She obeyed his coaxing without hesitation. What he was doing felt better than she could believe, better than anyone had ever done for her, better—she thought with astonishment—than she could do for herself.

Maybe she should have tried a Frenchman long ago.

A particularly sharp ache of pleasure dragged his name from her throat. His eyes came up, shocking her with their fire. His face was strained, his lips pressed whitely over his teeth. The sight told her how selfish she was being.

"You don't have to do this," she said.

He laughed and she realized with something like awe that he was shaking. "You don't know me very well if you think that."

"But you—"

"*I* want to watch you come."

She had an orgasm as he said it, a sweet, unexpected burst that seemed to swell just from the husky growl of his voice.

When it ended, his tongue curled out to wet his upper lip. "There's a start," he said with a humor that robbed her embarrassment of its sting. "In case you haven't guessed, however, I'm a bit more orally fixated."

Any question about what he meant vanished when he yanked her sweaty chinos down to her knees. His hands slid up to caress her legs, kneading deeply where they met her torso. She fought an urge to close her knees, unable to doubt he liked what he saw. His eyes were glittering with admiration. With a salacious grin, he squeezed her admittedly well-formed thighs.

"Must be the bike," he said. "Bet you'll wrap me good."

"Bastien—" Her protest was lost as he dropped down on his knees. Abruptly off balance, she grabbed his hair. He had swooped onto her without warning, but any thought of objection dissolved into a soundless *wow*. Everything he'd put into his kisses, he brought to this. And this was a man who could tie cherry stems in double time.

She gasped as he found her favorite spot and teased it with his tongue, faster and faster, one hand massaging her sheath while his second formed a V pointing downward from above his mouth. Those fingers pressed broader, subtler nerves, spreading sensation throughout her groin. The pleasure was almost frightening. Her skin was humming, her toes curled hard. She tried to keep quiet but could not, mewling and twitching until her hips bucked upward and her body seized deliciously from head to toe.

He gave her a second to gulp for air, then pushed her over again.

This climax was even sweeter, more than her greediest hunger could have asked. She was helpless beneath the spasms, gripped by ripples of joyous surfeit for long minutes. Her muscles were as warm as cinnamon when she relaxed.

"Wow," she sighed, the word coming out at last.

He was quiet, but she felt him smile, his cheek resting on her pubis, his hand spread across her abdomen.

To her surprise, she was stroking his decadently lengthy hair. She didn't know when she'd started and wasn't sure she could stop, though it seemed—perversely, perhaps, given their recent actions—a too-intimate thing to do. His hair was thicker than she expected but just as silky. The strands felt strong when she combed them up off his back, more like a cat's than a human being's. She smiled to herself, thinking she'd better not let Pirate Vic suspect he had competition.

"Thank you," Bastien said in a sleepy tone.

Mariann had to laugh. "You know, I'm pretty sure that's my line."

When his head came up, a trick of the light set his eyes aglow. "I wish I could stay, but dawn is coming, and I know you still have to work."

Mariann's hands clapped against her cheeks. How could she have forgotten so completely who and where she was?

"Don't worry," he said, helping her slide off the table and into her clothes. "Emile will have made certain Heather didn't hear. No one will gossip about what we did."

"Nice friend you have." She fought a wisp of unease as he turned her gently to do up her bra.

"The best," he reassured her. Momentarily shy, she tucked her T-shirt in by herself. When she faced him again, he cupped her face in his big, smooth hand. His skin was warm now, just as he'd vowed. "I meant it when I said thank you. I know you don't trust lightly."

"I feel bad. You didn't . . . I mean, it's not like I think we ought to be going at it in my kitchen, or that you should risk, uh, aggravating your allergy, but—"

He stopped her nattering by taking her hand and placing it squarely over his crotch. He didn't have to encourage her more than that. Her fingers curled around his huge erection of their own accord, surrounding his balls and shaft in summer-thin Italian wool. There was, she realized, nothing under that cloth but him. She remembered her dream, where she'd seen the furry hang of him from behind. He was just as hard as she'd imagined then, though she hadn't imagined quite so much of him. Within her hold, his blood pulsed with enthralling steadiness and force.

It would have taken a stronger woman than her to resist the chance to explore.

He didn't wince when she squeezed him, though his normally ivory face turned a dusky rose. Mariann's throat tightened with excitement. She sensed he'd let her do anything, try anything, and never utter a complaint.

"Don't you wrinkle?" she asked, suddenly noting the state of his shirt.

Eyes dancing with laughter, he shook his head. "I'm preternaturally tidy."

"Preternaturally, huh?" The catch in his breath delighted her as her nails dragged back along his trouser's seam. "You know that makes me want to muss you more."

He caught her hand before she could. "I should warn you," he said with a hint of roughness. "If you were touching me this way, skin to skin, with your bare palm against my cock, I wouldn't care where we were or what work you had left to do. I'd throw you down and fuck you on the village green."

His slurred Parisian accent made the words sound like poetry. She had a feeling he meant every one.

"Boy, oh, boy," she said once she caught her breath, "do you make a girl want to play hooky!"

His smile could only be described as wolfish, his eyes once again catching some stray gleam. He lifted her hand from between his legs, making an oddly sexy gesture of licking her palm. "I look forward to you making this up to me," he said, "when your schedule allows."

He was smart to leave the timing up to her. If he'd been pushy, she might have balked. Now she wasn't sure how long she could wait. Right then, a minute sounded like an eternity.

"I could maybe leave a little early—"

"No," he said, caressing the side of her neck as he kissed

her brow. "Don't regret leaving me this way. You've satisfied at least one of my appetites. In fact"—his lips curled against her forehead—"you're the best breakfast I ever had."

She wasn't used to men being this nice. Flustered but secretly pleased, she searched for a joke. "Just don't expect me to be serving this to your guests."

To her pleasure, he left on a laugh.

As Bastien neared the hidden entrance to his and Emile's quarters, the sun was trembling behind the trees, declaring its approach by adding heaviness to his limbs. Contrary to current fictional belief, the first few rays would not kill him, merely make him drunk and rob him of the sense it took to know when he'd had enough. Thirty minutes of full exposure would probably prove sufficient to set him alight, and less for serious burns. The more power an *upyr* had, the more sunlight he could withstand. The danger lay in growing addicted. *Upyr* who did that tended to die young.

Despite the risk, Bastien felt the lure of oblivion now.

Being in love was a powerful lot of work. His emotions were rocketing up and down like a roller coaster. Yes, he was happy he and Mariann had finally connected, but he couldn't fight his sense of waiting for the other shoe to drop. Would the gods grow jealous and yank her away? Could someone like him deserve to be content?

Screw deserving it, he thought. He'd take what he wanted and be damned.

Emile broke into his distraction. "Bastien," he called. "It's time to get underground."

He waited by the entrance to their retreat, a cleverly fashioned boulder that swung around on a pivot to reveal a flight of black granite stairs. In case this camouflage was not enough, magic also hid the opening from human eyes, runes so old their origins were lost in myth. Bastien had inscribed them reluctantly. Experience had taught him to be mistrustful of magic's power.

"I'm coming," he said and descended behind his friend.

He gave his shoulders a shake. No doubt the dawn was aggravating his moodiness.

As soon as his head was clear of the door, an electric eye instructed it to swing shut. Just as convenient were the tiny lights set into the stairway's arched ceiling. Arranged to resemble the constellations, their low illumination was perfect for *upyr* eyes. The electricians had done a marvelous job, as had all his builders. Bastien regretted that he had to thrall their memories when they were done. Proficiency like theirs deserved to be recalled.

Then again, it was Bastien's power—and Bastien's bite— that had spurred them to their best. Nothing like a dose of blood-enhanced *upyr* mind power to keep your hired hands in line.

Once they stepped off the long stairs, a handsome Indian carpet lined the tunnel's heart-of-pine floor. Despite the obligatory lack of windows, the twelve-foot ceilings made the passage appear spacious. With the ease of long acquaintance, Emile and Bastien's footsteps fell into synchrony.

"This place is great," Emile crowed as he often did upon coming home. "Much more comfortable than Ulric's cave."

Though true, the reminder of Bastien's exile increased the leadenness in his gut. His legs temporarily refused to go on.

"She's the one," he announced hollowly.

Emile stopped a second after he did. "The one what?"

"My queen. Mariann is my queen. She makes me want to claim my destiny."

Emile snorted and resumed walking.

Bastien hastened to catch up. "You think I'm delusional."

"I think you're the slowest *upyr* I ever met. You should have claimed your kingship centuries ago."

"You of all people know why I can't."

"I know why you believe you can't. My opinion diverges."

Emile was probably the only *upyr* alive who could contradict him with impunity. Even with their long friendship, Bastien's hands balled into angry fists. "If I can't win her—"

"Yes, I know," Emile sighed, "you'll throw yourself off a cliff."

His condescension made Bastien grab his arm. To his annoyance, Emile's eyes were laughing when he spun around. "How can I win her when I can't tell her who I am?"

"Today you can't tell her. Next month or next year may be a different story." Emile rubbed his arm as Bastien released it. "Leave it to time and nature. Be satisfied you made a start."

"She does like me," Bastien said, his memory of her smile making him bounce on his toes. "More than I thought. But maybe I rushed her. She hasn't been divorced very long. Maybe I took advantage of her loneliness."

"Mon Dieu!" Emile exclaimed, forking his hands through his hair. "All's fair, you idiot. How do you think people fall in love?"

"I don't know," Bastien said, taken aback by Emile's ire. "I've never tried to do it before."

"Pah. You are a shame to your countrymen. I don't know why I stay friends with you."

This time Bastien knew Emile was teasing. He slung his arm around the other's shoulder. "You stay friends with me because you love me . . . almost as much as I love the fair Mariann."

"Oh, no." Emile shook his head. "The good Lord save me from that!"

Chapter 4

ROUND about two in the afternoon, once Heather's tattooed boyfriend had loaded their last delivery into his van, Mariann was ready to call it a day.

Heather and Eric had been full of giggles, chasing each other around the lot like kids. Their antics made her smile in spite of her fatigue. She'd gotten through her work on automatic pilot, luck and experience all that kept her from culinary catastrophe. Her thoughts had been too occupied with Bastien to try for more.

She could still feel his hands smoothing up her thrumming body, still taste his kiss in her mouth. What she couldn't decide was whether giving in to him had been wise. He had been considerate, even endearing in his pursuit. Since when, after all, could a woman like her make a man like that so shy? But was it instinct that urged her to trust him, or should she chalk the inclination up to lust?

If she were honest, the answer would probably have little to do with what happened next. With a philosophic shrug for her libido, Mariann tipped two fingers to Harv, their senior citizen counter guy.

The bakery's tables were mostly full, and a family of rumpled tourists had their noses pressed with complete enchantment to the display case. Standing slightly behind her brood, the harried mother smiled. She looked as if she could identify with Mariann's long day.

"Lemon meringue pie," Mariann suggested, grinning back with equal fellowship. "Loaded with vitamins. Hardly any calories at all."

When the woman laughed, Mariann knew she'd pleased her.

"Ice cream's sellin' good," Harv called as she slipped out. "Better make another batch tonight."

"Will do," Mariann agreed.

Outside, her momentary cheeriness drained away. Her weight was barely enough to depress the pedals of her bike. Luckily, the ride home was mostly downhill. Too tired to cook just for herself, she made a meal of soup straight out of the can, peeled off her clothes and fell into bed.

To her disappointment, she didn't dream of Bastien. Instead, sometime past ten her eyelids flew up.

"Crap," she said to the ceiling. "Crap, crap, crap."

Pirate Vic, who must have curled up at her feet while she was sleeping, mewed politely in inquiry.

She'd left her grandfather's recipe book at the bakery, right under the counter where Arabella had watched her take it out. Groaning, Mariann shoved off the covers and got dressed, too annoyed with herself to laugh at Vic's attempts to steal her socks. She pulled them on, cat spit and all, then stroked his scruffy head in consolation. It was too much to hope that the journal would be safe where it was. As far as Mariann knew, her former partner still had her key.

She'd been meaning to change the locks, in a vague sort of I-should-get-to-that way. Other things had always seemed more important and then, as month after month went by without incident, it seemed silly to bother. In the end, she'd forgotten the whole idea.

Unfortunately, with her new career at stake, and her dubious sense of honor, Arabella was sure to heed temptation's call.

She biked to the bakery in a sweat, only to find the journal exactly where she'd left it. Relieved, she hugged the book to her breast.

"Thank you," she breathed to whatever guardian angel was watching over her. She didn't think she could bear to let Arabella steal any more than she had.

Tucking the journal safely in her basket, she reversed direction, pedaling slowly to enjoy the ride. Since Maple Notch wasn't known for its nightlife, she had the two-lane road to herself. She patted her fanny pack to check the presence of her cell phone, then just relaxed. Tourist season was good, but so was this emptiness. More at peace than she'd been in months, she filled her lungs with sweet rural air. The temperature was balmy, the stars like gems in the ribbon of black the treetops left. She was young—more or less—and healthy and quite possibly about to embark on a hot affair. Small-town Betty Crocker or not, she doubted life got much better.

The approach of a car behind her seemed no cause for fear. Her bike had reflectors, and her shirt was white. Certain she could be seen, she shifted onto the shoulder without bothering to look around.

Only when the car revved its engine did her adrenaline begin to spurt.

BASTIEN'S muzzle came up as his wolf-nose caught Mariann's scent. Appetite sated by a fat raccoon, he and Emile had been chasing rabbits playfully through the woods, racing back and forth, and generally having fun. He'd welcomed the distraction, but now the hope of seeing the source of his romantic worries seemed fortuitous.

Chocolate! thought the part of him that was not man, and, *Get a scratch behind the ear!*

Heedless of whose land he ran on, he galloped eagerly toward the smell.

He found it just in time to see the car roar around the bend.

It was a big, black Mercedes, running fast without its lights, nearly invisible on the mountain road. If that weren't alarming enough, its wheels suddenly swerved toward Mariann. An instant of denial paralyzed him in his tracks. Why was the driver going so fast? Surely whoever it was had to see her! But the bike fender twanged as it was clipped. Mariann went flying into the trees, farther than he would have thought she could, too shocked to cry out.

His world dimmed sickeningly at the sound of her skull hitting a rock, knowing at once that it wasn't a mild injury. Back on the road, brakes whined to a stop.

No, he thought. *No, no, no.*

A car door opened. A woman's heels clacked hurriedly.

"Jesus," muttered Emile. "She isn't calling 911. She's rummaging through the bike."

The words meant nothing. Though Bastien had no memory of changing, he knelt in human form beside Mariann. He was lucky he was in the habit of using his glamour. Otherwise, he would have lit up the road. Mariann lay sprawled and awkward behind a screen of weeds, a broken marionette smeared with blood and dirt. This couldn't be happening, not when he'd finally found her.

"Yes!" hissed a voice that seemed familiar. A car door slammed. Tires spun. The Mercedes scattered gravel as it left.

Bastien tried to breathe.

"She's gone," Emile said, appearing beside him. "She took Mariann's book. Is Mariann still alive?"

Her pulse beat so feebly in her throat that even with his *upyr* senses, Emile had to ask.

"Yes." Bastien's voice was a croak. He didn't dare touch her pallid cheek. "Barely."

Emile sank to his knees and gripped Bastien's shoulder. "Do it," he said. "Change her. If you wait any longer, there won't be time."

"I can't." Cold tears trickled down his face. "She's unconscious. She can't say yes or no. The *Upyr* Code—"

"Fuck the Code. In all the time I've known you, she's the only woman you've ever loved. If she wants a choice, she can have it after you save her."

Bastien lifted her limp, curled hand as if it were glass. For once, her skin was chillier than his. She did not move as he pressed her fingers to his heart. "I've never transformed a mortal. I've only watched others do it. If my power isn't up to it—"

"Your power is fine. All you need is the will."

Emile coaxed the hand that cradled Mariann's up to Bastien's mouth. Cold though it was, the scent of her flesh made him tense with longing. "Drink, Bastien. Just a little. It will make changing her easier."

This, too, was forbidden to Bastien's kind: to feed from humans when they had no chance to resist. He discovered he did not care. Whatever happened, he would carry a part of her within his being.

He moaned in anguish as his fangs slid free, praying to he knew not what. Let her live, he thought. *Let her live.* Within his gentle hold, her wrist bone was as delicate as a bird's. He pierced the vein and took a single swallow. She tasted of joy and sorrow, sweet beyond his wildest dreams. Despite everything, there was pleasure in the act of feeding, a quickening of sense and flesh. He had to force himself to release her. Her strength was too slight to risk taking more.

Emile's eyes glowed in sympathy. "She is inside you," he said huskily. "Use the bond of blood to make that of flesh."

Bastien thought her eyelids fluttered, but could not say for sure. Death was close to her, that he knew, like smoke clinging to his tongue.

He had no more hesitation, only the certainty one feels in dreams. With a slow exhalation, he let his physical form dissolve into light, the way all *upyr* did before turning wolf. Then, rather than reach for his beast, he sent his spirit flowing into Mariann, into the spaces between the molecules that made her up. By uniting their energies, he would leave behind the essence that made him immortal—like a yeast, Mariann would have said, that causes a bread to rise. The melding was unexpectedly sensual, a penetration beyond what solid bodies could achieve.

He expected to see visions of angels or stars such as other *upyr* had reported—though no one knew if these images were real. Whether they were or not, no visions came to Bastien. What he registered most was her: her broken body, her struggling mind blurring with his strong one. The ground was hard beneath them, the leaves a thin, damp mat. Without his presence she would not have felt anything at all. He had to fight not to lose himself in the link.

I love you, he thought at her with all his might. *Let me heal you. Let me bring you back.*

Gramps? said the tiny spark of her consciousness.

I love you, he said again, uncertain how to respond. If her grandfather could call her back, that's who he'd be.

She made a sound no mortal could have heard, a broken whimper that felt as if it issued from his own throat. Her pain ripped at his heart. Bonded with her as he was, he could not doubt she was his mate, the woman who could be his queen. Every instinct he had screamed out that truth. He couldn't lose her. He'd rather follow her into the dark. Had he been certain they'd be together . . . but he was not. Death, and the rules by which it worked, was as much a mystery to him as to anyone.

His words came from the deepest recess of his soul.

I've been waiting for you, he pleaded. *Don't you want to stay with me?*

SOMEONE held Mariann, someone with a strong, warm chest and a deep, male voice. Another man was answering, a gentle murmur above her head. Pine needles muffled the tread of their feet. She was being carried through the woods. A fired burned in her ribs and along one arm, her bones crackling oddly like Rice Krispies in milk.

They're broken, she thought, the pain as distant as a dream.

She didn't have the energy to open her eyes. She tried to

remember if she had rescued her grandfather's book, if she'd gotten to the bakery on time.

In the jumble that was her mind, she kept seeing a running wolf. The funny thing was, as soon as she thought it, she knew who her rescuer was. She couldn't understand why that felt so right.

"You're fine," said Bastien Luce, pressing his lips to her hair. "Even now your injuries heal."

Her temple rested on his shoulder, barely jogged by his tireless steps. When she listened for his heart it beat very slowly, though his body had none of the coolness it had shown before. Maybe he was a yogi to control such things. Maybe he slept on a bed of nails. She smiled at the silly thought. The way he carried her made her feel as safe as a child.

"Always," he said. "You'll always be safe with me."

She knew she was dreaming then. No one could be safe always.

WHEN she woke, Mariann could not for the life of her think where she was. She felt really good—which didn't seem right—as if she'd been to an expensive spa. Wherever she was, the room she'd slept in was completely dark, and the bed definitely wasn't hers. The sheets were silk: impractical, heavy silk, their weight like sun-warmed water on her naked skin. Aroused by their slippery clasp, she had a powerful urge to pull them closer and roll around.

Instead, she forced herself to be still, her nipples sharp, her belly and knees tingling with unusual sensitivity. As she lay there, listening, she couldn't shake the sensation of being watched.

This, strangely enough, was the most erotic awareness of all.

The rasp and flare of a match confirmed her suspicion. Bastien Luce stood by what turned out to be a low platform bed, as gloriously naked as any daydream she'd ever had. One shade paler than his sheets, his skin was a pure, rich ivory, his eyes like jewels cut out from a Caribbean sea. His long, glossy hair shone black with garnet undertones, a cape around his broad shoulders. She felt ashamed for calling him pretty. In this light, on this night, he was heartbreakingly beautiful.

As if his appearance—and never mind his presence— were natural, he touched the match to a beeswax candle, which he set into a sconce that curled from the wall.

Despite her curiosity at her surroundings, her gaze couldn't stray long from him.

She noticed her eyes weren't working the way they should. Colors danced around him sheer as veils, the likes of which she hadn't seen since one of her more adventurous boyfriends had convinced her to try a funny mushroom. She felt a bit like she had then, just a heck of a lot less queasy and a hell of a lot more turned on.

"Don't be afraid," he said. "You're perfectly safe where you are."

Maybe she should have been afraid. Maybe she would be once whatever this was wore off. For the moment, she could only feel ebullient. She looked at his shapely arms and hands, at the cloud of hair on his chest and the mouthwatering six-pack to which it led. His navel caught a pool of shadow that made her throat too tight to speak. Whatever mickey Bastien had slipped her, he had gotten his money's worth. As her gaze trailed irresistibly down the furry line to his sex, she imagined she could actually see his veins expand. When he noticed her attention, she definitely saw him swell and lift.

And lift and lift, she thought, her teeth catching her lip until it bled.

The wound inspired a breathless laugh from him.

"Ah," he said, "I see you are experiencing some side effects of the change." He swung one knee onto the silk-sheeted bed, his erection bobbing at the move. Its head was shiny and taut. Obscuring her fascinated view, he propped one arm beside her and bent to drag his tongue across her bleeding lip. The action made her shiver violently. "Perhaps I could help you get through them."

She had no idea what he meant, nor did she care. She grabbed the arm on which he was braced, yanking it toward her as she rolled his torso under hers. She wanted to crow as she straddled him. For a man of his size, he'd proved surprisingly easy to pin.

Happily, his arousal didn't fade at all. His penis thrust straight as an arrow up from his groin, hard enough that it didn't lay on his belly but hung an inch above, vibrating like a tuning fork. Mariann wanted to taste it so badly, her mouth watered.

"I'm going to give you what I owe you," she warned, her voice gone thick with lust. "And after that . . ." Unable to resist, she bent to nip his neck. "After that I'm going to ride you till you hobble like a cowboy at a rodeo."

"Ah," he said even more breathlessly than before, "I guess the answer to that is 'yee-hah.' "

CONSIDERING her fangs were already a trifle sharp, what Mariann proposed to do was on the daring side. Bastien could not have cared less. When her greedy mouth plunged over his aching cock, he simply arched his back and groaned. Her tongue was a touch of heaven on his throbbing shaft.

"God," she said, drawing back from the first tight pull. "You taste like ambrosia."

He probably tasted slightly of blood, that fluid a part of everything they were. Since she immediately sank down again, he decided he should be glad.

She had him trembling at the dozenth stroke, had him grabbing fistfuls of the sheets and holding his breath. She was deep-throating him without an effort, her newly tamed head of curls a silky tease against his abdomen. He could tell she'd been good at this as a human. As an *upyr,* she was sublime. Not satisfied with her amazing oral gymnastics, she cupped his balls, pressing them gently but firmly between his legs. That pressure increased the one inside him until, pushed to the shuddering edge of bliss, he started to relax and let go.

To his dismay, she took this as a signal to call a halt.

He cursed as his glans popped free of her clinging lips.

"I want you to last," she growled, crawling over him on all fours. "I want you to go all night."

He didn't have the breath to tell her he would no matter what she did.

"Wait," he gasped as she poised herself.

Her eyebrows rose until they disappeared behind the tendrils of her hair. "If you're about to say you're 'almost afraid' to make love to me, you're going to be on my sh—, uh, bad-person list."

He laughed at her determination not to curse, running his hands in admiring circles around her hips. She made a beautiful *upyr,* a bit more rounded but just as strong, the white glow of her skin faintly touched by peach. "I know you're eager," he said, "and, believe me, I am grateful. My only request is that you come down slowly for that first thrust."

Her grin was crooked. "Scared I'll hurt you?"

Happiness swelled inside him at her teasing, beyond any emotion he thought he'd know. "I think I'm up for whatever you can dish out. I just want to savor this. No lovers have more than one first time."

Her eyes filled unexpectedly, her pupils shining within their newly crystalline blue. "You know, you're pretty sweet for a weirdo."

"Honey, you haven't begun to taste how sweet I am."

She shivered at the roughness of his voice, her delicate fangs making dents in her lower lip. The evidence of her lust sent his sex surging painfully. He could hardly wait for her to discover the rest of her powers.

Her teeth bit a little deeper as she took him into her palm. The clasp had him quivering exuberantly.

"Can you hang on?" she asked, her forehead pinched with a crease of doubt. "If you need a break—"

He pulled her down and kissed away her breath, careful

to lick the sensitive spots behind each eyetooth. More than a little affected himself, he broke free with a gasp. "No breaks, Mariann. Take me slowly, then ride me hard."

"All right," she said, "since you asked for it."

When she put his tip against her entrance, both of them jerked. She was ready for him, hot and generously wet. His fingers tightened on her hips as he watched her thigh muscles tense. Her eyelids fluttered when she pushed down.

True to her promise, she took him languorously.

"Oh," she said at the reach and stretch of him deep inside. Her head dropped back and rolled. "Oh, boy."

"A little more," he whispered, devastated by her clasp, by the tempting arch of her neck. "Push all the way."

She planted her hands on his shoulders and did as he asked. For just an instant, he had a sense of how he felt to her: her instinctive caution at his male invasion, her more modern shame at her delight. His size seemed too much for her—too thick, too hard—and at the same time just enough. Her eyes went round, her fingers kneading fretfully by his neck.

"Wow," she said. "I think—" She stopped to give her hips a delicious grind. "I think whatever you slipped me made me grow a few extra nerves. I can feel you up to my throat."

He laughed. "I didn't slip you anything but this, love." The upward swivel he used to illustrate made her groan. "What you're feeling is who you are."

Her head was shaking from side to side, her distress obvious to see. Her nipples stood out like pale pink cherries against her breasts. "I've got to take you," she said almost fearfully. "Now. And I've got to take you really hard."

"I wouldn't stop you if I could."

He slid his hands up in encouragement, over her new and slightly lusher curves. The moment he brushed her nipples, she went wild. She didn't even wait for him to pluck them. She bucked on him like the rodeo cowboy she'd threatened to make him earlier: hard, merciless thrusts that had his body screaming with pleasure and his teeth gritting for control.

He clung to that control with all his will. After her talk of needing a break, he was damned if he would come first.

She went over with a muffled scream, her body stiffening with her head thrown back, her nails breaking his skin. Not yet knowing why it excited her, she licked her lips at the scent of blood. "More," she said, her hips going even faster. "I can't—I have to have more."

Snarling with a response he could not control, he rolled her under him and began to pump. He had more strength than her, more speed. He shoved an arm beneath her waist to tilt her for the best angle, the one that let him bury all his length. Thankfully, her hands braced on the wall to help. The arch of her back lifted her breasts. She shuddered when her nipples scraped against his chest hair. His fangs were so sharp he could not have hid them if she chose to look.

"Harder?" he said because he wanted to hear the hunger in her response.

"Yes," she gasped. "Oh, yes."

Their madness could not have been more in tune. She came again and it made him crazy, the shudder of her belly, the way she moaned and pulled him in for more. He'd never felt anything like this, not even with his own kind. His body ruled him. He literally could not have stopped what he was doing. He couldn't bring himself to want to. This leap into the void was pure, carnal joy, especially knowing she needed it as much as he did. Her heels dug into the mattress, one hand clamping on to his buttock for leverage. He grabbed the bedframe and prayed it wouldn't break. He was slamming into her with all his strength, his orgasm swelling with tsunami force.

"Feed," he said, the order harsh. "Sink your teeth in my neck and drink."

He had so little control he'd thralled her without meaning to, and she was still young enough to go under. Her head snapped up and her fangs broke through his *upyr* skin. Fire burst in his body, a long, hard groan burning his throat. He hung on the edge of jubilation.

"Drink," he rasped and she did.

He came like the world was ending, one cock-wrenching spasm after another as she took his lifeblood into her veins. His pleasure was a spur to hers. He felt her quiver and heard her moan. The grip of her luscious, climaxing flesh returned him to full erection before he could fade.

Upyr weren't known for being swiftly sated, but this surprised even him.

Her mouth fell away as she collapsed beneath him, her lips reddened by his blood. She licked them and blinked in wonderment, the blue of her eyes turned to flame.

"What," she said, "did we just do?"

He kissed her before her wonder could turn to fear, discovering he couldn't quite stop thrusting. Slower was the best he could manage, and hopefully with more finesse. When her arms came hesitantly around his back, he moved his kiss to her neck. His beast panted in approval. This was what he needed: to put his mark on her, to drink in her vibrancy.

She turned her head to give him access, wanting his bite even if she didn't realize what that meant. He dragged his tongue along her tendon, tracing a delicate line of blue. Her calves tightened invitingly behind his hips.

"Ooh," she said, unable to put into words how nice what he was doing felt.

"You promised I'd hobble," he murmured against her pulse. "Why don't we see how long that will take?"

He sucked her skin, hard, lingering over the anticipation. She was his now, after all the centuries of loneliness. A heartbeat longer was all he could bear. With a groan of triumph, he claimed his prize. To his relief, her sigh at his bite was long, her fingers twining in his hair. As he fed, he tasted a hint of himself. Most of all, though, and most arousing, he tasted her surrender.

Chapter 5

THE outraged female shriek dragged Bastien from his rest. It came from his simply appointed bathroom, a match for his spare, Japanese-style room. Bastien enjoyed the massaging shower jets, but didn't have much use for plumbing aside from that. Whatever he consumed, in either of his forms, his body converted to energy.

Thinking Mariann must have seen her reflection in his full-length mirror—a myth he enjoyed debunking—he rubbed his face and sat up. His room was shaped like a dome, with recessed golden lighting that mimicked the rays of the sun. Thus lit, Mariann looked quite fetching when she stomped back in.

"Eight pounds," she huffed, fists planted firmly on her naked waist. "How can a person gain eight pounds overnight?"

He'd forgotten about the digital scale, acquired for an experiment to see if he could gain weight. He couldn't, as it turned out, but he'd thought the device so clever he'd kept it around. Both he and Emile loved technology.

"Surely you don't think you're fat," he said reasonably.

"That's not the point. I never gain weight. Never. It drives everyone who knows me mad."

"I expect they'd be interested to hear you enjoy it."

"Well, of course I enjoy it. I'm a woman!"

He could see this discussion was veering off track. He patted the futon beside his hip. "We should talk. Come sit down."

"I don't think it's nice of you to hide your toilet," she added as she complied. "Plus, I couldn't find a comb or brush. My hair came out all funny this morning. I look like a poodle."

He pulled her hand from where it was tugging her glossy curls, which were transformed just like the rest of her. When humans changed, they became the ideal expression of their genetics. Height, weight, even age shifted to conform to rules for beauty that transcended culture and time. That being the case, it amazed him that she could complain. Women were stranger creatures than he had guessed.

"You look wonderful," he said, kissing her knuckles. "Absolutely flawless. And you obviously needed those extra pounds or you wouldn't have them. I promise you, though, you'll never have to worry about gaining another."

She stared at him. "No man can promise a woman that. What if my metabolism is getting slower? This could be the start of my downhill slide. Pretty soon I'll be as roly-poly as people expect."

He didn't know whether to sigh or laugh. Of a certainty, the next few minutes were going to be more difficult than he thought. He put his hand on her perfectly rounded thigh. "Mariann, what do you remember about last night . . . before we burned up the sheets?"

"I remember you must have slipped something into my drink."

"You remember drinking?"

"No, but—" A strange expression crossed her face, her brain trying to remind her of the seemingly impossible. Grimacing, she pushed the prodding away. "It has to be that. I never act the way I did with you—not that it wasn't fun."

Her faint peach blush charmed him to his toes. He patted her leg in thanks. "I appreciate the compliment. Now think back, don't you remember riding your bike home from O'Faolain's? Don't you remember being struck by a car?"

"Of course I don't. I . . . oh, my God. Arabella. She ran me down." Her mouth dropped open and her hands went to her breast. "Please tell me she didn't get my grandfather's book. Damn it. I'm going to wring her stupid, lying neck!"

"Mariann! There's a bit more going on here than your vendetta against your ex-partner. The injuries you took were fatal. If I hadn't changed you, you would be dead."

"Don't be ridiculous. If I'd been that badly injured, I'd be in a hospital."

Even when he explained, she fought belief. He had to take her through the proof step-by-step: how she felt, how she looked, how thoroughly she had enjoyed biting his neck. Judging it too much to absorb, he refrained from telling her about his wolf. The omission didn't seem to help. Finally, he pricked his forefinger and waved it beneath her nose.

She shrieked as her fangs shot out.

"I can't be a vampire," she wailed behind her hand. "Who's going to feed my cat?"

He would have laughed except she began to weep. Feeling helpless, he pulled her against him and rubbed her back.

"How can I run O'Faolain's?" she sobbed, her tears running down his chest. "You can't be a pastry chef if you can't eat. That bakery is my life!"

"You'll have a new life, I promise. You can't begin to imagine how much fun you'll have. Please stop crying, love. I don't think I can bear it."

"You don't understand."

"Tell me then," he said.

She sat back and frowned at him, clearly deciding how to explain. "When I was eight," she said, her palms rubbing at her knees, "I baked my first dessert for my parents. It was a caramel apple tarte tatin—a fancy apple pie, I guess you'd say, though the presentation was tricky. I practiced for weeks with my grandfather. I was convinced it had to be perfect.

Only then would my parents understand why I had to spend summers in Maple Notch. Only then would they realize there wasn't any point in sending me to camp. I didn't *want* to be like other kids."

"And was it perfect?"

"It seemed that way to me. Slid right out of the mold with every apple slice standing straight. I can remember my mother's reaction like it was yesterday. 'Why, that's pretty enough for a restaurant,' she said like I'd performed a miracle. My dad—who was a big, tough factory foreman—took a bite, set down his fork and teared up. He said he was honored I would bake for him.

"That's when I understood about cooking coming out of love. My parents and I were very different people. My mom thought baking was something you did with a mix, and only because you *had* to. When I made that dessert for them, that was the first time I could share my heart."

By now, the evidence of her tears was gone. Unfortunately, forgiveness had not replaced them.

"You did this," she said, in a frighteningly level tone. "Without my permission. Knowing full well I'd be forced to give up everything I care about."

He didn't want to feel defensive, didn't want to acknowledge she might be right. Instead, he folded his arms across his chest. "Call me crazy, Mariann, but I thought you cared about your life."

"You had a thing for me. You said it yourself. You'd been thinking about kissing me since we met. You . . . you . . ."

"Changed you?"

"You changed me because you wanted me to be your sex slave!"

She bit her lip as if this sounded silly even to her. Bastien might not have handled this situation as well as he could, but he knew enough not to laugh.

"You aren't my sex slave," he said. "What happened last night happened because you are *upyr.* All your appetites will be stronger. You'll control them better as you go along." He laid what he hoped was a calming hand on her upper arm.

"Until that happens, I assure you, I'd be happy to help you out."

Unamused, she swatted away his touch.

"I'm going home," she said, rising to gather her discarded clothes. "I need to think."

A panic he tried to subdue welled in his throat. "You'll have to return by sunrise. We're twenty meters underground here. Your house isn't shielded. It will be years before you can risk more than a few minutes out."

She stopped with her T-shirt half pulled down. In her expression, he could see the truth hitting her again. "Will sunlight kill me?" she asked. "Is that part of the stories true?"

He turned away to hide the agitation her question stirred. When Emile spoke of giving Mariann a choice after Bastien changed her, he hadn't thought she'd truly want one. He'd thought he could make her happy. He'd thought she would fall in love. He saw now how naive he'd been.

Pressing his fist to his breastbone, he released a breath. "Yes," he said as steadily as he could. "Emile and I have some resistance, but young as you are, you could burn completely within ten minutes. Immolation is painful, to say the least, but if you were determined, you could succeed."

She said nothing, as if the answer sobered the last of her rage. After a pause, he heard her pulling on her pants. The sound of her zipper preceded her voice.

"Is it nighttime now?"

"Yes," he said. "You slept through the day. When the morning gets close again, you'll feel sleepy. You'll have more than enough warning."

"Even if I can't see the sun?"

"Even then."

He didn't know the words to stop her, and wasn't sure he ought to say them if he had. Instead, he watched her walk to the door. She paused on the threshold, one pale, perfect hand curled around the frame. Every one of the dings and cuts she'd been so proud of had disappeared.

"I understand why you saved me," she said quietly. "I might not approve of the way you did it, but I understand."

He had no response for that. Grateful though he was, her understanding was a million light-years from what he craved.

MARIANN found her way out of Bastien and Emile's outrageously elegant subterranean residence without consciously knowing how. The bunker was, she gathered, a serious of domes connected by tunnels. The various halls bent like a maze, the dozens of doors suggesting the prospect of future residents.

During the course of his explanations, Bastien had said they "weren't very many." She hadn't had the presence of mind to ask what he meant. Were there hundreds of *upyr* in the world? Thousands? Intuition told her there couldn't be more than thousands or people would have noticed. Not sure she wanted to dwell on that, she let her body lead her, her nose sensing the dew-soaked night beyond the earth and rock.

The secret door moved at the touch of her hand. She suspected it wouldn't have if Bastien hadn't allowed it.

Once outside, she followed a slightly overgrown walking trail through the woods. Her sensitivity to sound was eerie. Every creak and crackle registered. This was not, however, the only change in her perceptions.

Her brain itself seemed sharper than before.

The accident—if Arabella's actions could be called that—was coming back in vivid detail. Despite the technicolor memory, she was having trouble believing it had occurred.

A vampire. Bastien Luce had made her a vampire.

Upyr, she corrected herself, wishing mere semantics could ease her mind. Though she tried, she could not imagine how she would cope with being one. Every turn of her thoughts brought another obstacle into view.

She reached the back of her house much sooner than she expected, her new and improved legs having eaten up the

distance in record time—yet another trait she'd have to learn
to hide from her friends.

The mere idea overwhelmed her. How on earth was she
going to face people she knew? Her friends weren't stupid.
Linda at the Clip 'n' Curl noticed if Mariann even thought of
cutting her own bangs.

A rising and falling growl of feline discontentment
snapped her gaze to the porch. To say Pirate Vic was bristling was like saying the Sahara was dry. Her poor cat looked
like someone had stuck his tail in a socket. The last time
he'd puffed up like this, he'd been the sorriest abandoned
kitten she'd ever seen, spitting behind her Dumpster at the
bakery.

Obviously horrified by her appearance, he'd backed up
all the way to his kitty door.

With a lump in her throat, she hunkered down before the
steps. "It's me," she cooed. "Mariann. The one who feeds
you kibble when you're worn out from chasing mice."

At her voice, the low yowling stopped. Though his tail
still twitched, his fur went down to half-mast.

"That's right," she said encouragingly, "come sniff my
fingers and see it's me."

After a few false starts, he came, giving her one aggra-
vated nip before butting her knee and breaking into a noisy
purr. She hadn't realized how much he meant to her until she
hefted him in her arms. She refused to acknowledge the fact
that he smelled sort of yummy. Vic was her pet and she'd
protect him no matter what. It wasn't like she'd ever felt the
need to eat everything in sight. Vampire or not, there were
rules.

"You still feel heavy," she said tearfully into his ruff. "I
guess my vampire strength's not all that."

She carried him into the kitchen and fed him with extra
scratches and praise. She left him crunching happily while she
went upstairs. Her bedroom mirror was not full-length, merely
a waist-up square above her chest of drawers. She figured this
would be less intimidating than the tall one in Bastien's bath.

Even so, she gritted her teeth to brace herself once she pulled off her clothes. Her eyes went wide as she took in the view.

She was hot. More than hot. She was curvy, something she'd never been in her life. Stepping back, she turned to the side to check out her breasts and butt. J Lo's rep was safe but, honestly, she was fine! She slid one hand over her stomach, which—to her relief—she didn't have to suck in. She had to admit she didn't hate the hint of voluptuousness. She did notice she wasn't creating a light show the way Bastien had last night, but maybe that was because she was new.

No doubt about it, though: her skin was seriously pale, more cream than white but close enough. Then again, for all she knew she would look snowy to human eyes.

I'm not a human, she thought, her knees giving out so that she had to sit on the bed. I'm not a human and if I were I would be dead.

She pressed her hand over her heart. Despite being upset, it beat slow and steady behind her ribs. Curious, she stretched her legs off the floor. Those were nice legs: hairless legs, so she guessed vampires didn't shave. She supposed she'd figure out the rules for why as she went along.

"You need to do that," she said to herself aloud, then rose to put on a fresh outfit. Her clothes were tighter than she was used to but they looked all right—sexy, if she told the truth.

Arabella would die of envy to see her looking this good.

She wrinkled her nose at the reminder of their enmity. Right now getting back at Arabella didn't seem important, no matter what she'd tried to do. Mariann had a date with her refrigerator. Bastien could drink espresso . . . and wine, as she recalled. Before she gave up her old life she was going to see just how much of it was ruined.

As Gramps liked to say, "If the third time's not the charm, go ahead and try the fourth." That philosophy had made him a patient teacher. She was counting on it to keep her from despair tonight.

*   *   *

THE Night Owl's reception area was Bastien's favorite part of the inn. The first section to be refurbished, it was a cozy Gothic hall with star-shaped ribbing on the ceiling and a carved oak desk like something out of a rectory. Though it was a romanticized Victorian version of the Middle Ages, Bastien took no offense at inaccuracies. For him, the style was a bridge between the modern day and his birth, a place he could feel at home but not out of step.

Behind the desk, fifteen cubbyholes waited for messages; before it, a Persian rug would welcome weary feet. Bastien didn't mind that he would never gaze out the mullioned windows during the day, or that he would have to turn much of the business's running over to others.

He had conceived this, had made this bed and breakfast a place where humans could step out of the humdrum and into another time. If it never made a penny, he'd still be proud of the accomplishment. To his mind, its greatest value was not as a potential profit center, but as a window on the mortal world. Humans and *upyr* shared the planet. In order for his kind to thrive, more of them needed to understand their fellow travelers. For those *upyr* who agreed with him, his door would remain open.

The ambition of the project occasionally took his breath away—his first taste of running anything in a thousand years. He had enjoyed being in charge more than he should. Whatever denials he'd given Emile, he had been born to rule. He could not doubt it standing in this tiny kingdom that he had made, certainly not with Mariann's accusations ringing in his ears.

You did this. Without my permission. Knowing full well I'd be forced to give up everything I care about.

She'd hit the target truer than she'd known. He'd thought himself beyond such dictatorial behavior, but he'd been wrong.

Regrettably, being born to rule didn't mean being born to rule well.

Impatient with his mood, he dropped into the reception desk's swiveling chair, rolling back and forth on its bronze casters. Despite his regret, he didn't see what else he could have done. Did it make him a horrible person to admit he preferred Mariann's resentment to her demise? That regardless of what she wanted, he'd do everything in his power to keep her alive? He couldn't bring himself to alter his decision, even knowing it might be wrong. In truth, what he wanted more than anything was to grab the scruff of her neck and drag her safely home.

She *was* his pack, he thought stubbornly, just like Emile. Never mind the *Upyr* Council had not approved his elevation to the rank of leader. Never mind he didn't entirely approve of it himself. Nature was nature. If it wasn't a higher law, at the least it was a law that shouldn't be ignored.

He stood abruptly with his resolve, his hands spread across their as-yet-empty reservation book. He would go to her. It was madness to leave her alone in her current disheartened state. Now was the time to press his case. She might have been a vulnerable human before, but tonight she was strong enough to fight.

As far as he was concerned, that was all the fairness she would get.

BASTIEN had never been in her home before, though he'd spent a night or two staring longingly at the windows. Considering his intent, he didn't wait for an invitation to poke his head into her bright kitchen. Its simplicity surprised him. Apart from a serious-looking stove, everything in it could have been found in any aging farmhouse.

He was disconcerted to find her sitting cross-legged on the linoleum with an array of dishes scattered around her. She looked up at his appearance, then shoved back her curls and sighed. Seeing how weary she was threw a wrench in his plans to bully her into his arms. Quite obviously, she wasn't up for that.

He could, however, take comfort in that fact she didn't appear annoyed to see him.

"I thought you might be thirsty," he said, lifting the bottle that swung in his hand.

Mariann eyed it suspiciously. "Wine?"

"Better," he said and popped the cork with his thumb.

The blood was dark as he poured it into a clean jelly glass. He had bought it—like the rest of his stash—from a local blood bank employee, one he'd thralled into believing he had a strange fetish. Bastien didn't bother feeling guilty at taking advantage of this convenience. It wasn't always practical to feed directly from humans. Besides, with what he paid for a single pint, the bank could purchase three more. Blissfully ignorant of these considerations, Mariann accepted his offering. She sniffed the drink, grimaced, then downed it in a single toss. A delicate flush rose to her cheeks.

"Jesus," she said against the back of her wrist. "It's totally disgusting how good that tastes. I think my mouth just had an orgasm."

He smiled, glad she was comfortable enough to speak that way to him. He poured himself a glass, this one decorated with a creature named Porky Pig. That done, he crouched down to refill hers.

"You know," he said, remaining where he was as she took a more moderate sip. "I could tell you which human food is edible. Save you the trouble of trial and error."

"Nah." She shook her head. "I'm kind of enjoying figuring it out for myself. So far I've got watered-down coffee, consommé, pulpless orange juice, and unsweetened Kool-Aid, weirdly enough. Apparently, anything with milk is totally repellent. I haven't figured out chocolate yet, but I'm thinking the pure cocoa liquor without the fat might be doable."

"That could be," he said. "I never met an *upyr* who tried."

"That's because you've never met an *upyr* pastry chef."

Despite her attempt at humor, he heard the fear and bitterness in her tone, the unspoken implication that *former* pastry chef might be a more accurate term. With a gentleness he hoped would convey his sympathy, he drew one knuckle along the side of her down-turned face. Mariann closed her eyes.

"I didn't mention this before," he said, "because it seemed too much to explain right away, but my line of *upyr* are shape-changers. We need to, er, form a connection with a real animal before we can do it, but once you take your wolf soul, you'll be able to eat what you like."

At this her head came up, her wide blue gaze zinging into his. "Take my . . . ? You mean, *you're* the wolf who ate from my hand? I should have guessed. You both have the same green eyes."

Emile would have laughed to know how flattered he was that she noticed.

"That was me," he agreed, trying to hide his pleasure by being businesslike. "So, conceivably, you could cook in your human form, then change into your wolf to taste what you'd done."

"Well, that shouldn't cause any comment!" She laughed but not happily. " 'Could you turn your back for a moment, Heather? My wolf has to see if this batter needs more salt.' "

"I didn't say it was a perfect solution—"

She stopped him by touching his arm. "No," she said softly. "It's a great deal more than I had when I was vomiting ice cream into that sink. Thank you for letting me know."

Her sincerity embarrassed him. His shoulders lifted in a shrug. "We'll probably have to go to Canada to find your familiar. There isn't much open wolf territory in the States."

"That's all right." She ventured an awkward smile. "I hear Canada is nice. And, hey, you already speak French."

"Mariann." He wasn't sure what he meant to say, but found he couldn't go beyond her name. This stilted conversation, while nowhere near as bad as it might have been, was hardly what he'd had in mind.

She must have sensed his frustration. "I'm sorry," she said. "I didn't mean to sound flip. You saved my life. I should be grateful."

"No." He dropped from his crouch onto his knees, wanting with all his heart to touch her again. "I'm the one who's sorry. Not that I saved you, but that I can't give you back what you lost."

"I'm stuck," she said with the sheepish air of someone making a confession.

"Stuck?"

"In the past." She spread her hands to indicate her surroundings, from the dated cabinets to the noisy old Frigidaire. "This is my safety blanket, this house and the bakery. All I ever wanted was to be like my Gramps. Daniel O'Faolain was a great guy, Bastien. The greatest. Give you the shirt off his back and the last brownie on the plate. Listen to you talk till his ears fell off. My parents were good people, but from the time that I could toddle, Gramps was my best friend. Grams used to say we must have been siblings in another life. Every year, I'd cross off the days until I'd come back here. If I lost the bakery . . ."

Fighting tears, she pressed her fist to her teeth. "If I lost the bakery, it'd be like losing him again. Everything I do, he's with me. Everything I know, he taught."

In spite of her best efforts, her tears spilled over and her voice wobbled. Without an instant's hesitation, Bastien pulled her against his chest.

"Crap," she said, "I'm sorry for being so weepy."

"Don't worry about that. *Upyr* shoulders dry very fast."

"So I noticed." Her laugh was muffled in his shirt. "Kind of handy."

He felt such complete devotion as he kissed her hair, he could have wept himself. "You'll find new things to love. I know it doesn't seem that way right now, but you will. And in the meantime, I'll do everything in my power to make sure you keep as much of your old life as you can."

She pushed gently back from him, her eyes glistening like rain-kissed aquamarines. "You're being really good to me," she said as if afraid of making it a question.

"It isn't hard," he assured her, coaxing her back.

He was, after all, only following his heart.

Chapter 6

Mariann let herself rest against him, not crying anymore, but enjoying the way his shoulder seemed specifically formed to cradle her cheek.

Though her nose was sharper than before, he smelled better: not just like a forest, but like a man—a slightly salty, slightly musky scent. Just as nice was the strong but easy circle of his arms. With a soft, satisfied sigh, he tilted his head against her hair. If she'd ever felt this comforted by her ex, she couldn't recall it now.

Though the contentment she felt might be an illusion, she was reluctant to let him go.

"This place is a mess," she said with no particular compunction to clean it up. "If someone came in now, they'd think I'd been attacked by hungry thieves."

"I'll help you straighten it," he said.

She smiled to herself when he didn't move either. Then her gaze fell on the oven clock.

"Shoot," she said, sitting back. "It's four a.m. I should be at the bakery. Heather will think I slipped a gear."

"I can call her like I did last night. Tell her you haven't fully recovered from your accident."

"I can't do that. Heather's never done all the baking by— Oh, no." She hit the center of her forehead. "Last night. I slept through my shift."

"I'm sure she managed," Bastien said, but she was already stuffing trash into a Hefty bag. "At least let me go with you. You'll need my help to look human."

"Damn it," she said, annoyed afresh by the reminder, then quickly apologized. She wasn't used to depending on other people for things like this, important things, things she couldn't do without. Her nerves didn't settle until they were walking side by side on the road, and his hand reached to clasp hers.

"You can count on me," he said, but that wasn't the problem.

Allowing him to comfort her was way too easy, way too pleasurable. Power flowed across the link between their fingers in smooth, warm waves. She'd felt the tingling before, but her perception of it was stronger. She wondered if he was trying to calm her, if that was among his gifts.

"Just how old are you?" she asked, looking up at his starlit profile. His features could have been cut from marble; they were that motionless and serene. Seeing him this way, she realized how much of his nature he'd hidden up until now.

"I was born around eleven hundred or so," he said. "Anno Domini. I was a forester—a gamekeeper, you'd call it—to a large estate in Burgundy." His mouth twisted wryly within his otherwise unmoving face. "I was not a popular figure, since my job was to prevent the starving rabble from poaching my lord's *lapins,* sometimes by rather Draconian means.

"One day, I caught a wolf who was not a wolf in one of my traps. The jaws of the trap were iron, a weakness of ours, which sapped his *upyr* strength. Unfortunately for me, as soon as I opened it to remove what I thought was a carcass, the wolf sprang up and changed into a man. Because I had more stubbornness than sense, I fought him . . . nearly to my death.

"I suppose my ferocity impressed my opponent. Auriclus decided to change me rather than let me die of my wounds."

"That was his name, Auriclus?"

He shook himself from the past and met her gaze. Watching him, she couldn't tell what he thought of his sire. "Yes. We do not have many elders, but he is one. Only an elder can change a human to what we are."

"So you're an elder."

"Not officially, but yes."

She knew this answer only told part of the story. His fingers were noticeably stiffer within her own. "Could you get into trouble for saving me?"

"That is conceivable, but not likely. Many of the *upyr* on the Council are my friends. I suppose I must pray they trust me to know what I was doing."

A gravity she didn't understand shadowed his words. "Well," she said, hesitant to pry, "I suppose I should be extra grateful you stretched the rules."

He stopped and turned to her, his back to the darkened road, his hand closing tight on hers. The glow she had seen the other night flared in his eyes. "It was my choice to do what I did. I couldn't have let you die. I love you, Mariann. In all my years, I've never felt anything like this."

The passion in his voice struck her speechless. He sounded like a crusader before a war. At that moment, she could imagine him living a millennium ago.

He loves me, she thought, the truth of it sinking home. Her happiness at hearing the declaration, her need to believe it, put a knot of wariness in her neck. Who fell in love like this? And with her?

"That's . . . quite . . . flattering," she said, the words coming out on separate puffs of air. "Considering you've been around since way back when."

She didn't see his expression shift, but between eye blinks it turned sad. His right hand rose to brush a curl the breeze had blown across her cheek. "My words weren't meant to flatter."

"Bastien," she said.

Maybe he sensed she intended to warn him he was going too fast. She wasn't ready to give him the trust a good relationship required. If this was what he expected, he didn't want to hear. He waved toward the intersection that marked the edge of town.

"We should not dally," he said. "Heather will be concerned."

SOME *upyr* were born with a knack for glamour, but Mariann wasn't one of them. Bastien suspected she was going to have to learn the hard way, by experimenting over time. While he could cast the illusion of normalcy over her himself, he had to be touching her to maintain it, a requirement that would make working with her assistant impractical.

"No kidding," Mariann burst out once he'd explained. "Why did you even bother to let me come?"

They stood outside the bakery door, speaking in tones no human could have heard.

"I could thrall her," he said. "That lasts longer than a glamour."

"Thrall her?"

"It's a form of hypnosis, of brainwashing. It changes what people believe, as opposed to just what they see."

Mariann wrinkled her nose.

"It requires that I bite her first," Bastien added, wanting to be clear. "A blood-bond helps cement my power." She opened her mouth, then shut it when he laid a hand along her jaw. "There's something else you should know. Your friend is pregnant. From the looks of her aura, the father is the boy with the tattoo."

"Pregnant." Mariann's voice was so breathy even he had trouble hearing her response. "And you can see that? Wow." She rubbed her arms as if they were cold. "She'll want to have it. She's crazy about Eric, and she loves kids. But she'll need her job more than ever. She has no other experience. If I can't keep the bakery going, I don't know what else she can do."

"Emile and I could hire the boyfriend as our handyman. Make sure he gets a good, steady paycheck."

"That's very kind, but not as good as Heather being able to support herself. Frankly, I can't imagine her swinging a hammer."

Bastien smiled, wondering if she realized how modern such sentiments were to him.

Mariann looked up, her brows drawn together above her nose. "Would biting Heather hurt the baby?"

"Not physically. After a brief period of weakness, being bitten strengthens the human immune system. The baby would benefit as well. Chances are good, though, that the child would be born with a predisposition to my influence. Among our kind, in part because of my age, I'm a skillful shaper of minds. The question is, do you trust me not to abuse my power?"

He shoved his hands in his pockets to keep her from seeing them shake. Though he hadn't tried to read her, her doubts—about him, about men in general—were obvious.

She stared at him, her gaze as sharp as a knife. That was one trait she'd kept from her human days.

"Heather is yours," he said, "just as Emile is mine. I wouldn't do this without your approval."

"Mine to protect, you mean."

"Yes."

She paced away from him and stopped, head bent, arms crossed, the toe of her silly blue sneaker tapping the grass. "You've never thralled me," she said without turning around.

"I wanted to win your love, not compel it."

She sighed and faced him again. "I want that, too. I want Heather to interact with me just as she would have before, even if she sees me as human. I don't want her free will diminished in any way. If you can promise it won't be, my answer is yes."

He released his breath gustily. "I can promise. I'm very, very good at what I do."

She laughed, though he hadn't meant to be funny. "Modest, too."

He discovered her gift then, the particular *upyr* talent that expressed itself most strongly in her. She came to him with a swiftness that was little more than a blur, a movement that to humans would have seemed instantaneous. Putting her hands on his shoulders, she rose on tiptoe to kiss his cheek.

"I trust you to keep your word," she said, "which is more than I'd say about most of the world."

He pulled her to him and held her tight, thinking she'd never know what a gift she'd just given him.

H E had tears in his eyes when he pulled back. Mariann could hardly believe it. Apparently, her approval meant a good deal.

"Do you want to come in with me?" he asked.

She shook her head. "I said I trust you. Plus"—she rubbed one finger across her lips—"I, uh, don't think I'm up for watching you enjoy it. If my experience with a cold glass of the stuff is anything to go by, it's pretty much impossible to take blood without pleasure. But don't worry. I'm not the kind of girlfriend who freaks out over every smile. I'm a mature modern woman. You go do your thing."

Amusement had been playing around his lips. Now it broke into a grin. " 'Girlfriend,' " he repeated. "I can live with that. But don't *you* worry." He leaned close enough to whisper in her ear. "I fully expect, even hope, that you shall come to be possessive."

His shift to teasing rattled her. She could only watch as he stepped jauntily into her bakery. Remaining outside while he went in might have been her most surreal experience yet.

"Mature," she said to the swinging O'Faolain's sign. "I am entirely grown up."

She let five minutes pass, then ten, before her curiosity drove her in. The front room was clean and quiet, the floor recently swept. In spite of being left to her own devices, Heather had managed to stock the displays. Mariann saw an awful lot of cookie bars, but they seemed to have sold well enough.

"Checking up on my goods?" Heather said from the

kitchen door. Mariann wasn't sure what she'd been expecting, but Heather's grin was the same as always: wide and full
of sass. She looked her employer up and down. "You look
good, boss. Playing hooky must agree with you."

"I . . . I didn't—"

Before she could stammer out an explanation, Heather
squeezed her into a hug. Behind the girl's back, Bastien
smiled at her and shrugged. He looked, Mariann thought,
extremely pleased with himself.

"I'm glad you're all right," Heather said. "Not that I be-
grudge you your night of fun. You and Bastien are made for
each other. It's just that working on my own was, like, totally
horrible. I miss it when you don't teach me the baking stuff.
Those jerk-offs at the cooking school were way too stick-up-
the-butt, expecting me to be, like, Ms. Cordon Bleu before I
even got there. You made me believe I could learn."

The compliment affected Mariann more than she expected. Blinking hard, she patted Heather's back. "I won't
leave you alone again," she promised. "At least not for a
while. You don't need to be overstressed."

Heather fell back from her, mouth agape, then turned ac-
cusingly to Bastien. "You told her! It was bad enough that
you guessed. I wanted to break the news myself."

Bastien pressed his hand to his heart. "My heartfelt
apologies, Mistress Heather. How may I make amends?"

"You can't," Heather said. "And don't call me that goofy
name. Man. Old people think they don't have to ask permission for anything."

Ignoring the jibe at Bastien's age—more appropriate than
Heather knew—Mariann assured her she was happy if
Heather was. Heather turned pink and mumbled a response,
something about Eric and her not getting married yet, but
being prepared to "act like a team." Whatever Bastien had
done to impose his thrall, he hadn't changed the real her.

"I'm proud of you, kiddo," Mariann said, "keeping this
place together by yourself. A lot of employees would have
thrown in the towel. That tells me you and Eric should do
fine. Why don't we—" She paused to take a breath. "Why

don't we go back in the kitchen and I'll show how to make my grandfather's famous Vermont Mountain Fudge Cake."

"Really?" Heather cocked her head. "Your Gramps's recipe? Like, can I copy it down and all?"

"You bet," she said, feeling strangely light. "You're part of my team, too. It's time I treated you that way."

"Wow," said Heather. "Cool."

"SHE thinks I'm a good teacher," Mariann said, still hugging the memory to her. "And she didn't seem to find it odd that I made her do all the tasting. I know it's early yet, but maybe this will work out."

Bastien squeezed her hand, then let it swing between their hips. He didn't have to say a word. She knew he guessed how sweet her optimism felt, as sweet as knowing their thoughts were in harmony. Every time their fingers twined, the contact felt more natural—until she gave up on trying to fight her pleasure. Now they were climbing the grand main staircase at the inn, following the curve of mahogany risers to the second floor. The Night Owl was dark, but Mariann could see everything perfectly, down to the muted greens and browns of the wallpaper.

She had to admit she liked her new hypersenses. Her nose had told her the state of her cooking almost as well as Heather's tastebuds.

At the top, they stopped to admire the black-and-white diamond patterns in the marble floor below. Apart from a few empty spots in the decor, the renovations looked done. Seeming nervous, Bastien released her hand. Mariann pretended she didn't mind.

"So," he said, "how does the place strike you?"

"Quiet. Plush. Even though a lot of this stuff is new, it looks like the real McCoy. I feel like I'm time traveling."

"Good," he said. "That's what I wanted."

"Figure you'd get the humans to meet you halfway?"

"Perhaps. Of course, halfway for me would be more like the Renaissance."

"I'm afraid I never was much for counting if it didn't involve spoons and cups."

"Ah," he said, a sound that came out as awkward as it was pleased. She suspected he was leery of putting a foot wrong. Their new rapport must have seemed as delicate to him as it did to her.

"Bastien," she said, hoping to make him relax. "Why do you want an inn? It seems a peculiar business for a . . . an *upyr* to have."

"Do you want the easy answer or the hard?"

"Both."

She turned to him, resting her side on the banister. He was gripping the rail with both hands. A human's knuckles would have been white. "The easy answer is that I wanted a window on the human world, a place where my friends and I could learn to pass unnoticed among mortals. As the years go by, we tend to lose touch with what we used to be."

"And the hard answer?"

He let out a rueful laugh. "The hard answer is that I wanted a little kingdom. I need to rule, Mariann. That drive is as strong in me as the one for survival."

"You say that like it's bad."

He pushed off the banister to scrub his face. "Neither Emile or I like to talk about it, but once upon a time, during a struggle for dominance, our pack leader in France put a curse on Emile that weakened him bit by bit until it threatened to end his life. To die quickly is one thing. To die slowly we find particularly gruesome. For us, pain truly can last an eternity. Hugo chose this form of torture to intimidate me and anyone else he viewed as a rival. Emile and I escaped to Scotland, but getting away proved no cure.

"Because I was desperate, I tried to take over an established pack. I intended to use its members as soldiers to defeat the man who had cursed my friend. I employed magic and force and any trickery I could think of to get my way. In the end, I showed myself no better than my enemy."

"You used magic?" The word had rolled more easily off his tongue. "Isn't being a vampire magic enough?"

"There are spells we can do," he said, his eyes showing his awareness of her discomfort, "to increase our natural powers: our thralls, our glamours, all our inborn abilities. Most are forbidden, but people do break the rules."

"And you used these forbidden spells."

"I would have committed any act short of murder to save Emile." He signed. "I started my own little reign of terror, against people who had done me no wrong. I hope I've changed since then, but I can't say for certain how much."

Mariann pressed her thumbnail against her teeth. "What happened to the *upyr* you hurt?"

"They forgave me, even the man whose pack I tried to steal. They welcomed Emile and me to their home and found a way to heal his injuries. It was a miracle, for both of us, one I doubt I'll ever repay. Unfortunately, the years have made me too powerful to share our new pack leader's territory. Inevitably, we would clash. That is why Ulric banished me to America."

Sorrow roughened his voice, a regret that held the weight of all his years. Whoever this pack leader was, Bastien admired him. She suspected being exiled had cracked his heart.

She was beginning to understand just how big a heart he had.

"I don't know," she said, striving for lightness. "It sounds as if Ulric might have meant you well. Maybe he didn't want to fight you any more than you want to fight him. Maybe he sent you here because he thinks you'd make a good leader. It might have been his version of a friendly kick in the pants."

Bastien wagged his head. "I wish I could believe that."

"Please forgive me if this offends, Bastien, but I haven't met anyone who's terrified of you now. You treat Emile like a valued partner. You thralled Heather, and she's still not afraid to yank your chain. On top of which, there's me. I may be a pipsqueak compared to your pack leader but, trust me, I'm no patsy."

"No, you're not. You're the most wonderful woman I've ever met. I wish—" He stopped himself, his expression turning serious.

"I know what you wish," she said, her voice as soft as she could make it. "And I can hardly express how gratifying I find that. All I can say is, give me a chance to catch up with you. I've only known you liked me for two days."

"Do you think you can catch up?"

For all his beauty, for all his power, he was as bashful as a French schoolboy. Smiling, Mariann laid her hand on his cheek.

"Oh, I'm pretty sure of it," she said, "almost sure enough to promise."

He caught her up and laughed exultantly, swinging her around on the broad landing. Midspin he started to kiss her, adding a light-headedness of another sort. The instant she kissed him back, she was slammed against the wainscoting.

"You'll break something," she protested breathlessly.

His hips undulated between her thighs. Somehow he'd managed to work his hand under her waistband, and was cupping her bottom beneath her pants. The seam wasn't up to the added strain. Stitches tore as she licked him behind the ear.

"Never break things," he gasped when she added the scrape of her teeth. "I'm very careful of my strength. Lord. Help me get you out of these clothes."

Released from his hold, she peeled out of them, then stared pointedly at his crotch. His erection stretched his trousers impressively. He rubbed his palms along either side, the muscle and hair of his forearms exposed by his rolled-up cuffs. She could learn to love this look: half lusty business-man, half sex god.

Not that he needed those business clothes now.

"You, too," she reminded.

"What? Oh. Right."

His zipper whined down and parted, allowing his shaft to bulge from the opening. Before he could release himself completely and charge ahead, she put her hand on the throb-bing arch. "Take everything off, Bastien. Including socks."

"What socks?" he muttered, then wrenched and shoved and hopped on one foot until he was bare.

She had barely drawn breath to comment on his magnificent naked state when she was kissed and lifted, her thighs pressed smoothly to either side of his hips. The tip of his penis nudged her, shifted to find its aim, then pressed thickly inside.

Groaning with gratitude, Bastien ground her against the wall. She had a second to savor the penetration before he began surging in and out. Then she could have groaned herself. The sensitivity she'd thought she must have imagined the other night had her shuddering on the brink by the fourth forceful stroke. Her whole sheath was as responsive as only a tiny part of her had been before. The effect was maddeningly sensual.

It did nothing for her control to think his nerves must be similarly multiplied.

"Don't crack the plaster," she said as her hands clutched his back and neck. To her dismay, half the words were wailed.

"Paper . . . covers it," he huffed, but he cursed and dropped with her to the floor.

There the only danger was carpet burn.

"Wider," he demanded, his hair falling around them, his grip already stretching her thighs.

"Yes." She gulped for air as he slammed in deeper, the head of him pummeling some secret pleasure spot. When her neck arched up uncontrollably, his mouth immediately nuzzled her pulse.

"Should warn you," he said against its frantic drumming. "The first time of the night can be very fast for *upyr.*"

"The first time?" Her heels climbed to midspine.

"Believe me, once is never enough."

The warning was hardly unwelcome, especially when his hand slipped between them to find her clit. She groaned at the help she didn't even need. "How many . . . times . . . do you think you'll want?"

His kiss shut her up, his fangs sliding longer around her tongue. "Can't talk," he said. "Really . . . need to fuck."

He suited his actions to his words, his thrusting growing

more urgent, his breath beginning to break in swallowed grunts. As if his life depended on more access, he grabbed one of her knees and shoved it higher still. Both of them moaned at the new angle. Supernaturally strong or not, she knew mere seconds lay between them and a genuinely explosive climax.

When he screwed his eyes shut and sucked a breath, she had to grab her chance.

"Wait," she said on her very last burst of air.

"Wait?" His disbelieving gaze burned into hers. His movements slowed but did not halt. "Mariann, this is not a good time to be testing me."

She flinched at his intensity, but didn't withdraw her demand. Tom had never let her try new things. If she couldn't claim more freedom as an *upyr*, when would she ever? At her silent insistence, Bastien's hips slowed to a stop.

"Suck my finger," she said, a little breathless for an order.

His brows went up. Then he nipped it instead.

Yelping, she yanked her finger back trickling blood. Her sex contracted hotly at the tiny pain. That was unexpected but interesting. Apparently, she was going to have all sorts of new tastes.

"I can heal it," Bastien suggested hoarsely, unable to resist probing in and out of her flickering sheath. "It wouldn't take but a minute."

Mariann pursed her lips in refusal. "That's very kind of you, I'm sure, but I have other uses for this."

"Other—ah!" He jerked as she found the tiny opening between his buttocks, the instinctive clenching of his cheeks unable to keep her completely out. "Ah, okay. Other uses." He laughed at her when she stopped. "Now, now, don't lose your nerve, love. I think you must have figured out I'm rather hard to shock."

"I don't want to hurt you."

"Can't," he said with a telling squirm. "Not like this."

Still she hesitated.

"Need a road map then? Or do you have a fair idea where you're going?"

"I know," she snapped. "Theoretically."

This made him laugh again, a reaction she silenced by forging determinedly ahead. From the sound of his gasps, he was far from minding. His muscles were trembling.

"You can feel everything, can't you?" she said, her voice dark with lust. "Every inch of you is sensitive."

"Yes . . . oh, God. We're all like this. We love being touched."

His passage was satiny and tight, twitching around her intrusion as if it were hungry for every stroke. The cut on her finger was as good as oil.

"Uh, Mariann . . ." He ground himself deeper into her body. "Would now be the time to mention that the presence of blood makes everything more intense?"

"Sh," she said, hiding a grin. "I'm trying to concentrate."

He was panting for air by the time the pad of her longest finger found the firm, almond-shaped gland. She stroked his prostate very gently, delighted by the way his cock thumped heavily in response.

"Well," she whispered. "Vampire or not, I'm glad to see you've got all your parts."

"Mari–ann." Her name was a groaning plea.

"Do you like it?" she asked more shyly.

Despite his obvious frustration, he smiled beatifically, fangs and all. "I adore it, love. And I'm thinking . . ." He slid slowly out of her and back in, his girth notably increased. "I'm thinking if I like it, maybe you will, too."

She squeaked as he made good on his threat—very good, as it happened, his wriggling finger clearly more experienced than hers. Sensation spread through her like clove-spiced wine. When he withdrew his hardness and thrust again, she thought her spine would melt at all the pleasure bombarding it. It was quite impossible to restrain a moan.

"Tit for tat," he murmured against her neck. "And please do keep rubbing me."

"My toes are going to come," she warned, feeling them curl into the back of his calves.

"Be my guest, because I'm not stopping again."

Despite his threat, he stroked into her with a fond half-smile, balanced on one elbow, not quite pumping but getting there. His gaze held hers captive, his muscles tense beneath their shimmer of faint pink sweat. She licked his shoulder to see how it would taste and nearly climaxed just from that. Sensing her reaction, his pupils expanded over his irises.

When she squeezed herself around his penis, they went startlingly black.

"Bite me," she said, knowing only this could make the act complete.

For a moment, she thought he would tease her for her choice of words. Instead, his face abruptly changed: darkening, tightening, his lips pulling back in a feral snarl. He seemed more inhuman than she'd ever seen him, and she seriously doubted any force on earth could stop him now.

The realization was more thrilling than she would have guessed. She wanted to be claimed, to be ravished in the fullest sense of the word. She threw her head back in invitation. Bastien muttered a curse and struck.

Like white-hot lightning his fangs pierced her skin while his lower body worked furiously. The first suckling pull threw her into bliss. The second had her crying out. He groaned in answer and shoved so deep they both slid along the carpet. He was gone then, over the edge, coming in time with his swallows in bursts so long and hard she could count each one. The knowledge that he was taking his pleasure set her off again. She clung to him as if her orgasm were an ocean she could drown in, the waves rolling over each other in crashing spumes.

When she cried his name, he shuddered and collapsed. Silence reigned for long minutes. His head came up weakly at last.

"Whew," he breathed, sounding amusingly American.

"I'll see your 'whew,' " she said, "and raise you a 'holy cow.' I thought vampires couldn't sweat."

He laughed and rolled her atop him, his hands already sliding into new mischief.

"We can sweat," he said. "We just need a good reason."

Chapter 7

GIVEN their recent sexual olympics, sleeping through dawn was no great surprise. The first dusty rays were creeping across the foyer when Bastien roused. Though he gave it his best attempt, the stupor that came with daylight could not be cursed away.

Fortunately, no windows overlooked the balcony where they lay. Unfortunately, if they didn't leave the Night Owl soon, they'd be forced to spend the day in the basement.

Bastien looked down at Mariann, now metaphorically dead to the world. He doubted she'd enjoy waking up covered in cobwebs . . . or being spotted by a contractor.

His bleary mind saw only one solution. As quickly as he could, he rolled her in an area rug, yanked on his clothes and tossed a blanket over his head. Carrying her fireman style, he ran across the grounds and through the woods to his residence.

This would have gone smoothly except for the fact that, midway through his mad dash, Mariann woke and began to scream. He had to use his mind-voice to keep her from alerting any early dog walkers who might be out.

When he unrolled her at the bottom of the hidden steps, she stumbled like a drunkard. She wagged a finger unsteadily.

"A secret passage," she said, "connecting the inn to here, might not be out of place."

Bastien caught her elbow as she swayed. "Emile and I are still debating that. We're not sure we want to risk the possibility of a human guest accidentally finding the door. A single entrance is easier to guard."

"Fine," she said, bending to collect his blanket. "Let your girlfriend burn up."

Her irritation pleased him. They were squabbling like a real couple. He had to wipe off his smile when she snapped around. This time her accusing finger was completely straight.

"You spoke in my head."

"That I did."

Her eyes narrowed as she tucked the blanket beneath her arms. "Next time you do it, try saying something nicer than 'shut up.' "

"I will, love," he promised. "Any time you like."

He steered her toward the great room, hoping to grab a glass of sustenance before bed. They'd both wake happier if they weren't starved.

"Wait till you see this," he said, looking forward to her response. "I think it will reassure you we aren't stuck in the Victorian age."

Apart from its dome construction, the design of their largest room was classic Frank Lloyd Wright: stone floors, substantial leather furniture, lots of simply finished solid wood. Lush potted palms made up for the lack of windows. Discreetly screened, the refrigerated walk-in could store a year's supply of blood. The true pièce de résistance, however, was the wide screen, wafer-thin plasma TV.

Like their human counterparts, Bastien and Emile had been helpless before its siren call.

From the sound of things, Bastien assumed Emile had forgotten to shut it off.

This turned out not to be the case.

"Perfect timing," Emile exclaimed, surprising them both as they walked in. "I've got something you'll want to watch."

BASTIEN'S friend sprawled in the corner of a cavernous leather sofa, shirtless but clad in his usual faded jeans. In the light from the nearest Tiffany lamp, he looked as fresh as a daisy—not what Mariann expected in a subordinate vampire after sunrise. Seeing him so casual and assured, the thought came to her that he might not be Bastien's junior in power by much. Maybe he deferred to Bastien because he would rather his friend be in charge.

By contrast, Bastien looked slightly haggard as he plopped beside him. "You're sure whatever this is can't wait?"

Emile's grin was devilish. "If you don't watch now, you'll miss it. You see, while you two lovebirds have been shagging each other senseless—congratulations, by the way—yours truly has been a busy boy. *En voilà*." He pushed a button on the remote. "It's time to see my work bear fruit."

The opening credits to *Cooking with Arabella* appeared on the screen: Arabella dazzling her numerous male guests, Arabella making sultry faces while she licked her finger, Arabella wiggling her curvy butt as she served a gooey slice of Vermont Mountain Fudge Cake.

The reminder of her perfidy was more than Mariann could stand.

"Crap," she said and turned to walk out the door.

Emile caught her wrist before she could. "No, no," he said. "Trust me. You're going to enjoy this show. It's very special and very 'live.' "

"What did you do?" Bastien demanded as Mariann allowed herself to be coaxed onto the couch between them. Big as it was, both men contrived to bump her knees.

"Do? Well . . ." Emile laid one finger along his cheek. "I might have paid the divine Arabella a visit after I traced her licence by hacking into the DMV. I might have bitten her and, yes, it's possible that, in passing, I could have mentioned it would be nice if she confessed her thefts and—just in general—told the truth."

"You thralled a human to tell the truth." Bastien's tone was a mix of incredulity and awe.

"Well . . . yes, but I mentioned the part about confessing to stealing recipes first. She didn't know she'd nearly killed you, by the way," he said to Mariann, the twinkle bright in his eyes. "She thought the worst she'd done is knock you out. Eaten up with envy, if you're interested. Evidently, her subconscious considers you to be indestructible."

"Well," Mariann said at this irony, her hand spread across her chest. Because Arabella had been so hell-bent on protecting her lie, Mariann practically was indestructible now.

The commercials over, the show was everything she could have hoped in her wildest dreams of revenge. Not only did Arabella confess to taking credit for Daniel O'Faolain's work, she also felt compelled to share her not very flattering opinions of her producers, her assistant, and her goggle-eyed audience. When she began to describe her fiancé's unfortunate shortcomings in bed, the station developed mysterious technical difficulties and went to black. When it returned, a repeat of *Emeril* was shouting "Bam!"

Emile quickly switched it off.

"Wow," said Mariann, "I almost feel sorry for her. She'll have a heck of a time digging out from this."

"Not to worry," Emile dismissed breezily. "I am not the strongest spinner of thralls. The effect should wear off within a month."

"A month!" Mariann couldn't help it. She covered her mouth and laughed. "Thank you, Emile. That's the second-nicest present I ever got."

"I have your book, too, if you want it." He flashed his teeth at her gasp of delight. "You may kiss me, if you like. Here, on the cheek."

She felt Bastien relax when Emile specified the spot, but a kiss was not enough for her. She hugged his friend as well, with all her rib-cracking *upyr* strength. As she did, a pecu-

liarly vivid image flashed through her mind, of herself handing the recipe journal to Heather. The idea made her happier
than she would have thought.

Maybe it was time to share her legacy.

"Oof," Emile complained laughingly. "And welcome,
sweet Mariann, to Bastien's pack."

"My unofficial pack," Bastien corrected.

"That's what you think, old friend. Ulric—our previous
pack leader—and I had a little talk before we left Scotland.
Then Ulric had a little talk with the Council. You have been
approved to act in your full elder capacity. They sent word
by e-mail last night."

Bastien looked completely stunned. "You did that? For
me?"

"Of course I did. You think I want someone else bossing
me around?"

Bastien rubbed the side of his head. "I'm an elder. Me.
I'm approved to run my own pack."

"You could have run one at any time," Emile pointed out,
"with or without their approval. You only needed to trust
yourself. Then again, maybe you settled that when you decided to change Mariann."

"Surely you didn't tell them I did that."

Emile reassured him with a shake of his head. "I'm not
crazy. Better the Council think they had the power to say
'yea' or 'nay.' You were born today," he added to Mariann,
"in case anybody asks."

"Is it just me," Mariann asked, "or is our pack really
small?"

Bastien laughed and kissed her noisily on the mouth.
"What an ambitious *upyr* you are. Already thinking like my
queen."

"Wait a second," she protested. "I didn't say I wanted to
be anybody's—"

He picked her up and kissed her more soundly. Even with
Emile watching, even with the sun high in the sky, her insides began to melt. By the time he'd released her, her legs
were firmly wrapped around his waist and the blanket had

drooped dangerously. She suspected more than daylight had made her dizzy.

For one thing, his excitement was prodding her pointedly. He hitched her higher to improve the fit.

"I love to work," she warned, gasping just a bit. "My ex didn't like that at all."

"You'll get your work done faster than you ever did," he countered. "And I fully expect to provide you with good incentives for coming home."

The gleam in his eye made the hottest part of her squirm.

"All right," she surrendered. "I'll be your queen, but only if you dig that tunnel and make a room for my cat."

Bastien's grin was as broad as his friend's. "You'll be my queen because you almost love me, because you're nearly positive you will soon."

"You're a bully," she said, but she could see he didn't believe her. His arms tightened teasingly beneath her rump.

"I'm the man who will love you till the end of time."

This was an awful lot to take on faith but, as she laid her cheek in her favorite spot on his shoulder, Mariann thought she might manage.

Seduction's Gift

ANGELA KNIGHT

Chapter 1

WHEN the Jaguar X-Type blew by Grace Morgan going seventy in a forty-five, she stared at its receding taillights in disbelief. He'd crossed a double yellow line to pass her on the two-lane road, a flash of red zipping through the illumination of her headlights.

"Oh, rich boy," Grace purred as she reached down to flick the switches for her patrol car's siren and blue lights, "you have transgressed."

A feral grin twisting her lips, she hit the gas and grabbed her mike to radio Tayanita County Dispatch that she was pulling over a speeder. The Ford Crown Victoria accelerated with a happy roar as it filled with the rapid rise and fall of the siren. Adrenalin surged through Grace's bloodstream at that police version of a battle cry, and her heartbeat began to bound.

What does it say about my love life that the closest I get to sex is pulling over some guy compensating for the size of his penis? She curled her lip.

The two cars shot through the darkness, weeds and trees

blurring to either side. Just as Grace was starting to think he was actively running from her, the Jag's speed dropped in surrender.

If anything, her tension increased as he pulled onto the shoulder. Grace whipped in after him, parking her car behind and slightly to the left of his in a position designed to protect her if he opened fire when she got out. The guy was probably just late for something, but there was always the chance he'd knocked over a convenience store and thought she was trying to bust him for it. Ninety-nine percent of traffic stops were mind-numbingly boring, but that one percent could kill you. Which was why her car's video camera was designed to cut on automatically when she activated its blue lights.

Eyeing the speeder's tail, Grace cut off her siren and picked up her mike. "Tayanita, Bravo 10. I'm out with a red two-door late-model Jaguar, California tag number Kilo November India Golf Hotel Tango 1." KNIGHT1. *Uh huh.* And what was a California rich boy doing all the way out here in the sticks of South Carolina, anyway?

She gathered up her pen, hat and ticket pad while the dispatcher started his computer check to discover whether the car was connected to a crime. Unfortunately, they wouldn't know the results until Grace was already talking to the speeder. At which point, things could get dicey in a hurry.

Senses on high alert, she swung the door open and stepped out onto the blacktop. A night breeze blew into her face, carrying the bark of a distant dog and the scent of roadside honeysuckle. The cruiser's cooling engine ticked. Settling her round-brimmed deputy's hat over her eyes at the regulation angle, Grace started toward the Jag, her gaze focused on the back of the speeder's head. Her hand eased to her holster with the automatic wariness instilled by five years as a cop. Yet despite the danger, some part of her enjoyed the singing rush of risk, the sharp awareness of her own beating heart.

But the speeder made no suspicious moves.

The Jag's powered window slid down with a mechanical

hum. Grace's gaze swept the speeder's lap and the seat beside him. No weapons, nothing suspicious "License and . . ." She lifted her eyes to meet his.

Time seemed to elongate, stretching between one thumping heartbeat and the next. She knew him, knew that elegantly angular face with its wide cheekbones and narrow nose, recognized the temptingly curved lips and the devilish arch of dark brows. Something intensely female heated in Grace's belly as she looked into sherry eyes that knew far too much about her secret dreams. Dreams the big, long-fingered hands resting on the Jag's steering wheel were very capable of fulfilling.

She found herself wondering what so many others had, men with fear, women with anticipation: *Is he here for me?* It was a double-edged question, since he could kill as easily as he could seduce. She'd seen him do it.

"Hello, Grace," he said.

Despite the danger, her inner sixteen-year-old gave a happy squeal. She mentally snarled at it, then stiffened in genuine dismay. *Oh, hell, the camera.* It was rolling quietly away on the patrol car's dashboard, picking up every word they spoke through her shoulder mike. And there was no way to turn it off. "License and registration," Grace said again, keeping her voice cool and crisp. Then she mouthed, *"We're being recorded,"* before continuing aloud, "Do you know how fast you were going, sir?"

His eyes flicked down to the pad. "About seventy, I'd say." His voice sounded like sin and silk sheets, rich and smooth and seductive.

"The speed limit for this section is forty-five," she told him.

He reached for his wallet with the prince-of-darkness grin she remembered so well. "I don't suppose you'd consider letting me off with a warning?"

She gave him her best cold, emotionless stare from beneath the brim of her hat. "No, sir." *I'm not sixteen anymore, damn it.*

His eyes widened in surprise. *Good.* Grace took the ID

from those clever fingers, turned and stalked back to her car
to fill out the ticket.

Settling in the driver's seat, she studied his license in the
dome light's illumination. John Lance, 120 Avalon Way,
Brentwood, California. Our hero was just too cute for words.

And Grandma was getting too damn clever.

Not that Grace had any intention of giving either of them
what they wanted.

*W*HAT *the hell was she playing at?*

The man who called himself John Lance glowered at the
rear of Grace Morgan's Crown Vic. Having presented him
with that $150 ticket, he'd expected her to head for some se-
cluded spot where they could talk. Instead, she'd continued
her patrol, ignoring the headlights in her rearview mirror despite his dogged tailgating.

Why?

She had to know what he was here for, the opportunity he
was offering—a chance other women begged and schemed
and fought for. You just didn't walk away from that kind of
power.

What had happened to the Grace of twelve years ago
who'd thanked him for saving her life with such adoration in
her eyes? There'd been no trace of remembered puppy love
in that cool cop gaze tonight. Or even gratitude.

And now she was ignoring him.

Suddenly aware of his own offended masculine ego, Lance
grinned. *When did I start taking myself so damn seriously?*
Grace was probably doing him a favor by deflating him.

Yet, she had to know the chase wouldn't end until he got
what he'd come for. He didn't quit. Ever. He couldn't afford to, and they both knew it. Sooner or later, she'd have to
give in.

So he stayed on her bumper, silently willing her to pull
over. Grace kept right on going just as stubbornly, never
varying her speed.

Lance found himself beginning to enjoy the pursuit as he imagined her inevitable erotic surrender. It would be well worth waiting for; his experienced eye had detected some very enticing curves inside that stern black uniform. The coltish young girl he'd known had grown into a luscious Amazon.

The sudden rising yelp of her siren jolted him out of his lustful preoccupation. He looked up just in time to see her speed off, blue lights revolving. *Oh, good,* he thought, grinning. *Another chase.* He shot after her like the hungry predator he was.

They'd only gone a block or two when the Crown Vic screeched into the parking lot of a long, low brick building. He followed, one brow lifting as he glanced up at the sign over the entrance. Hot-pink neon formed a curvy female silhouette draped languidly over the word HOTRODZ.

A strip club? This should be good.

Lance parked the Jag and got out as Grace stepped from her patrol car. She didn't even look back at him as she settled her black hat over her blonde head, squared her slim, uniform-clad shoulders, and strode toward the door. He paced after her, eying that businesslike walk.

No doubt about it, his little Grace was all grown up.

She had the most delicious legs, even in polyester uniform pants and black cop shoes. In a miniskirt and red heels, she'd be deadly. She wouldn't even need the big gun holstered at her hip. *Maybe I'll suggest it to the sheriff.* Lance grinned, suspecting bad guys would happily follow those endless legs wherever Grace Morgan led—including jail. His eyes lingered on her tight little behind as she pulled open the door and walked in. Come to think of it, he didn't mind letting her take the lead himself.

A female scream cut the air, wiping the amusement from his face. *Grace!* Heart in his throat, Lance charged inside, ready to kill any man who touched her.

He relaxed only slightly when he saw her, unhurt, pushing her way through a crowd of male backs. He was tall enough to see over them to the other side of the room, where a big, beefy man in a white T-shirt had a cowering, bare-breasted brunette backed against the stage. She must be the one who'd screamed.

Automatically, Lance inhaled, testing the air. It smelled of booze and blood. Never a good combination. Looking closer, he saw that the brunette's lip was split, her chin smeared wet and red. She touched it with shaking fingers. He rolled his shoulders and fought a familiar kick of hunger.

"Leave the chick alone and let her dance!" someone yelled.

"Shut the hell up!" the man snarled, his voice slurred. "She's my woman, I'll do what I want. Give me the fuckin' money, Jen!"

He was evidently referring to the bills tucked in the stripper's G-string. Lance curled a lip, but before he could shove his way through the crowd and teach the bastard how women should be treated, Grace stepped out of the pack. "Police!" she said, her voice cool, controlled. "What's going on here?"

The man whirled on her, his florid face reddening even more. "Back off, bitch, or I'll give you what I gave her!"

"That's Deputy Bitch to you." She bared her teeth in something not even a drunk could mistake for a smile. "And you're under arrest."

"No!" the stripper said. "That's okay, I'll give him the money."

Ignoring her, Grace told the man, "Hands behind your head, sir." Despite her controlled tone, she stood like a du-elist, loose-limbed and watchful. "You're under arrest."

"Fuck you!" the drunk growled. He started toward her, his fist lifted.

Grace stepped to meet him, grabbed his wrist, spun him around, and cranked his arm up behind his back, using the leverage to slam him facedown across the stage. "I said," she gritted, reaching for her handcuffs, "you're under arrest!"

Lance damn near applauded. *That's my girl!* If he hadn't already known what she was, that move would have told him. Folding his arms, he rocked back on his heels to watch. Directly behind him, somebody in the crowd booed. Without looking around, Lance shot an elbow back, hitting something beer-belly soft. The same voice strangled out a gasp of pain.

"Has he ever been charged with criminal domestic violence before?" Grace asked the stripper, not even breathing hard. Her captive was struggling, and she bore down on his pinned arm.

"Yeah, and he don't need to get busted again." The woman took a step back toward one of the tables near the stage, where several empty bottles stood like chess pieces. "You're just gonna make it worse."

Lance's instincts went to high alert. He started forward. "Grace . . ."

"Lady, the way I see it—relax your arm, sir!—his spending the night in jail will save you a night in the emergency room. Sir, if you don't—"

"You're not locking him up, bitch." The woman spun, grabbed a bottle and swung it hard, right at Grace's head.

Faster than even Lance could come to the rescue, Grace released the drunk and pivoted to deflect the bottle with a thrust of her palm. It spun out of the stripper's hand and smashed on the floor in an explosion of jagged glass.

The drunk's swinging fist smacked into Lance's hand on the way to Grace's jaw. An instant later, the bruiser was sprawled across the floor, out cold from a hard, clean punch to his misshapen nose.

Lance turned, but Grace already had the stripper down across the stage, snapping on the cuffs she'd intended for the woman's abuser. Her hat had fallen off, and several blonde strands had escaped that ruthless French braid. Her elegant, delicate profile was tight with anger, blue eyes burning hot. "Lady, you just broke Grace's Eleventh Commandment," she snapped over the woman's sobbing obscenities. " 'Thou Shalt Not Coldcock The Nice Deputy.' That means your first stop is jail. As your second stop, I suggest a therapist for that codependency problem you have with Mr. Wrong." Grace looked around at the crowd. "Hey, somebody get her something to wear."

As she dragged the cursing stripper onto a chair, a redhead dressed in a thin, flowered robe tottered up on six-inch heels, a terrycloth bundle in her arms. "I hope you're still gonna take Darrell to jail, too," the redhead said, shaking out the white robe and settling it around her friend's shoulders. "He's always beatin' up on her. He's such an asshole."

"I noticed. And yeah, he's definitely going to jail." Grace reached for her shoulder mike.

As she radioed for help transporting her prisoners, Lance sauntered over. Scooping her hat off the floor, he presented it with a flourish. "Nice work."

"Thanks." She settled the hat precisely on her head. Her eyes flicking over to the unconscious bruiser, she keyed her mike again. "Oh, and send an ambulance. We've got one Signal Eight." Releasing the button, Grace looked at him. "Which means 'knocked cold.' Very pretty punch, by the way. Looks like you broke his nose."

Lance shrugged. "Judging by the interesting contours, that's been done before."

She smiled, full lips curving. "Probably by half the people who know him. And the other half have thought about it."

"And should have followed through on the impulse." Staring at that soft, unpainted mouth, Lance considered kissing her. He really wanted to find out how she'd taste.

She'd probably slug him.

Might be worth it, though. Grace had been pretty even as a teenager, but as a woman, she was lovely. In contrast to that tough, athlete's body, she had the face of an art deco wood nymph. Her cheekbones were delicately curved rather than sculpted under that creamy, fine-grained skin, and her nose was slim and straight above sweetly seductive lips. Her eyes shone a translucent, crystalline blue that was almost gemlike. Lance wondered how long that honey-blonde hair would be, freed of its vicious braid. He'd love to run his fingers through it and find out.

But he was even more interested in getting that black uniform unbuttoned. Even through its thick fabric, he could tell Grace had very pretty breasts.

"When is your shift over?" Lance cleared his throat, trying to rid his voice of its low growl of need. "I'd like to talk."

"I wouldn't." She lifted her stubborn little chin. "I know what you're going to say, and I'm not interested."

He'd played the game far too long to believe that lie. Lance took a step closer, dipped his head to her ear and purred, "Are you sure?"

Her pulse began to pound beneath the satin skin of her throat. Before he could yield to temptation, she took a step back. "Very. Excuse me, I think the Duke of Budweiser is regaining consciousness." Without another glance at him, she moved away to kneel beside her weakly stirring prisoner.

Lance's narrowed eyes swept from her long, delicate nape to the enticing curve of her ass. He started toward her . . .

"Damn, Xena, who'd you beat up this time?" a deputy demanded, stepping out of the crowd.

Lance stopped short as the cop swaggered toward her. The conversation he had in mind definitely didn't need witnesses. Muscles coiling in frustration, he turned and stalked for the door.

Luckily, there was plenty of time before dawn.

GRACE escorted the now fully dressed stripper out to her patrol car. Rod Smith had parked his vehicle beside hers, its rotating light bar sending blue and white light chasing one another across the surrounding cars. Smith and the rookie he was training sat in the front seat, the drunk in the back. Paramedics must have decided Sir Drinksalot was up to a night in jail after all.

He was lucky. Lance could have shattered his skull.

Mrs. Drinksalot had sunk into a sullen silence. As Grace opened the rear car door and guided her inside, the woman said, "He's just going to beat the hell out of me when he gets out tomorrow." Tears had tracked white paths through the blood drying on her face.

"Probably. Which is why you need to leave his ass. You can stay at the women's shelter until you get a place."

"But I love him!"

Grace rolled her eyes and slammed the car door. People thought love was an excuse for anything.

Staring into violet eyes blazing with jealous rage, she felt long fingernails bite into her jaw. Waves of another woman's madness crashed over her mind. Grace knew her own sanity was about to be seared away.

Then Lance's big hands wrapped around her attacker's head and . . .

She shoved the memory aside.

As Grace stalked around to the driver's door, she heard the rookie say, "Man, she's hot. Is she married?"

"Who, the stripper?" The windows of Smith's patrol car were rolled up, but Grace's inhumanly keen hearing picked up the conversation anyway.

"Nah, the deputy. What's her name?"

"You mean Xena?" Smith snorted. "Hell, boy, you don't want nothing to do with that. She's a ballbuster. Does steroids, the whole bit."

The rookie snorted back. "You're crazy. Testosterone didn't have nothing to do with *that* body."

Grace smiled slightly as she pulled open her door and tossed her hat inside. *Thank you, rookie.*

"Nah, man, I mean it. I've seen her bench-press two-fifty in the department gym. That's got to be twice her body weight. No normal chick could do that. Not one built like her, anyway. I'm thinking maybe she had the surgery."

"Surgery? What surgery?"

"You are such a fuckin' idiot. Like to cut off her dick, genius. Like I think she was a guy."

"You're so full of . . ."

Grace snarled as she slammed her door on the rest of the conversation. "Bet you say that about all the girls who kick your sexist ass, Rod." He'd grabbed her butt once, and she'd bodychecked him into a locker. Maybe she should have reported him instead, but there's nothing cops hate more than a snitch with a badge.

"What?" Mrs. Drinksalot asked from the backseat.

"Nothing." She threw the car into gear with a vicious slap of her palm. "Just a little department in-joke, that's all."

As she turned her head to pull out, she saw the Jag sitting in the parking lot behind her. She could feel the burn of Lance's stare even through its tinted windows. Despite her irritation with her coworkers, something within her melted and ran hot. Grace jerked her eyes away and hit the gas. *You are* not *sixteen anymore.*

But the heat didn't go away.

T HE house stank of mildew and human waste, and a roach crawled past the toe of her shoe. Grace kept her eyes focused politely on the old woman's wrinkled face, illuminated solely by the beam of her flashlight. The power had been cut off.

"All hours, I'm telling you," the woman said, her voice cracking. There was only one tooth visible in her mouth, and it had gone brown from years of dipping snuff. "All hours they're playin' the music and flashin' lights into my house." A sheen of tears rimmed her faded blue eyes. "I can't sleep. All I want to do is sleep."

"Yes, ma'am. Have you got any children? Does anybody come to visit?" Grace headed through a doorway, following the smell of rotted food. Sure enough, the scent trail led to the kitchen. She stepped to a cabinet and opened it, but her flashlight beam illuminated nothing but a dusty stack of cracked dishes and something that scuttled. Grace closed the door and opened the one next to it, shining the flash inside to pick out a sagging bag of rice and a few dented cans. "When was the last time you bought food?"

"Hear that?" The woman's voice rose. "There it is again—that music! All hours, I'm tellin' you!"

Grace glanced back at her sharply. There was no music.

"How long has it been since you had anything to eat, Mrs. Lacey?"

"Sometimes he parks that truck of his right on top of my house. Right on the roof! Races the engine all night long . . ."

Oh, hell, the old woman was delusional. "Mrs. Lacey . . ."

"I deserve better." She straightened her pitifully thin shoulders and lifted her sunken chin. The southern drawl faded as her voice took on a trace of a regal accent, clipped and familiar. "I am the daughter of Lord Galahad. I danced at the vampires' ball. They shouldn't do me this way."

Carefully, fighting the impulse to slam it, Grace closed the cabinet door. "No, ma'am, they shouldn't. And if you'll wait right here, I'm going to do something about it."

"You should have seen me at my debut." Slowly, the frail figure began to sway back and forth. "I wore a beautiful dress. All lace and silver, and I danced . . . oh, how I danced." A tear rolled down her seamed, dirty face, shimmering in the flashlight beam.

"Yes, ma'am." Grace gave her a tight smile. "I'm sure you were lovely. If you'll excuse me, there's somebody I want you to meet." She strode for the front door.

Outside, just as she expected, she saw the Jag parked behind her patrol car. Setting her jaw, she stalked across the weedy front yard Mrs. Lacey was too sick to cut.

The passenger-side window hummed down. She bent and aimed a snarl at Lance's inquiring eyebrow. "Get out of that car and come with me. There's somebody you need to meet."

Grace spun without waiting to see if he'd obey and marched back to the house. His door opened and closed with an expensive thunk. And damn it, every nerve cell in the nape of her neck broadcasted his potent male presence to her brain. *Shake it off, Grace.*

She shoved the warped screen door open and led the way inside.

As he followed her, Grace directed her flash at the ceiling and turned to study Lance in the spill of its beam. His nostrils flared in aristocratic disgust at the smell of age and rot.

"Nice, huh?" she said. "Brings back my childhood." Then she deliberately flicked the beam directly into his face and looked at Mrs. Lacey, who blinked at them both in bewilderment.

The old woman's eyes widened. Grace knew to the second when she recognized him. Astonishment filled the faded eyes, then delight—then a heart-wrenching shame at her surroundings. "Lord Lancelot!" Grace had to grab her arm as she attempted a tottering curtsy. "I didn't know you were comin'!"

"This is Mrs. Ruth Ann Lacey." Grace aimed a tight, polite smile into Lance's startled eyes as she supported the woman's bird-frail body. "She's Galahad's child—and your granddaughter."

To his credit, Lance didn't cavil at what needed to be done. As soon as Grace explained the old woman's circumstances—the lack of food and utilities, her poor physical health—he pulled what looked like a cell phone out of the pocket of his overcoat and pushed a button.

That the device was much more than a phone became instantly obvious when an elegant, well-lit hole opened in the middle of Mrs. Lacey's shabby living room.

Framed within the opening, a slim woman in ice-blue silk looked up from a massive ebony desk and the thick book open on its surface. She frowned, brows pulling low as she pushed the dark hair back from her face. She looked no more than thirty. "Lance, is that you? Where are you, anyway? Who is that woman?"

He placed a big hand on Mrs. Lacey's shoulder. She gazed up at him, trembling, dazzled, tears sliding in a slow, constant stream down her cheeks. "I'm requesting transport for myself and one of my Line to the Elysium Sanctuary."

"What about my granddaughter?" the woman demanded. "Where is she?"

Grace stepped into the phone's pickup range. "Right here, Morgana." She bared her teeth. "And I'm still not interested in anything you have to offer." She turned the snarl on Lancelot. "Either of you."

And if that last sentence was a lie, she intended to make damn sure he never found out differently.

Chapter 2

THE witch wasn't happy about expending so much magic, but she transported Lance, his granddaughter and the Jag to Sanctuary, the elder-care center in Brentwood, California. The High Court had established the sprawling stucco facility for those who were refused the Gift, and it looked more like an upscale hotel than a nursing home. Sanctuary's large nursing staff included one undercover Maja whose healing spells ensured the residents stayed healthy and active until their aging bodies simply gave out. Ruth Ann would finally get the care she needed.

Lance got her settled and filled out all the required paperwork, then notified Galahad of his daughter's arrival, adding a steely suggestion that he pay her a visit. His son agreed, startled that fifty years had passed since he'd sponsored the girl at her failed debut.

No one at the High Court had a particularly good grasp of the passage of time.

Knowing Morgana expected a progress report, Lance drove home to Camelot Courts. In contrast to Sanctuary, the subdivision they all called home was pointedly middle-class, filled with cookie-cutter ranches and split-levels as bland and colorless as only American suburbia could be. Ordinarily, none of the Magekind would have been caught dead in one of those houses, but a more opulent display would have attracted mortal attention nobody wanted. Besides, no one actually lived there anyway. They weren't really homes.

They were doorways.

Lance drove to his own nondescript little bungalow and parked in its enclosed garage, over the spell-generator set in the cement floor he would use to return to South Carolina. Too bad there were no generators in Tayanita County; he'd have to beg the witch's help again to get back home. And owing Morgana for anything was not a good idea.

As it was, he needed a drink before their meeting. Going hungry to any confrontation with the Liege of the Majae's Council was very bad strategy.

The garage doors slid closed behind him as the house sensed his presence and unlocked with a soft click. He stepped inside and walked through the kitchen, ignoring the dishes that had occupied the sink for the past twenty years. Like everything else in the house, they were props, designed to make burglarizing mortals think the residents had just stepped out the door.

Positioning his feet precisely over a pattern of blue tiles inset in the floor, Lance murmured, "Lords' Club." The generator in the floor obediently made the world go white as its magical energies sliced a passage between one universe and the next.

When the light faded, he was surrounded by the expensive leather and antiques of the Lords' Club—and the sustaining energies of the Mageverse. Lance sighed as the tension he always felt on realspace Earth drained away. He often imagined a fish might feel the same, flipping from a bass boat back into the cool, dark waters of a mountain lake.

The club was largely empty tonight except for Reece

Champion and a man Lance had never met, sitting at one of
several circular tables. Arthur stood beside them, in the act
of putting down a bottle and three glasses on the table.

Physically, the former High King hadn't changed at all
from the man who'd won Lance's loyalty sixteen centuries
before. He still had the same stocky, powerful musculature
he'd built trying to beat back the tides of chaos after Rome
abandoned her British subjects. Since Lance's last visit,
he'd shaved his dark beard again, revealing a round, boyish
face with a mouth bracketed in laugh lines. He looked
more like an English country squire than a hero out of
myth, but behind those cheerful brown eyes lay a ruthless,
brilliant mind utterly dedicated to the survival of the human race.

Arthur had been Champion of Britain for sixteen hundred years, working behind the scenes to guide the country
through every major crisis in its long history. He'd used a variety of names, but never his own. Even the mortals who'd
realized he was something more than human had no idea
they were dealing with the legendary King Arthur of
Camelot.

And a vampire.

He looked up. For an instant, the smile he wore cooled
when he saw Lance. After so many centuries, his hostility
had largely lost its ability to wound, but for some reason it
stung tonight. And because the sting made Lance feel obsti-
nate, he sauntered over to join the trio, snagging a wineglass
from off the long mahogany bar as he went.

Meeting Arthur's eyes, he gave his forelock a mocking,
subservient tug like the medieval peasant he'd never been.
"My liege," he said, then smiled at the others. "Reece.
Killed any Redcoats lately?"

The American Champion smiled slightly. "I gave that
up." Rising, he shook Lance's hand with all the warmth
Arthur had withheld.

Reece was a big, brawny, dark-haired man, his face still
subtly battered from some mortal adventure back during the

French and Indian wars. Almost every nation had a vampire Champion like him, working undercover to help guide it through crises and to serve as a voice of sanity. In Reece's case, he'd just returned from a year-long mission in the Mideast hunting terrorists.

Lance didn't envy him. A Champion's role wasn't an easy one, since you often ended up revealing more about your nature than was safe to mortals from your client country's government. Yet you were forbidden to let them discover anything at all about Magekind. It was a tricky path to walk.

Turning, Reece clapped the strange vampire on the shoulder. "Lance, this is Captain Antoine Foster, U.S. Marines. Antoine, Lancelot du Lac."

Foster stood for the handshake. "That's retired Captain," he told Lance dryly.

"Thanks to an Iraqi hand grenade, which he tried to punt when some terrorist rolled it into the room," Champion added, "thereby saving the three men in there with him. One of whom was me. I told the council he'd make a good addition to our ranks." He must have been convincing; the Majae's Council wasn't usually that accommodating.

"When you told me that chick was going to make me a vampire, I thought she was going to bite me," Foster told Reece as they all took their seats. Despite his recent Change, his dark, handsome face showed the mark of suffering, as if he'd been very ill for a long time. Even so, his body was fit and muscular under the khaki pants and black knit shirt he wore. "You didn't tell me she was going to screw my brains out until the power of God slapped me into the middle of next week."

Lance considered the simile. "I think that's the best description of the Change I've ever heard."

Foster shrugged. "That's how it felt. One minute I'm a one-legged gimp bouncing on this blonde for something like the fourth time that night. Then all the sudden I'm at ground zero of a lightning blast that hurt worse than the fucking grenade had. When I finally stop screaming, damned if my leg's not back, just as quick as that Iraqi sumbitch blew it off."

"As your Gift triggered, there was a moment when you became pure magical energy—that was the lightning blast you experienced," Reece explained. "When the magic re-assembled you in your new form, it re-created your leg. Remember, I told you that would happen when I approached you about joining us."

"Well, yeah, but . . . I pictured it regenerating or something." Foster shook his head. "This Gift is the vampire thing, right?"

"More or less."

"Because, you know, I'm definitely a vampire. I was still staring at my new leg when I realized I could hear the blonde's pulse. Next thing I know, I'm biting her and . . ." He grinned, his eyes kindling with the memory. Every other man at the table grinned back, knowing exactly what it had been like. "So after we bounce around again, she opens this hole in the air, and we're here. Wherever the hell 'here' is." He lifted an eyebrow at Reece. "Then she handed me off to you and left without so much as a 'Call me sometime.' I'd be crushed if I didn't have such a healthy ego."

"That's a Maja for you," Lance said dryly.

"No, she said her name was Isolde."

He smiled. "I mean she was a Maja. Plural's Majae."

"Which is what—a code word for drive-by fuck bunny?"

"Drive-by fuck bunny," Arthur drawled, eyeing Lance. "What an apt term for a Council seducer."

Lance barely resisted the urge to flip his liege off.

"I thought you had to be bitten three times or something," Foster continued, glancing at them curiously as if wondering what was behind the byplay. "She never even tried to drink my blood."

Champion was frowning at Arthur. "That's because she isn't a vampire. Remember, I told you ninety percent of all the folklore about us is wrong. Vampires aren't evil, we're not undead, crosses and garlic don't bother us . . ."

"And there are no female vampires," Arthur put in.

"They're all Majaé. You could call them witches, but I wouldn't if I were you."

"Not to their faces, anyway," Champion agreed. "We don't consider 'vampire' a polite term either. It's Magus or Magi."

"I'll keep that in mind." Foster sat back in his chair. "So she put some kind of spell on me?"

"No," Arthur said, sipping from his glass. "She only triggered what was there to begin with. You were a Latent, which means you're one of the very few who carries Merlin's Gift in your genes."

"And Merlin's Gift is . . . ?"

Arthur put his glass down and raked his fingers through his hair in a gesture Lance had seen a thousand times. "About sixteen hundred years ago, Merlin and his partner Nimue came to Earth . . ."

"Wait a minute—are you saying they were *aliens*?"

"Basically. And missionaries of a sort, I suppose. Their people, the Fae, had seen countless intelligent races destroy themselves once they got technologically advanced enough to do it. The Fae got the idea to create a race of Champions for each species who could guide it through its racial adolescence. So Nimue and Merlin tested groups of people all over Earth, and those that passed, got the Gift. A number of people at my court—you'd call it Camelot—"

"You're *that* Arthur? King Arthur?" Then he sighed. "Okay, that was a dumbass question. If there was a Merlin, and I'm talking to guys named Arthur and Lancelot . . ."

Arthur's mouth took on a dry twist. "At any rate, about fifty of us, male and female, were chosen to drink from Merlin's cup. Whatever it was in that cup genetically changed us. From then on, all our descendants carried the Gift gene, but it remained latent unless they were selected to receive the Gift. Meanwhile Merlin and Nimue went on to the next planet, leaving us here with the mission of saving the human race."

"*I* am a descendant of one of the Knights of the Round

Table?" Foster couldn't have looked more stunned if he'd been told his father was the Easter Bunny.

"Bedivere, judging by your scent," Lance told him. "It was a while back. At least four hundred years, since he's been dead that long."

"Shit." Foster sat looking dazed for a long moment before he roused. "So let me get this straight—this gene is activated when a Latent has sex with one of y'all?"

"Yeah, except once won't do it," Reece said. "It takes repeated sex with a Maja—or, if you're female, a Magus. In men, the Gift manifests as vampirism, but in women, it confers the ability to use the energies of the Mageverse to work spells. Vampires can't do that. Our magic operates only within our bodies, like the ability to shape-change and heal damn near any injury. Missing legs, for example."

"Change shape?" Foster sat back in his chair and stared at him. "Into what? Wolves and mist and all that stuff?"

"Wolves, yes. Mist no. The form has to be alive."

"Okay, so what's this Mageverse?" The young vampire rubbed his temples as if developing a headache. "Y'all have more bullshit terminology than the Marines, by the way."

"The Mageverse is a parallel universe existing alongside our own, where the laws of physics allow magic," Reece explained. "This is Mageverse Earth, which occupies the same location in the 'Verse as the realspace version. You can cut between the two with spells . . ."

"Wouldn't it be easier to let Grim explain it?" Lance interrupted. "It makes more sense when you see the illustrations."

Champion sighed and rose from his seat. "Probably. Come on, Antoine, I'll introduce you."

The two men rose from the table, leaving Arthur and Lance behind. The tension immediately escalated, bubbling like heated syrup.

"Making progress with your seduction of Grace Morgan?" Arthur asked at last. His tone was cool.

Lance studied him warily. "Since when are you interested in my assignments for the Majae's Council?" The Majae's

Council decided who received the Gift and who didn't.
Arthur, as Liege of the vampires' Magi's Council, was pri-
marily concerned with the day-to-day operations of the Mission—their efforts to save humankind from itself. Normally,
his only interest in Lance's work for the Majae was making
sure it didn't conflict with Mission assignments. The two
councils voted together on overall policy.

Arthur shrugged. "The Majae are in a tizzy. Apparently
somebody's had a vision, and none of them likes the looks
of it. They're convinced something's coming, something
nasty. And for some reason, they all believe we need Morgana's granddaughter to stop whatever it is."

Lance snorted and poured himself a glass from the bottle.
"Something nasty's always coming. We've been trying to
keep the human race from committing mass suicide for sixteen hundred years, and they're only getting more inventive
at it." He swirled the rich, crimson blood in his glass, savoring the anticipation of his next sip. When he finally lifted the
goblet to his lips, the liquid bit into his tongue, intoxicating
and fiery. He sighed in appreciation. "Nice. Who donated
this?"

Arthur gave him a mocking smile. "You mean you don't
recognize the taste?"

He stiffened. "Contrary to popular belief, I haven't actually fucked every Maja in the Mageverse."

"Just all the ones that matter."

Carefully, Lance put his glass down. "As many times as
we've had this conversation, I'd think you'd have it memo-
rized by now."

"I do. I just haven't started believing it."

"It was once, Arthur. Just once. Sixteen hundred years
ago."

"Which is what makes it so impressive."

"Guinevere didn't give a damn about me, and you know
it. All she wanted was to force you to Truebond with her."
Initially, the High King had refused to enter into one of the
new psychic bonds with his wife, thinking she had enough

power over him as it was. Guinevere seduced Lance in an attempt to force his hand. And Lance, new to his vampire nature, had been unable to resist the woman he'd loved. He'd been so damn naive. "I meant nothing to her then, and I mean nothing to her now . . . Oh, hell, why am I telling you this?" Lance flung up both hands in disgust. "You're the one in the Truebond. You've touched her soul, linked with her mind-to-mind in a union nobody can break. You know exactly what happened between us."

Arthur bared his teeth. "Oh, yes," he said. "Every last second."

"Look, I've begged your forgiveness so many times I've lost count. What the hell more do you want?" He bolted to his feet as his temper snapped. "Do you want to call me out again? Fine, I'll fight this time. I'll even let you kill me. It'd be worth it, just to get you off my ass."

Arthur stared up at him, his face expressionless. "But if I kill you, who'll Gift Grace Morgan?" A small, cold smile twisted his lips. "After all, nobody else makes as good a . . . what was the term? . . . 'Drive-by fuck bunny.' "

Aching to call his Liege out, Lance instead punched his fist up, slapping his biceps with the other hand in an Italian gesture he'd learned years before. Ignoring Arthur's astonishment at being so spectacularly flipped off, he spun on his heel and strode toward the door. On his way out, he passed Reece Champion and Foster, standing before the thick, sentient tome that was Merlin's Grimorie. An image of a man and woman floated over its pages, neither of them looking older than seventeen.

"*That's* Merlin and Nimue?" Foster demanded, staring at the three-dimensional image in shock. "And they were aliens from another planet?"

"From another world in the Mageverse, yes," the book said. "Oh, Lancelot—have you seduced Grace Morgan yet?"

He snarled at it and kept going.

"Hey, isn't he the one who screwed Arthur's wife?" he heard Foster whisper just before he slammed the door.

*   *   *

HE had never cared for Morgana's new chateau. She'd
built it from Mageverse energies four hundred years before,
and he'd never gotten used to it. Her previous home had
been constructed in the style of a Roman villa, its coolly elegant mosaics and frescos a welcome reminder of a time
when they'd all been merely human. This one was filled
with art she'd commissioned during the Italian Renaissance, handwoven rugs and tapestries, and fussy French antiques. Walking through its cavernous rooms, Lance didn't
see a single chair that looked as if it could support his
weight.

Not that he really gave a damn about the decor, given that
every breath he took carried the Maja's intoxicating scent.
Fighting the lust that rose with each inhalation, Lance
silently cursed his unruly cock. Only a fool went to a meeting with Morgana Le Fay with an erection. Like Gwen, she
wouldn't hesitate to lead him around by it. And he'd learned
his lesson on that score.

He wasn't surprised when her most recent scent trail led
down a marble inlaid corridor to her bedroom. She was
probably sprawled across the velvet canopied bed wearing
only her endless hair and a taunting smile. Morgana liked instant results, and she tended to punish and tease when she
didn't get them.

Surprisingly, this time the bedroom was empty. Looking
out through the French doors, Lance saw her standing on the
balcony where the true face of Avalon sprawled on glittering
display. As far as the eye could see, Italian villas stood next
to French chateaus or Spanish castles, all constructed of
pure alien energies that shimmered in the light of the
Mageverse moon. Magekind from all over the planet lived
here, all of them united in one goal: to save mankind from itself. As elected Liege of the Majae's Council, Morgana was
one of the most powerful of them all. And one of the most
capricious.

Taking a deep breath, Lance stepped out to join her. As he'd expected, she was dressed to tease in a long silk nightgown that lay like mist over her impressive curves, its neckline a low-cut frame for her cleavage and long swan's throat. She smelled of sex and blood and that undefinable something that was uniquely Maja. The dark hunger that had been nagging Lance intensified into a feral kind of lust, lengthening his cock and fangs until they ached. Even as his body leaped, it occurred to him that something in his spirit remained curiously uninvolved.

The same something that had responded to Grace with such famished eagerness.

Before Lance could explore that thought, Morgana turned and gave him her best look-but-don't-touch smile, posing against the balcony railing in a way calculated to make her breasts strain to escape that tight bodice. "Why aren't you off seducing my granddaughter?"

"I had to take care of mine," he said, moving to lean against the rail himself in a position he knew emphasized the width of his shoulders. The witch was not the only one who could play the game. "You do realize Grace wants nothing at all to do with the Gift?"

"If she had, I could have sent any Magus with a cock." Morgana being Morgana, her lips lingered on that last word. Her lids lowered over green eyes that seemed to glow like a cat's in the moonlight. "Don't tell me she refused the High Court's prize stallion?"

"I'm also the High Court's prize killer, which might explain her reluctance. Especially since she's seen me in action." He hated to expose the fear that had been nagging at him to a woman who would happily turn it against him, but Morgana was the only one who could give him the answers he needed. "Is Grace afraid of me?"

The witch's cupid's-bow mouth curved in that delighted smile that meant she'd just found a weakness. "You mean for snapping poor, mad Clarice's neck before her impressionable sixteen-year-old eyes?"

"Yes," he said, trying to sound as if the answer didn't matter.

Morgana lifted a creamy shoulder. "No. Grace worships you, my fine stud, though she'd rather eat glass rather than admit it. You killed your lover to save her life. That does tend to impress a girl."

He relaxed fractionally. "Then why . . . ?"

She looked off across the softly glowing landscape. "I denied her mother the Gift, and Grace blames me for her death. Never mind that Jenae was even less suited to becoming a Maja than Clarice."

Lance grimaced. "I can see why she wouldn't be thrilled at the opportunity now." An image flashed through his memory: Grace as a young girl, her face parchment white after her encounter with Clarice's Gift-addled mind. "Particularly since she knows what the Mageverse can do to someone who can't handle it."

"That won't be a problem for Grace. She's got enough strength and self-control not to be overwhelmed. And her potential is breathtaking." Turning that molten smile on him again, Morgana stepped close enough to cup his sex with one small, cool hand. "All you have to do is use your considerable . . . talents until you trigger her Gift."

Lance kept his body relaxed and still, though he ached to snatch her into his arms and sink his fangs into that white throat, grind his erection into her hot, welcoming sex.

That, or retreat to the other end of the balcony.

Since either would demonstrate just how much power she had over him, he stayed where he was and arranged his features into an expression of boredom, keeping his mouth firmly closed. A waste of time, of course, since she probably knew his fangs were lengthening as rapidly as the cock under her palm.

"Mmmm." Morgana's lashes lowered as she squeezed ever so gently. "How long has it been since you've drunk from a Maja's throat, Lord Lancelot?"

Her truth spell shot from those long fingers and sank into his body like a flaming dart. "Twenty-two days," he spat, unable to disobey. Withholding sex was a favored Majae trick that kept the balance of power weighted in their favor.

Red lips pulled into a moue of mock sympathy. "So long? The Craving must be intense." She stepped away from him. Lance knew better than to snatch her back. "Grace should satisfy it nicely."

"Somehow I doubt she's going to be that easy."

"It's up to you to persuade her. Latents are naturally hot-blooded. Once you get her into bed, you can use that luscious cock of yours to make her lose count of the rides you give her. She'll be one of us before she can drag herself away."

"And if her mathematical skills are stronger than you expect?"

Something ugly moved behind Morgana's lovely green eyes. "Don't take no for an answer."

Lance stiffened. "I'm not a rapist."

The seductive mask dropped entirely, revealing the cold determination beneath it. "We need that girl, Lord Lancelot. There's something coming, something evil. If we're going to defeat it, we have to have her." Her lovely eyes turned ugly. "If you fail me, I'll see to it you face the rest of the Table for it."

Lance looked away to hide his instinctive flinch. More than once, the Majae's Council had ordered the twelve remaining Knights of the Round Table—including Lance himself—to mete out justice to errant vampires. Armed with enchanted swords that inflicted wounds even a Magus couldn't heal, they could butcher a man in less time than it took to say the words. Alone, even Lance would have no chance against them.

But one did not show fear to Morgana Le Fay. "The rest of the Table has as little love of rape as I do."

"But my brother has wanted a piece of you for a very long time—particularly your head. And I don't think Arthur would be all that picky about how he got it."

The truth of that statement sent a twist of pain through Lance, but he denied it anyway. "You underestimate him, Morgana."

"Perhaps. And perhaps not." She smiled ever so slightly. "The problem with a Truebond is that it leaves no room for comfortable illusions. And Arthur knows exactly how Guinevere feels about you."

He snorted. "Don't try to play me, Morgana. Gwen's like you—ice and ambition all the way to the core. I was nothing to her except a way to force a Truebond out of Arthur."

"Perhaps." She stepped in close again and directed a feral smile into his eyes. He managed not to back away. "And perhaps Arthur is afraid you could melt sweet Gwen's ice. If you want to keep everyone's comfortable illusions intact, I suggest you get Grace into bed. And keep her there until she receives the Gift, no matter what you have to do."

GRACE pulled up in front of the white two-story Victorian she'd called home for the past five years. The evening air was cool, but she felt hot and sticky after wearing her bulletproof vest all night, and her hips ached from the weight of her equipment belt. All she wanted was to climb into a hot bath and soak for at least an hour.

She realized she wasn't going to get her wish when she pushed open the front door and smelled roasting meat. Something popped. Despite strong suspicions about the identity of her culinary burglar, Grace drew her weapon as she made for the kitchen.

Lance looked up from the glass of champagne he was pouring just as she pointed her Smith & Wesson between his eyes. He wore only a pair of black slacks and a robe loosely belted around his narrow waist. A delicious swath of tanned muscle showed between its velvet lapels.

"Oh, look," she said, managing a snarl despite the mouthwatering view. "There's a half-naked vampire in my house. Maybe I'll shoot him."

He smiled slowly. "I always thought there was something erotic about a woman with a weapon."

"If the rest of that kinky little fantasy deals with a riding crop, I don't want to hear about it." Snorting in disgust, she holstered her gun. She should have known better than to try to bluff Lancelot du Lac. "How's Mrs. Lacey?"

"Clean, fed and settling in nicely." He sauntered around the kitchen island to hand her a glass of the champagne. "I checked on her this evening before I came here. Galahad had dropped by to visit. She was . . . glowing."

"Princely of him." She curled her lip. "Too bad she had to spend all those years in abject poverty before he deigned to give her any attention."

"When you've fathered as many children as we have over sixteen hundred years, it's easy to lose track," he said mildly, picking up his glass.

"You know, a crack dealer told me the exact same thing the other day. Well, except for the 'sixteen hundred years' part." Grace took a sip of her own. She wasn't surprised to discover it was Dom Perignon. The High Court had expensive tastes. "He was very proud of the fact that he bought shoes for all his kids once a year." She let an artistic pause develop. "Come to think of it, I guess that does put him one up on y'all."

"Touché." Some subtle movement made the tie of his belt slip free. His robe fell open, revealing more of that breathtaking chest. The ridges of his pecs and abdomen looked as though God had sculpted them personally. Somewhere inside Grace, the girl who'd adored her handsome savior ached to run her fingers over them.

Damn, Grace thought. *If I had a dollar for every dream I've had that started just like this.* Lord Lancelot, barechested and bent on seduction . . .

Unfortunately, he was more interested in doing Morgana's dirty work than making her teenaged dreams come true. She wrapped her fingers tighter around her glass and took another sip. "Nice six-pack. You'll be very popular in prison. First-degree burglary carries twenty years in this state."

His lids lowered lazily over eyes the color of heated

sherry. "I can hear your testimony now—'Judge, he broke into my house and forcibly cooked filet mignon and artichoke hearts in my kitchen.' The headlines will look a little strange, don't you think?"

"Not as strange as the one after you're caught munching on some greasy fellow convict in the state pen."

He laughed, the sound more wickedly seductive than another man's nudity. "I'd never see the inside of a jail, and you know it. The High Court's lawyers would make O.J.'s dream team look like third-rate public defenders." His eyes glittered as he moved closer, a corner of that elegant mouth kicking up. "But if you'd like to handcuff me anyway, be my guest."

Love to, a hot little voice whispered as Grace's eyes dropped helplessly to that marvelous chest again. A thatch of fine dark hair stretched across it from nipple to nipple before trailing toward his waistband. Her gaze following the tempting path it drew, Grace swallowed. He had an erection. A very, very impressive erection. Thick, hard and promising.

It made her remember just how long it had been since she'd made love. And just how unsatisfying she'd found it. Lance would see to it she was very, very satisfied.

Grace wanted to hit him.

He knew about her ferocious adolescent crush, of course. He'd been kind and pointedly avuncular about it when she'd been sixteen, but she suspected he was trying to take ruthless advantage of that old infatuation now. And she didn't dare let him. The man was a human crack pipe; one kiss, one taste, one ride on that thick cock, and she'd be unable to stop until it was too late. She carried Merlin's Gift in her genes, and allowing Lance to come too many times within her body would trigger it.

Oh, the Gift sounded like a great package to the unwary; immortality, the ability to manipulate Mageverse energies that modern physicists didn't even know existed, not to mention that secret, romantic battle to save mankind from itself. There was the increased stroke risk, too, of course, since a

Maja was genetically programmed to produce more blood than she needed in order to accommodate vampire needs. You had to either donate or allow a Magus to feed from you in order to avoid putting your health at risk. But since Magi liked to feed from their partners during mind-blowing sex, that wasn't exactly a hardship.

Unfortunately, it all came at a very high price Grace had no intention whatsoever of paying. She didn't think her sanity was up to it. And she didn't want to end up like Clarice.

Lance was looming subtly now, looking down into her eyes, surrounding her with muscle and strength and that curious heat Magi always seemed to radiate. His eyes were fixed on her mouth in an unblinking gaze that made her think of wolves and ancient hunger, sensuous and devouring. His lips parted. She saw the tips of his fangs.

Her nipples peaked.

I've got to tell him to get out. Any woman would have had a hard time saying no to Lancelot, but those of the Line were especially vulnerable. There was no way to suppress her body's instinctive response to the exotic Magus pheromones he exuded. She could already feel herself going hot and ready for him.

To make matters worse, Lance wasn't just any Magus—he was a Knight of the Round Table. *The* Knight of the Round Table, Lord Lancelot du Lac, vampire assassin and High Court seducer. The High Council sent Lance out when they wanted a man dead or a woman Gifted. And Grandmother Morgana, one of the leaders of the Council, badly wanted Grace Gifted.

The thought made her spine stiffen. "Get out."

LANCE cursed silently. He could taste Grace's hunger in the air, a hot, subtle musk. Despite her resistance, she was creaming, readying for him. Behind that uniform shirt and thick, businesslike bra, the nipples of her full breasts were erect, begging for his fingers, his mouth, his flicking tongue.

Her pulse throbbed under the thin, fine skin of her long throat, waiting for his fangs. Latent as she was, she would taste as rich and intoxicating as any vampire's dream. The young girl he'd once pitied and befriended had grown into a lush, lovely feast, both for his famished body and for that something within him that was even more endlessly hungry. And he had no intention of being denied.

Oh, he'd never use force, Morgana's blessing notwithstanding—the idea of making Grace a victim was nauseating. Luckily, he wouldn't have to. She had one weakness most Majae did not: she wanted him more than she wanted power. And she'd be even hungrier before he was through.

"You don't want me to go," he said, pitching his voice to the low, velvet register that never failed.

Grace wasn't his usual Latent prey. Her crystalline eyes glittered. "Oh, yes I do. Get out, Lance."

But to his delight, her stomach picked that moment to growl. Ignoring her demand, Lance smiled slowly and eased a little closer, making sure his scent flooded her sensitive nose. "Sounds like your body has other ideas. And I worked so hard to prepare this lovely meal, too." *Of which you are the main course.* "Won't you at least let me watch you enjoy it?"

Grace bared her teeth. "You've obviously mistaken me for somebody polite."

That surprised a laugh out of him. "You do make a point of not playing by the usual rules, don't you?" Taking a chance her desire was stronger than her temper, Lance reached out to caress her jaw. Her skin felt so warm and soft under his fingers, he couldn't wait to bare her breasts. "I wonder—is that because you like it out on the edge?" The velvet rumble was beginning to degenerate into a feral rasp. He stopped and cleared his throat. "Do you find something seductive about taking a chance? Seeing how far you can go before you fall?"

"Sounds like you're speaking from personal experience."

Since she hadn't batted his hand away, Lance slid his fingers around to brush the nape of her neck. "Now that you mention it, I *have* taken that tumble a time or two." Lowering his head, he inhaled, drinking in the sweet scent of her, the spice and musk of a Lineage woman. "And to tell the truth, sometimes I enjoy it." He stepped fully against her, letting her feel the length of his erection against her soft belly. "What do you say, Grace? Want to fall with me?"

Chapter 3

WHY not? the reckless cowgirl inside Grace whispered. Once wouldn't trigger the Gift; she'd have to sleep with him at least three times for that, maybe more. Too, there was something deliciously tempting about the idea of sampling Morgana's forbidden fruit—and walking away before the Gift could kick in. God, that would piss the witch off.

Besides, this was Lancelot, her hero, her handsome girlhood fantasy. To finally touch him after all these years of distant yearning, to run her hands over that powerful body, taste his kiss, ride that thick cock . . .

Later she would realize Lance was too skilled a seducer not to know when his prey was weakening. His dark head dipped and his mouth took hers in a sweet, silken slide.

Before the voice of logic had a chance to even squeak a protest, he'd wrapped her in himself. The feel, the taste, the scent of him burst across her famished senses. The velvet of his robe contrasted with the hard muscle of his chest and the soft thatch of hair that covered it. His tongue slipped between her lips, tasting of champagne and hunger, swirling around her own, tempting her to pursue it back between his teeth. When she did, she touched the exotic length of a tooth. A Magus's fangs, she knew, slid to full extension only when lust rode him hard.

They were fully extended now.

Those big, long-fingered hands moved over her body, pausing here to stroke her thigh, there to squeeze her bottom, here to thumb a nipple to aching erection. Her overwhelmed senses spun, slinging fire through her mind.

Then everything was spinning as he lifted her effortlessly and laid her down on the table. Something poked her in the back, and he swept it out of the way with one hand. It fell to the floor and shattered. She didn't care.

The cool wood of the dining table pressed against her back as those seductive fingers started in on the buttons of her uniform shirt. It occurred to her she should protest, but he was kissing her again—clever man—nipping, suckling her lips as if trying to keep them too busy to say no.

God, he felt so good.

A button went flying. She was too busy trying to drag off his robe to notice, both fists wrapped in the velvet collar, wanting only to see his magnificent body naked for the first time. Frustrated, she panted, "Get this off, dammit!"

Laughing softly, he pulled back just long enough to obey. She sat up to touch him, and he used the opportunity to peel her shirt off, too. Hypnotized by his perfectly defined contours, she ran her fingers over the thick plates of his pecs, the ridges of his ribs and abdominal muscles. His skin felt like hot, rough silk stretched tight over tempered steel. Touching him, running her fingers through the soft ruff of hair covering his chest, she barely noticed as he flicked open the back clasp of her bra.

"God," she murmured. "You're so beautiful." And wondered if she'd sounded like that idiot teenager again.

"No," Lance said, pulling away to gaze hungrily at her naked torso. "*That's* beauty."

He reached for her. His fingers still retained the tan they'd had when he'd been Gifted, and they looked strong and dark cupped around the pale, sleek curve of her breast.

"Perfect," he breathed. His sherry eyes burned with hunger. She could see his fangs peeking beneath his full upper lip as he spoke. His thumb brushed across the sensitive peak of her nipple once, then again. And again. Back and forth, each pass sending luscious little zaps of pleasure through her nervous system. She realized she was panting and tried to stop, until she saw he was breathing hard, too.

"That deputy was an idiot." Both big hands cupped her breasts together. "Concentrating on what you bench-press when he could have been looking at these."

"You heard that?" She caught her breath as he rolled both pink tips between his fingers.

"I'm a Magus. Of course I heard it."

Grace let her head fall back as pleasure steamed through her, all force and hot pressure. "They all know I'm not like other women."

"Well, they're right on that point." Lance lowered his head to her breast. "You're more responsive." His tongue flicked her nipple once. "Sensual." Flick. "Delicious." Flick. "A feast for a poor, famished vampire." His mouth closed fully over her to suckle with such head-spinning strength, she was driven to grind her hips against him in hunger.

He began playing clever games with his fangs—pressing their slick front curves against her nipple until the peak pouted up between them for his swirling tongue, then raking the sharp points across her skin in an almost-bite that made her squirm.

"Damn," she groaned breathlessly when he stopped just long enough to unbutton her pants and jerk off her shoes. "You're good at this."

"So are you," Lance said roughly, and grabbed the waistband of her slacks to drag them ruthlessly down. "You're very, very good." Straightening, he looked down at her as she sprawled there, naked except for her panties. "And you've made me very, very hungry."

Then he wrapped a big hand in that last bit of thin silk and ripped it away.

* * *

BREATHING hard, Lance stared at Grace lying spread and naked across the dinner table like a vampire's fantasy feast. She was hardly the first Latent he'd been sent to seduce, but none of the rest had ever affected him with this much raw power. There was something special about her—the brash honesty, the sensuality, the keen intelligence. And, of course, that long-legged Amazon's body.

Not to mention her utter lack of the calculation and manipulation that seemed bred to the bone in most of the Majae he knew.

He could feel his control fraying with each hungry throb of his cock. His fangs were aching. Even his hands shook with the force of his raw need. If he wasn't careful, he'd plunge right into her without making sure she was ready for him.

To give himself time to recover, he pulled up a chair and seated himself at the table between her widespread thighs like a man settling down to dinner. As she watched, wide-eyed, he took her tight little ass in his hands, dragged her closer to the table edge, and buried his face right between her thighs.

He tried to keep his eyes locked on hers over the arch of her body, but her taste detonated in his senses. His eyes slid closed. Forgetting his usual tricks, he spread her creamy folds with two fingers and feasted, licking, nibbling, wanting only to make her share the lust he felt.

He had to make sure she didn't deny him.

GRACE writhed, fire trails of pleasure streaming through her mind with every pass of Lance's clever tongue. She found herself bending and spreading her legs, opening herself even more to his magical mouth. He took the movement for the wanton invitation it was and slid one big finger into her sex. She swallowed a shivering moan.

He reached the other hand around her thigh and found one of her desperately hard nipples again. Rolled and twisted it even as his tongue swirled wet fire over her clit and that finger rotated deep inside her.

It felt like the top of her head was about to blow off. "Oh, God, Lancelot!" She dropped her thighs, draped them over his broad shoulders and hooked them against his back so she could drag him even harder against her sex. And he gave her exactly what she needed, driving a second finger into her as his mouth closed ruthlessly over her clit. Slowly, he stroked and rotated and sucked and—

Arching her spine off the table, she drowned in fire, screaming her climax at the ceiling.

Grace was still riding the downslope of the peak when she looked up to see him standing between her limp thighs. His impatient hands unzipped his slacks and jerked down his briefs just enough to free his shaft. Her eyes widened at his size. He leaned down to position himself. She felt the thick, rounded head press against her sex. Then, with a deliciously agonizing pressure, he sank slowly inside.

The sensation was unbelievable. Heat. Thickness. Strength. Opening and stretching her. She screamed again, her orgasm clenching tighter, harder. He snatched her off the table with that effortless vampire strength and seated his cock to the balls.

"Now," Lance growled, as she hung stunned and impaled in his arms. "Now I've got you." Sherry eyes locked ferociously on hers, his strong hands gripped her ass, holding her poised as he began to lunge in and out of her like a pirate bent on conquest. "I've got you—" Thrust. "—and you're mine—" *Thrust.* "—and you're not getting away—" THRUST. *"—until I'm satisfied!"*

"Jesus, Lancelot," she whimpered, letting her head fall back. "Who the hell wants to get away?"

He chuckled in her ear, his voice an erotic purr almost as maddening as the deep, silken strokes of his cock. His hand closed around the back of her skull, threading through her hair, holding her neck arched. She felt his lips against her throat. He licked her banging pulse. Grace caught her breath, realizing what was coming.

The tips of his fangs touched her skin. He bit deep.

She screamed in arousal and surrender.

Heat. Pounding pleasure. His cock pistoning away in her cunt, his torso rolling against hers, his arms hard and strong around her. Satin lips, tongue moving on her throat, sucking, drinking greedily. The icy prick of his fangs.

Too much, all too much. She felt her consciousness splinter under hammer blows of fire and pleasure. Convulsing yet again, she cried out, her voice hoarse and helpless.

Lancelot dragged her so tight her ribs creaked. He stiffened and came, buried to the balls, growling against her throat.

W HEN Grace became aware of herself again, she still hung in Lance's arms. Looking around, she realized he was sitting down with her draped across his lap, impaled on his erect cock. Though she was naked, he still wore his slacks; she could feel his open zipper digging into her bottom. She felt so weak and stunned, all she could do was hang there in his embrace.

He nuzzled the underside of her jaw, his tongue tracing leisurely patterns on her skin. Suddenly he bent her back in his arms and buried his face between her breasts, inhaling as he cupped one of them in a big hand. Wallowing in her like a cat in catnip.

Something about that curiously feline gesture reminded Grace of Morgana's warning years ago, when the witch had noticed how infatuated she'd been with him. *"Never forget that no matter how brave and handsome and heroic they are, Magi are not human. They're predators. And we're their favorite prey. They crave us. Our blood, our taste, our scent, our bodies. Ordinary humans are a poor substitute to them."*

If the witch was right, Lance would have wallowed like that in the scent of any Latent female. Had the experience Grace found so profoundly sensual and romantic been, for him, the equivalent of fast food?

Instinctively, she put her feet down and tried to rise off his lap. His grip tightened, holding her in place. "Let me up," Grace said. Her voice emerged as a hoarse croak, a reminder of ecstatic screams.

"Wouldn't you like to . . ." He looked over her breast at her and rolled his hips. She could feel him hardening even more inside her. Magi never needed much recovery time.

"No," Grace said, assuming the tone of cold command she used on drunks and recalcitrant teenagers. "Let me up. You don't get seconds, Lance."

He gave her that seducer's smile again, flicking her nipple with a thumb. "I could change your mind."

Something in that smile brought it all crashing back—the savage pleasure, the dark, uncontrollable hunger she'd felt for him.

Give in, her body whispered.

Oh God. She thought she'd gotten over him, outgrown the infatuation, but she hadn't. "No!" She tried to spring off his lap. His big hands tightened, holding her effortlessly still. She realized that if he didn't want to let her go, she'd never get away. Panic rose. *"No!"*

Instantly he released her. "I'm sorry," he said as she scrambled up, instinctively wrapping her arms around her body. He frowned and stood, zipping his pants. "Did I hurt you?"

Grace looked away, spotted her uniform shirt lying on the floor, and snatched it up. "No. No, you didn't hurt me." *You only gave me the greatest sexual experience of my life. And I'm still in love with you.*

She didn't dare let him know, she thought, frantically buttoning the shirt. He'd gained too much power over her as it was. He'd play on her weakness like the seducer he was until she found herself drowning in the Mageverse.

Mad as Clarice.

"You enjoyed it," Lance said, in a tone somewhere between accusation and demand. Grace looked up from her buttons to find him watching. She stilled her hands, knowing they were shaking.

"Yeah, well, you're good." She glanced around for her underwear, didn't spot them, and grabbed her pants instead, stepping into them quickly. "But I'm sure you know that."

"I may have heard it a time or two," he admitted. Though she didn't look up, she could hear the smile in his voice. "But I like knowing you loved it as much as I did."

"Probably more." She mentally cursed the admission the moment she made it.

Lance moved closer. Grace edged away. He began to stalk her in that long-legged, graceful, pacing-tiger stride. "In that case, why don't we *both* have seconds?"

Her belt buckle rattled nervously as she zipped her pants. "Not without a condom."

"That would rather defeat the purpose."

"That's·the idea."

Instead of answering, Lance reached out and gently slipped the rubber band off the tail of her braid. "Doesn't it make your head hurt, having your hair all wrapped up so tight?" Long fingers ran through her hair, loosening it, gently massaging her scalp.

His touch felt so good she found herself struggling to maintain her resistance. "I don't want the Gift, Lance."

"Why not?" Those fingers stroked and rubbed. "Judging from what I've seen, you'd like saving the world. And being immortal is not exactly a hardship."

"Maybe, but I've also seen the High Court in action. I don't want anything to do with them."

"That's understandable," he said, circling his thumb into a knot of muscle he'd found at the base of her skull. "Sometimes I don't want anything to do with them, either. But we have managed to keep the world from blowing up a time or two. The Cuban Missile Crisis, the time the Chinese were set to nuke the Americans, that incident last year when Al Qaeda got its hands on those vials of Russian smallpox . . ."

Startled, she frowned. "Smallpox? And when were the Chinese going to—?"

"Oh, that sort of thing happens all the time." His matter-of-fact tone made his words all the more chilling. "The human race is by turn stupid, careless, murderous and suicidal, and it takes the High Court all the muscle and skill we can summon to keep it from self-destructing." Gently, he turned her to look up into his eyes. "Morgana says we need you, Grace."

For just a second, she wavered.

Then she remembered a beloved face gone gaunt and skeletal against a mound of pillows. "The way you didn't need my mother?"

He winced. "Majae have a lot of power. We have to be careful about who we give it to. Given what happened with Clarice, I'd think you'd understand that."

"My mother wasn't like Clarice." Pulling away, Grace stalked to the butcher-block island where the dishes he'd prepared stood. "Mom kowtowed to Morgana her entire life, hoping for the Gift. Even married the guy Grandmother picked out, though God knows she didn't love him. Why would she? He was an abusive bastard and a drug addict. Being Latent was the only thing he had going for him."

"Morgana probably thought they'd produce Gift-worthy offspring." She glanced up to see Lance watching her, his sherry eyes warm with sympathy. "Which they did."

For something to do, Grace started filling the china plate sitting beside the food. "Yeah, well, he wasn't father material in any other way. He sure ran out on us in a hurry. Remember Mrs. Lacey's house? I wasn't kidding when I said it brought back my childhood. Sometimes in the winter we slept in the kitchen with the stove on and the door open because Mom couldn't afford fuel oil. It's a wonder we didn't burn the place down around our ears."

When she looked up, Lance was staring at her, appalled. "I didn't know, Grace. I would have—"

"It wasn't your business, Lance. It was Morgana's if it was anyone's, but she'd cut Mom off because of her drug addiction."

"You had nothing to do with that. And you were a child. If it was that bad, Morgana should have taken you away."

"I didn't want her to." She banged the spoon hard against her plate. "Morgana would not have been an improvement. At least my mother loved me; dear Grandmother just loved saving the world."

"Aren't you selling her a little short? After all, Morgana did arrange for Janae to get into Sanctuary after she developed ovarian cancer. And she did take you in."

"Yeah, but then she ignored me about half the time. You were the only one who gave a damn what happened to me." Picking up a knife, Grace got to work cutting a thick slice of the perfectly browned meat, sawing at it viciously. "You know, the night she brought me to the Mageverse for the first time, I begged her to let my mother have the Gift. She turned me down flat." Her knuckles went white on the hilt from the force of her grip as she remembered the helpless rage of that moment. "Then she said, 'But when you're grown, I'll give it to you.' I was sixteen—I didn't want the fucking Gift, I wanted my mother. And Morgana let her die. Her own daughter, and she didn't give a damn."

Gently, Lance took the knife and fork from her hands. "Give me that—you're butchering that meat." He began slicing it with neat, practiced movements. "Morgana has been doing a very difficult job for a very long time. It's made her . . . hard. But not all the High Court is like that."

"Lance, don't try to sucker me. I lived among the Court for five years after Mom died, until I was twenty-one. I know exactly what they're like. Yeah, there are some who seemed decent, but the majority are cold, ruthless and manipulative. They're so busy trying to save the planet, they don't give a damn about people."

He eyed her as he forked a slice onto her plate. "I do."

She dipped out a spoonful of tiny carrots that, even cold, smelled delicious. "Yeah, okay, you do seem a little more emotionally connected than the rest, but . . . You know, I asked Morgana once who my mother's father was, and she said, 'I don't know. What difference does it make?' That just says it all, doesn't it? The woman has so damn many kids, and yet family means nothing to her whatsoever."

"He was probably a Magus. Morgana rarely sleeps with mortals."

Grace turned to stare at him as a horrible thought occurred to her. "Oh, Jesus, it wasn't you, was it?"

Lance drew himself to his full height. "Do you really think I'd seduce my own granddaughter?"

"Well, Arthur slept with Morgana."

"And we all know how that turned out." One of the few accurate elements of the Round Table legends was Arthur's betrayal by Mordred, the product of his unwitting incest with his sister while the two of them were teenagers who didn't even know they were related. What the legends didn't say was that Mordred rebelled because he had been denied the Gift. He died in the war he started—the same war that cost Arthur his rule of the High Court. "I know the scent of my own Line, Grace. You're not on it. Not within the past six or seven generations, at least."

She relaxed and spooned artichoke hearts onto her plate. "That's something, anyway."

"On the other hand, you could be pregnant."

Grace damn near dropped the plate, barely managing to slide it into the microwave in time. "Luckily, I'm on the Pill. I've watched you boys in action too long."

He stepped up behind her and slipped his arms around her waist. Bending his head, he whispered, "You know, the second time won't trigger the Gift, either."

Damn, but he felt good. Warm and strong and hard. She ached to let herself relax against him.

Instead Grace stiffened her spine and punched the buttons on her microwave. "No, but the third time could. I'm not going to let you snake charm me into forgetting how to count, Lance."

"Sometimes it's weeks before the Gift kicks in."

"And sometimes it's the third time." She turned and propped her hands on her hips, shooting him a stern glare. "Go away."

He extended both brawny arms and braced them against the cabinet, bracketing her in muscle. Slowly, he leaned closer, so close she found herself focusing helplessly on his seductive mouth. "But you don't want me to."

Grace managed not to lick her suddenly dry lips. "Yes, actually, I do."

Lance bent his head and nuzzled her ear, sending prickles of sensual heat dancing down her spine. She swayed. He smiled. "Is that your knees going weak?"

"Blood loss." She didn't dare let him get her into bed again. He wouldn't let her out. "And you're not getting dessert."

"But I'm a growing boy." Lance rolled his hips against her, making it clear he was not a boy of any kind.

"Too bad." Grace ducked under his arm and retreated to the refrigerator. She needed something cool to drink. "Go snack on somebody else."

His eyes dropped to her breasts, swaying unbound under her uniform shirt. "Oh, sweet, you are not a snack."

"Do I need to get my gun?" She meant it. A bullet wouldn't hurt him—much—and was one of the few things that would get him out of the mood.

Lance stared into her narrowed eyes like a wolf sizing up a deer, then laughed, throwing up his hands. "You win. Let me get my shirt and I'll go."

Chuckling, he sauntered toward the living room. Before he stepped out, he aimed a wicked look at her over his shoulder. "But I'll be back."

When he'd stepped from view, Grace blew out a breath and muttered, "That's what I'm afraid of."

She realized she hadn't spoken softly enough when she heard his rich, tempting laugh.

DRESSED again, Lance strode out of Grace's house. He'd parked the Jag a block or two away, not wanting her to spot it before she walked into his sensual ambush.

Which, as such things went, had been a delicious success. Grace had a very strong will, but being Latent her body responded to his instinctively. The fact that it had obviously been so long since she'd had a partner of any kind also worked in his favor.

Unfortunately, he had no illusion that getting her into bed the second and third times would be as easy. When she said she didn't want the Gift, she meant it. And there was no guarantee that even if he managed two more seductions, they'd be enough to trigger her change. With some of the Line, it took up to ten encounters, though it never took less than three.

Unfortunately, Morgana had been serious when she'd told him she wanted Grace Gifted even if he had to use force. God, he hated that idea. The very thought of hurting any woman like that—especially Grace—made his stomach twist.

Besides, he admired her. The courage, the blunt wit, the utter lack of artifice. He'd known Majae with that kind of bedrock integrity, but most of them were already True-bonded. The ones who weren't tended to be so focused on the Mission, they could have given a Borgia pope lessons in ruthless manipulation.

Which was why he couldn't afford to fail. He might end up facing the Table but Grace's fate would be even worse. He wouldn't put it past Morgana to order a gang rape that would trigger Grace's Gift in one swoop. And he knew three or four of the Knights who were just fanatical enough to do it.

Lance understood all too well the philosophy behind that cold-blooded willingness to do whatever it took to get the job done. He lived by it himself. Chivalry was a lovely ideal, but preventing the extinction of the human race was much more important. If you had to commit a few gut-churning atrocities along the way, so be it. And he had, though none of his own midnight regrets had included the rape of an inno-cent. He'd killed men the Council wanted dead, and not al-ways in fair battle. He'd seduced, he'd lied, he'd schemed, he'd planted evidence, he'd ruined reputations.

And he'd saved a lot of lives in the process. That thought had always kept him going, despite the nasty taste his as-signments often left in his mouth.

But he absolutely refused to rape Grace. He remembered the child who'd adored him far too well, and admired the woman she was now far too much. He wasn't sure he could survive adding that particular regret to his collection.

On the other hand, he wanted to watch her become the centerpiece of a Round Table gangbang even less. Which meant he needed to craft at least two of the most skillful, creative, wicked seductions of a very long, wicked, creative career.

A grin of anticipation spreading over his face, Lance slid behind the wheel of his Jag and drove off to plot.

Chapter 4

GRACE stood slumped under the hot, pounding shower spray, hoping its stinging stream would erase the vivid sense memory of Lancelot's hands, mouth . . .

Thick, beautiful cock . . .

Damn, the man was lethal. She'd never experienced anything like the passion she'd shared with him. Even aside from the whole biting-the-neck thing, the intensity had been staggering.

And what was worse, she wanted more. A lot more. She wanted to be engulfed by the erotic storm of his hunger again, wanted to let him sweep away her self-control. Wanted him to turn her back into that burning creature she'd become in his arms, the Grace she'd never even glimpsed before. When she'd imagined making love to him as a horny, lonely teenager, it had never been anything like that.

She could still remember the first time she'd seen him. He'd been trying to teach swordplay to some newly Gifted young vampire who'd never picked up a blade in his life. Lance had taken his shirt off sometime before she'd walked up, and his beautiful body was on sweaty, magnificent display. Grace had taken one look and fallen for him with the embarrassing intensity only a teenager can manage.

After that, she'd followed him around like a puppy every minute she wasn't with her dying mother. He'd rebuffed her clumsy adolescent advances with such delicacy he barely broke her heart at all. Then, realizing the depth of her loneliness and grief, he'd taken her under his wing, teaching her swordplay to keep her busy when he wasn't running interference between her and Morgana.

So finding herself the target of Lance's determined erotic pursuit put a serious strain on her emotional defenses. It was far too tempting to give in, especially when he made the experience so utterly delicious.

Unfortunately, Grace couldn't afford the price of another surrender. Not when she risked ending up like Clarice—a psychotic threat to anyone with the misfortune to cross her path.

Sighing, she stepped from the shower and began to towel off. Though her mind spun in worried circles, her body still floated in the boneless relaxation that follows really good sex. When she glanced up at her own face in the mirror, her eyes looked heavy-lidded, sated. "You are not going to let Lancelot du Lac get within twenty feet of you again," she told her languorous reflection sternly.

She thought it sneered.

With a grimace, she grabbed another towel and flipped it over her wet hair. "You're a cop, Grace Morgan," she muttered at herself sternly, briskly rubbing. "And a cop is all you'll ever be."

Finished, she lowered the towel and straightened, glancing toward the mirror.

Her own reflection was gone. In its place, the mirror showed the darkened front of a building with a wide stone staircase. A blonde woman descended the steps, a backpack stuffed with books slung across her shoulder.

Grace froze, staring at the mirror, feeling every hair on her body rise to attention. She knew that building. It was the library on the Tayanita Community College campus.

The image moved, as though the viewer walked quickly toward the blonde. The girl glanced up. She looked young, nineteen or twenty at most, with a delicate cameo face and a small mouth. Her eyes shone a clear green in a shaft of light from the building's windows. Then she was gone as the viewer continued past her, up the steps toward the library door. A male hand reached out into the frame to pull the door open . . .

And Grace was staring into her own stunned face.

"Shit!" She jumped back. "What the hell was that?" Obeying an instinctive impulse to get as far from that mirror as possible, Grace shot out of the bathroom.

She'd never had a vision. Had the contact with Lance triggered the latent psychic abilities that were part of being a Maja? The raw panic of that thought made her want to break into a run.

No, dammit. She stopped in midstride, fists clenching. Grace Morgan was not a coward, and she didn't run. Not from a fight, not from witch grandmothers, and certainly not from whatever was happening to her. Straightening her shoulders, she wheeled around and marched back into the bathroom to glare defiantly into the mirror.

Which showed nothing but her own reflection.

Had she imagined it? Was she beginning to get the Gift? Or—and a chill blew across her skin—was she just losing her mind?

Like Clarice . . . Oh, God.

No. She dragged her galloping imagination back under control. She'd heard Latents sometimes had fleeting psychic experiences following sex with a Magus, but the powers weren't permanent. Not, anyway, if you didn't sleep with him again. She'd just have had to make sure she stayed the hell away from Lancelot du Lac.

Whether she liked it or not.

IT was three in the morning before she managed to get to sleep. And even then, her dreams were far from restful, a

disturbing mix of erotic images of making love to Lance
and . . . something else. Violent, half-seen glimpses of
blood, of the blonde college student, of . . . someone. A
man. Not Lance, but someone else, someone whose face she
never quite saw.

And a knife.

She woke too early the next morning, though she worked
second shift and wasn't due at the station until three o'clock
in the afternoon. She tried to keep busy and avoid brooding,
but her thoughts kept drifting to Lance. And worse, to those
disturbing dreams.

It was a relief to finally slide behind the wheel of her blue
Honda Prelude for the drive to the station. As she buckled
the seat belt, she absently looked into the rearview mirror to
check her hair.

Instead, she saw the blonde girl walking down the sidewalk, holding hands with a tall, handsome boy, smiling up at
him with adoration.

Grace jerked her gaze away from the mirror and stared
down into her lap. When she finally forced herself to look
into the mirror again, her own eyes stared back. She started
the car, trying to ignore the way her hands shook.

The day went straight to hell from there.

GRACE was trying to avoid glancing at her patrol car's
rearview mirror when she heard the call over the radio.
"We've got a reported 10-50 with P.I.s at the I-85 overpass
on Silvercreek Road," the dispatcher said.

Traffic accident with personal injuries. Which could
mean anything from a bloody nose to death. She scooped up
her radio handset and keyed it as she hit the gas. "Tayanita,
Bravo Ten. I'm just around the corner. I'll respond."

"Ten-four, Bravo Ten. HP's on the way." The South Carolina Highway Patrol had jurisdiction over accidents on state
roads, but troopers were usually spread so thin it took them
time to arrive, so deputies and local police also responded to
accidents to help out.

Grace switched on her siren and blue lights, feeling the familiar rush of adrenaline she always felt going on a call. When she rounded the curve that led to the bridge, the car's headlights picked out a Toyota, passenger door crushed in, sitting at an angle to a pickup truck with a crumpled hood.

A stop sign stood at the nearby intersection. From years of working accidents, she suspected the pickup had run the stop and T-boned the Toyota.

Then she saw something that made her belly clench in dread: a figure hunched beside the car with its back to her, cradling someone. All that was visible of the second person was a pair of small, limp, jeans-clad legs.

Grace snatched up the handset. "I need an ambulance."

"Rescue Six is on the way. What have you got?"

"Don't know. Looks like a kid. And it's not good." She threw the handset aside, hit the brakes and killed the engine, then jumped out of the car without bothering to put on her hat.

As she ran toward the two figures, she realized the adult was a woman. Round, plump shoulders shook as the victim rocked back and forth with her small burden, her voice a thin, hopeless wail. "No, Jesus, no, Jesus, no, please . . ."

When Grace crouched beside her and got a good look at what the woman held, she had to clench her teeth against a curse.

The ambulance would not be needed.

"Who gives a shit."

Startled, Grace snapped her head up. A man stood over them. Her cop's mind automatically ticked off his descriptors: white male in his fifties, thin, wearing blue jeans and a workshirt. His nose poured blood, and he swayed visibly, the smell of alcohol rolling off him in waves. Fear stirred in his bloodshot eyes even as he sneered at her. "It was her fault. Don't care what she says, it was her fault."

Before she could answer, Rescue Six roared around the corner and slid to a stop behind Grace's patrol car. Which left her free to deal with the asshole who'd just committed felony D.U.I.—and would, given the chance, run like hell.

Grace stood and walked toward him. Behind her, the woman screamed hopelessly at the paramedics who were coming at a dead run, "Somebody help my baby!"

"Were you the driver of the pickup, sir?" Grace asked, keeping her voice calm and level over the woman's heart-breaking sobs as the paramedics coaxed her into putting down her little girl.

The drunk's eyes flickered. "Naw. There was another guy. He . . . ran off."

"Lying son of a bitch!" The woman rose ponderously to her feet. Her eyes were dull and empty with shock, despite the tears shining in the headlights. "There wasn't nobody else. You was the only one in that truck!"

"So what?" the man roared back. "Who gives a shit about some brat anyway?"

The woman lunged for his eyes with hands curled into claws. Grace was seriously tempted to let her do her worst, but leaped to restrain her anyway, knowing she'd have to charge the mother if she hurt her child's killer.

While she was wrestling with the woman, the drunk whirled and took off. Cursing, Grace released the sobbing mother and sprinted after him.

He disappointed her. When she caught him, he didn't re-sist arrest.

FOUR hours later, Grace returned home with impotent fury still sizzling through her veins.

She knew there was a good chance Richard George would avoid paying for the death of four-year-old Tanisha Miller, despite his five previous convictions for driving un-der the influence, his suspended license and his utter lack of contrition. In court, his defense attorney would attack both Grace and the highway patrolman on the stand, trying to paint them as Nazis picking on his hapless client. He'd say they were lying about the choking cloud of alcohol around the defendant, then argue the unreliability of the urine test that showed George had twice the legal limit of alcohol. The

attorney would cap off his performance by telling the jury
his client had refused to take the more reliable blood test because he really was as afraid of needles as he'd claimed.

And there was a good chance the jury—which would
probably include at least one person who'd driven drunk
without being caught—would gleefully turn the bastard
loose. George, being George, would promptly head to the
nearest bar to celebrate.

Grace had seen it all before. She knew she'd see it all
again.

Most days she could hack the job, even at its worst. She'd
long since learned how to turn off the emotion, how to keep
the death and stupidity and pain at a distance behind an insu-
lating shield of cynicism.

But then, when she least expected it, something like tonight's fatality would punch through that shield, and it
would take everything she had not to detonate like a pipe
bomb with a badge.

Grace opened the front door half hoping to find Lance
waiting for her. She wasn't sure if she'd rather take him to
bed or plow her fist into his face. In her current mood, she
suspected either would do.

Instead she stepped inside to see a dark, hulking shape
waiting in her living room. Every muscle instantly knotted.
She flicked on the light.

The shape resolved itself in a massive chunk of granite
with a sword thrust through it.

Grace straightened from her instinctive crouch and
dropped her hand from her holster.

"Okay, what the hell is this?" Despite her irritation, some
part of her sang in anticipation. Count on Lancelot to give
her exactly what she desperately needed.

She swung the door closed behind her and stalked toward
the stone with its embedded weapon. She wasn't at all surprised to see an inscription cut into the granite: *Whosoever
pulls the sword from the stone will have a very good time.*

Grace studied the sword, adrenaline surging through her

blood. The simple cross-guard hilt was plain, unadorned, without the gems and runes she'd seen on enchanted blades like Excalibur. It looked exactly like the blunted practice weapons Lance had used to teach her swordplay.

Her lips peeled back from her teeth. Without hesitation, she scrambled up on top of the stone until she could get a good grip on the sword. "Want to play, Lance?" she muttered, heaving upward. "Okay, let's play."

The blade pulled free of the rock with a slow, sliding sensation, as if it had been buried in peanut butter. The instant the point cleared the granite, light exploded in Grace's eyes, brilliant and cold. Blinded, she was aware of a spinning sensation she recognized as a dimensional doorway. *Must be a spell generator in the rock,* she thought.

When the purple flashes faded from her dazzled vision, she found herself standing in a huge space that reminded her of a medieval castle's great hall, complete with arched walls and a curving staircase running up one side.

"Jesus," she muttered, turning in a slow circle with the sword still gripped in one hand, "I've been transported into an Errol Flynn movie."

A loud, warning creak made her spin warily just as a wooden door swung slowly open.

Lance sauntered in carrying a sword just like the one she held—and just as she'd thought, it was a practice blade.

But he'd never dressed like this when she was sixteen.

He wore only a leather loincloth, soft, knee-high boots, and thick straps buckled around his wrists, biceps and thighs. His skin gleamed as if oiled. It was the kind of getup that would have looked utterly ridiculous on another man, but adorning Lancelot's sculpted body, it looked like an invitation to break a few commandments.

Grace grinned. "Well, well. If it isn't Leathergod Ken."

He smirked back. "I suppose that would make you Bondage Barbie."

As she swallowed a bark of laughter, she looked down and realized he was right. She, too, wore nothing but a few

strategically placed pieces of hide set off by thigh-high
boots. "What is this, Lance?" Grace demanded. "You guys
didn't wear this crap."

"No." He strolled toward her, a wicked glint in his eyes as
he admired her barely clad body. "But then, if any of my op-
ponents had looked like you, I might have been willing to."

"Uh huh." She felt a feral smile spread across her face.
God, after the day she'd had, she needed this. "What have
you got in mind—as if I need to ask?"

"A duel." He lifted the sword, his sherry eyes lighting
with laughter. "Winner fucks the loser."

The fury that bubbled under the tight lid of her control
turned her smile into a savage grin. "That's what I thought."

Leaping forward, she swung her own sword at his head
with every ounce of her strength.

"Jesu, Grace!" He retreated, lithe as a tiger, his blade
shooting up to block hers. In his eyes was a hint of offended
astonishment, like a big predator suddenly attacked by
something small and delicious that should know better.

"Hey, you're the one who wanted to fight." Grace went
after him again, hacking at his head, watching those powerful arms lift his weapon to beat hers effortlessly away. She
licked her lips, admiring the sheen of torchlight on his oiled
skin. "So let's fight."

"Actually," he snarled, blocking another attack with a
ringing parry, "the operative word in my challenge was
'fuck.' "

Well, they might get around to that, too. Eventually. But
all she wanted right now was to burn off some of the rage
roiling in her belly, wipe out her galling helplessness with a
good brawl. And Lance could give it to her without getting
hurt. She didn't have to hold back. With a happy growl, she
banged her blade into his, enjoying the hard impact of steel
on steel as he parried with no particular effort.

Apparently realizing she needed to work off her anger
before he attempted his seduction, Lance started circling
her. But as he tested her guard with flicks of his sword, he
seemed more interested in the sway of her breasts and the

bunch of her thighs than her blade. His sensual smile suggested he was imaging what he'd do when he won.

And they both knew he would win. He could end their mock duel in a dozen ways, either through sheer vampire muscle or his overwhelming experience in gutter fights spanning sixteen centuries. And when he did . . .

Grace felt her nipples harden and rasp against the rough hide of her bra.

Common sense told her she should throw down her sword and cry off before he claimed his inevitable prize. Each time he emptied himself inside her brought her that much closer to the Gift.

But just as that shaft of sanity penetrated her reckless mood, she saw Lance's gaze sharpen. Predator that he was, he had no intention of letting her get away.

He began stalking her. It seemed his every move became a dance of seduction, a display of muscle rippling under gleaming, oiled skin. When she inhaled, her lungs filled with the hot scent of leather and Magus. And her body responded just as he intended, growing so wet and ready she was tempted to drop the sword and surrender to whatever he wanted to do to her.

Instead she lunged at him, refusing to yield, either to her hunger or her common sense. Her sword slammed against his, skated down the length of it until Grace was nose to nose with him. "You do know what I'm going to do to you when I get tired of this?" He flashed his fangs in a dark smile.

"The question is," she growled, "what am I going to do to *you*?"

He laughed and tossed her back with a thrust of his weapon that forced her to scramble to keep her feet. As she steadied herself, he came after her, that smile stretching white and hungry. She danced away, knowing he allowed it.

"You know, this would be a good time to consider surrender," Lance drawled. He wasn't even breathing hard, the bastard. That wolf-smile broadened. "Spin it out much longer, and I may have to punish you."

Stung, Grace slammed a quick, hard one-two combination strike against his blade, trying to knock it aside. She would have had better luck beating down an I beam. "You really need your arrogant ass kicked."

Lance had the gall to laugh. She used the instant's distraction to snake through his guard. Would have hit him, had not those vampire reflexes carried him neatly out of the path of her blade. He shot her that annoyed predator glower again. "I can think of better uses for all that energy."

"I can't." She attacked again, mostly for the sensual enjoyment of watching those powerful thighs bunch as he leaped back.

This is stupid, a small voice whispered as she charged recklessly after him. She ignored it.

DAMN, he didn't think he'd ever seen anything more delicious than Grace wearing nothing but three bits of leather and thigh-high boots. Her hair had worked free of that French braid, long, blonde wisps floating around her lovely face. A sheen of sweat gleamed on her thighs and the full curves of breasts quivered with every attack and parry. God, there was something about a mock brawl with a beautiful woman that got his blood pumping. For one thing, there was the tantalizing prospect of what he'd do for his victory celebration.

Lance hadn't expected to take this much time getting to that. He'd intended no more than a couple of exchanges, just enough to get past her wary self-control, then a quick disarm and a segue into seduction.

He had to admit, this was much more fun. He wanted to pin her down and redirect all that hot passion toward doing something besides taking his head off. Though judging from the way she kept stealing glances at the massive erection behind his loincloth, she was already headed in that direction as it was.

Then her recklessness provided him with the chance he was waiting for. When he blocked one of her wild hacks at his head, she kept trying to bull past his guard until she slammed chest to chest with him. Her eyes glittered as she tried to force aside his sword.

"Come on, Grace, you know better than that," he said, and hooked a foot around one of her ankles. She tumbled. He pounced, locking one hand around her sword wrist and pinning her on the ground.

Snarling a curse that made his eyebrows rise, she twisted under him, slim and wild as an infuriated cat. His cock hardened even more as his fangs slid to full extension in his mouth. Still holding her sword arm, he used his free hand to hook one cup of her leather top and tug it down. A sweet, pink nipple popped free.

It was, he saw as his hunger spiraled, almost as hard and eager as he was. He bent his head to feast.

GRACE gasped at the sensation of Lance's wet mouth claiming her breast. At the same time, his free hand roamed down her body to cup her sex through her bikini bottom. One long, strong finger slid under the leather, eased between her lips, stroked deliciously. She caught her breath and let her head fall back, arching her body under his. He felt so damn big, so damn good. Rock hard and sweaty and strong. And when he touched her, tasted her, the bitterness of the night fell away.

Stop him before it's too late, the voice of sanity whispered.

But it had been too late since the moment she'd watched him swagger in wearing only a loincloth and a fine layer of oil.

Besides, she'd only had him once. And she wanted him again.

She fisted her free hand in his dark hair as he devoured her breasts. His middle finger was buried deep in her sex, while his thumb strummed her clit. Pleasure curled and snaked through her veins.

Something wild escaped the tight control she'd kept on it. She slid a hand up and jabbed a thumb hard into a nerve bundle in his chest. He jerked away with a gasp. Grace used his momentum to shove him over on his back and straddle his thighs. Spotting a glint of silver in the top of his boot, she reached back to snatch it free.

It was a dagger. And unlike their swords, it was stiletto sharp. She grinned.

Chapter 5

SUCKING in a breath, Lance looked up to see her crouching across his hips with his knife in her hand. "Oooh," she purred. "I wonder what you were gonna use *this* for?"

He lifted a brow. "Surely you don't think I'll tell you?"

"You don't have to." A wild-thing smile curled her lips. "I know exactly what you had in mind. Something like . . ." She slid the knife's sharp blade between the leather cord of his loincloth and his skin. "This." A flick of her wrist cut the cord as she flipped the cloth aside with her other hand, revealing his cock straining toward his navel.

"Actually, it wasn't *my* clothes I planned to cut off."

That wicked smile widened. "Oh. You mean . . ." She reached down and cut the cord around her own waist at one hip. "This." The triangle of leather drooped even as a second flick of the knife cut the cord on the other side. She whipped the bottoms off. With the same breathtaking ruthlessness, she sliced the cords holding up her top. Her lovely breasts bounced free, pink-tipped and gleaming with sweat. "And this."

Lance swallowed, taking in Grace's lush body dressed

only in leather boots. His shaft jerked against his belly, heavy and hungry. "Yes," he managed, his voice strangled. "I think I did have something like that in mind."

"Too bad." She stroked long fingers over the arch of his sweat-slicked chest, then bent down. "Because I seem to have won, and we're going to do what *I* want."

Slowly, she extended a pink tongue and gave one of his tight male nipples a lick. He arched under her with a gasp of pleasure. She grinned. "You like that?"

He rolled his hips until the head of his rigid cock brushed one of her full breasts as she bent over him. "Can't you tell?"

"Let me see." Sitting up straight, she eyed his straining erection as it lay pointing at his chin. "Mmmm. You do look . . . interested." She ran a fingernail up the length of the flushed shaft. As it grew even harder, she cupped his balls in one long-fingered hand.

"Oh, I'm interested, all right," he growled. "So interested I'm about to demonstrate just what happens to tasty Latent girls who cocktease vampires."

"Why, Lance—that sounded like a threat." He felt cold steel against his throat again. "Not a good idea, when I'm the one with the knife."

He smiled slowly into her eyes. "But can you keep it?"

"Oh, I think I can." Still holding the dagger beneath his chin, she reached for his cock with her free hand and aimed it skyward as she rose off his thighs. "I'm really good with blades." Pressing the rounded head to her nether lips, she sank slowly down, impaling herself.

"Yeah," Lance groaned. "Oh, yeah, you certainly are!"

God, she felt so hot and tight and wet. Long, luscious thigh muscles bunched as she rose off him and bent forward. Lance was still gasping at the sensation when he felt the knife press harder against his throat, almost drawing blood. He jerked in shock and stared up at her, about to knock the blade away.

"You're at my mercy, Sir Lancelot," Grace purred. "Are you going to be a good, obedient captive?"

He was strongly tempted to roll her over, tie her up with what was left of her bikini, and show her who was whose captive. Instead he arched his hips and slid slowly deeper. "Your wish is my . . . pleasure."

Her soft mouth fell open at the sensation as her eyelids drifted to half-mast. "Good. Ohhh, good." A pink tongue flicked out to wet tempting lips. She bent until her breasts hung lusciously over his mouth and pressed the knife's cool mock threat to his throat. "Then suck my nipples, captive."

With a groan of hunger, he lifted his head and obeyed the rough command, swirling his tongue over and around each hard little peak in turn as he simultaneously rolled his hips upward, driving his shaft even deeper into her slick, clamping depths.

His head spun. She felt so damn good. He couldn't remember the last time a woman had turned the tables on him so deliciously. *Two of a kind,* he thought, drowning in heat as he stroked harder, faster. They were two of a . . .

LANCE bucked against her, his skilled mouth locked on the tip of one quivering breast. The raw, unbelievable pleasure made her shiver. Made her burn.

Until she had to have more.

Grace threw the knife aside with a flick of her wrist and leaned back to grab both ankles. Circling her hips, she ground down hard on his thick width. "God, Lancelot," she whimpered. "You make me . . ."

"Yeah," he said roughly, deepening his rolling thrusts. Strong male hands clamped over the tops of her thighs, holding her captive for his cock. His voice dropped to a guttural purr, rumbling an incomprehensible torrent of words in a language that hadn't been spoken in centuries. She could feel her orgasm building, hot and cold and blinding, a corkscrew of pleasure twisting up her spine. Until she heard herself begging in a hoarse, broken voice, "Lancelot, please . . ."

"Yessss." A big hand snapped up, wrapped around the base of her skull and jerked her down. Then his mouth pressed against her throat with the quick, dark pleasure-pain of his fangs sinking into her pulse.

She jolted in surprise, but she was caught in those powerful arms, impaled on his shaft—helpless.

He began to feed as he fucked, his mouth moving hot on
the thin skin of her throat as his body jolted hers. Burning,
prickling waves of pleasure spread from the contact points
of his cock and fangs. Grace keened at the furious storm of
sensation.

Arching his spine, he forced his full length to the balls
and held it there, growling out his orgasm against her pulse.
Her climax exploded through her body in a shower of hot
sparks to burst from her mouth in a helpless scream.
"Lancelot!"

LONG minutes passed before Lance became aware of the
press of cold stone against his back and the heat of a limp,
sated woman draped over his chest. "Grace?"

She moaned but didn't stir.

He rolled carefully over with her, laid her down just long
enough to rise to his feet. "Floor's cold," she said grumpily.

"I know." He bent and picked her up again. She draped an
arm around his neck and curled in his arms as he walked
through the castle doorway and into his own opulent bedroom.

Putting her down on the furs piled in barbaric luxury on
his massive bed, he slid in next to her. When he gathered
Grace against him, he discovered she was already asleep.

It didn't take him long to follow.

"YOU need to watch your guard," Lancelot told her, pulling
off his helmet and wiping his forehead with a swipe of his
hand. "It keeps dropping. An opponent could drive a blade
right through that opening and—"

"Cut out my heart, I know, I know. I heard you the first
dozen times, Coach." Grace's gaze lingered on his handsome face. He's so . . . cute. She sighed as he turned away
and sauntered off across the Lords' Club practice arena.
And he thinks I'm just a kid.

But she wasn't. She'd be seventeen in three months.

That thought brought another, less welcome. Would Mom be alive to see her birthday?

"Grace?" Lancelot said suddenly. She looked up to see him start across the sawdust-coated floor toward the door. He was frowning. Distracted, it didn't occur to her to wonder why. "Stay put, would you? I . . . hear something. I need to check it out."

"Yeah, okay." Frowning, she worked absently at the buckles on her leather breastplate with sweating fingers. Mom had looked so sick today when Grace had arrived at Sanctuary after school, so thin, so old. Like she was—

No, Mom isn't going to die, *Grace told herself fiercely.* Grandmother will let her have the Gift, and she'll be okay. Things will be like they'd been before, only without the booze and drugs and bastard boyfriends. Morgana can fix all that, too. And then we'll be happy . . .

"It's you, isn't it?"

Frowning, she looked up, directly into the weirdest gaze she'd ever seen. The black part took up the Maja's entire eye, leaving only a thin ring of violet. Tiny lights flashed inside her pupil like heat lightning on a dark night. "It's you," the woman said again. "I saw you in my vision. He's going to love you."

Clarice. *Grace realized, recognizing her at last.* Lancelot's girlfriend.

Only . . . *Automatically, she backed up a pace. Something was wrong. Clarice's red hair, usually perfect, was matted and tangled, and her skin clung almost as tightly to her bones as Mom's. She wore some kind of flowing white filmy thing that showed a whole lot of cleavage, but it was wrinkled and stained. She stank of vomit and something rotten, like Dad the time he'd spent the night in a Dumpster. Come to think of it, she had the same kind of look in her eyes Dad did when he went too long between fixes: mean. And not quite sane.*

"Hi, Clarice," Grace said, forcing a bright tone. Her heart was pounding. Bad. This was bad. "You want me to get Lancelot for you? I think he's right outs—"

"He's going to fuck you." Lightning forked through those black eyes.

Oh, this was definitely bad. *"Who?"*

"Lancelot."

Grace might have her dreams, but she wasn't stupid. "Clarice, I'm a kid. He's not interested in me."

"You'll be older when he loves you. I see it in my vision. But where am I? What happens to me?" She moved closer, her mouth twisting as her red brows drew down over those wide, crazy eyes. *"He didn't take me the last time, you know. They sent somebody else to give me the Gift. He wouldn't do it. Was it because of you?"*

Oh God. *"Why don't I just get Lancelot, and you two can talk—"*

A hand flashed out and wrapped around her jaw, sharp, red nails digging into her skin. "I wonder if I can change the future." Clarice lifted, cranking Grace onto her toes with a Maja's superhuman strength. She stepped closer, the lights flashing faster in her violently expanded pupils. *"I wonder if I could make it so he never looks at you."*

Screw this, *Grace thought, and swung a fist right at the Maja's jaw. A wave of heat blasted out of the fingers around her face and froze her arm in midair.*

"I wonder," Clarice whispered, *"if I could burn your mind away."*

Something reached out of the witch's mind and wrapped around hers, something black that writhed like a nest of maggots. Grace tried to scream, but the only sound that escaped her open mouth was a hoarse, gasping whimper.

Then the pain started. It felt like her bones were turning into red-hot pokers, burning her from the inside out. Unable to speak, her mind gibbered a helpless plea: Stop it stopit stopitSTOPITSTOPIT.

Clarice smiled slowly. "No."

Images began to pour from her captor, raining into Grace's mind like flaming hail: herself bursting into flame, skin cracking and falling away from her bones like the layers of a burning onion. Screaming and begging while Clarice laughed.

Then it got worse.

Swirling, horrific images of blood and suffering, not just hers but everyone Clarice hated, even Lance, all dying before the power that blazed in the new Maja. Grace couldn't stop her, no one could, Clarice was invincible, she had touched the face of God, she was God, she—

A pair of strong male hands wrapped around the witch's head. Her mad eyes widened. The hands jerked. Something snapped. Clarice . . . folded and fell like an empty suit of clothes.

The fire, the pain, the madness was gone. Powerful arms encircled Grace, lifted her half off her feet, swept her toward the door. She struggled, panicked, until she heard Lance's soothing voice. "It's me, baby. It's okay, I've got you."

He started telling her something, something about some kind of spell Clarice had worked that had distracted him until he'd realized what she was doing. Barely listening, Grace turned to look over his broad shoulder as he carried her out. A body lay on the gym floor, its head at an unnatural angle.

But the hair wasn't Clarice's red. Somehow, it had turned into a pale tangle of blonde. Grace looked closer . . .

SHE woke screaming, Lance's arms tight around her. "It's all right, I've got you," he said, his voice sounding so exactly as it had in the dream that she felt disoriented, unable to unable to tell what was real. "You're having a nightmare."

"God." Grace wrapped shaking arms around his shoulders and clung, trying to anchor herself to his warm strength. "That was horrible."

"What on earth were you dreaming?" She could hear his heart pounding almost as hard as hers was. "I've never heard you scream like that."

"Clarice. I was dreaming about Clarice. Only . . ." She tightened her grip on his shoulders and shuddered.

"Only?"

"At the end, when I looked back at the body . . ." She swallowed. "It was me."

He pulled her closer. "Grace, you're not like Clarice," he said, his voice so utterly sure she felt comforted. "There was a weakness in her you don't have. Hell, I warned the Majae's Council she wouldn't be able to handle the Gift, but they refused to listen. When I wouldn't sleep with her the third time, they sent another Magus to finish it."

"But why? Why didn't someone get a vision or something?"

Lance snorted. "Vision, hell. Anybody with a brain should have seen that coming. But she was Percival's daughter, and he was bound and determined his baby would receive the Gift."

"Whereas Morgana wouldn't give it to Mom even to save her life." Brooding, Grace stirred a forefinger through the ruff of hair on the strong, hard arch of Lance's chest. "After Clarice . . . I wouldn't admit it, but I understood why Morgana refused to help my mother. The Gift would have destroyed her the same way. Things . . . took Mom over. She had a drug problem. She kept saying she was going to quit, but she never could. If Morgana had given her the Gift, she'd have gone right over the edge like that. I just couldn't admit it."

Lance angled his head until he could meet her eyes, his own calm and understanding. "And you were afraid Morgana would give in."

"Yeah. God, I felt guilty. That was the real reason I was so damned angry at Morgana." She looked away from his perceptive sherry gaze. "Deep down, I was afraid Mom would go off like Clarice—but you wouldn't be there to save me. I hated myself for feeling that way. She was my mother. I should have been willing to take the risk."

"Why? None of the rest of us were." Soothingly, he stroked her hair. "You were absolutely right. The Gift would have driven your mother insane. She would have been a danger to us all."

"Which is why I don't want it, either." She rose on her elbows to better search his gaze, looking for . . . she wasn't sure what. "I touched Clarice's *mind,* Lance. And what I saw there scared the hell out of me. I don't want to end up like that."

"But you wouldn't. There's a bedrock strength in you that will not break. You're one of the ones that can handle the Gift."

"Don't be so sure about that." She rested her fist on his chest, then propped her chin on it. "There was a man I arrested today. He killed a four-year-old in a drunk-driving accident, and it meant no more to him than running over a dog. It was all I could do not to draw my weapon and put a bullet right between his eyes." Sighing, she sat up to slump. "Lance, I can't even be trusted with a nine-millimeter Smith & Wesson, much less a direct pipeline to the energies of the Mageverse."

"Did you shoot him?"

"Of course I didn't shoot him, but—"

"Then you can be trusted. The point is not whether you're tempted, but whether you give in."

She snorted. "Yeah, and I've been giving in to temptation since I met you."

"It was my pleasure." He shot her that flashing grin before he said more seriously, "It's also not the same thing. Look, I've been watching people get the Gift for sixteen hundred years. I've learned to spot who can handle it and who can't. You can."

Grace rolled off the bed and snatched up his velvet robe off the floor. "But I don't *want* it." She jerked the robe on and whipped the belt into a knot. "I don't want the power, and I don't want the responsibility, whether or not I can manage them. And I sure don't want to spend the rest of eternity entangled in High Court power plays."

He rose up on an elbow to meet her gaze. "Grace, sometimes you don't always get what you want."

"This time I'm going to." She stalked toward the door, determined to find the nearest spell generator and go home. "Stay the hell away from me, Lance."

Please.

* * *

LANCE lay back across the furs, frowning up at the ceiling. He should probably go after her, but after the last few minutes, he needed the space as much as she did.

A moment later, he heard the telltale whoosh and pop of displacing air that meant a dimensional gate was opening and closing. Grace must have found the spell generator in his library.

His mind circled restlessly back to the moment just before she'd woken from her nightmare. Something had roused him; he never slept deeply at this point in his cycle. It was a couple of hours yet before he'd have to enter the daysleep, when it was practically impossible to rouse him while his body absorbed the energies it needed from the Mageverse.

For several languorous minutes, he'd lain there with Grace curled against him, her head resting on his shoulder. Her scent surrounded him as her heartbeat thumped in his ears. A sense of peace deeper than anything he'd ever known had slipped over him.

Then she'd woken from her nightmare with that look of helpless horror in her eyes, and he'd felt her fear all the way to his soul. Comforting her, making that terror drain away, had been deeply satisfying.

Now he felt the stillness of the castle more than ever in her absence. He hadn't realized how damn lonely he'd been until this moment.

Lance stirred restlessly against the furs, wondering when she'd come back. The daysleep was an hour away yet; he could feel it in his body. He found himself hoping she'd be there when he woke, even if it was just to give him the sharp edge of her tongue. She . . . added something to his life even when she was in a tearing snit. Perhaps because he understood her as he understood so few of the Majae. Despite differences in gender—and vast differences in experience—at the core they shared more similarities than differences. Like him, she was a warrior, a protector, someone who found her purpose in helping the helpless, making their lives a little bit better.

Unfortunately, he also knew that after she gained the Gift—and control of the Mageverse energies it brought—he would see her only rarely. The High Council would send him on to other missions, and she'd have her own.

That thought left him feeling surprisingly empty. Unless . . .

He kept her. He sat up in bed, staring sightlessly at the opposite wall. Yes, it would be possible. Some part of that puppy love she'd held for him years ago still survived. He could build on that feeling, use it to keep her with him.

But there was a very big fly in the ointment. Hell, it was more like a pterodactyl: he'd have to have the High Council's approval. Considering two of its most powerful members were Guinevere and Arthur, he was unlikely to get it. Luckily, Grace had given him a pair of aces to play; that lovely infatuation with him, and Morgana's determination to see that her granddaughter got the Gift.

He rolled out of bed and headed for the shower, knowing he'd need to prepare for the coming meeting as carefully as he'd readied himself for battles in earlier years. He might wear Armani rather than armor now, but the stakes were just as high.

He couldn't shake the feeling that his life was on the line.

"I'VE got her," Lance told Morgana an hour later. If he could get her approval of his plans for her granddaughter, the rest of the Council wouldn't stand in his way. "She's still resistant, but she's also weakening. When I go to her the third time, she won't say no."

Morgana smiled her smug cat smile. "I knew she wouldn't be able to resist you."

"I appreciate your confidence," Lance said, seeing his moment. "But once she's Gifted, I want something from the High Council in return."

The witch's dark brows lifted as she leaned back in her massive desk chair. Her long, slender fingers toyed with the string of white pearls that imparted a touch of femininity to her stern white suit. "And what would that be, Lord Lancelot?"

"Grace." Lance leaned forward and braced his Armani-clad arms on her desk. "I want the Council's permission to marry her."

Morgana's eyes widened. "Has the Assassin of Avalon fallen in love?"

He straightened. "Don't be ridiculous. I'm just tired of being alone. Grace and I . . . suit each other. She's intelligent, she's sensual, she's courageous . . ."

"And I have other plans for her." Morgana pulled the massive illuminated tome on her desk a little closer and picked up a pen as if preparing to write. "Will that be all?"

"Not if you want her Gifted." He folded his arms and braced his legs apart in the pose of a man who would not be moved. "I'll have your vow on it, or I will not touch her again."

"You are not the only Magus in Avalon."

"But I am the only one she won't refuse. She's still infatuated with me."

"That may be." Morgana's expression was absolutely cold. "But there are those who are loyal enough to do whatever the Mission demands, whether Grace likes it or not."

Lance stiffened. Here it was, the threat he'd been expecting. His fangs slid to full extension. "Then you'll be losing a fanatic, because I'll kill any Magus who tries to lay one finger on her."

Morgana rose slowly to her feet. Sparks of power snapped in the darkness of her expanding pupils. "Do you dare turn rebel, Lord Lancelot?"

With a thought, she could fry him where he stood or summon the rest of the Table to butcher him. Lance refused to flinch. "I have always been loyal to Avalon. Everything the High Council has asked of me, I have done, no matter how distasteful, for the past sixteen hundred years. Even when it left me broken. Now I ask one thing." He leaned forward again, focusing his gaze, his will, on Morgana's. "You owe me."

Slowly, the deadly energies died in her eyes. Her lids dropped, veiling the green in long, thick lashes.

As he watched in increasing unease, she started around the desk toward him. With every feline pace, the white suit glowed brighter and brighter against her skin. "Yes. Yes, you have served these many centuries. Perhaps you do deserve a reward."

It was all Lance could do not to retreat a wary step.

To his amazement, Morgana began to sink slowly to her knees before him as the glow faded from around her body. Her spell had transformed the stern white suit she'd worn, turning it into a sheer, white lace robe that lay open over a breathtaking sweep of tempting skin.

Involuntarily, Lance's gaze tracked down from long throat to bare, pink-tipped breasts to endless legs and the dark triangle between them. "Morgana, you can't buy me off with a quick screw."

"Not a 'screw'—and what a vulgar term. No, I'm willing to take an Oath of Service to you." Her voice seemed to spin a web of temptation and seduction around him—not quite a spell, but damn close. "Think of it, Lance. Morgana Le Fay, yours to command for one year. An offer I assure you I made to no other man."

Lance looked down into her lovely face. For an instant, dark images wheeled through his mind. He would be able to take her, drink from her, extract any delicious revenge he wanted for the abuse she'd heaped on him over the centuries, as many times as he chose.

A few days ago, he would have jumped at the chance to get the witch so completely at his mercy. Now he thought of Grace, curled against his chest in sleep, her breath warm on his skin.

And found, to his shock, that Morgana's seductive offer had no real interest for him.

"You are too generous," he said smoothly, despite the cold refusal on the tip of his tongue. He knew better than to offend a Maja of Morgana's power. "I would never dream of making such a demand of you. Grace's hand is more than enough."

For an instant she stared up at him, incredulity widening

her eyes as if she was unable to believe he'd dare turn her down.

Then Morgana barked out a harsh laugh and rose to her feet, fury blasting off her with such heat, even battle-hardened Lance flinched. "You *are* in love with her!" Whirling, she stalked back behind her desk and threw herself into her chair. "Oh, that's rich! My granddaughter has brought the High Court's killer stud to his knees!"

Lance clenched his teeth against an instinctive denial. "Her hand, Morgana."

The witch studied him with glittering eyes. "Will you Truebond with her, then?"

Enter a psychic bond with Grace so she could touch his mind any time she liked? Until he became even more vulnerable to her than he already was? Lance knew too well what a witch could do with that kind of power. He'd watched Guinevere use it on Arthur for centuries. "Not likely."

"Her Gift is strong, Lance," Morgana said, her tone warning. "She may not be able to manage it without your anchor."

"Her Gift may be strong, but she's stronger. Are you going to let me marry her or not?"

"I told you, I have other plans for her."

"Then I won't touch her until you change them."

She sneered. "Don't hold your breath, Lancelot du Lac."

He snarled. "Don't hold yours."

Lance wheeled and stalked out the door. He barely got the heavy oak panel closed behind before something heavy and fragile smashed against it, hurled by the witch's infuriated hand.

GRACE lay curled on her bed, watching the morning sunlight pour through the windows. She still wore the robe she'd snatched from the floor of Lance's bedroom. It wrapped around her in velvet sensuality, reminding her of him, caressing her bare skin, smelling of his dark, seductive scent.

God help her, she had never gotten over him. And how was she supposed to tell him no the next time he came after her, all sin and seduction distilled into two hundred pounds of muscle?

"My girl," she whispered to herself, "you are in trouble."

No sooner were the words out of her mouth than the world went mad.

Light stabbed into her eyes, blinding and vivid, accompanied by a swirl of dark, vicious emotion—lust, hate, a craving to watch another human writhe in agony and die.

Madness.

She was leaning on the fender of a car, watching a blonde woman run toward her, breasts bouncing behind the thick sweatshirt she wore.

Grace realized two things simultaneously: this was the girl she'd seen in her visions. And she was watching her through the eyes of a man who meant to kill her.

He was fantasizing about torturing her, watching her writhe in agony. In his mind, he could already hear her screams. His zipper dug into his erection.

Grace, locked inside the vision, yelled a warning even though she knew the girl couldn't hear it.

Concentrating hard on getting through her morning run, the little blonde didn't even realize death waited on the sunny sidewalk. Coiled like a snake, he watched her run as he'd been watching her for days. He knew she always used the same five-mile route at the same time. He'd set his trap here, when she was almost back to her dorm, knowing she'd be too exhausted to put up much of a fight when he took her.

She ran past, blonde hair whipping. He let her go one more stride before he pounced, grabbing her from behind, whipping the chloroform-soaked rag from a pocket and clamping it across her nose and mouth. Startled, she screamed, sucking in an involuntary lungful of the drug. Working fast, he dragged her to his car despite her weakening struggles, popped the trunk with his key fob and threw her inside. Triumphant, rock-hard with lust, he looked down into her dazed, terrified eyes and slammed the lid down.

WHEN Grace came to herself, she was standing halfway across the room from her bed, sweating and shaking.

God help her, she could still feel him. Feel what he intended to do.

He would play with the girl, build her terror, feed off her pain and his power. And then, sometime tonight, he'd kill her.

Just like he had all the others.

Grace barely made it to the bathroom before she threw up.

Chapter 6

"WHAT do you mean, there's nothing you can do?" Grace demanded, staring at Morgana across the gleaming width of the witch's desk. She'd used the stone spell generator Lance had left in her living room to make the trip to Avalon. "If you don't help me find him, that bastard is going to torture that girl to death!"

"I'd help if I could, but I can't," the witch growled. "First, it's daylight in Tayanita, and you know how the sunlight interferes with Mageverse energies. It's damn near impossible to work a spell when the sun's up on realspace Earth—"

"If we wait until dark, she'll be dead!"

"And second, there are six billion minds out there," Morgana continued, ignoring her outburst. "How can you expect me to zero in on a man I've never even touched?"

"Well, *I* made contact with him, and I'm not even Gifted! It can't be all that damned difficult."

The Maja rubbed her temples with both hands and sighed as though striving for patience. "Grace, every mind is like a radio—"

"And they broadcast into the 'Verse on different frequencies. I know that, dammit. But if I can feel him, I don't understand how you can't. Especially considering how powerful you are."

Morgana glared at her in frustration. "For one thing, this monster of yours must be a particularly strong broadcaster. For another, you evidently have the profound bad luck to share his mental frequency at a time when contact with Lance has triggered latent aspects of your Gift."

"So touch me and see if you can't lock on to him, too."

The witch shook her head. "It won't work."

"Try!"

Morgana sighed and moved around her desk to lay cool, long fingers against the side of Grace's face. As she met her grandmother's gaze, the witch's pupils expanded to wide black lakes lit by flashes of lightening. Despite a too-vivid memory of the last time a Maja had touched her mind, Grace forced herself to remain still and reach for the kidnapper. She could just barely feel him, a dark, malevolent presence . . .

Morgana jerked her hand back. "Merlin's Gift, that *is* nasty."

"Did you feel him? Where is he?"

The witch shook her head, flipping her fingers like someone trying to rid themselves of something rotted and clinging. "I felt . . . someone thoroughly unpleasant. But I get no more sense of where he is than you do. Perhaps after the sun has set and solar radiation no longer interferes—"

"By then she could be dead." Grace coiled her hands into tight fists. "Besides which, I want to get her away from him before he has the chance to torture her any more."

"In that case, your best bet is to accept the Gift and find her yourself. Considering you've already got a link with him, you may find it possible to locate him even with the sun still up."

She drew back with a chilly memory of the mental maggots eating at Clarice's thoughts. Even in her egomania, a part of the Maja had known she was mad. Grace could still remember her psychic wails of horror. "Assuming I don't become an even bigger threat than he is."

"You needn't worry on that score," Morgana said. "Lance wouldn't let it come to that."

"And what a comforting thought that is." Grace winced, remembering the wet *snap* as Lancelot's big hands broke Clarice's neck. The wailing thing had been grateful.

Yet Grace couldn't just stand by and let the killer murder his victim; that would drive her just as mad as the Gift. She frowned. "Would it be possible to wake Lance this early in the day?"

"I didn't think of that." Morgana frowned, nibbling a long nail. "He'll be in the daysleep now. This being Avalon, though, you may be able to rouse him an hour or so before nightfall in South Carolina, but no sooner."

"I can't wait that long." She straightened shoulders that ached with tension. "Send me back. I'm damned if I'm going to sit on my hands while that girl suffers."

A headache pounding viciously behind her eyes, Grace drove through Tayanita County in her patrol car, trying fruitlessly to hone in on the killer's location. She'd searched all morning and through the afternoon even before going on duty at 3 P.M., using her personal car to quarter as much of the area as she could.

Over the radio, she could hear the sheriff directing the other searchers from his command post. When the killer had snatched Deborah Keller off the street, half a dozen people had witnessed the crime. Unfortunately, none of them had gotten his car's license tag number, and the description they'd given could have been any one of a thousand men.

Grace had kept her mouth shut. They'd have slapped her into a padded cell if she'd tried to report her visions, and in any case, she had no solid information to share. She'd never seen the killer's face because she'd looked through his eyes, not his victim's. She didn't even know his name. The only thing she was sure of was that he didn't need to be on the planet with everybody else.

And if she found him, he wouldn't be. She was going to

put a bullet in his brain, even if it meant going to jail herself. She couldn't take the chance he'd get off through some legal maneuvering, or be found not guilty by some gullible jury. She'd spent too many hours drowning in his sick fantasies, his craving to see Deborah writhe and die simply because she aroused him.

Unfortunately, the diseased son of a bitch had never once thought about his own name or address. And strain though she might, Grace could not get a lock on his location. She'd driven along every back road in Tayanita County, but the signal she got from him never got stronger or weaker.

And every second that passed was another second closer to nightfall—another second closer to the moment on his sick timetable when he'd rape that girl and hack her to death with the Bowie knife he'd used to taunt her all day.

Grace was damned if she'd let that happen.

Watching the sun sink closer to the horizon, she knew she had only one option left. Whipping the car into a U-turn, she headed for home. All she had to do was climb onto the stone spell-generator and say Lance's name. It would send her straight to him—and her appointment with the Gift she'd never wanted.

Picking up the handset of her radio, she said, "Tayanita, Bravo 10. I'm going 10-8 for dinner."

LANCE woke to the hot sensation of long fingers stroking his cock. "Come on, Lance," Grace said, sounding amazingly grim for a woman who was all but jerking him off. "Rise and shine."

Feeling so sluggish he knew the daysleep wasn't yet over, he struggled to pry his lids open.

She crouched over him, deliciously naked, her long pink nipples a tempting invitation to his mouth. He hardened in a rush as his vampire body shook off the daysleep and woke to hunger.

"That's better." But her mouth was drawn into a hard line, and her eyes were cold. Inhaling deeply, he could detect no hint of arousal in her scent. She lifted his erect cock and rose over it, preparing to impale herself anyway.

Lance jolted awake. He'd sworn not to touch her unless Morgana allowed them to wed. If he let her do this, he'd lose her.

Though his body howled a protest, Lance locked his hands around Grace's forearms and held her back from him. "Grace, what the hell are you doing? This is the third time!"

"I need the Gift, Lance." He didn't think he'd ever seen a woman more determined to have sex—or less aroused by the prospect.

Gently, he pushed her back and rolled off the bed, looking around for his robe. "This is really bad timing, Grace."

She lifted a brow, eyeing his erection. "You seem divided on the issue."

"Despite rumors to the contrary, that particular part of my anatomy isn't the brains of the operation." Spotting the robe, he snatched it up and jerked it on. "What's going on? I thought you wanted nothing to do with the Gift."

"I don't," she told him grimly. "Unfortunately a certain psychopath hasn't given me a hell of a lot of choice."

Five minutes and one explanation later, Lance's heart sank with the realization that she was right. It meant the end of any hope he'd had of forcing Morgana to approve their marriage, but he had to give Grace the Gift. As a Magus, he couldn't allow this Deborah Keller to be butchered, of course, but as a man, the ragged desperation in Grace's eyes scared the hell out of him. He had the ugly suspicion she was clinging to sanity by her fingernails. Hours of contact with that monster's mind had worn her down. They had to sever that connection fast.

"Fuck," he snarled in fury.

"Now would be good," Grace agreed. Lying back on the bed, she drew her thighs apart. "Let's get it over with."

He eyed her. "That is not a phrase a woman has ever used to me before—and I'm sure as hell not taking it from you."

"Dammit, Lance, we don't have time for candlelight and flowers."

Sliding the robe off his shoulders, he eased onto the mattress and lowered his head between her legs. "Candlelight was not what I had in mind."

"We don't have time for *that,* either." Grace tried to sit up, but he wrapped his hands around her thighs and held her still. Using two fingers, he spread her delicate folds and studied the pink lips.

"You're dry, darling—I'd hurt you, and I've never hurt a woman that way in my very long life. Besides which, for this to work, you need to come. It jump-starts the Gift."

"I'm not exactly in the mood, Lance."

He gave her his best darkly seductive smile. "Let me worry about that."

Lowering his head, he stroked his tongue between her lips. She quivered against him. Feeling the slight motion under his hands, Lance smiled.

And got to work doing what he did best.

AFTER the day she'd spent, Grace hadn't thought it would be possible to wring arousal from her battered mind. She'd underestimated Lancelot du Lac.

With all the skill gained over sixteen hundred years as the Seducer of Avalon, Lance used his clever tongue and wicked hands to drive her ruthlessly into arousal. He knew just where to lick, where to stroke, where to drive two long fingers, using tongue and lips and teeth to drag her into lust with a speed she would have thought impossible. He filled her so thoroughly with himself there was no room for anything else, not even her awareness of the killer. And Grace was almost pitifully grateful for the respite.

As she moaned helplessly, he licked and swirled his tongue over her clit, lapped slowly between her creamy lips, rumbling deep, masculine purrs of approval. "You taste so good," he lifted his head to say, and reached up her torso to cup her breasts in both hands, thumbed her nipples in skilled flicks.

She reached down to fist her hands in his dark curls,

rolling her hips, silently begging for more. "Damn, Lance," she gasped, "you're good at that."

He smiled at her wickedly over her belly. "I've had a lot of practice." Then he buried his face against her and thrust his tongue deep. His fingers pinched and twirled the burning tips of her breasts. Pleasure coiled and lashed inside her like a tiger's tail until she twisted helplessly on the sheets. The hot, dark surge went right on building, fiercer than anything she'd ever felt before. She realized dizzily the Change was beginning, prepared by her previous exposure to his saliva, his sperm, his pheromones. She could almost feel the rising snap and crackle of the Gift surging through her on a wave of silent hormonal signals. She found herself going helplessly limp, dazzled by the sparks bursting in front of her eyes.

Lance lifted his head from between her thighs and gave her a hot, predatory smile. "*There* you are. I knew you were going to be one of the ones that go over fast." He sat back on his heels with a surge of muscle, caught her by one hip, and flipped her over on her belly. She moaned helplessly as he piled a mound of pillows on the mattress.

Dazed from the strange, hot sensations pouring over her, she couldn't even move as he lifted her effortlessly and arranged her bottom-up across the pillows. Big hands spread her thighs wide.

Then, at last, he covered her, gathering both wrists in one hand while he wrapped the other around her chin and turned her head. She licked her lips and lifted her spinning head. "What? Why are you . . . ?"

"I want you helpless," he growled in her ear. The heat from his breath made her shiver, like a tiger's exhalations. "I want you to feel my cock driving you into the Gift. Me, Grace. Nobody else." Her dazed eyes focusing on the mirror of his oak bureau, she saw him angle the thick length of his erection, aiming it for her creamy core. "You may be doing this out of duty, but you're damn well never going to forget this moment," he said, his voice rough with submerged anger. "Even if it's all I'll ever get of you."

He entered endlessly, stuffing her with a slow, relentless thrust until his hard thighs pressed against the back of her legs as his muscled body blanketed hers.

Overwhelmed, she squirmed, but he had her thoroughly captured, pinned beneath his strength, wrists cuffed in one hand. He purred male pleasure in her ear as she moaned. The long fingers under her chin angled her head to arch her neck. "Now," he said, in a low, rough rumble, as he leaned down to bite, "let's see how unforgettable I can make this ride."

She sucked in a breath at the sharp sting of his fangs slicing into her throat. Dazed, she stared into the mirror as he began to drink, simultaneously easing his long shaft out of her wet sex, then sliding it back inside.

He started slowly at first, letting her adjust to him, find the pleasure in his thorough conquest. Easing in and out, stoking her to sensual delight until she whimpered mindlessly.

He rumbled something triumphant against her neck. His thrusts deepened, roughened, until he was pumping hard, rolling his hips against her ass. Until her whole consciousness centered on the fierce strokes of his big cock, on his lips moving on her throat as he drank in long, rippling swallows.

Inside her, that hot, alien energy grew, swelled along her nerves, filling every inch of her he did not. Too much, too much . . . "God, Lancelot," she gasped. "What's happening?"

He growled something and rammed his hips hard against her ass, once, twice, again. And stiffened, driving to the balls as he came. Grace felt the familiar pulses of her own orgasm break free. The long, sweet waves deepened and intensified until she screamed.

But just when it should have begun to die, the climax grew hotter, more overwhelming, building like a sexual storm surge in her mind. Her next cry mixed ecstasy and terror as the fire seemed to pulse out of her on a searing wave of heat. It surged into Lance, and he jerked against her with a muffled bellow. Then the energy came raging back out of him again, a blazing, molten tsunami that ripped a shriek from her.

In the mirror, she saw their bodies begin to glow, brighter and brighter until she had to squeeze her eyes shut against the glare. She writhed in the ferocious grip of her transformation, shattering under him as he screamed hoarsely in her ear.

And the world went out.

MAJAE could mentally draw on and control the energies of the Mageverse in working their spells, but for the vampire Magi, the connection went all the way to the cellular level. In a sense they *were* the Mageverse given human form. They could use its otherworldly energy to power their feats of superhuman strength, to heal otherwise fatal injuries, even to assume new forms. And they could use it to bring a Maja into her Gift.

When Grace's body produced the first signaling pulse of her transformation, Lance's reacted. He could no more control what happened next than a woman can control labor. Mageverse energy poured from his body into hers, surging through her cells, changing her. For a moment, both of them became raw energy, blending into one white-hot creature. One mind. One heart. One soul.

Lance had Gifted more women than he cared to remember, but this was different. As their minds fused, he touched her, felt her. Knew her fire and strength and vulnerability, just as she knew his. He heard a voice whisper, *Mine* . . . and had no idea whether it came from himself or from her. In truth, it didn't matter.

Then, between one fiery instant and the next, she was gone. Something in him screamed a protest as he became himself again, his face buried in her slim throat, his cock clasped in her tight, wet grip.

"Lance?" She whimpered it, sounding broken, lost. He knew exactly how she felt.

Another long moment passed before he had the strength to pull his fangs from her skin. At the same time, he found himself tightening his grip on her slim body out of some instinct to keep that final connection. It took him two tries to manage speech. "Here."

"I feel . . ." She stopped, swallowed. "I feel really strange."

"I know." Carefully he withdrew from her, wincing in regret for the lost connection between them. He turned her in his arms, though his aching muscles protested, strained after the violent effort of her transformation.

Her wide, unblinking eyes made his breath catch. Their normal crystalline blue was skimmed over by a lake of black, shot through with flashes of alien lightning. She blinked once, blindly. A tear tracked down her cheek. "Where did you go? I need you."

"I'm here, darling."

Her throat worked as she swallowed. "I don't think I can do this."

He could sense her terror, the fear that the energies she'd tapped into would destroy her identity. Gently, he took her face between his hands and met those black-swamped eyes without flinching, determined to reach her. "No, Grace. You have the strength—I know, I touched it in you. I've helped so many to the Gift, women with much less will than you. They made it. You can. Believe. Reach for it."

STARING blindly into Lance's demanding, sherry stare, Grace swallowed. If he thought she could do it, she had to try. But God, the Mageverse roared and burned like a cataract of lava. Her instincts screamed that any second it would sear her to ash.

But Lance thinks I can do it.

Then she sensed it—a tendril of malevolence so intense it made her breath catch.

As soon as she became aware of it, the connection popped to full force. She realized her link with the killer was even stronger.

And he was about to kill the girl.

Grace could feel his craving for murder, for the power he

felt when he watched life drain from a woman's eyes and knew he was the cause. To him, it felt like being God. Everything in her recoiled from his sheer sadistic evil, but she knew she couldn't afford to flinch. He was minutes from raping the girl, drunk on the hours of terror he'd wrung from her with the threats and cruelty that had grown worse as he anticipated the conclusion of his ritual.

Feeling like a woman deliberately plunging into a lake of sewage, Grace reached for him, touched him. The fantasies spinning through his mind made her gorge heave, though she was no stranger to horror after her years in law enforcement.

She knew she had to get to him—now. She had to stop him.

"I've got to go," Grace muttered blindly, trying to pull out of Lance's hold.

"What?" She was dimly aware of his expression of alarm, his hands tightening on her face. "Where are you going?"

"I've got to stop Gordon Childers from killing the girl. Let me go."

He obeyed. "I'm going with you."

"Good." She sat up. It seemed the room was full of snapping sparks of energy. Grace stared at them blankly, realizing they'd always been there; she'd simply been unable to see them. "Uniform. Where's my uniform? My gun?"

"I'll get them." He rose, muscular and naked, and moved around the room collecting her scattered clothing and equipment. Grace found herself watching the sparks as Childers's mind spilled visions of gut-tearing horror. Her skin quivered and jumped like a horse's stung by flies, reacting to the constant hot currents of the Mageverse roiling around her.

I'm in no shape to tackle this guy. The thought was sharp and clear and gut-level, and Grace knew it was dead on. Unfortunately, she had no choice. There was no time to search out any of the other Majae, explain the problem and link with them so they could find the killer to stop him. It had to be now.

She'd just have to trust Lance to keep her pointed in the right direction. Fortunately, after touching his mind, she knew he'd never fail her.

He helped her fumble into her uniform, then snatched a shirt and pants out of his own closet even as she reeled to her feet. The sun was just about to slide behind the horizon back in Tayanita; she could feel its disruptive energies fading. She and Lance had to jump *now*. Childers was about to make his first cut; there wasn't even time to get to Lance's spell generator. She had to work the spell herself.

"Oh, God, Lance," Grace moaned in sudden panicked realization. "How do I open the gate?"

"Calm down," he said soothingly, jerking up his zipper and stomping into his shoes. "Just reach for the energy. It'll tell you how to use it."

Reluctantly, she opened her mind to the boiling energies—and saw at once how to create a tunnel boring through time and space. She flung up a hand and mentally grabbed a passing current, jerked.

And the door was there, hanging in the air of Lance's bedroom. On the other side, a lanky, round-faced man stood over a sobbing naked woman, his pants unzipped, his penis jutting. His face ugly with power and lust, he held a gun pointed down at her head. Grace could feel the girl's abject terror and shame just as easily now as she felt Gordon Childers's craving for murder.

The emotion dug into Grace like a spur, driving her to draw her gun and head for the gate.

She heard Lance roar, "Grace, dammit, wait!" And almost ran into his back as he leaped ahead of her. Annoyance flashed through her as she stumbled through behind him, gathering her breath to yell "Police!"

Over the Magus's broad shoulder, she saw Childers whip around as they plunged into the room. His gun tracked toward them . . .

BLAM! The thunder of its rolling boom made her recoil. Lance fell back against her.

"Lancelot!" she screamed.

"What the fuck?" Childers yelled. "Who the hell are . . . ? Where did you . . . ?"

She was scarcely aware of his babbling voice as she

fought to support Lance's sagging weight. Looking down as she lowered him to the ground, she saw with horror that his eyes were glazed with pain. There was a neat, dark hole squarely in the center of his muscled chest, left bare by the shirt he hadn't bothered to button before the jump. Blood was already pumping from the wound.

"Knew that was going to happen," he husked.

And she should have, too; it was a rookie's mistake, to surprise a man with a gun in his hand. The 'Verse energies had distracted her.

"I *said,*" Childers snarled, shoving the gun against her head, "who the fuck are you?" His eyes widened as she looked up, and she knew he'd seen the Mageverse in her gaze.

Grace's lips drew back in a snarl as she caught those primordial energies in a web of her will, harnessed them tight in the space of a blink. "I'm the woman who's going to kill you, you sick little bastard."

Her spell smashed out, grabbed him, wrapped tight. The killer yelped, the cry spiraling into a scream as the pressure increased viciously around his bony torso. Grace ground her teeth, barely able to breathe herself from the energies she was channeling.

Yet even through all that, she could still feel Lance's agony like a spear through her own chest. Fighting to breathe, she looked down to meet her lover's eyes, ignoring Childers's whining gasps. "Hold on," she husked. "I can heal you." And she knew she could, could feel the way to do it in the paths of swirling energy.

"Don't bother," Lance whispered. "I just have to Change."

Of course. Changing would heal his injuries as the Mageverse reshaped his body.

In the next instant, she felt the 'Verse boil around them as his cells drew on its dark energies, channeled them, used them. A white-hot light burst in her face in a massive, silent detonation.

When she could see again, she realized two things simultaneously; there was a huge black timber wolf resting across her lap . . .

And her distraction had broken the spell holding Childers.

Stunned, disoriented, she looked up at the massive bore of his gun as the killer pointed it dead center of her forehead. His eyes were wild with terror. "Die, you fucking bitch!"

As his finger tightened on the trigger, Grace reached desperately for the Mageverse, knowing she'd never be able to shield herself in time.

Wolf Lance catapulted from her lap in an explosion of fur and muscle, slamming into Childers with such force he staggered back and fell. The gun went off. The echo of its rolling boom competed with the killer's terrified screams. Then the screams cut off as Lance's fanged jaws clamped on to his neck.

Which was when Grace realized the link between her and Childers was still fatally strong. To her horror, it seemed the wolf's teeth had sunk into her own throat, cutting off her breathing, ripping her flesh. She tried to tear her mind away from the killer's, knowing that to share his death in a deep link could kill her. In the distance, she could hear Deborah Keller screaming in horror, high and hopeless. Her mind echoed the sound . . .

*L*ANCELOT!

The telepathic cry punched through Lance's killing rage. He lifted his bloody wolf muzzle, knowing his victim would be dead in seconds anyway.

Grace lay in a crumpled heap on the floor. He could hear the whistling wheeze she made as she struggled to breathe.

Oh, Merlin's Gift, he thought, horrified. *She's still linked with the bastard.*

Lance leaped for her, changing back to human between

one step and the next, the pain of the process so hot and familiar he barely noticed it. "Let him go, Grace! If you maintain that link while he dies . . ."

Her panicked eyes met his. Though her throat was undamaged, her mind was treating Childers's fatal injuries as her own. Curled in the corner, Childers's victim made a choked sound of horror.

Lance cursed himself. He should have realized this would happen, should have known . . .

Kneeling, he snatched her into his arms. "Breathe with me. Please!" She was going blue. "No! Grace, I love you!"

The Truebond. If he could get her to Truebond with him, he could help her cut her mind off from Childers. Desperately, he opened himself, sought her consciousness. Felt her reaching for him . . .

And they surged together with a silent psychic *snap* like two pieces of a puzzle clicking together. As the power of the Truebond rolled over them both, he sucked in a deep breath and saw her chest copy the motion. In the link, he could feel air flooding her throat, cool and life-giving.

Relief flooded him, just as sweet and welcome. *Thank God, thank God,* he babbled mentally, mind to mind with her. *I thought I'd lost you. Everything in me just . . . stopped.*

Sorry, she thought back. *Boy, I really screwed that one up. Is the sonofabitch gone?*

Lance looked up at the crumpled body on the floor. *He's gone.*

Good. I love you.

He pulled her close, savoring her soft, warm weight. *And I love you.*

A sudden loud sob jolted them out of their warm nest of relief. They looked up just as Childers's erstwhile victim leaped up and ran for the door. *Hell,* Lance thought. *She saw me turn into a wolf. I'd better stop her.*

Which would freak her out even more. She's been traumatized enough. I'll do it. Grace sent out a wave of Mageverse energy. She felt Deborah Keller run into her makeshift barrier, heard the woman's terrified yelp as it wrapped around her and held her still like a silken net. *Oh, hell,* she thought to Lance, *so much for not scaring the crap out of her.*

Grace tried to sit up, only to find her body was still too oxygen-starved to readily obey. Lance slipped out from under her and gave her a hand. "You're going to have to alter her memories," he said. "Or she's going to tell everybody Childers was killed by a werewolf."

"And whatever I come up with is going to have to be consistent with the fang marks in his throat." At least she could talk, since the damage she'd felt had been more virtual than real. With Lance's support, she trudged into the hall.

Deborah Keller waited for them, her huge green eyes swimming with tears, panic on her face. "What are you people?" she demanded, her voice high and frantic. "Why are you doing this?"

Between her weakened body and the Mageverse's distracting heat, Grace discovered her capacity for sympathy wasn't what it should be. "To start with," she snapped, "we're the people who saved your ass. Which resulted in one of us getting shot, I might add. And we did it so Gordon Childers wouldn't cut you up like a Christmas turkey. You got a problem with that?"

The girl blinked. "Uh, no." She hesitated, her gaze flicking from Grace's uniform and badge to Lance. "But he's a werewolf! And you're . . ." She trailed off.

"A witch. Yeah. It's hard for me to believe, too." With a gesture, she released Deborah from her spell. When the girl made no effort to run, she felt faintly encouraged. Maybe she was calm enough to listen now. "Look, would you like to forget most of this crap—what Childers did to you? I could make it like a dream. You'd think he kept you heavily medicated. You wouldn't remember . . . that other stuff."

"You could do that?" Deborah bit her lip, visibly torn as she shifted from foot to foot.

"Yeah."

"I wouldn't normally . . . I don't like the idea of somebody . . ." The girl swallowed as her eyes filled. "But I don't think I can handle this. What he did. Remembering what he was going to do. The pictures he showed me of the others he'd . . ." Her shoulders began to shake. She sobbed, slumping. "Please . . . please help me! Whatever you have to do, just . . ."

"It's okay." Grace stepped up to her and caught Deborah's face between her hands. For a moment she remembered standing in just this pose with Clarice. *But I'm not Clarice.* She'd faced her fear and the Mageverse, and she'd won.

As she reached for the girl's thoughts, she was sharply aware of Lance's mind in the Truebond as he stood watching them, still and powerful and as deeply rooted as an oak. "Neither of us has to be afraid now."

Chapter 7

THERE were loose ends to be tied up after that, such as explaining how Childers's throat had come to be ripped out by a wolf. They'd decided to blame his injuries on an invented attack dog. Grace had altered Deborah's memories until she believed Childers had threatened to have the dog tear her apart. While he was tormenting the animal to work it into a frenzy, it had instead attacked him. She remembered very little else, and Grace's and Lance's involvement not at all. As far as Deborah was concerned, they'd never even been there.

They watched through the upstairs window as she ran next door to call police, eyes wild and clothes torn. "At least my psychic surgery worked," Grace said. "She remembers only the bare minimum about what happened." She rolled her shoulders restlessly. "We'd better get out of here. Every cop in Tayanita County will be here in about two minutes."

"Better transport us to the Mageverse," Lance said. "We've got to deal with Morgana next."

She rolled her eyes. "Must we?"

"I'd say so," Lance said grimly. "Particularly since we

Truebonded without the Council's permission. Even though I was following orders when I Gifted you, they tend to get touchy about that kind of thing."

Grace winced. "Good point." Sighing, she reached for the shifting swirl of energy she could feel dancing just out of sight. "Let's get this over with. I need to come back and put in my resignation to the Sheriff's Office."

He looked at her. She actually heard his thought. *Are you sure about that?*

Oh yeah. She grinned at him. *I've had a better offer.*

TRANSPORTING herself and Lance to the Mageverse damn near drained Grace of everything she had left. When the spell faded, she saw it had brought them to her grandmother just as she'd intended.

What she hadn't expected was to find Guinevere and Arthur in Morgana's office when they arrived. Evidently, she realized giddily, they were all sharing a friendly drink.

"Hi, Grandma," Grace said, and felt her knees buckle.

Lance caught her before she could fall and eased her into a chair. She looked up at him and tumbled into the rich, heated sherry of his gaze. She could feel his love wrapping around her like a shimmering cloak.

When they finally tore free of each other and looked around, it was to find themselves the focus of three sets of speculative eyes. "Well," Morgana said. "You did Gift her, didn't you?"

"And rather more than that," Guinevere added, lifting a brow. "Unless I miss my guess, they're Truebonded."

Arthur's eyes widened with surprise. He barked out a laugh, the sound short and a little nasty. "Well, well. The Seducer of Avalon has been gelded at last."

Beside Grace, Lance stiffened. In his memory, she could see all the little digs the king had inflicted over the years. Suddenly she felt her exhaustion wash away on a swelling tide of anger. "Oh, believe me—he's far from gelded," Grace said, managing a sensual purr despite her exhaustion.

Arthur made a dismissive gesture. "No offense meant, my child. I simply meant that husbands the world over may at last rest easy."

"Okay, that's it." Grace shot to her feet. From the corner of her eye, she saw crackles of Mageverse energy gather around her. She could feel herself drawing on their power as she took a warning step toward Camelot's royal vampire. "This shit is coming to an end right now."

Arthur's eyes widened in offended astonishment. "What?"

"You heard me," she snapped. Through the link, she could sense Lancelot's amused approval. "We all know exactly what happened sixteen hundred years ago, and we all know it's over. It's time for you to drop it."

"You insolent little chit," Arthur said in a low, deadly voice that made the hair rise on the back of her neck. "How dare you address *me* in that tone?"

Oh, God, what am I doing? a small voice wailed in Grace's mind. She ignored it. "I'm not a chit, Arthur. I'm a cop. And I've been dealing with bullies long enough to know one when I see one."

That storied Pendragon temper exploded. Arthur took a single step forward—

Right into Lance's swinging fist. Blood spurting from his nose, the Liege of the Magi's Council fell on his royal ass.

"If you ever threaten my Bonded again, I'll call you out," Lancelot said, the words all the more chilling for their cold control. "And don't think I won't kill you."

"Arthur!" Guinevere swept around Grace and ran to her husband. She crouched beside him, examining his bloody face. "Oh, Lance, you broke his nose."

"Get me Excalibur," Arthur snarled.

"Don't be an ass, darling," she told him tartly, slapping her hands on his chest to hold him down before he could explode to his feet. "You had that coming, and you know it."

Arthur's furious eyes met his wife's for a long, tense beat. Until they slowly, reluctantly, softened. "I suppose I did." With a sigh, he rose in a lithe, powerful movement and turned to help her up. "Over the years, needling him got to be a habit," he told Grace, as if by way of apology.

"Break it," Grace said crisply.

The former High King looked up at her in surprise. Then he laughed, a great boom of sound, and Grace realized suddenly how he'd won Lance's loyalty all those centuries ago. "You know, I think I like you, child. You'll do."

"I always said she would," Morgana said smugly. She lifted a black brow. "Now, isn't it time we started discussing the wedding?"

Lance relaxed subtly. Grace felt his relief as they realized the Majae weren't going to fight them over the Truebond. "Didn't you say you had other plans for Grace than marrying the likes of me?"

"Did I?" Morgana's cat smile widened.

He exchanged an exasperated look with Grace. "I think I've been played."

"Get used to it," Arthur said, smiling down at his wife with dry affection.

"So if you always intended we marry," Grace demanded, shooting her grandmother a hard look, "why did you try to seduce Lance?"

The Maja shrugged gracefully. "If I was to give my granddaughter to the Seducer of Avalon, the least I could do is make sure he wouldn't take up old habits after you're wed."

"Believe me," Lance said, moving to take Grace in his arms. "Old habits no longer hold any appeal."

As they sank into a long, fiery kiss, Grace heard Morgana say smugly, "You see, Gwen? This has all worked out exactly as I said it would."

Grace slid one arm out from around her love and flipped her grandmother off.